The Viper Amulet

The Viper Amulet

The sequel to *Rubies of the Viper*

Book Two of The Ruby-Viper Trilogy

a novel by

Martha Marks

The Viper Amulet

———

THE RUBY-VIPER TRILOGY consists of *Rubies of the Viper, The Viper Amulet,* and *The Ruby Ring.* For more information, including a glossary of names and terms used in all three books, a map, personal photos of featured places, book club discussion topics, and *The Purple Parchment* blog, see MARTHAMARKS.COM.

Also by Martha Marks
Betting on Bernie, A Memoir of a Marriage is a double gold-medal award winner in international book competitions and also an international top seller in several categories on Amazon. Learn more at BETTINGONBERNIE.COM.

To BERNARD ("BERNIE") MARKS,
the talented, patient, and supportive love of my life.

And to DR. JULIE BREER, who read *Rubies of the Viper*
and asked the key question that set up this sequel.

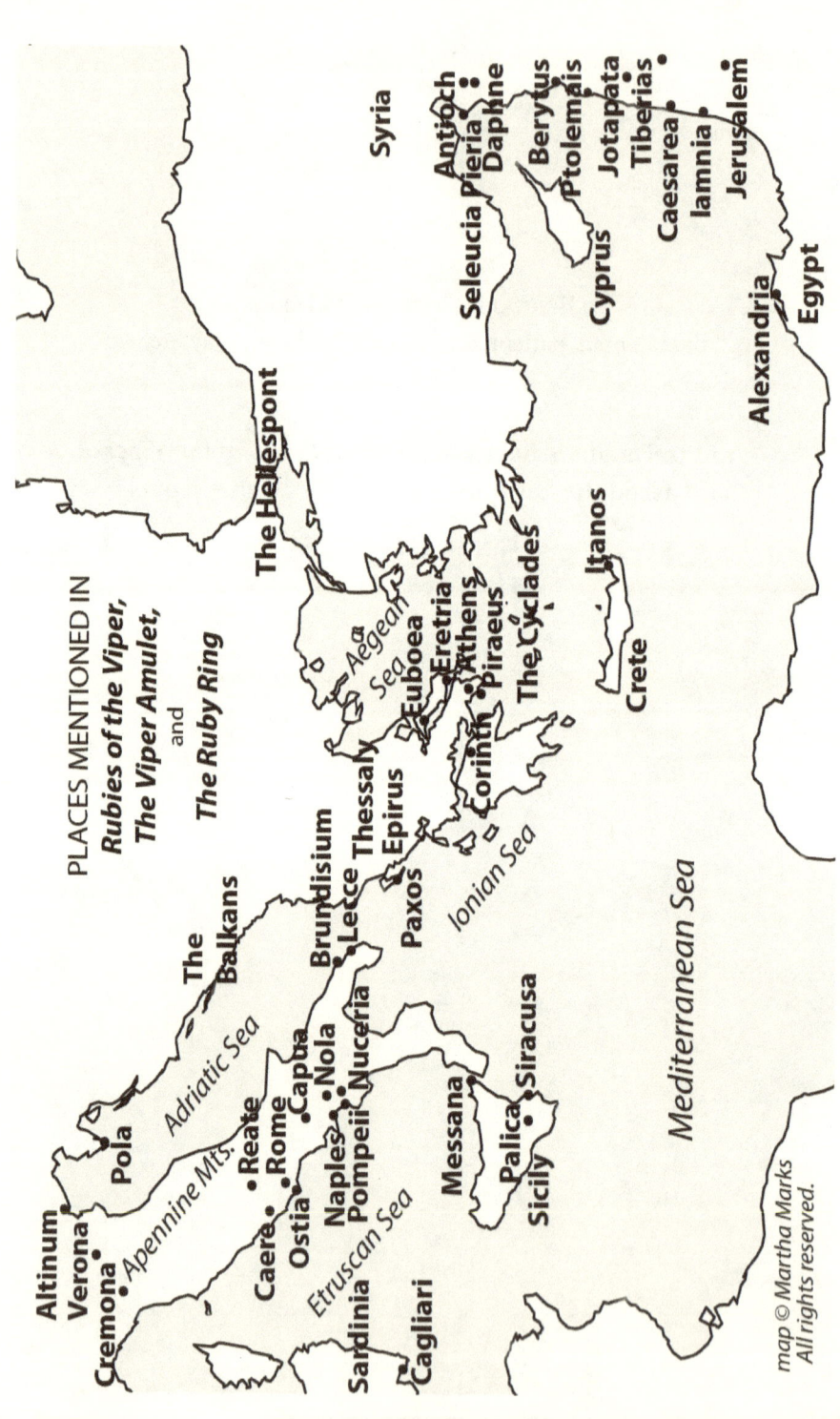

PLACES MENTIONED IN
Rubies of the Viper,
The Viper Amulet,
and
The Ruby Ring

Altinum
Verona
Cremona
Pola
Apennine Mts.
Caere
Ostia
Rome
Reate
Capua
Naples
Nola
Pompeii
Nuceria
Sardinia
Cagliari
Etruscan Sea
Adriatic Sea
The Balkans
Brundisium
Lecce
Thessaly
Epirus
Paxos
Messana
Palica
Siracusa
Sicily
Ionian Sea
Mediterranean Sea
Euboea
Eretria
Athens
Piraeus
Corinth
Aegean Sea
The Cyclades
Itanos
Crete
The Hellespont
Syria
Seleucia Pieria
Antioch
Daphne
Berytus
Ptolemais
Cyprus
Jotapata
Tiberias
Caesarea
Iamnia
Jerusalem
Alexandria
Egypt

Contents

For a glossary of names and terms used in this trilogy,
see *marthamarks.com/glossary/*

PART I

JUNE TO DECEMBER 56

ANYONE CAN HOLD THE HELM WHEN THE SEA IS CALM.
—PUBLIUS SYRUS, 85 BC - 43 BC

CHAPTER 1

L ife is a journey, the wise men said, and Theodosia Varro knew it was true. She had endured too many journeys already in her twenty-two years.

But philosophy wasn't on her mind that morning, five hours into the escape from her ancestral villa, when the thing she feared most in the world rose up in front of her.

At first it was just a rumble. Then a slow, steady pounding. Fish fled. Seabirds screamed. Waves rocked harder. The massive ship picked up speed as it headed toward the fishing boat hired to spirit her away, along with two men who had risked their own lives to save hers.

Dearest Juno, I'm really not much of a threat to him.

She clutched the skiff's splintered wales as blood from her palms and fingertips smeared its peeling green paint.

Why can't he let us be?

The boatman took the paddle from Stefan's hand. "They'll spot you first. Get down and stay still."

Stefan slipped off the seat and wedged his bulky body into the narrow space between the benches.

Alexander tossed a blanket over him, piled nets on top, and turned his gaze to the fast-approaching ship.

Theodosia wiped her red, wet hands on the knitted cap that the boatman had given her at dawn and tugged it over her ears. "First time I've appreciated my chopped-off hair," she said.

Alexander's bearded face lost a bit of its tension as he leaned over to caress her neck. "Best you not look too beautiful right now, my love."

"Could a captain on the water get the word this fast?" She buried her legs in the jumble of nets and accepted the paddle that the boatman handed her.

"Maybe." Alexander straightened again. "If Titus spoke to Nero last night."

"Titus was furious with me."

"And Flavia had told him the whole plan."

The short, tow-headed boatman, whose name Theodosia didn't want or need to know, began rocking back and forth on his bench.

He's been so steady to this point.

Somehow, Flavia had found this runaway-slave-turned-fisherman and paid him to carry out the critical first stage of Theodosia's escape from the Italian Peninsula. In many ways, the boatman was a perfect match for his passengers, all of them desperate to avoid attention.

"It's a bireme," he said.

"A warship?" Alexander asked. "So close to Rome?"

"There's several in these waters. Usually, they pay no attention to me."

But this warship was bearing down on them.

Mercilessly, the wind whipped the bireme's plumped-out mainsail as the pounding in its belly grew louder. On each side of the hull, two banks of oars sliced the whitecaps in perfect unison and at full speed, driving its bronze battering ram ever closer. The hammer pacing the rowers' strokes accelerated with the ship. If it continued on course, the ram would pierce the air over the boat moments before the bow crushed it.

Then, suddenly, "Rowers, halt!"

The order blasted across the top deck and echoed on the water. After a second shout in the hold, all the oars rose in precise formation and hovered in midair until, still in perfect alignment, they rotated, plunged into the water, and stopped the forward movement.

The bireme quivered and glided the last few feet until its port side came smoothly to rest an oar's distance from the boat.

Another command—"At rest!"—rose from deep within, followed by an audible sigh as scores of rowers relaxed. Pale, gaunt faces squinted through each oar hole as if starved for a glimpse of sunlight, a breath of clean air, or an explanation for this break in their relentless routine.

The rowers—all condemned criminals, for sure—sat one or two levels below the uniformed officers on deck, almost parallel to the fishing boat, as the stink of their combined sweat, urine, and feces billowed out.

As rancid as my cell in the Carcer.

Theodosia peered through the oar holes into their eyes… poignant reminders of miseries recently escaped and traumas yet to come if this latest journey didn't go well.

Alexander and Stefan could wind up rowing a galley like that.

The boatman, too.

A grunt from Alexander drew Theodosia's attention. Nothing in the thin line of his lips, the protruding tendons of his neck, or his rigid posture suggested that things were going well.

Did we really get away from Nero only to be netted like fish?

An officer in a hip-length red cape strutted to the top-deck railing and glared down at the three supposed fishermen sitting among a pile of nets in the tiny green boat.

"Where're you from?" he called.

"Sardinia, sir." A wide grin broke over the boatman's face, and there was no wobble in his voice. "Cagliari, to be precise."

Gutsy fellow.

"Who are you?" the officer demanded.

"Name's Fulvius." The boatman pointed at Alexander. "My partner's Sabbas." He jabbed his thumb in Theodosia's direction. "His son's Doros."

Such clever names we invented.

"Been out of port long?"

"Fourth day."

"Long way in a short time."

"We pushed it this morning."

Theodosia let her head droop and shook her arms as if worn out with the speed of their paddling.

When she raised her eyes again, the officer at the railing was staring at her.

Idiot. Mustn't call attention to myself.

"Stand up, boy," the officer said in that same imperious tone.

Her body froze. Heart and lungs and limbs and brain… all paralyzed. The only functioning parts were her eyes, which darted from one face to another.

"Up," the officer barked, "now."

Alexander eyed Theodosia levelly and held out his hand.

She managed to take it and also grab the wale with her other hand. Ignoring the splinters that gouged her fingers, she pulled her legs out of the net pile, propped the bent right one on the flattest part of the hull, braced the twisted left one against the side, and rose halfway. The maneuver would have been tough for her under any conditions, but Stefan's bulk beneath the nets made it even harder.

Please, Juno, keep him still.

Clinging to Alexander, she willed herself to stand. Every man on the ship, from the officers and sailors on the two upper decks to the criminals at their oars below, was inspecting her now. The knee-length boy's tunic she wore offered no camouflage for her deformed legs.

And that's how they'll identify me.

Unable to maintain her grip on the wale, she let go. Supported only by Alexander's steady hand as the boat rocked in the wind and waves, she reached her full height, lifted her head, and returned the stares of a hundred gawking men.

It's over. We're caught. But I will not flinch.

She stood in silence and concentrated on not toppling over as the voice of her long-dead father whispered in her ear.

"Theodosia, no matter what happens in your life, never forget—"

"Our cabin boy just died," the officer yelled from the railing.

"You're a Varro."

"We need a new one."

Father must've known my life was going to be a challenge.

"You'll do fine, boy."

Theodosia gasped as the officer's words sank in. "That's not possible."

Did they divert the ship just to find a cabin boy?

"Watch your tongue." A scowl darkened the officer's face as his cape flapped hard in the wind. "Captain decides what's possible and what's not."

"No, I mean— Physically, I can't do that kind of work. It's my legs."

"How old are you?" The officer's eyes bored into her.

"Fourteen." That was part of the agreed-upon story.

"Don't look fourteen."

Good thing I'm scrawny right now. No feminine curves to give me away.

At that moment, a man in an even-longer, even-noisier cape swaggered to the railing. He waved his hand, and the other officer retreated.

The captain. Nero's agent on the sea.

"What happened to your legs, boy?"

"An accident, sir. I can't walk well or stand for very long." That part of the story, at least, was true.

Juno, help me spin the lies equally well.

"Years ago," she said, "I fell off the roof of our barn. Ma tried to straighten my legs, but she only made 'em worse."

Alexander gushed fake enthusiasm. "Despite all that, my son's a superb fisherman!"

The captain switched his eyes to Alexander. "You don't sound Sardinian. More like a Greek."

Alexander responded with his usual wry smile. "We Greeks do have some experience fishing these waters."

"And now you live in Sardinia?"

"Yes, sir. Came for adventure. Met a girl. Had a son. Never went home."

Who knew he was such a proficient liar?

A deep ache pulsed up from Theodosia's knees to her hips and spine. "Please, sir," she said, "it hurts me to stand. May I sit down?"

The captain frowned but made no haste to answer. At last, he shrugged. "I need a new cabin boy, but not one who can't stand or walk."

Theodosia collapsed onto the bench and held her breath as the captain focused his attention once more on the boatman.

"Where're you heading?"

"Thought we'd make it to Capri today, but the wind's against us."

"How's the fishing?"

"No good. Going back to where we had better luck yesterday."

"Got anything to sell?"

"No, sir."

"Damn!" The captain banged his palm on the railing. "An ocean full of fish and our stock runs out."

He hasn't heard of our escape.

She struggled to breathe normally.

And he came this way in search of a cabin boy or a fish dinner, not a woman fleeing for her life.

"Just a ways north of here—" The boatman gestured and grinned anew as even more lies poured out. "We passed a fellow with a huge catch. Headed to Ostia he was."

"Guess we'll head in, too," the captain said, "a lot sooner than expected."

"Good journey to you then." The boatman dipped his paddle into the water and nodded for Alexander and Theodosia to do the same.

A shout rang out from the high deck, followed by another in the hold. The long oars pierced the water on both sides, splashing the tiny boat as they maneuvered away from it.

"You handled that well, my love," Alexander said when the bireme was out of earshot. "Looks like we're safe."

Safe for now, but we must never let ourselves be trapped again.

***

Thousands of stars silvered the night sky as the fishing boat floated through the volcanic Aeolian Isles on its course for the Sicilian port of Messana.

Dawn still hadn't arrived when the boatman pointed to an odd orange light floating above the water in the distance.

"There's our beacon," he said. "The Greeks built that stone structure centuries ago. It's been protecting ships out here ever since."

Even more eye-catching than the brightest star, the flame that flickered atop the famous light tower at Pelorus was a welcome sight after five days and nights at sea.

"You'll have us ashore by sunrise?" Alexander asked.

"Expect to, but there's some bad currents to come before we reach the north end of the channel."

For the last hour of this first phase of their escape, with the boat slipping and swirling toward the Strait of Messana, Theodosia gripped the peeling wales with both hands, squeezed her eyes shut, and forced herself to envision a better future. At last, as the first pink rays edged over the mainland, the boat eased into the calmer waters separating this northeastern tip of Sicily from the Italian Peninsula and on to a sandy cove beneath the bluff.

High above them, the immense fire glowed atop its tower.

The boatman let his passengers off on the beach, accepted their thanks and a tip of a few coins, and pushed out toward the channel.

Soon, he vanished into the mist, leaving Alexander, Stefan, and Theodosia Varro—refugees from the might of Imperial Rome—on their own near the town of Messana, a place where none of them had ever been before.

Clutching Alexander's hand, as she always did these days, and with Stefan close by in case she needed extra help, Theodosia made her way across the sand, around a series of tide pools, and up a jumble of rocks. At the top, moments after the sun popped into the eastern sky, she collapsed onto dew-covered grasses, massaged her aching legs, and looked across the water.

Somewhere back there were all the places she had loved and hated in her life. Her villa and the coastal land around it. Rome's glorious Forum. That stinking cave cell in the Carcer Tullianum.

And Otho would be back in Rome by now, nursing his own injured leg, fuming over last night's humiliation, and conspiring with Nero to recapture the woman with a secret that could topple the emperor from his throne.

***

"You two stay here," Alexander said. "I'll check out the situation in Messana while you catch your breath."

"No, wait." Theodosia reached for his hand again and tugged him into the grass beside her. "There's something we promised we'd do as soon as we landed."

Had she been a typical Roman maiden, marrying a typical Roman man under normal circumstances, she would have come to this moment prepared to murmur the traditional wedding vow: "Where thou art Gaius, I am Gaia."

But these were not normal circumstances, and Theodosia and Alexander were anything but a typical bride and groom. So she improvised.

"I pledge before Jupiter, the father of gods and men—and with Stefan as my true witness—that I freely accept you, Alexander, as my husband. I will love and respect you every day of my life and be a loyal and caring wife to you."

"And obedient?" Alexander's deep-set eyes twinkled.

Even for a man who relished irony, this turn of events had to be beyond belief. But still…

How much obedience can I bring myself to promise?

She gave him a half-shy, half-sly smile. "I ask the blessing of Juno, who held me close through so much turmoil and pain, to restore my body so I can give you, my beloved husband, many fine sons."

"But no obedience, I suspect." His eyes teased her again.

She touched his beard, her fingers lingering for a moment on that old, deep scar on his jaw where hair no longer grew. "I'll need some time to get used to this new life and our changed relationship. I will do my best to be an obedient wife, but I am who I am and what I am." She gestured for him to help her stand. "As you know very well."

"Better than anyone else alive." Alexander stood, pulled her up, and planted his lips on hers.

She smiled when he released her. "That's the first time you've ever taken the initiative to kiss me."

"First of many." He winked. "Well, for my part, I pledge my love to you before Apollo, our great Greek god of healing and music who guided me back to you when all seemed lost."

Alexander motioned for Stefan to come closer. The big man wrapped his long arms around them, as if binding the bride and groom in a marriage knot.

Despite the significance of their unorthodox ceremony, Theodosia couldn't help chuckling to herself.

This may well be the strangest wedding that ever took place on Sicilian soil.

"I utter these words," Alexander continued, "so Apollo will know—and also with Stefan as my true witness—that I freely take you, Theodosia, to be my stubborn, impetuous, and occasionally disobedient wife. I will love you, care for you, protect you, honor you, and be faithful to you through all the days of my life, wherever the Fates may choose to take us."

And so, with humor instead of fanfare, Theodosia Varro—the last surviving member of a long, illustrious line—and a man known simply as Alexander—whom she once had owned as a slave—became husband and wife in the eyes of the gods of Greece and Rome.

A short time later, Alexander left Theodosia in the care of Stefan, also her former slave, and went to investigate the port city of Messana.

THE FARMHOUSE OF LEIOS BRYAXIS
ON THE ISLAND OF EUBOEA, NORTH OF ATHENS

Nikolaos entered the kitchen, bowed to his host, and took his regular seat at the end of a long wooden table. As usual, none of the men munching figs as they awaited Hebe's hot pancakes and fragrant fennel sausages bothered to acknowledge his presence.

The cooking fire that shot sparks out of the hearth never failed to overheat the kitchen, even on the coldest winter day. But on that bright mid-June morning, both front and back doors stood open, filling the air with cooling breezes, the chirps of birds in the eaves, and a not-so-welcome odor from the livestock pens behind the barn.

My master never would've dined in a room that reeked of pig shit.

Although Nikolaos had lived on the Bryaxis farm for a year, the crudeness of Greek country life still astounded him.

The man at the head of the table—the short-statured, square-headed, thick-necked Leios Bryaxis—owned one of the largest farms on the island of Euboea. But still, he was a barely literate peasant, nothing at all like the refined magistrate whom Nikolaos had served for a decade in Daphne, a lovely, leafy, popular-with-Romans suburb of Antioch, the capital of the province of Syria. And in every possible way, Bryaxis's manners and house and slaves reflected that contrast.

Ignoring his young guest, Bryaxis spoke quietly with his two sons-in-law, who had arrived last night, accompanied by their wives and children. From the women's quarters above came the voices of Bryaxis's daughters, jumbled with the sounds of screaming babies and inconsolable weeping.

Damn near drowns out the men's conversation.

It wasn't that Nikolaos cared about their conversation, which would be just more death talk. Scary tales of the plague that had reappeared on the north coast of Euboea last spring. Names of islanders lost in this latest round, including Bryaxis's wife, who would be buried on the farm today.

His mind shifted to a matter of greater concern to himself.

Where's Lycos?

Every other morning for the past two months, Nikolaos and Lycos had conducted one-on-one tutoring sessions with the goal of teaching each other all the different things they knew. But today, with so much grief in the house, spending even an hour that way would offend their hosts.

Hope he doesn't have the plague, too.

It wasn't that Nikolaos cared about Lycos, either. Didn't actually like him. Couldn't understand why his father had taken such pains to bring him along on the flight from the Italian Peninsula two years ago.

But lately, despite his young age, Lycos was growing in Nikolaos's esteem. The boy had turned out to be a talented tutor, and Nikolaos wanted to keep learning, even in this second-hand way, the things that Alexander had taught Lycos back in Rome and surely would have taught his own son if they had been fortunate enough to enjoy a normal family life in years gone by.

Father'll be impressed at how much I've learned while he's away.

From the stairway in the hall behind him came the smack of large bare feet, an announcement that Myrine—the buxom, left-handed slave girl who waited table—had arrived at last.

Late for her duties. Wonder if Bryaxis will slap her.

After profuse apologies to her master, Myrine filled plates with her mother's pancakes and sausages and rushed them, still steaming, to the men.

As usual, Hebe the cook kept a close watch on her daughter and everyone else in the kitchen.

Myrine's bulbous nose and downcast eyes flushed even more florid than normal as she carried food around the table.

Nikolaos had never found Myrine pretty. The girl shared a distinctive look with most of the other human chattel on the farm, a shape both square and squat with enormous hands and feet, pink-blotched skin, and ragged hair in the drabbest shade of brown he had ever seen.

Absolutely bovine.

But bovine or not, Myrine was, at fourteen, the youngest female slave on the Bryaxis property and thus of great interest to her master's house guest.

Just a year younger than me.

Myrine stumbled on the uneven floor, as if her thoughts were far away.

My master never would've put up with such a sorry excuse for a servant.

For the briefest moment, as the girl reached Nikolaos's end of the table with his plate of pancakes and sausages, she paused. Then, clearly preparing herself for what she knew was coming, she moved closer to serve him.

As always, he watched her face, which betrayed no emotion as his hand grazed the back of her thighs, slid up to her round posterior, and probed its hidden parts through the thin fabric of her chiton. After all his months of residence here, this intimate little moment was now an appealing, routine feature of every meal.

Nikolaos knew the slave was braced for it, but still he took pleasure in the twitch of her buttocks under his fingers.

Just like they always do.

Without a word, Myrine set the plate in front of him, stepped back, and moved away.

Not interested. Never interested.

He smiled to himself, jutted his jaw, and reached for a bowl of honey to sweeten his pancakes.

But she'll be interested soon enough.

***

Bryaxis and his sons-in-law were just finishing breakfast when Lycos slipped down the stairs and joined Nikolaos at the end of the table. His tardy arrival escaped no one's notice.

"You spent the night in the women's quarters," Bryaxis said. It was a statement, not a question. He wasn't usually quick to anger, but...

Still, it was a stupid thing to do. With a crotchety old Greek like Bryaxis, you never know how he'll react.

"Yes, sir, I did." Lycos's face was now as red as Myrine's. At age ten, he occupied an awkward spot between the world of a small boy—free to visit the women's quarters without permission—and the very different world of the grown men seated at this table. "I didn't think you'd mind."

Good thing he's still a child, or Bryaxis would flog him like a slave.

The master of the house eyed his youngest guest. "My wife was fond of you. My daughters are, too. Glad you were there to comfort them."

Lycos blinked back tears, tore off a piece of the pancake that Myrine set in front of him, and crammed it into his mouth without dipping it in honey.

"How're they doing up there?" asked the husband of one of Bryaxis's twin daughters.

"Iocaste was out of her mind when I left." Lycos glanced at the ceiling and cocked his head to listen. "That's her you hear wailing."

"Last of the three still at home," said the other son-in-law, "and very close to her mother."

"Iocaste's got female issues," her father said in his usual flat way. "Needs to be married off, and soon."

Nikolaos mopped up the last bites on his plate and licked his fingers. *Old man's been saying that a lot lately.*

"I told her," Bryaxis went on, "Stefanos better be back by harvest time."

"You're letting her pick her own husband?" asked one of the sons-in-law.

"And then wait for him?" asked the other.

"Well, she made such a fuss about it." Bryaxis pushed his stool away from the table. "But I told her, if Stefanos ain't here by September, there's a fellow on the other side of the island keeps asking to marry her."

Without another word, the three men left the kitchen.

Hebe immediately loaded a tray of food for the women and headed upstairs. The dirty plates clanked in Myrine's hands as she hauled them from the table and washed them in a tin pan of water. By their master's rule, neither of the slaves was allowed to do any cleanup or leave the kitchen until the adult males in the family were gone. Young guests, of course, didn't count.

Lycos flicked the long brown curls that hung around his face and raised his green eyes to Nikolaos. "I know what's wrong with Iocaste. It's not just that she loves Stefan, but—"

"Time to break that stupid old habit," Nikolaos said. "You're living in Greece now, so call him *Stefanos*, not that childish version, *Stefan*."

Lycos ignored him. "She's afraid of that man who keeps asking for her hand. They only met once, but Iocaste can't stand him. She keeps telling me she won't marry anyone but Stefan, no matter what her father says."

Myrine walked across the room and rested her palms on the table. "At her sister's wedding last summer, that man from the other side of the island done something that really pissed off Mistress Iocaste."

"What?" Nikolaos asked.

The slave turned her bovine eyes on him. "Can't you guess?"

"No." He smirked at her. "You'll have to tell me."

"Young master—"

"Not all that young. I'm absolutely taller than you and absolutely stronger than you and absolutely—in every way that matters—a man."

"And *absolutely*," she dared to mock him, "not my master."

"Close enough." He grabbed one of her wrists and held it while he rubbed up and down her arm with his other hand. "So, Myrine, if you know something about this fellow who wants to marry Iocaste, you must tell me."

"I don't know nothing." Myrine yanked her arm away and stepped out of reach. "Just that he made her feel dirty. She told her ma 'bout it, not her pa."

"That's why she's so upset," Lycos said. "That and… well, she's lost her mother now, but even more, her mother was the only one who could reason with her father."

"She's fearing her pa." Myrine's brow furrowed as if her own future were at stake. "Thinking he'll force that scummy fellow on her."

And if that scummy fellow marries Iocaste, Bryaxis'll probably give him Myrine, too. Fun to imagine all the sexy stuff he'll make her do.

"Bryaxis waited this long." Lycos turned as a clatter sounded on the stairs. "I bet he'll hold off a bit more."

Iocaste's unstrapped sandals hit the kitchen floor. "Is Pa still here?"

The others shook their heads.

"I gotta talk to him before the funeral." Iocaste lowered her thick frame onto the bench and bent over to fasten her sandals as a black tangle of hair spilled over her shoulders. Her nose seemed to stick out from her face even more than usual, and after a day of intensive weeping, her red face outshone even Myrine's.

If Myrine's a cow, Iocaste's a rooster.

"There's something Pa don't know," she said. "A big secret Stefanos shared with me before he left. Pa's gotta hear 'bout it before he goes and does something crazy."

"It can wait," Nikolaos said.

"Not if you'd heard Pa. He said, just like this—" Iocaste lowered her voice and scowled in perfect imitation of Leios Bryaxis. "You're seventeen, girl, and no man wants an old bride."

Nikolaos snickered.

With a fat enough dowry, any girl can catch a husband, no matter how old or ugly she is.

"I begged Pa to let me wait till Stefanos gets back, but now he's saying—" Iocaste's voice cracked. "That dirty dog's gonna be at Ma's funeral." She leaped to her feet. "So, Pa's gotta hear this before he—"

"None of that makes any sense." Nikolaos didn't care if he cut off her babble.

"It makes sense to me," Lycos said with his usual smugness.

Can't believe I have to explain something so obvious.

"Why wouldn't Bryaxis want Stefanos for a son-in-law?" Nikolaos laughed. "Huge body. Strong muscles. Great work habits. What farmer wouldn't welcome a man like that into his family?"

"Pa did feel that way when Stefanos was here," Iocaste said. "But now that he's been gone a whole year—"

"So," Nikolaos interrupted her again, "what's your big secret?"

She aimed her puffy rooster eyes on him. "If I tell you, it won't be a secret any more."

"If you tell me, I'll talk your father into letting you wait longer." Nikolaos jutted his jaw. "He'll listen to another man."

"Can't reveal Stefanos's secret."

"I won't help you unless you tell me."

"Stefanos said to keep it to myself."

"But you'll tell your father."

"Sure, to keep him from marrying me to the most repulsive man I've ever met."

"But what if Stefanos and *my* father…" Nikolaos always made a point of emphasizing his relationship to Alexander, whom everybody on the Bryaxis farm seemed to adore. "What if they never make it back here? Aren't you afraid of dying a childless crone?"

"No, because I trust Stefanos to come back. And I trust Alexander, too. A whole lot more, it seems, than you do."

CHAPTER 2

Sitting stiffly side by side on a flat rock surrounded by mats of yellow wildflowers, neither Theodosia nor Stefan spoke as the morning sun lifted the dampness from the northern Sicilian coast and warmed the salty air around them.

Just like old times.

"My dear old friend," she said at last, as the silence grew awkward, "Alexander and I owe you so very much."

Stefan lifted one of her hands and kissed it. "If things had turned out different, I'd be the one taking you to my bed tonight."

Theodosia retrieved her hand. "Don't ever say such a thing to me again."

"Can't I even think it?"

"No."

"But—" He lowered his voice, even though no one else was around to hear. "I *do* think it."

"By all the gods, Stefan, you're shameless." She erupted in peals of laughter that threatened to go on and on until they reached the ears of the captains and sailors and rowers on ships in the harbor at Messana and beyond.

How wonderful to be free and able to laugh again!

"And you haven't changed a bit," she added.

"Why change? Women love me as I am."

Theodosia stared into his bright-blue eyes. "Good thing you'll soon be married to Iocaste. Just please be smart for once."

"I'm always smart."

"No, sometimes you're a fool." She tried to stifle her amusement and sound more serious. "Now, listen to me. What you're about to do—marry into a free-born, land-owning, slave-holding family—would've been unthinkable for you not long ago, and all you have to do to make a success of it is be faithful to Iocaste. No messing with her slave women."

"Iocaste will nail my hide to the wall if I ever mess with her slave women."

"She must be a lot tougher and meaner than I ever was."

"She is." He grinned and changed the subject. "So, tell me what you hope to find in Greece."

Theodosia shrugged. "Haven't had much time to think about it."

"You can't just show up there, you know. Gotta have a dream."

"Well." She plucked one of the yellow flowers and twirled it in her fingers. "In my dream, if you want to call it that, Alexander and I make our escape to some lovely, peaceful place where Nero can never catch us and Alexander is free to use his talents any way he pleases. No more slavery for him."

"He'll like that."

"Along the way, I plan to give him lots of children." That old, familiar flush crept up her neck and cheeks. "And build a happy home for him and them… and Niko, too."

"What if some bad person shows up to spoil that dream?"

"Other than Nero and Otho, I can't imagine who would." She tossed the flower over her shoulder. "But you know me. I've always had to fight for what was good in my life. So, I'll fight a bad person, too, if he shows up."

Stefan reached into the breast of his tunic, as if he had been waiting for the perfect moment, and pulled out a small leather pouch. "Here's something to help with that dream." He tugged its cord over his head and handed it to her. "Not sure how you'll feel about it, but it is yours."

Theodosia opened the pouch and turned it upside down. Out slid a silver amulet in the shape of a twisted viper. In its mouth… a tiny ruby.

Long-forgotten memories rushed back.

Otho's bribe to Lucilla.

"Do you know what this is," she asked, "or where it came from?"

"Alexander told me all about it after we got to Greece. Before that, I didn't know nothing."

Not sure I believe that.

"You said it would help with my dream." She tossed the amulet in her hand. "But how could something created for such a wicked purpose bring anything but grief?"

"While I was away, I learned all sorts of strange things about the Greeks. They scare their little ones with stories of sea monsters covered with snake heads and an ugly woman who grows serpents instead of hair, but then they turn around and talk about how great vipers are, not bad creatures at all."

"You don't mean vipers like my brother?"

"No." Stefan made a face. "Real-life vipers kill rodents, so the Greeks welcome 'em into their farms and gardens. They also talk about 'em as guardians and healers, especially for women in childbirth."

"I never knew that."

"During our first escape, Alexander kept telling Lycos how this little viper thing was gonna look out for us."

Lycos. Haven't thought of him in years.

"Whenever the boy got sick or scared or cold or hungry, Alexander always told him, 'Don't worry, we've got our viper amulet.' Or 'No matter how bad things are right now, our viper amulet will see us home.' And I guess it worked, 'cause we did make it all the way to Greece."

"I never knew Alexander was superstitious."

"He's the one insisted on bringing it when we came back for you. For protection and good luck, he said."

Theodosia studied the viper amulet as if she had never seen it before.

Beautiful texture in the silver skin. And with that tiny ruby, it's perfect.

"I should hate this thing," she said, "but I don't."

"What'll you do with it?"

"If it means so much to Alexander, I'll wear it every day." She returned the amulet to its pouch, draped the cord around her neck, and smiled at Stefan. "And let it take us to a happy place where he'll earn a good living as a free man, I'll bear him many children, and neither of us will ever have to deal with powerful Romans again."

***

The sun blazed high overhead. Sweating profusely, Alexander tossed a rolled-up bundle onto the yellow flowers and dropped to the ground beside it. "There are reward signs painted on walls all over Messana. Nero's offering an immense bounty." He wiped his sleeve across his forehead. "Five hundred gold coins for *each* of you."

"Never knew I was worth so much." Stefan chuckled sourly. "He sure must want us caught."

"He does." Alexander nodded. "You're well described, Theodosia. A gaunt woman. Chopped-off hair. Early twenties. One leg bent, the other twisted. Believed to be traveling with a gladiator-size escaped slave."

"That would be me." Stefan dropped his head and scratched his scalp.

Theodosia looked at Alexander. "Any mention of you?"

He shook his head. "Nero and Otho didn't notice me at the banquet, so—unless Titus told them later—they have no idea I'm anywhere around."

"I reckon it's time to split up," Stefan said. "You two will be safer without me. The boatman had the right idea. Make like you're father and son, and nobody'll question you."

"I'm reluctant to separate, but—" Alexander untied the bundle. "Let me show you what I picked up in town." He unfolded a long, cheap cloak made of undyed wool so recently spun that it still smelled of sheep. Inside were two rolled parchments, two knives, and a cooked fish wrapped in cloth. He stuck one knife under his belt, gave the other to Stefan, passed the cloak to Theodosia, and spread out one of the documents over the flowers.

Theodosia and Stefan leaned over the parchment, which featured crude black ripples, brown-shaded areas, and scrawled place names.

"This is the Italian Peninsula." Alexander outlined it with his forefinger. "Greece is over here. North Africa, down here."

Theodosia had trouble making sense of the drawing.

Never saw anything like this.

"What's it for?" she asked.

"Navigation. The shopkeeper claims every ship at sea these days has at least one of these on board. They're copies of a drawing done by a fellow named Pomponius Mela during the reign of Emperor Claudius. Some enterprising Roman bought the original ten years ago and has had his slaves reproducing it ever since. All the major cities and ports are marked. This is Ostia, see, right next to Rome." He moved his finger slightly and thumped it on the northwest coast. "Your villa is somewhere around here."

Alexander kept his finger on that spot and extended his thumb down to where the island of Sicily tipped closest to the Italian Peninsula. "We're right here now, at Messana. Shows how far we rowed in five days."

"That's a long way," Theodosia said, "so maybe the worst is behind us now."

"Afraid not, my love. With reward notices for you and Stefan going up in every major seaport, these last few days may turn out to be the easiest part of our journey." He circled his fingers over Greece, then pointed to an indistinct shape in the Aegean Sea. "This is the island of Euboea, north of Athens, where Niko and Lycos are waiting for us, not to mention a certain young lady named Iocaste." He gave Stefan a knowing look, then turned apologetic eyes to Theodosia. "See how much farther we still have to go?"

"Hope I can make it."

"Let's be honest." Alexander's eyes crinkled at the corners. "There's plenty of risk to such a trip, even under ordinary circumstances, which these most definitely are not."

"Tell me," Stefan said, "where in the Italian Peninsula should a gladiator-size escaped slave go if he wants to get to Greece without being caught."

"By an odd coincidence, I asked the shopkeeper that same thing."

"I trust," Theodosia said, only partly in jest, "you left out the gladiator-size-escaped-slave part of the question."

"I did." Alexander reached for a broken seashell lying in the grass and used its edge to gouge a dent in the parchment on the east coast of the Italian Peninsula. "According to the fellow in the shop, the fishing village of Lecce, south of the big naval port at Brundisium, on the Adriatic Sea, is remote enough to be safe."

"Lecce." Stefan pointed at the marked spot.

"Lecce is your best bet and ours, too." Alexander dug his sharp shell into the island north of Athens. "And here's our ultimate goal, the island of Euboea."

Stefan nodded. "Island of Euboea."

Alexander squinted at his friend. "Can you remember that?"

"Euboea. Euboea. Euboea. I ain't educated, but that don't mean I'm stupid."

"How long will it take him to get there?" Theodosia asked.

"Hard to say exactly, but moving by himself, Stefan should get to Lecce, and maybe all the way to Euboea, while you and I are still trudging across the southern mainland."

"Because of my legs?"

Alexander patted her shoulder. "Sorry, my love. Didn't mean to say that the way it came out."

She tilted her head and laid it against his arm. "I'll try not to be too much of a drag on you."

"Well, as for that—" Alexander chuckled. "If you're my son, I'll shout at you and push you along and rough you up and make you keep pace and teach you a good lesson if you ever fall behind."

Theodosia made a show of pouting. "Not sure I'm going to like being your son."

He leaned over and kissed her lips. "Only in public, sweet wife."

∗∗∗

An hour later, after they shared the fish, Stefan set off on his own, armed with the knife, an assortment of coins, and his gouged-up drawing on parchment.

Once he was gone, Alexander cast a flirtatious eye at Theodosia. "What say we find a place in town for a couple of nights. Somewhere to bathe and eat and rest and just be alone."

"Think it's safe?"

"Without Stefan, yes. That long cloak will hide your legs. If we keep a low profile, there's no reason a man and his son should attract attention."

"You're serious about keeping up that story?"

"It's our best chance, my love. Will you play the part?"

"If I must. Just don't thrash me too often."

He grinned at her. "Only when you're disobedient."

∗∗∗

"We're full up," the innkeeper said to the bedraggled father and son on his doorstep. "Got a dozen big ships in port with their crews billeted all over town. Got sailors bunked ten to a room."

"Perhaps," the father said, "you could suggest some other place that might have a spare room."

"Nobody has spare rooms." The innkeeper shut the door.

The father strode down the street as his lame son limped behind.

The afternoon was too warm for such a hot, smelly cloak, but still Theodosia kept it on.

They heard the same answer at two adjacent inns and five more around the harbor, including several with signs describing the fugitives on walls near their doors. The ninth inn they approached was a prosperous-looking, two-story establishment identified by a comically illustrated placard as The Petulant Pelican. But the man who opened the door wasn't patient enough even to find out what they were looking for.

"No room," he said curtly. "Overloaded."

Theodosia tugged at Alexander's sleeve. "Father, let's find something to eat."

Without looking at her, Alexander nodded.

"No, wait." The innkeeper's voice lost its sharpness as he gazed down at Theodosia. "My wife might be willing to share space in our apartment, as long as you swear you're not sailors."

"Definitely not sailors," Theodosia said.

"I'll have to charge you double, of course." The innkeeper offered an oily smirk. "For the intrusion into our home."

Alexander cupped his hand under the small money bag looped around his belt and jingled the coins inside. "We're not rich, sir, but not beggars either." His voice was tight, his forehead furrowed. "We can pay."

The man motioned them in. "My name's Carbo. Wife's Candelora. Let's see if she's agreeable today."

Carbo led them through the atrium and up a flight of stairs to a bright sitting room where a woman in pink reclined on a couch with red cushions. An open window framed both the waterfront and a distant mountain on the mainland. A stooped, white-haired maidservant lurked in one corner.

"These travelers are looking for a room," Carbo told his wife. "They swear they're not sailors."

"It's been a long journey," Alexander said, "and we need to rest, but the town's packed."

"I thought," Carbo said, bobbing his head toward his wife, "maybe you wouldn't mind if they stayed up here with us for a few nights."

Candelora swung her legs to the floor and patted the cushion beside her. "Come on over, boy, and have a seat."

Theodosia's left hand guided her onto the couch as her right hand clutched both pieces of the cloak at her knees.

Candelora wrinkled her nose at the sheep-stink and brazenly pulled the fabric aside. "How'd you get so hurt?"

"Long time ago," Theodosia launched into her memorized story, "I tumbled off the roof and smashed myself up. Ma did her best to fix things, but some of my body parts still don't work right."

Candelora clucked as she inspected Theodosia's misshapen legs. "It's an awful warm day. Care to shed your cap and cloak?"

Theodosia glanced at Alexander. Without hesitation, he helped her out of the cloak, tugged the cap off her head, and turned back to face Carbo.

"This is my son, Doros, the gods' finest gift to me. With those legs, it's hard for him to keep up, especially on cobblestones and stairs, so he wears out fast." Alexander extended a hand to his host. "I'm Sabbas, a merchant from the island of Corfu, on the west coast of Greece. Doros and I have been in Sardinia for a month, working out shipping arrangements with a commercial captain there. We're on our way home now, but first, we need some sleep. It never occurred to us that every inn in Messana would be crammed with sailors."

Carbo eyed Candelora, who nodded. "Wrapped around the chimney wall," she said, "is a small space with a single bed. Our daughter slept there until she married. It's far enough from our room that we didn't bump into each other in the night. Best part is, it faces away from the street. Overlooks the alley and the quiet rear of the building."

"Whatever you're willing to share." All visible signs of tension had drained from Alexander's face and voice.

"There's a special benefit to sleeping up here with us," Carbo said, "as opposed to down there with the sailors. No bedbugs!" He chortled as if that were the wittiest thing anyone had ever said. "Assuming, of course, that you didn't bring any with you."

"No bedbugs on us." Alexander chortled a bit, too.

"You'll bathe before turning in, I trust," Candelora said, "just to make sure."

"Of course," Theodosia was breathing easier as well.

Nothing in the world I'd like more right now than a hot soak in a tub.

***

Three hours after the funeral, once the extended Bryaxis family had left, Nikolaos stretched out in a bare patch of dirt and closed his eyes. Listened as bees buzzed from the flower-fragrant trees to their hives in a nearby meadow. Enjoyed the solitude. Waited for Lycos.

Their chosen tutoring space was located on the front side of the house, beside the path at the edge of the apple orchard, and as far as possible from the pig pen and poultry coops behind the barn. Like the bees, Lycos moved at his own speed. Nikolaos was accustomed to waiting for him, but still...

Is the brat intentionally annoying, or does it come naturally?

At last, hearing voices, he opened his eyes in time to see Lycos amble around the corner of the house, accompanied by Myrine and Hebe.

Obvious what Myrine will look like when she's fifty.

Heavy, gray, and stooped, Hebe was just what one expected of a slave who had labored for decades in her master's kitchen and given birth to over a dozen of his children.

Pleasant enough way to build a labor force.

Especially if you've got an attractive—and fertile—slave girl.

All five of Hebe's surviving sons toiled in Bryaxis's orchards, barns, sties, folds, coops, hives, and fields, while Myrine—her youngest child and only living girl—stayed busy in the kitchen and nearby butchering hut. Each one was short, square-headed, and thick-necked, with straight hairlines that emphasized the overall boxiness of their appearance.

Six perfect replicas of Bryaxis.

Nikolaos sniggered as he always did when confronted with the reality of life on a remote farm. By his recently deceased wife, Bryaxis had three weepy daughters. By his slave concubine, five robust sons and one voluptuous, hard-working daughter... none of whom he ever would acknowledge.

Wonder which gods conspired to make that happen?

Carrying a branch the length of his forearm, Lycos dropped to the ground. "Myrine's amazing with a knife. Quickly put a fine point on our writing stick."

"So, a slave did a job for you. Why spend so much time talking to her?"

"Myrine's smart, and I like her." With the palm of one hand, Lycos smoothed the dirt and scratched Myrine's name into it with his newly sharpened stick. "Time spent with her is always time well spent."

Nikolaos exhaled a disparaging *pffffh*. "She's just a slave."

"You and I were slaves once, too." Lycos's scarred face contorted. "Not so long ago, Niko."

"I've told you a hundred times. Don't call me Niko. I'm a man now. My name is Nikolaos."

Lycos shook his long, unruly curls. "You don't look like a man."

"Been marking my height on the barn wall. I'm lots taller than I was six months ago."

"Doesn't mean you're really a man."

"My arms and shoulders are bigger. Stronger, too. I'm more man than boy right now, which isn't something you can say."

"Are you going to insist that Alexander call you Nikolaos when he gets back?"

"Sure, why not? He gave me that name to start with."

"So, anyway, *Ni-ko-laos*." The boy stressed each syllable, as if adding one more was terribly inconvenient. "What makes you think you're too good to spend time with Myrine?"

"I'm a man. She's not. She's a slave. I'm not. I've got a fancy manumission paper all written out and stamped. She doesn't."

"And you think that means—"

"It means I'm better than her."

"Better than me, too, I guess, since I don't have a fancy manumission paper all written out and stamped."

"Which means, legally, you're still a slave." Nikolaos sneered. "And that means, legally, I *am* better than you."

"Nobody else around here knows that."

"And nobody else ever will unless you piss me off too much."

"How do I piss you off?"

"You keep me waiting while you chat with a slave. You insist on calling me 'Niko' and Stefanos 'Stefan'. And you just act obnoxious."

"You'd turn me in to the Romans for that?"

Better not vex Lycos too much.

Need him for more tutoring sessions.

"No, of course not." Playfully, Nikolaos punched Lycos in the shoulder. "You're almost like my little brother. So, no, I'm not going to turn you in, no matter how annoying you are."

A long silence followed, which Nikolaos finally broke with a laugh. "Well, my annoying almost-brother, what are you going to teach me today?"

"Maybe nothing, if you keep threatening to turn me in. That wasn't the first time, you know."

"Just teasing you." Nikolaos ruffled Lycos's curls. "I appreciate how well you're tutoring me."

In reply, Lycos pounded the blunt end of his stick into the ground.

"And don't forget," Nikolaos went on, "these sessions benefit you, too, on days when it's my turn to be the teacher. My father will be proud of us both when he gets back."

Lycos kept hammering the ground.

"And also don't forget," Nikolaos added, "my master in Antioch had me *professionally* tutored in mathematics and Latin. He wanted a first-class secretary, and he saw great potential for that in me."

Lycos groaned. "I know, I know. I know all about how he made his Hebrew slaves teach you their language and history and culture, and how that made you so very, very much more valuable to him, and so on and on and on."

"Glad you pay attention when I tell you things. Actually, the Hebrew language, history, and culture *are* interesting. Maybe I'll teach you all that some time, too, if you ever stop acting like a brat."

***

"Tell me about the Roman woman," Nikolaos said as they strolled through the aromatic orchard after their session ended. "The one Father went back to rescue."

"She's nice."

"Nice? That's the best you can do?"

"Yes, because she *was* nice to me."

"How, exactly, was she 'nice' to you?"

Lycos shrugged. "The cook made me carry heavy buckets of water that hurt my arms and banged my legs, and the mistress put a stop to that. And she let me read Homer without slapping me, like her brother did. And she let Alexander tutor me without slapping him, like her brother did. And she—"

"Her brother slapped my father?"

"Lots of times. Over and over."

"In the face?"

"In the face. That's how Alexander got that bad scar on his jaw. I had to stand there and watch him take it."

"Hard?"

"Very hard. The master was always wearing his heavy gold ring. But the mistress never did that even once, not to Alexander or to me, and she kept her brother's nasty friends away from me, too. She was just… nice."

"So, fine, she was nice to you."

"And she was beautiful." Lycos giggled. "Alexander and Stefan were both in love with her."

"No! Father was never in love with *her.*" The moment the words slipped from Nikolaos's lips, he realized his tone was too sharp, so he softened it. "My father loved my mother, and he never stopped loving her."

"Well, he sure did act like he was in love with the mistress. Everybody saw it but her, and nobody was surprised, because she was so beautiful and nice."

She couldn't possibly have been nicer or more beautiful than Mother was.

They reached the end of a row of trees and turned the corner.

"Actually," Lycos went on, "the last time I saw the mistress, it was Saturnalia and she looked awful."

"Why?"

"The soldiers carried her to her balcony to watch the bonfire, because she couldn't walk."

"Why couldn't she walk?"

Lycos ignored his question, as he often did. "Later that night, I found her rubies, and we took off."

Her rubies?

Nikolaos glanced at the boy, who appeared lost in reverie.

Her rubies sound like something worth learning about.

Before they reached the house, Nikolaos draped his arm around Lycos's shoulders. "You mentioned finding some rubies at Saturnalia. Where did they come from?"

"From her. The mistress." Lycos stopped walking.

"I understand that, but— How did *you* wind up with them?"

"She's clever. She figured it out."

Nice. Beautiful. Clever.

None of this improved Nikolaos's opinion of the woman whom his father now had returned to Rome to save, but he kept that to himself.

"Where are those rubies now?" he asked.

"We used a few little ones in our escape."

"And the rest?"

"I don't know. Ask Alexander when he gets back. Or Stefan."

There was a long silence.

"I bet you were scared that night," Nikolaos said.

Anything to keep his tongue moving.

"Not me, but the mistress was."

"Why was she scared?"

"Because she was trying to help us get away, but she wasn't sure we could. And because she knew the Romans would crucify us if they caught us."

"Crucify you?"

"That's what Alexander kept telling me, so I wouldn't make noise."

"Why would they have crucified you?"

"They'd have claimed we were thieves. Runaway slaves, you know, carrying a fortune in stolen rubies."

A fortune in stolen rubies.

"I hope she knows we got away." Lycos started moving again toward the house. "Hope she got away, too."

"Why would she need to get away from the Romans?" Nikolaos followed closely behind him. "Isn't she one of them?"

Father never mentioned any of this to me.

Lycos sighed, as if Nikolaos should already know this. "The full-blooded Romans don't like her, because she's half Greek."

"And we full-blooded Greeks don't like her," Nikolaos said, "because she's half Roman."

"Well, I'm a full-blooded Greek, and I like her, and so does your father, and he's a full-blooded Greek, so I think you'll like her, too, once she gets here."

"Not likely, especially if my father takes it into his head to marry her."

"Can he do that?" Lycos's expression brightened. "I mean, since Alexander was her slave, will the Romans here in Greece let them do that?"

That's a very good question. And maybe a way to stop them from marrying.

CHAPTER 3

The elderly maid entered Theodosia's bedroom with a flask of oil, a strigil, a pitcher of water, and several cotton towels.

"Mistress said you was wanting to bathe." She set her burdens on a three-legged table beside the door and gawked at her master's guest. "You need help, boy? Looking mighty tired."

"I can do for myself. It's just climbing stairs that's hard for me."

"Where's your pa?"

"He went to the public baths. For me, it's easier to wash up this way."

"Mistress said I was to stay and help you."

"I'm fine, really."

"I raised two boys." The woman moved to the room's generously sized window and tied back its sheepskin curtain. Light flooded the space. "Real used to bathing 'em."

Theodosia turned her back. "Please leave."

"Mistress was amazed how good you speak Latin. Better'n your pa, she told the master."

"I've spent more time on the Italian Peninsula than Father has."

"Mistress said your accent's native."

Theodosia tried to ignore her, but the woman wouldn't stop.

"Mistress said you don't look like your pa at all."

"You may leave now." Instantly, she knew her tone was wrong. *Mustn't act like an adult with experience commanding slaves.*

"He's got a Greek nose, Mistress said, but yours is Roman."

"I take after my mother's side of the family."

Why am I making things up just to satisfy the curiosity of a slave?

Before the maid had time to comment again, a new worry crept into Theodosia's head. "Did your mistress tell you to find out about me?"

"Nah, she don't care nothing 'bout you. I'm just curious."

"Well, if you don't mind leaving, I'd like to get on with my bath."

"Sure you don't need help? I got time. Not much else to do right now."

"No, as I said, I can bathe just fine on my own."

The slave angled toward the door, then looked over her shoulder. "Mistress said you're kinda odd for a boy."

"Please go now."

"Got some mighty messed-up legs."

"Get out!"

"Well, boy, you just yell if you need me. I won't be far."

***

Alexander returned to The Petulant Pelican shortly before dark, freshly bathed and shaved. He wore a new gray linen tunic and carried an identical one for Theodosia, plus a cloth packet of food, a wineskin, and a pottery cup.

Wrapped only in a couple of long towels—because she couldn't stand to put on her fisherman garb again, much less the sheep-smelly cloak—Theodosia rose from the bed that offered the only seating in the room.

Evening light filtered through the wide-open window that the slave had left uncovered.

With a finger to her lips, Theodosia pointed to the wall.

No telling where that woman sleeps.

"Take a whiff of this." Alexander extracted the cork from the wineskin.

Theodosia went to him and, for the first time in years, inhaled a delicious aroma she had taken for granted long ago. "Falernian. Can we afford it?"

He replugged the wineskin, laid it on the table, and drew her closer. "On our wedding night," he whispered, "we can afford it."

Theodosia gave him a kiss that ended only when her legs began to shake.

"Not even a bedbug will come between us tonight, my love." Alexander's voice was barely audible. "But first, we need to eat."

He helped her back to the bed, filled the cup, wiped its edge with a cloth, and presented it to her with all the polish of the attentive steward he had been. Then he fetched the three-legged table, unfolded the cloth on it, and set out a modest feast of olives and cheese, smoked fish, and fragrant Sicilian bread.

Theodosia took a few sips before passing the cup back to him.

Alexander downed what was left and refilled it.

Without saying another word, they devoured every bit of the food.

"That was wonderful," she said when the last crumb was gone. "I could eat the whole thing again right now."

"Our first meal alone as husband and wife." He kept his voice low as he caressed her cheek. "Not rich and elegant as my mistress would have expected, but served with a kind of love that lady never knew."

He returned the table to its place and gazed at her from across the room. A smile slowly spread over his lips.

Theodosia's neck and face flushed as they always did at awkward moments. Shyly, she stretched out one hand.

He approached, took both her hands, and knelt before her.

"We'll eat again tomorrow, and the day after, and the day after that. Simple meals until I can afford to give you—every single day for the rest of your life—the kind of food and wine and home that you deserve." He turned her hands over and kissed the palms. "Please believe that, Theodosia. We have nothing right now except our love, but I promise you… better days lie ahead."

"Mistress said you don't look like your pa at all."

"I will work harder," Alexander went on, "than ever before to give you a good life. So for now, let's just enjoy the miracle of being safe and together at last."

"Mistress was amazed how good you speak Latin."

Theodosia leaned closer. "You really think we're safe here?"

"Better'n your pa, she told the master."

"Nobody's hunting you and me. All eyes are out for a gladiator-size man and a lame woman, not for a normal-size Greek and his skinny adolescent son."

"Mistress said you're kinda odd for a boy."

"If we stick to our story," Alexander said, "we should be fine."

"Got some mighty messed-up legs."

Theodosia decided to ignore the words echoing in her ears.

I won't let that woman ruin our wedding night.

Alexander untied the curtain so they still had a bit of air and light, but also more privacy. Then he sat beside her on the bed, wrapped her in his arms, and nuzzled the top of her head.

"I've waited a long time for this." He gazed into her eyes at close range. "First imagined doing bold things—holding you, kissing you, making love to you—that night of the big storm. But you were so impossibly high above me. So far beyond my reach. Whatever god has brought us to this point, I will praise his name forever."

"Perhaps it was a goddess. I suspect Juno had the most to do with it."

"Then I will praise her name forever." Alexander stood, pulled off his new tunic, draped it over a nearby chest, and touched the towels wrapped around her. "Do you wish to remove these, or shall I?"

"What's your pleasure?"

"You do it."

Feeling the wine, she giggled a bit too loudly. "Yes, Father."

Alexander pressed a finger to her lips. "Keep your voice low if you want to continue enjoying these luxurious, bug-free accommodations. And don't call me Father, please. Not at this moment, anyway."

"Yes, Father." Theodosia grinned at him, dropped both towels to the floor, and came close to him. She ran her hands up and down his chest a few times before letting them slide to his thighs.

Alexander released a muted moan.

"I used to be so much more beautiful," she said. "Just wish you'd seen me naked like this, back then."

"Oh." Another moan. "I saw enough of you through those slinky fabrics you liked to wear. Wasn't hard to imagine the rest." His eyes caressed her breasts before his hands did. "These attracted my attention on the very first evening that we met. The way they moved under your garments. It took some serious effort to keep my interest from showing."

He ran his lips down her throat to her breasts and beyond, as Theodosia responded with her own soft noises.

"You are still beautiful, my love," he said, "inside and out. There are some things not even the Roman Empire can destroy."

"Let's pretend we're at the villa again, in the library on the night of that big storm. I'm playing my cithara and singing to you and Stefan, the rain and wind are pounding the walls, and you're having thoughts no self-respecting steward would ever allow himself to have."

"I'm having those same thoughts right now."

"So, please, picture me as I was that night and then do everything you wanted to do to me but didn't dare."

"Very well, Mistress, but don't forget…" He winked. "You asked for it."

***

If only I could put the slave woman's words out of my mind.

Theodosia lay awake with her arm across Alexander's chest and her ear over his heart, enjoying its beat even as she brooded over their situation.

As the hours passed, one thought resonated in her mind.

We should leave tonight.

Last evening, before he returned from the baths, she had evaluated two escape options. Only a few feet separated their window ledge from the flat roof of the back wing of Carbo's inn, so leaving that way would be easy, even for her. She would face a more challenging drop from the tile-topped parapet into the alley, but with Alexander on the ground to catch her, she felt sure she could manage it.

The other way—to sneak past Carbo and Candelora's bedroom in the dark, descend the narrow stairs without a lamp, and get out through the locked front door without raising a ruckus—seemed more perilous.

She couldn't bring herself to waken Alexander. He needed to sleep, and so did she, but she couldn't, so she lay quietly, listening and worrying.

After a few hours, he stirred, kissed her hand as he moved it aside, and went to use the chamber pot.

"You've been deep in sleep," she said when he came back to bed.

"I awoke a couple of times. Kept pinching myself. Had I dreamed this wonderful night?" His voice was groggy.

Still, Theodosia didn't let him doze off again. "I hate to keep you awake, but there's something you need to know."

He rolled onto his side and held her close as, in an undertone, she recounted her conversation with the slave woman.

"It was 'Mistress said this' and 'Mistress said that,' over and over. Clearly, Candelora didn't believe our story."

"Good thing you told me, because it heightens the importance of something I noted last evening." Alexander seemed fully awake now. "When we first reached the wharf yesterday, did you see any legionaries in the streets?"

"I wasn't paying much attention, but I don't believe so."

"Neither do I. Wasn't specifically watching for them, but if they'd been there I'd have noticed. When I came back here in the evening, I spotted a pair of soldiers on each end of this street. Quite sure they weren't there when we arrived, or even when I left for the baths."

"Think the slave turned us in?"

"More likely her master. No chance Carbo missed those signs around town. He's the kind who'd kill his only child for five hundred gold pieces."

"So, why haven't the soldiers come for us?"

"They're not looking for a man like me. I'm definitely not gladiator-size."

She gave him a quick kiss. "Your presence may have confused Carbo, but it does seem like Candelora identified me."

"If that's true, why didn't they send the soldiers in here for you while I was out?"

"Maybe you came back too soon, before they were ready. Or maybe they're just waiting till morning." Theodosia thought about it for a while. "Wonder if they know their servant tipped me off."

"Can't imagine she did that on purpose. For sure, she wouldn't have told her masters if she did."

"You think she was just curious, as she claimed?"

"I doubt she even knows about the reward. There's no way she can read the signs. More likely, she's just eager for something to gossip about. 'Master's got a guest with twisted legs' or something like that. Wherever there are slaves, there's a slave grapevine." Alexander crawled over Theodosia and swung his feet to the floor. "Trust me. I do know. By noon, every slave in Messana will be spreading the word that Carbo has a guest with messed-up legs."

"So, we've got to get away. Slip out through the window while it's still night." Theodosia rested both hands on the mattress and eased herself into a standing position. "Nobody'll know we're gone until well up in the morning. We'll have a good head start."

"My love." Still sitting, Alexander reached for her hand. "Let's think this through."

"What more is there to think through?"

"What if we're wrong?"

"What if we're *not* wrong?" Theodosia sat down beside him.

"What if it turns out there's no problem? What if the slave woman really was just curious?"

"It's still fine for us to leave."

"Not if our abrupt departure—out a window in the dark hours, no less—becomes the very thing that gives us away."

"Carbo and Candelora won't care as long as we leave double payment for one night."

"I wouldn't count on that. A reward of five hundred gold pieces beats double rent any day." Alexander released her hand. "What if Carbo turns us in and every Roman soldier in Sicily winds up chasing us?"

"Guess it's a matter of figuring out the greater risk."

"How do you calculate a risk like that?"

"Either we wait here," Theodosia said softly, "to find out if our suspicions are correct or not… and if they *are* correct, we're trapped. Or we leave while we can and take charge of our fate."

Alexander said nothing, so she leaned over and kissed him.

"You and I know exactly what they'll do if I'm caught. Nero and Otho will have a grand time with me. But what if we're both caught? How long before the local authorities discover you're an escaped slave and chain you up in some galley like the one we saw that first day at sea?"

Still, he remained silent.

Theodosia dropped her voice even more, to the barest whisper. "I could take whatever came to me, but I couldn't stand seeing you thrown back into slavery."

"You think I could stand seeing Nero and Otho get their hands on you again? I'll gladly die, Theodosia, before I let that happen."

"So, we're in agreement." She rose and tugged him to his feet. "We haven't struggled so hard and come so far only to be caught simply because we needed a little more sleep or because we were lucky enough to find a bedbug-free bed."

"We can't leave from the port, you know. They'd nab us there in an instant."

Good thing I developed a plan before he woke.

"So," she said, "we take a land route to the southern coast of Sicily. Nobody would expect us to head that way when we're so close to the mainland."

"Sicily's mostly mountains. Can you cross them on those legs?"

"They have horses on this island, don't they?"

"Of course, but—" Alexander chuckled under his breath. "Don't tell me you're itching for another hard ride."

"Itching for it, no. Up for it, yes. Riding's one of the things I do best. Lying around waiting to be captured is not."

***

They dressed in the dark. Alexander left double payment on the table and handed Theodosia some coins.

"In case we get separated," he whispered.

She dropped them into the leather pouch, where they clinked on the viper amulet. Then she hung the strap around her neck and secured its pouch under her tunic, between her breasts.

Meanwhile, Alexander lifted the sheepskin, crawled through the window, and lowered himself to the first-story roof. There was no moon, but the stars provided light.

Theodosia watched as he peered into the alley below, then returned and held his arms up to her.

Balanced on her semi-reliable right leg, she hoisted the left one with both hands and straddled the ledge. She wedged her right knee into the opening, lifted it through, and slipped silently down to him.

But a few moments later, as she followed him over the parapet above the alley, her left foot hit a large tile. It fell and shattered on the ground an instant before she landed, rather awkwardly, in Alexander's arms.

They clutched each other as a wave of sound rose around them.

One neighborhood dog barked, then another, launching a clamorous canine cacophony throughout the city. Angry shouts erupted in response from nearby houses. Footsteps crunched in the main street that ran along the front of the inn.

Without waiting to see who was there, Theodosia pulled away from Alexander and flattened herself against the rough stone wall.

Soon, a uniformed legionary stepped around the corner, drew his sword, and strode into the alley, straight toward them.

He must've been stationed there to make sure I, or we, didn't escape.

In the next instant, Alexander's demeanor changed. He hiccoughed loudly and lurched in the soldier's direction, all the while gesturing behind his back for Theodosia to move on down the alley.

Willingly obedient for perhaps the first time in her life, she slid along the wall, increasing the distance between herself and the legionary.

If he spots me, I'm dead.

But even so, she couldn't take her eyes off Alexander.

Like a drunken sailor about to pass out, he dropped to the ground. Rising again, he propped one unsteady arm on the wall and waved the other at the soldier in a broad, brash gesture of camaraderie.

"Evenin', ossifer."

The legionary leveled his sword at Alexander's chest and shouted a few commands.

Blatantly, Alexander ignored him and staggered forward with an air of jovial, inebriated joy. Brushed the man's sword aside. Draped an arm around his shoulders. Patted him on the chest. Steered him toward the main street... even farther away from Theodosia.

A quick memory flashed from another moonless night. She was sitting between two guards on the balcony at her villa, as a drunken-sounding Alexander cajoled a soldier on the ground to let him approach.

"What'sa madder, ossifer? Don'cha see 'er?"

And now, that same ridiculously merry, half-coherent voice floated back to her from the end of the alley.

"What'sa madder, ossifer? Lookin' fer a drink?"

At the corner, Alexander maneuvered the legionary to the right, toward the front door of The Petulant Pelican.

Meanwhile, Theodosia crept on down the block, turned left into a new one, and walked as fast as she could through several tangled passageways, doing her best to parallel the main street that ran in front of the inn.

Finally, reaching a spot with a clear view, she stopped to rest.

Some time later, Alexander passed through the intersection, still staggering along.

Theodosia sneaked down a few more twisty blocks until, from a different angle, she caught another glimpse of him. She licked her lips, placed two fingers of each hand next to her teeth, and blew through them several times, whistling long and low as an old family slave had taught her years earlier.

Without turning his head, Alexander pointed forward, toward the next intersection. Theodosia stopped whistling and kept moving until their paths crossed some distance ahead.

By dawn, they were far away, well past the stinking slums that ringed the port town of Messana, leaving behind the legionaries, the Imperial Navy, the bounty signs, the talkative slave, her sharp-eyed mistress, and her money-grubbing master.

***

Soon after cock's crow on the day after the funeral, Nikolaos reached the dirt patch beside the orchard where he and Lycos held their tutoring sessions.

Despite the boy's usual tardiness, he was there already, energetically scratching the bare ground with his stick.

What bee buzzed over his bed to get him out so early?

"Welcome, Ni-ko-laos."

Rubbing it in that he got here first.

It was the kind of obnoxious behavior that drove Nikolaos crazy.

But I need to learn everything I can, and there's no one around to teach me except this damn brat.

"Last time," Lycos said as Nikolaos squatted beside him, "we covered everything your father taught me about Greek history. Today, we're going to talk about literature." He pointed to the letters in the dirt. "Can you read that?"

Nikolaos struggled to make sense of the scrawl.

Wish I could read and write Greek as well as I can read and write Latin.

"It's a man's name," Lycos hinted.

"Homer?"

"That's it. And who was he?"

"A poet."

"What's he known for?"

"*The Iliad. The Odyssey.*"

Lycos handed him the stick. "Write those titles."

Nikolaos struggled to carry out the assignment.

"Pretty good," Lycos said. "What are those stories about?"

"The Trojan War."

"And when was that?"

"A thousand years ago."

"By all the gods!" Lycos shouted as he slapped his forehead with dramatic flair. "Something stuck from our history lesson!"

I hate this little brat.

As if unaware of the anger he generated, Lycos pushed on with his questions. "Did Homer live through the Trojan War?"

"Guess so, since he wrote about it."

"Wrong." Lycos popped his pupil on both shoulders with the stick, just as a true pedagogue would do. "He lived hundreds of years later."

"You mean… recently?"

"No." Lycos rolled his eyes. "Homer couldn't have lived recently, because boys like us have been studying him for hundreds of years."

"Speak for yourself, boy. I'm not a boy." Nikolaos slouched back on his elbows. "So tell me, when and where did Homer live?"

"Right in the middle of the time between Helen of Troy and us."

"That's the *when*. What's the *where*?"

Lycos shrugged. "I have no idea."

"How can you *not* have an idea? You're supposed to be educating me."

"Look, Ni-ko-laos, I'm the pedagogue today. I ask the questions, not you. What dialect did Homer speak?"

"Greek."

More rolls of the eyes. "That's his *language*. What's his *dialect*?"

"You're the pedagogue today. You teach me."

"Homer spoke and wrote in the Ionic dialect."

"How do you know that?"

"Because Alexander told me."

"And how did *he* know that?"

"His pedagogue taught him."

"My father studied with a pedagogue?"

I never knew that.

"Yes, with a pedagogue," Lycos said.

"You mean, my grandfather had enough money to send his son to a *real* pedagogue?"

"Sure." Lycos snickered. "Any moron can figure that out just talking to Alexander. It's obvious he was properly educated." The boy paused and looked at Nikolaos. "You sure don't know much about your father, do you?"

"It's a wonder I know anything about him, since he was in Rome the whole time I was growing up in Syria, and later he abandoned me a second time to chase back to Rome after that woman."

"He didn't abandon you either time."

"Yes, he did."

Nikolaos gazed into the orchard where two of Bryaxis's slave-sons were engaged in their regular routine: weeding, hauling water, pruning branches, wiping the sweat from their brows, laughing, and bantering back and forth with one another.

They know everything there is to know about their father, but they can't call him that. They can't read or write. They don't know anything about Homer, and they don't care.

But I'm meant for better things than farm work, so maybe I need to try getting along with this annoying boy if I want to learn everything I can from my father... through him.

"In Daphne," Nikolaos said after a while, "I actually did study for a while with a pedagogue, but my master hired him to teach me his stupid Latin language and culture, instead of our great Greek language and culture. He made his Hebrew slaves teach me Aramaic, too, so that's how I wasted my time all those years, instead of reading Homer."

"You know what?" Lycos's tone turned serious, and suddenly he sounded more like a wise pedagogue than his usual annoying self. "I bet some fluency with Latin and Aramaic could come in handy for you some day."

CHAPTER 4

No horses were available, but an amiable farmer south of Messana was willing to part with two of his donkeys. Theodosia relaxed under a gnarled olive tree, massaging her worn-out legs, as Alexander joked and haggled over the price.

Juno, please don't let us run out of money.

At last, Alexander counted the coins into the farmer's palm and led his two blanket-draped purchases to Theodosia. He helped her stand, kissed her lips, and lifted her onto the back of one of the scruffy beasts.

"Lucky for us," he said, "that you ride so well."

"But I've never tried *this* before." Theodosia patted her donkey's shaggy neck. His shoulders were narrower than a horse's, and he was shorter, so her feet hung close to the ground. To keep the rough-textured blanket from chafing her thighs, she drew the back hem of her gray tunic forward as a buffer.

Alexander mounted the other donkey. "Let's pretend these are noble steeds and see how much more distance we can put between ourselves and Nero's bounty hunters."

***

It was almost nightfall when they stopped at an inn at the base of the cone-shaped volcano that loomed over the island. Mount Aetna had been smoking all day and remained shrouded in clouds, but the friendly peasants they had bought food from around noon insisted there was no cause for worry.

Muncibeddu—Beautiful Mountain—does that all the time, the country folk said.

Beautiful Mountain gives good crops, they said.

Nothing to fear from Beautiful Mountain, they said.

But Theodosia wasn't convinced. "If Beautiful Mountain blows up on us tonight—" She patted the leather pouch that still hung between her breasts. "We'll know this viper amulet is worthless."

"And if it *doesn't* blow up on us tonight—" Alexander dismounted and helped her off her donkey. "We'll know there's a guardian snake watching out for us."

"You don't really believe in guardian snakes."

"I do." His eyes twinkled. "And I boldly predict that by the end of this journey, you'll believe in them, too."

After supper, they stretched out together in the grass behind the inn, enjoying the cool night air and whispering about the future. The moon hadn't yet made its appearance, but the stars put on their usual show.

"I want to give you sons, but there's a problem I haven't told you about." A tremble entered her voice. "My flow dried up in the Carcer. No idea if my body will ever function that way again."

"You're not even ten days out of there, my love. Your body needs good food and love and plenty of time to recover."

"But what if it doesn't?"

"Even if your body never fully recovers, I have a fine son waiting for me—waiting for *us*—on the island of Euboea and a beautiful wife at my side here in Sicily. What more could a man ask?"

"Most men don't think like that, much less say things like that."

"Well, don't get me wrong," he said. "It would be wonderful to have more sons, but I care most about you. If the gods choose to give us a child or two of either sex, we'll count that as a great blessing. And if not, we'll still have each other for all the rest of our lives."

Theodosia kissed him. "Tell me about that son waiting for us on the island of Euboea."

Alexander stretched back and stared at the sky. "Niko's fifteen now. He's smart. Educated. Speaks, reads, and writes Latin very well, and he's fluent in a couple of other languages, too."

"Greek and… what else?"

"Aramaic."

"Never heard of it."

"It's a Semitic language. Older than both Latin and Greek."

"Where did it come from?"

"The great empire builders of the past—the Babylonians, Parthians, Assyrians, and Persians—they all spoke some form of Aramaic and spread it as far as the Romans have spread Latin in the last two centuries."

"And nowadays?"

"It's common in the eastern Mediterranean. Niko got it from the Jews in Daphne. He said it's replaced Hebrew as their everyday language."

"Why would he want to learn that, of all things?"

"Actually, it wasn't his choice. His Roman master ordered the other slaves, the Jewish ones, to teach Niko to speak Aramaic. He also sent him to a pedagogue for Latin and mathematics."

"Sounds like the man was training him to be a multi-lingual secretary and accountant. I'm amazed he let you buy Niko's freedom."

"Well, he didn't make it easy or cheap." Alexander's voice grew hard. "But I was gratified, at least, to meet a patrician who actually valued the intelligence of a boy he owned."

"Unlike my brother, you mean."

I don't want to talk about Gaius tonight.

"Your brother had a smart boy in Lycos, too, but insisted on using him as a sex slave."

I especially don't want to talk about that.

She steered the conversation away from that old, unhappy topic. "I can tell you're proud of Niko."

"He's turning out all right, I think."

"You *think*?"

There was a long silence, which Theodosia did not try to break.

At last, Alexander did. "My son has endured a lot of trauma in his life. Experienced great losses and seen things no child—no person—should ever see." He paused. "Truth is, I really don't know Niko very well. We traveled together for a month, from Daphne to Euboea, but after that it was only a short time before Stefan and I left the Bryaxis farm for Rome."

"How did Niko feel about that?"

Alexander ignored her question. Instead, he rose and held out both hands to help her up. "We've got another long ride tomorrow, and both of us need to sleep."

Theodosia shot him a coy look. "I know you're tired, but… perhaps not too tired to practice making your next son? Just in case my body ever decides it's ready."

"Definitely not too tired for that."

Beautiful Mountain did not blow up that evening, although a heavy smell of ash hung in the air. And the viper amulet came in handy in a way that Theodosia had not anticipated.

She was already in bed when Alexander called across the room.

"Where's your leather pouch?"

"On top of my tunic."

He pulled out the amulet and brought it over, waggling it up and down, teasing her. "Viper magic." He lifted her side of the mattress and slid the little silver snake onto one of the wide leather support straps beneath it.

"I thought I was marrying a sane man, not a crazy one."

He crawled over her to the other side of the bed. "Time will tell."

"You don't really think that thing's going to help me conceive, do you?"

"Let's just ask it to get your flow started."

"I've been begging Juno for that ever since we reached Sicily. In the past, she answered my prayers, but maybe now I'm just too far away."

"So, my love, when your flow does begin, and later on when you finally do conceive—as I said earlier in a very different context—we'll know for sure that there's a guardian snake watching out for us."

***

Five mornings later, as they rode their donkeys through a lonely stretch of mountain trail in a pine-fragrant forest, Theodosia became aware of something warm and moist at the spot where her legs straddled the blanket. She held her breath and reached down. Her fingers, when she withdrew them, came out red and sticky.

"By all the blessed gods." She glanced at Alexander. "It's unbelievable."

He stared briefly at her hand, then averted his eyes.

"I'm going to need some loose cotton or absorbent cloth," she said. "Do you suppose there's a town with a store anywhere near here?"

"We could go back to last night's inn." He was still looking away. "They're bound to have something you could use."

"But the bedbugs were the worst we've seen." She scratched the newest bumps on her arms. "Wouldn't want to press anything from there up into my body." She wadded the lower length of her tunic into a ball and sat on it. "Damn that little viper. Did it have to pick this exact place and time to produce my first flow in years?"

"You believe in it now?"

Theodosia laughed. "Not really. I'd rather credit good food and love, as you said. But still, if that snake can find us a town with a store…"

***

Within an hour, they rode out of the forest and into a town. On the right side of the road stood a field-stone cottage with a garden and children playing in the dirt. Then two cottages on the left. Then four more clustered together. Then a rutted path winding off to the east. Then several larger stone-and-wood buildings flanking a communal well and a washhouse. And finally, the most welcome sight of all: a shop with an eye-catching red-and-white sign painted over its door and a display of goods on the ground outside.

I am beginning to believe.

Theodosia waited on her donkey while Alexander went in.

He came back with a bag of soft cotton, a vial of clove oil, and two lengths of olive-green linen. "We haven't seen bounty notices for days, so I think it's safe for you to start dressing like a married woman." He held up the linen pieces. "Think these will do for a stola and matching palla?"

She rewarded him with a bright smile. "They will definitely do."

He passed his purchases up to her and led both donkeys forward.

"This town's called Palica," he said over his shoulder. "There's an inn—small but comfortable, according to the store owner—tucked away, out of sight in the woods, on the west side of town."

Soon, they were settled into their seventh rented room in seven days.

Alexander fetched a basin of hot water and towels, then left to give Theodosia privacy and get a better fix on their location.

***

In their pleasant brown-and-white space, Alexander took one of the two wooden stools, unrolled the drawing on parchment across the table, and tapped the island of Sicily. "Let me show you something," he said.

Freshly bathed and draped in the new green linen he had bought for her, Theodosia bent over his shoulder to look.

"*Ummm.*" Alexander sniffed her fragrance. "I always enjoyed your clove oil, back in the bad old days."

She kissed him. "Now, thanks to you, we both can enjoy it again."

"Makes it rather hard to concentrate." He inhaled the scent a few more times, then with one finger traced a triangle in the bottom third of Sicily. "Palica's somewhere in here." His finger slid to the right. "The port of Siracusa is east, on the Ionian Sea."

"So, assuming this thing's accurate, it looks like we're well south of the peninsula now, with a straight shot from Siracusa across the sea to Greece."

"The innkeeper says we'll get to Siracusa if we head east on that rutted path we passed, follow it to the coastal road, and then go south."

"I'm not keen on that."

"What's our alternative?"

"We've done very well sticking to the rural roads."

"But at some point, unless we want to spend the rest of our lives in these mountains, we've got to go where there are more people."

"And more risk."

He tipped his head back, taking another whiff of cloves, inviting another kiss. "A Greek merchant and his quiet, obedient son won't be too conspicuous."

"I can't go back to that." She dropped onto the other stool. "It'll be even harder now that my body finally remembers it's a woman."

"Then let's try a different approach. You stay in Palica for a few days. Rest up and let your flow run its course while I go to Siracusa to evaluate the situation."

"You'd leave me alone?"

"I can travel faster by myself, even on a donkey. Make the round trip in six or seven days. And if I don't—"

"No, please."

"If I don't see signs—"

"What if something happens and you never return?"

"If I don't see signs, I'll find us a place in Siracusa and be back before you know it. This is our best inn yet, and out here in the heart of the mountains, it's probably the safest, too."

"No Carbos and Candeloras in Palica?"

"This innkeeper and his wife are the nicest yet. I'll pay them in advance for your room and meals, so all you have to do is eat, rest, and recover."

"No nosy slaves? No soldiers?"

Alexander drew the knife from his belt and laid it on the table. "Keep this near you, just in case. Given your proven skill with sharp blades, I pity anybody who dares intrude on your privacy."

***

The morning came when Nikolaos had promised to teach Lycos bits of Hebrew history and culture gleaned years ago from his fellow slaves in Daphne. He was scratching Latin letters into the dirt when he caught sight of Lycos—and Myrine—heading his way.

He glared at her as the two drew near. "What's this?"

"I invited Myrine," Lycos said. "She's interested in the Hebrews, too, so you may as well instruct us both."

"Can't see why she needs to learn about the Hebrews."

"I don't *need* to learn 'bout them." Myrine sat cross-legged on the ground. "I *want* to learn 'bout them."

"A slave," Nikolaos said, "has no right to *want* anything."

"Zeus!" She looked at him. "Why are you so rude? Even my master don't talk to me like that."

"Because I don't want you here. Don't want to teach you anything. Don't want to listen to your babble."

"I won't say nothing, I promise. Just sit quiet and listen."

"You must have work to do."

"Ma said I could come. She don't need me in the kitchen this early."

"If you won't let Myrine stay," Lycos said, "then I won't stay either."

Loudly, Nikolaos blew out his breath. "Will she keep her mouth shut?"

Lycos made no reply, but Nikolaos detected a smirk playing at the edges of Myrine's mouth.

She's as obnoxious as he is.

Ignoring her, Nikolaos pointed to the Latin word H-E-B-R-A-I-C-E scrawled before him. "What's that mean?" he asked Lycos in Greek.

"Something about the Hebrews."

"What else are they called?"

"The Jews."

"Where do they live?"

"There were lots of Jewish slaves in Rome."

"Sure, some live in Rome, others in Athens or Antioch, but where's their homeland?"

Lycos lifted his shoulders to his ears, so Nikolaos answered his own question.

"A long way from here, on the eastern end of the Mediterranean. Sometimes they call their land Judea, sometimes Israel. Sometimes they call themselves Hebrews, sometimes Israelites, sometimes Judeans, sometimes Jews."

"Why so many names?" Lycos asked. "Euboea is just Euboea. Greeks are just Greeks."

"The Jews are a whole lot more complicated than we are. Know who rules over them nowadays?"

"The Romans." Lycos made a face and stuck out his tongue.

"True, but the Romans have played a clever little trick on the Jews."

"What trick?"

"They let the local Jewish kings pretend to govern their people... just as long as they—those Jewish kings—swear allegiance to the emperor and send huge amounts of money to Rome."

"So, they're just make-believe kings?"

"No, they're real kings from real royal families, but the emperor in Rome holds all the power. And, of course, the common people get stuck in between. They pay big taxes to their local ruler so he can deliver the tribute that Nero demands to maintain his crown."

"The local ruler's crown?"

"Exactly. The local kings live in fancy palaces that the common people pay to build and maintain, but they would lose their power if they ever stopped being toadies to the emperor in Rome."

Lycos grinned. "Sounds like the Jews don't much like their rulers."

"The Jews hate the Romans, and the Romans hate the Jews, and they all despise the toady kings."

Myrine giggled at that, but Nikolaos kept ignoring her.

"My friends in Daphne told me," he said, "that the Jews are tough and always fight back. They never surrendered to the Romans like we Greeks did, and every so often, when the ordinary Jews get sick of the Romans' corrupt deal with the toady kings, they rise up. My friends said Jerusalem bathes in blood from time to time."

"What's Jerusalem," Lycos asked.

"Their capital. They call it the City of David."

"Who's David?"

"David *was* a shepherd boy who killed a giant with a slingshot and became king of Israel."

"What a joke," Myrine muttered.

"It's not a joke." Nikolaos scowled at her. "It happened a thousand years ago, but the Jews talk like it was yesterday."

"Do they tell their old jokes in Greek," she asked, "or Latin?"

"Neither one. My friends told me all their old stories—and even their old jokes—in Aramaic. They taught me to speak Aramaic, too, and made sure I got lots of practice."

The annoying girl kept on. "Did your friends also speak Latin and Greek?"

Nikolaos shook his head. "Just Aramaic."

"How could they follow their Roman master's orders?"

"Well, the steward was an educated Greek who also spoke Latin and Aramaic, so he was the only one who could talk with everybody."

"I bet that gave him a lot of power."

Nikolaos clenched his teeth.

Contrary to her promise, Myrine had inserted herself and was now a full participant in the discussion. He hadn't meant to interact with her, but he found he couldn't help himself.

"Languages are powerful things," he said. "I haven't used Aramaic since I left Syria, but I spoke it there for many years, and I still remember it."

"Why don't you teach us that language?" Myrine asked. "I'd like to speak something other than Greek."

Lycos looked puzzled. "You want to learn Aramaic?"

"Why not?" The girl's face brightened.

Nikolaos sneered. "You're a slave. On a farm. On an island. In Greece."

"So?"

"So, there are no Jews on this farm. Probably not a single one on the whole island of Euboea."

"So?" Myrine waited for Nikolaos to respond. When he didn't, she went on. "I'm going to leave this farm someday. Maybe even leave this island."

"You're planning to run away?"

"Didn't say that."

"I'll tell your master."

That'll chase her off.

She laughed. "I don't care. Just teach me something useful."

"How, exactly, would you use Aramaic?"

"Talking to people."

"Who?"

"You and him." Myrine jabbed her thumb in Lycos's direction. "You're people, aren't you?"

Lycos chuckled. "Might be fun to learn Aramaic. We three could have our own secret language."

"Think of that," Myrine said. "Talking to each other, and nobody else understanding a word of it."

Nikolaos was about to argue further when another idea came to him.

The more people around here who speak Aramaic—and the more I use it by teaching it to them—the less I'll forget and the better I'll speak it if I ever need to again.

"I don't read or write Aramaic," he said after a while, "but I'm good at pronouncing the words. It's not an easy language."

Lycos grinned again. "Myrine and I are both very smart."

"Teach us to speak Aramaic, Master Nikolaos" Myrine's eyes sparkled. "I'll be your best pupil, I promise."

"You promised you'd keep quiet, and look how that turned out."

She almost looks pretty.

Nikolaos wasn't sure why he delayed saying yes. Maybe he just wanted her to beg some more.

"Please." She flashed a bright smile. "Please do teach us!"

By all the gods, Myrine absolutely is pretty.

"Well, maybe it won't hurt you to learn a few basic words and phrases."

***

Time passed slowly in Palica. For a couple of days after Alexander left, Theodosia was content to stay in her room, napping, eating, and managing her flow. Taking it easy and having time for herself was a pleasure.

But by the third morning, she was bored and curious to see more of the town where six centuries earlier, according to the innkeeper, runaway slaves from the Italian Peninsula had taken refuge, only to be captured later and sold back into slavery.

A timely reminder of how easily freedom can be lost.

So she draped her olive-green stola around her body, flipped the matching palla over her head, and slowly made her way into the central part of Palica.

At first, she worried that someone might identify her by her limp, but nobody showed any sign of recognition.

She ended up strolling into town four mornings straight, savoring the sun, fresh air, and exercise. After thirty months in a prison cell, five days in a rickety boat, and seven more on a plodding donkey, the opportunity to walk about on her own was precious.

Besides, she found the mountain hamlet on the edge of the forest charming. Even in midsummer, the days were cool. A rainbow of wildflowers softened the edges of the roads and brightened the gardens around the small stone houses. Gray-and-orange butterflies fluttered down narrow lanes and feasted on the flowers. Nesting birds carried squirmy morsels to their demanding babies.

Palica's only store offered basic goods but also regional sausages and locally grown oranges and figs.

There were personal luxuries for sale as well, the kind of things Theodosia hadn't touched since that long-ago night when Nero's soldiers yanked her, without warning, from her villa. A tortoise-shell comb, a set of silver hairpins, and a polished-brass hand mirror enticed her to part with a few coins. But mostly she resisted the temptation to spend money or add to what she was already carrying. There would be time later for such pleasures.

She discovered a shady bench nestled against a high, moss-covered wall that formed a protective barrier between the forest and the community well.

To keep out wolves and bears?

She strolled to the bench each morning and lingered until noon as the people of Palica went about their daily activities around her.

Peasant men in plain work tunics and sturdy sandals hiked into town with farm tools on their shoulders or rolled through on loaded, creaking donkey carts.

Peasant women in cheerful colors arrived on foot, balancing terra-cotta water jugs on their heads, carrying bags of clothes, and chattering in a dialect that Theodosia did not understand. Some clustered around the well while others labored under the canopy of the open-air washhouse at one end of the wall.

At first, when she tried to engage with the women, they shied away and kept their distance. But by the third day, they allowed themselves to nod, establish eye contact, and greet her with timid smiles.

So good to see friendly female faces once more.

***

As the sun coursed higher on Theodosia's fourth daily visit to the well, a loud shout shattered the tranquility. Heavy footfalls shook the bench beneath her as a long line of soldiers marched into town from the south. At the head of the column, astride a prancing black horse, a centurion with the usual plumed crest on his helmet halted in the main intersection.

"At ease!" he shouted.

His men promptly dropped to the ground, laid down their shields and swords, and took long drinks from their water skins.

Theodosia glanced to her left. To her right. Back and forth a couple of times. But the wall behind her and the buildings on each end of it formed a barrier that blocked all hope of escape.

Trapped again.

She tightened the palla around her head and made sure the stola fully covered her legs.

Good thing Alexander chose a dull green, which blends with the trees and the mossy wall, rather than the bright color I would have picked.

The centurion leaped from his horse. Threw the reins to a subordinate. Strode toward the well. Approached the nearest cluster of women. Barked commands at the entire group. The women who had gathered for their pleasant everyday routine of laundry and gossip froze in position.

On the bench, Theodosia froze, too. Her breathing slowed. Heart almost stopped. Muscles locked up. The only movement she could manage was to raise her right hand and grip the pouch resting between her breasts.

Juno. Little snake. I need you both right now.

The officer interrogated the women, one by one, in their own dialect.

Unable to comprehend, Theodosia focused on their faces. Each woman reacted with an expression unique to herself. Shook her head. Or frowned. Or shrugged. Or made some other sign of negation.

He's hitting them all with the same question. Getting the same response.

For what seemed an hour, the centurion methodically worked his way through the crowd, asking his question, following up on each woman's answer, moving on to the next. None of the women glanced in Theodosia's direction.

At last, when all of them had been questioned to the centurion's satisfaction, he stalked away, bellowed to the men in the roadway, and remounted his horse as they formed up to continue their march toward the north.

Silently, the women filled their water jugs, gathered their laundry, and slipped away.

Once everyone else was gone, Theodosia took several deep breaths and leaned forward over her knees.

He never noticed me. Bless you, Juno. Thank you, little snake.

She remained on the bench as her mind ran through all the possible interpretations of this unnerving episode. Eventually, one thing became clear.

At great personal risk, not a single woman in Palica chose to give me away.

CHAPTER 5

All that afternoon and all that night and all the next day and all the following night, Theodosia remained in her room with the door bolted and the knife close at hand, eating, drinking, and bathing only when the innkeeper's wife brought her a tray or a pitcher of hot water.

And then, finally, on the eighth day after his departure, Alexander was back in the hallway, tapping on the door and calling her name.

At the sound of his voice, Theodosia briefly closed her eyes.

Thank you, Juno.

He wrapped her in his arms, and for a time they clung to each other, swaying slightly side to side.

"Siracusa's a perfect next stop for us," he said after a while. "No worrisome signs on the walls. No legionaries in the streets."

Because they were all here two days ago.

"Not even a garrison," he added. "A small harbor with fishing boats, but no naval presence." He tipped her head back and nuzzled her neck. "I found a high-quality inn called The Harbor Watch. We can stay as long as we like. It's quiet, private, and pretty, and the best part is… no bedbugs. The management actually guarantees that. I had to promise we'd go to the public baths first, get rid of whatever might be traveling on us, buy new clothes, and have our current ones cleaned."

"Sounds wonderful," Theodosia said into his chest.

Alexander seemed happy to be alone with her and make love in the afternoon, so Theodosia waited until after supper to tell him, calmly and unemotionally, about the incident at the well.

"Not surprising," he said when she had finished. "On the day I left and again this morning, legionaries stopped me on the coastal road."

"What'd they want?"

"To know if I'd seen a lame local woman traveling with a Greek man. The 'gladiator-size' part of the description had disappeared."

"That must be what the centurion was asking the women at the well, and if so—" Theodosia smiled. "They told him the truth, because even though they'd seen *me* limping around, few of them—or none—had laid eyes on *you*."

"Looks like they're combing the island from one end to the other." He stroked her hair several times. "My lame son and I should head east at sunrise tomorrow."

"Alexander, no."

"My lame son and I will make it to Siracusa. My lame wife and I will not. It's just that simple. The army in Sicily seems on full alert now. The soldiers who stopped me coming and going knew exactly who they were looking for. Someone tipped them off."

"Carbo?"

"Maybe, or any of the six other innkeepers along our route." He frowned. "I'm afraid your inquisitive centurion may have found more cooperative witnesses up north. He might well calculate when we were at each place and how fast we're traveling and come back to catch you right here at this inn."

"I can't play the role of your son anymore."

"You must, at least till we get to Siracusa."

She leveled her eyes at him. "You said there were no soldiers there. No garrison or naval presence. When were you planning to tell me the truth?"

"The truth about...?"

"Being stopped and questioned. If I hadn't told you what happened in Palica, would you have told me what happened in Siracusa?"

"My love, what I told you was the truth. The soldiers stopped me on the coastal road, not in town, and there really are no big ships there." One corner of his mouth turned up. "I don't like seeing you so distressed."

"You know I've always been a fighter, but right now—" Tears welled in her eyes. "I'm tired of running and whispering and hiding from the world and pretending to be someone that I'm not. I'm ready to settle into some kind of normal life."

Alexander tugged her up from the table and held her close. "The cottage I've rented at The Harbor Watch is perfect for us. Not the sort of place where anyone looks for fugitives. You can do whatever you wish there. Read for pleasure. Go for walks along the water. Talk as loudly as you please. And the owners will provide as much personal service as you want and need."

In response, she wrapped her arms around his waist.

"Please trust me, Theodosia," he said. "This difficult stage of our journey will soon be over."

***

The language lessons were going well.

Every other morning, as dawn washed Leios Bryaxis's house and fields with its golden light, Nikolaos and his two pupils arrived at the dirt patch for a couple of hours of practice, following a teaching method that he had devised just for them.

So far, they had acquired a basic Aramaic vocabulary. Words to describe people, places, and things. Ways to ask questions. Numbers one to ten. Colors. Body parts. Essential verbs.

Today, the three of them were playing a game that Nikolaos had introduced yesterday. He asked questions in Aramaic. Lycos and Myrine had to understand and respond appropriately. It was fun and worked well, even though isolated words and simple sentences were all the students had mastered up to now.

To encourage them to expand their vocabularies, repeating words was not allowed.

"Who is Lycos?" Nikolaos asked Myrine in Aramaic.

"Boy. Greek. Young."

"What is he like?"

"He is small." Myrine eyed Lycos. "Short. Thin. Weak."

Lycos made a show of reacting angrily.

"And his hair?"

"His hair is long and brown and curly."

"Can you touch his right hand?"

Myrine reached over and patted Lycos's right hand.

"Good." Nikolaos turned to Lycos. "Who is Myrine?"

"Girl. Slave."

"What is she like?"

"Myrine is strong and smart and pretty."

The brat's only ten and already a flatterer.

"What is the biggest thing above her shoulders?"

"Her nose." Lycos wrinkled his own very small nose.

Myrine punched him in the arm. Lycos pretended to keel over.

"What does she have two of?" Nikolaos asked when the boy straightened.

"Eyes. Lips."

"What else?"

"Hands. Feet."

"Anything else?"

"Ears. Arms. Legs." Lycos blushed. "Breasts!"

Myrine giggled, but Nikolaos kept up his rapid questioning.

"Where does Myrine live?"

"In Greece."

"More detail."

"On the island of Euboea."

"Be even more specific, and give me a complete sentence."

"Myrine," Lycos said, "lives on a big farm on the island of Euboea."

"Excellent." Nikolaos pointed to both of them. "Who owns the farm that Myrine lives on?"

"Leios Bryaxis!" they shouted in unison.

"What is he like?" He pointed first to Lycos, then to Myrine.

"Leios Bryaxis is generous," Lycos said, "and old."

Bryaxis's slave-daughter swallowed noisily. "He is rich and powerful."

Not by Roman-patrician standards. Only by Greek-peasant standards.

"And Iocaste, who is she?"

"The master— His child," fumbled Myrine. "Daughter. Mistress."

"She is," Nikolaos emphasized the correct sentence structure, "*your* master's daughter and *your* mistress. Now, repeat that the way *you* should say it."

"She is *my* master's daughter and *my* mistress."

"Good. What is Iocaste like?"

"She is sweet." Myrine sounded confident now. "And kind to me."

"She is good to Myrine," Lycos said. "Also sad and afraid."

"Why is she sad and afraid?"

"Stefanos is not here. He is in Rome."

"She soon have scary husband." Myrine made a faraway gesture with one hand. "From other side."

Time to introduce a few new words and raise the level a bit.

"Iocaste is sad and afraid," Nikolaos said, "because she thinks Stefanos is wonderful, but if he is not back here when the harvest begins in September, her father will force her to marry a man she does not like, and that horrible man will take her away to live on the other side of the island, and she may never come home again."

Lycos and Myrine recoiled at the length of his sentence.

"Say that in Greek," Lycos said in Greek.

"No," Nikolaos said in Aramaic. "You understood me."

Both Lycos and Myrine shrugged and nodded.

"So," Nikolaos went on, still in Aramaic, "tell me what Stefanos is like."

"Very tall and strong." Lycos flexed his little-boy biceps.

"He is a giant," Myrine said.

"Where does he come from?"

"From a villa in the country," Lycos said.

Myrine injected a question of her own. "What is a villa?"

"A large house for rich people."

"Where is the villa?" she continued.

"On the coast north of Rome."

"What is Rome?"

"Rome is a city on the Italian Peninsula." Lycos frowned. "A very bad place."

"Why?"

"Mean men live there."

This is starting to feel like a real conversation.

"Who is Stefanos's best friend?" Nikolaos pointed at Lycos.

"Iocaste."

"No," Myrine said, "Alexander is Stefanos's best friend."

"You are right," Lycos said. "Alexander and Stefanos are very good friends."

"Who is Alexander?" Nikolaos asked Myrine.

Myrine pointed to Nikolaos. "Your father."

Then she pointed her finger toward Lycos. "What is Alexander like?"

"He is smart and nice."

Myrine groaned. "Lycos cheats," she complained in Greek. "Smart and nice are repeated words."

"Well, Lycos, since you cheated," Nikolaos continued in Aramaic, "you have to say three entirely different things about my father, all in one complete sentence."

"*Your* father," Lycos began, "is *my* best friend and an excellent teacher and a very good person."

"Tell us more about him."

"Alexander is hard working and loyal." Abruptly, Lycos switched into Greek and also into the role of pedagogue. "Now, Nikolaos, you must tell us something else about your father."

Without thinking, Nikolaos responded in Greek. "My father's the most important person to me. The most special person in the world."

Myrine's face twisted into an impish grin as she added to the conversation in Greek. "And who is the most important person to Alexander? Is it Lycos, his former student, or Nikolaos, his son?"

"Theodosia Varro is the most important person to Alexander," Lycos shot back in Greek. "He cares the most about her."

Damn brat.

"You should have said *me*." Nikolaos jutted his jaw as he glowered at the boy. "My father cares the most about *me*."

"No," Lycos continued in his irritating way, "to your father, the most important person in the world is Theodosia Varro."

***

Much of Siracusa was built on the flat island of Ortygia—"quail" in the language of its long-ago Greek founders—which was separated from the mainland by a narrow channel fringed with marshes on both sides. A soft belt of tall grasses extended all around the shore of Ortygia.

Theodosia found the setting beautiful in a way that neither Messana nor Palica could match.

Feels good to be back on a natural, undisturbed coast.

The Harbor Watch stood by itself on a modest rise that fronted the southern marsh, where dark birds she had never seen before fished from partially submerged branches and spread their wings to dry in the sun. Larger white birds flew in and out at dawn and dusk. And all day long, small brown birds trilled and fluttered in the reeds.

A smooth, stone pathway curved through the marsh grasses on a gentle slope to the water. The journey down and back took Theodosia about two hours… challenging enough for therapeutic walks and, since she had it to herself, far enough away from other humans to ease her anxiety.

The cottage was the largest, brightest, and most appealing place that Alexander and Theodosia had occupied as man and wife. On its frescoed walls, yellow dolphins cavorted with orange fish and pink mermaids in the depths of a pale green sea. Embroidered cushions in the same tones softened the wooden chairs that flanked the fireplace. A mosaic floor carried the relaxing colors from the entry door through the sitting room, into the bedroom, and out across the wide, covered terrace.

But it was that outdoor space—with its fragrant pink-flowering vine hanging from the arbor, its tile-topped table, its cushioned lounge, and its soft breezes—that Theodosia most appreciated. Every morning when she stepped outside, the same two thoughts flitted through her mind.

Amazing that Alexander found a place with a pergola like the one at my villa. I would gladly spend the rest of my life right here.

Each day, a male slave served her breakfast and lunch on the shady terrace. Each afternoon, following her walk, a female slave flexed her legs and feet and massaged them with clove oil. And all day long, she savored the fresh sea air and long views across the water.

As July passed into August, her chopped-off hair grew out enough to shape and even style a bit. Thanks to the walks and massages, her gait smoothed out to the point that, on flat terrain at least, she moved almost normally. Most amazing of all, her body developed feminine curves once more.

She had no idea what the cottage, meals, and services cost, but Alexander dismissed her concerns. "We can afford it," he told her whenever she asked.

But still, his life in Siracusa was a mystery to her.

Every morning at dawn, he departed on errands that lasted all day. Every evening at sunset, he returned with special treats. Juicy oranges freshly plucked from a tree. Honey in the comb to sweeten her bread. Bright-colored pallas to drape over the long, leg-covering stolas that he also bought for her.

He even purchased a silver chain so she could rescue the viper amulet from its dark pouch and wear it as a sparkly ruby-and-silver ornament on the outside of her clothing.

Theodosia knew she would never walk without a limp, but now—for the first time in years—she also knew that she looked and felt like a lady again.

***

The fifth day of August dawned hot and muggy on the island of Euboea. Both kitchen doors stood open as the light picked out floating dust particles and the usual pig-stink blew through.

After breakfast, Nikolaos sat in the kitchen telling Myrine—in Aramaic, of course—odds and ends of things he had learned from his fellow slaves in Daphne. Somehow, the girl had the ability to chop meat and vegetables and mince herbs while at the same time asking him questions in Aramaic and turning her head to catch his answers.

Remarkable, really. She's absorbing the language and details of Jewish culture without ever meeting any actual Jews.

As they talked, Iocaste and Hebe arrived to check on preparations for the main meal of the day. They bent their heads to inspect a lamb that Myrine had slaughtered, cleaned, and cubed before the sun was fully up.

Once Myrine finished her chopping, her mother would dump all the ingredients into an enormous iron pot for a succulent stew that everyone in the household—first the master and his two young male guests at the kitchen table, then his daughter in her upstairs quarters, and finally their slaves from the house and fields—would enjoy late in the afternoon.

Suddenly, a shadow fell across the floor.

Although Nikolaos spotted it moments before the women did, he didn't immediately recognize the backlit figure that filled the doorway.

But Iocaste raced across the kitchen and threw herself into the man's arms. "Stefanos!"

***

As August slipped into September, Theodosia's financial and safety concerns returned. One morning, on her walk through the marshes, she spotted a column of soldiers marching along a road on the opposite side of the channel.

If there's no garrison in Siracusa, what are they doing here?

That evening, while Theodosia and Alexander dined under the pergola, she broached yet again the two subjects that most concerned her.

"Yes, we really can afford to live here." A rare edge of irritation crept into Alexander's voice. "Theodosia, you gave no thought to money at your villa. You were content to let me do the worrying back then."

"That was different. I knew the money was there. And these days, I can't help wondering—" Her face puckered. "Where is it you go each morning?"

"By all the gods, my love, you still haven't figured that out?" The edge disappeared, and his eyes twinkled as they always did when he was teasing her. "Actually, each question leads to the other's answer and back again."

Theodosia pursed her lips. "I've never been good at riddles."

He lifted her hands and kissed each one. "Soon after we got here, I took a job that allows me to provide for—and give a happy life to—the woman I love. That's what a free man with a wife is supposed to do, isn't it?"

For the first time since they arrived in Siracusa, she noticed ink stains on his fingers.

"You're working as a scribe?"

"And translator-interpreter. In the main public office in town. Same thing I did for half a year in Antioch when I went to rescue Niko."

"Are you sure it's safe, with me living so openly here and you working in town? I did see soldiers across the water this morning."

Alexander rose and, from behind, wrapped his arms around her. "Years ago, I shared with you the most important lesson that my parents taught me when I was a child in Corinth. Do you remember what that was?"

She nodded. "There is no place on Earth where the Romans can't find you if they want to."

"Yes, and that's just as true now as it was when I was a boy. So, let's be honest, my love. Given enough motivation and time, Nero *will* discover your whereabouts if he wants to." Alexander returned to his chair. "The good news is… the emperor's anger will fade in time. His desire to catch you will wane as other issues arise to bedevil him. That may already be happening."

Wish I could believe that.

"Do you have a plan for us?" she asked.

"For now, this place seems safe. But even so, I'd like to see us on our way no later than the end of November, before the sea lanes ice up. Otherwise we're stuck here all winter. I've investigated the cost of hiring a captain to take us—just you and me, no one else—to Eretria."

"Eretria?"

"That's one of the two main harbors on the island of Euboea. Traveling on a small ship, we'll skip the major ports and only put in at minor ones where the imperial navy doesn't land."

"Can you possibly save enough, on top of our expenses here, to hire a boat to make that trip just for the two of us?"

"Well, I'm working long hours, as you've noted. Earning more than enough to keep you comfortable while saving up for our voyage."

"What we're spending to live here makes that harder to do."

"True, but something else matters to me. My main goal from now on is to give you a good life. Of course, we'll never have the kind of wealth or villa or servants or social status that your family enjoyed. I can't bring that old-money world back to you, but for sure, we can be safe and secure and comfortable. Do you believe that?"

"Yes, I do believe it."

"We passed our first milestone on the way to that better life the moment we reached Siracusa. This is the start of the rest of our lives, so please relax and enjoy this lovely place while we wait to take our next step."

And so, as summer's heat gave way to the crisp air and warm colors of autumn—and with all the sweet, wrinkly-ripe persimmons she cared to eat—Theodosia continued her walks, read scrolls from the library at The Harbor Watch, and took restorative naps under the pergola.

She expected her monthly flow to return in September, as it had in July and August, but by the end of the month it has not appeared. She kept that news to herself, taking the absence for a fluke.

But in time, more signs presented themselves in her body.

Another month passed, with another missed flow and more unmistakable changes, before she told Alexander.

***

Each morning, when Theodosia dressed, she put on the chain that held the silver viper that was eating the tiny red ruby and, for the whole day, enjoyed their shimmer on the outside of her stola. Each night, as she prepared for bed, she set the amulet on top of her stack of folded clothing.

But on the evening of the last day of October, instead of leaving the snake in its usual location, she placed it in the center of the mattress.

Alexander pulled his tunic over his head, wrapped his arms around his wife, tipped her head back, and covered her neck and breasts with kisses.

She let him guide her backwards toward the bed until, at the last moment, she reached around, took the viper amulet in her fingers, and danced it up and down in front of him.

"What's this?" He grinned. "Don't tell me you've finally become a believer in guardian snakes."

"I have." She waggled it again. "And for a very good reason."

"Tell me."

"Guess."

"No idea."

"What did I say I wanted most in the world?"

Alexander turned his eyes away, then slowly brought them back. "We're going to have a baby?"

"A fine son for you, next June."

"You're sure?"

"As sure as a woman can be."

Alexander's hands rose to the sides of her face, slid through her hair to the back of her head, and drew her closer. "And I'm as happy as a man can be."

***

Alexander still left for work at sunrise and returned at sunset.

Theodosia still walked and read and rested.

But now she also threw up each morning and ached each afternoon. Her breasts grew tender, then painful to the touch. Her moods cycled from elation to depression and back, several times a day.

Then, without warning, on the cold eighth day of December, Alexander reappeared at the cottage only a couple of hours after he had left.

"Could you leave today?" he asked.

"What?"

"Could you leave now?"

Theodosia stared at him. "Right now?"

He nodded. "I've found a ship. Captain Aeton is very experienced, and he's willing to take us, all by ourselves, to the island of Euboea."

"But you said the sea ices up in December, too dangerous to sail."

"We'll hug the coast where it's safer, put in at the smallest ports. A much slower trip that way, but we should reach Eretria by February."

"You said it would be too late after November." Her eyes swept the room, taking in its cheerful frescoes and soft cushions and brilliant mosaics and the bright fire in its hearth.

I've come to love this place.

Alexander's eyes followed hers, clearly reading her mind. "I did hope we'd be gone before now. Just couldn't make it happen."

"The timing's terrible." She draped her hands over the bulge in her belly. "I'll be sick every day, all day, the whole way."

"Sorry, my love, but please—" Gently, he placed his hands on hers, over the bulge. "I was lucky to be the first one in Captain Aeton's office this morning. Another group showed up while I was talking to him. They're ready to sail right away if we aren't. I told him we'd make our decision within the hour. He promised to give me till noon, but no longer."

"Do we have enough money to travel all the way to Greece?"

"I've already paid him."

Theodosia looked down. "And once we're there, what'll we live on?"

"Again, I ask you to believe me. We have plenty of resources to start the next phase of our life." He cupped a hand under her chin and lifted it, forcing her to look at him. "Ship owners aren't willing to do this in good weather, because it ties up so much of their time and they don't earn much with just two passengers. I've been asking around for months. Captain Aeton's the only one who said yes. Winter's here, so most captains are already home with their families. It's our last chance to get away before March, when a sea voyage becomes reasonably safe again."

"Would that be so bad? Or even—" Theodosia reclaimed her chin. "Couldn't we stay here till the baby's born in June?"

"I've already been away from Niko for a year and a half. Add that to all the other years when I wasn't there for him and—" Abruptly, he stopped.

They'll both hate me if I refuse to go.

"I'm thinking of Stefan, too," Alexander went on. "He's bound to be back on the Bryaxis farm by now."

"Assuming he made it." Theodosia stared into the flickering flames.

"I'll bet you anything he did, months ago."

"Wish we knew that for sure."

"There's only one way to find out. Get to Euboea and see for ourselves." A pleading note entered his voice. "Everyone who cares about us—Stefan, Niko, Lycos, and even Bryaxis and his family—they'll all fear the worst if we don't show up by the end of this year."

Alexander has worked so hard.

"So," he said, "my beautiful, beloved lady…"

And given me so many luxuries. And paid already for our passage.

"Are you up for it?"

I'll never see Rome again. Forever be a stranger in a foreign land.

Alexander wrapped his arms around her and held her close.

I could say no.

Something rumbled inside her belly, like a warning from their babe-to-be.

But he might leave me here, and then what?

After a last moment of hesitation, she nodded against his chest.

Dearest Juno, I have no choice.

"Yes," she said, "I can leave this morning."

"Oh, my love." His lips grazed the top of her head. "My very dearest love, thank you."

PART II

WHEREVER THERE IS A HUMAN BEING,
THERE IS AN OPPORTUNITY FOR CRISIS.
—*SENECA, 4 BC - AD 65*

CHAPTER 6

THE FARMHOUSE OF LEIOS BRYAXIS

The baby came slowly. Too slowly.

Toward the end of her seemingly interminable labor—after baking on her bed all day in the June heat and crouching through the night over Hebe's well-worn birthing stool—Theodosia began to pray that Thanatos, the Greek god of death, would come for her, as he had come for countless other young women before her, including her own mother twenty-three years earlier.

But Thanatos never showed up this time. Only pain.

Intense pain was no stranger, of course. She had known it before. But these pangs were different. They attacked from within, rising and falling in cruel waves that smashed every nerve in her body, deadened her mind, and threatened to wipe out her very existence.

At the darkest part of that night—as Myrine's strong arms and huge hands supported her back and stroked her belly and Hebe lay on the floor beneath the birthing stool, quietly coaching and offering encouragement—Theodosia gave up on Thanatos and turned to the Roman goddess of women.

Beloved Juno, if you can hear me so far away from home, I beg you... bring me relief. Either a live birth or my own death.

And then, suddenly, after a final, enormous push, it was over.

Hebe caught the baby as it slid from Theodosia's womb, held it upside down for the ritual slap, and shouted with joy when it cried.

"Mistress, it's a boy!"

***

When Theodosia woke, Alexander was sitting in a circle of amber light, just as he had on that long-ago night at her villa, when she emerged from what had been, up to then, the worst experience of her life.

He pulled the viper amulet from beneath her mattress. "You've given me a second son, my love. A fine, healthy boy. I'm grateful for that gift."

Theodosia wrapped her fingers around the little silver snake. "And I'm grateful to have survived the experience of giving it."

He reached for her hand and treated her to one of his teasing winks. "Before the naming ceremony… do you have a preference?"

"It's your job to name him. I merely gave him birth."

"Then he will be Doros, because—of all your many gifts to me—he is the most marvelous."

Doros. A gift.

"That's what you called me, your alleged son, back in Sicily. I like it better on our baby."

It's definitely not a Roman name. No surprise there.

Alexander seemed to read her mind. "I intend to raise him as a Greek. No hint of Rome must ever shackle his thoughts or hang like a weight around his soul. I will insist on that, my love, even if you don't agree."

"Then we're in luck, because I do agree. We've both had our fill of Rome."

Except for Juno. I can still hold her in my heart, and praise and thank her, and call on her for help.

Myrine slipped through the curtain at the door and laid their newborn son—clean and snugly swaddled, with a beguiling tuft of soft brown hair and a mouth open in noisy protest—at Theodosia's breast. Then, silently, she left the room.

On his own, the baby found Theodosia's nipple and began to suckle.

"How did he know to do that?" Tears welled in her eyes as Doros took her milk for the first time. She smiled, then laughed very softly at the odd sensation. "I'll need some time to get used to this."

"And I'll need some time to get used to thinking of you as a mother."

For a while, neither of them spoke.

At last, Theodosia raised her eyes. "There's something I'd really enjoy."

"Another nap? A cup of wine? Say the word and you'll have it."

She smiled again and shook her head. "A brisk trot on a horse."

Alexander's mouth fell open. "After what you've just been through?"

"Morning rides together, like we used to take at home. I bet the Euboean countryside is beautiful."

"You've got to be joking."

"For the time being, of course, I'm joking. I couldn't even sit on a horse right now. But sometime soon, now that Doros is born—"

"There are no horses here, just donkeys, and you didn't appreciate that experience much in Sicily, as I recall."

"Somewhere on this island there must be a horse fit to ride."

"Don't even think that way, Theodosia. Not here. Not ever again. Doros must have a proper Greek mother, and proper Greek mothers do not go galloping around the countryside." Alexander arched his eyebrows. "Didn't you promise me you'd act like a respectable Greek matron?"

"It's one thing to say it and quite another thing to do it. Nothing in my life ever prepared me to act like a respectable Greek matron."

"You'll learn. You'll adapt. You always do."

"I don't always blend in well."

"Blending in isn't necessary, my beautiful lady. Adjusting to a different culture is, and Greek culture definitely *is* different from Roman culture, especially for women." He patted her shoulder. "You'll do fine."

***

After dawn crept in and Alexander departed for the lower floor—that mostly off-limits-to-free-women domain of free Greek men and their household slaves—Theodosia scanned her own living space.

Speaking of Greek culture…

The women's quarters occupied the entire east-facing second story of the Bryaxis farmhouse. Following centuries of custom, the free women and children of the Bryaxis household, including any female guests, were expected to stay upstairs, take their meals together, weave at their looms, and care for one another. Only on feast days or other special occasions were they invited to mingle with their menfolk on the ground floor or outdoors.

Theodosia herself hadn't set foot outside this space in the four months since her arrival, because, for sure, no visibly pregnant free woman—as she had been since the day she landed on the island of Euboea—would ever associate with any man who was not a close relative.

The few colorful items in this space—four small, blue-painted chests, four blue-dyed woolen blankets, and a blue-painted cradle—all but disappeared in the mass of plain wooden tables, stools, bed frames, looms, walls, and floor. Four lumpy bed cushions filled with duck and goose feathers, each suspended from its frame by four leather straps, spanned the interior wall. Four tall looms alternated on the exterior wall with four windows that admitted dappled sunlight through four mature chestnut trees, each one squared up in the frame as if deliberately planted to obscure the activities outside and the farm's other natural features.

Clearly, Greek men didn't want their women looking out at anything scenic, or even mildly interesting, just as surely as they didn't want their wives and daughters interrupting their own much-freer lives downstairs.

Everything in this space seemed to come in sets of four. There was a logic to that, of course, since all four free women of the family once had lived up here. But now, with Bryaxis's wife dead and his three daughters off in their husbands' houses, Theodosia had the whole long, boring dormitory to herself.

At the opposite end of the rectangular room, a coarse, undyed curtain hung across a doorway that led to a steep flight of stone stairs primarily used by the family's two female slaves, Hebe and Myrine.

Each morning, as soon as Theodosia opened her eyes, her thoughts drifted back to the cheerful frescoes and bright mosaics and shady pergola and salty breezes and expansive vistas and entertaining books and skillful servants of The Harbor Watch in Siracusa.

She especially missed that sweet cottage on days like this, when last night's mutton and onions lingered in the air. The smell had been worse in the winter, but even now, with the shutters removed and spring air blowing in, there still was a constant odor of food, because the women's quarters were located directly over the kitchen, where—as she had been told but hadn't seen, because she never had gone there—Hebe cooked the meals and Myrine prepped the food and waited on the men of the family and their male guests.

Alexander and Theodosia's two-month, mid-winter slog around the northern Mediterranean coast on Captain Aeton's unheated ship, lumbering from one tiny port to another with little privacy and neither time nor place for a hot, soaking bath, had been a terrible experience for her. And so, when they finally reached Euboea in February, this room—for all its food smells, cold corners, and lumpy beds—had felt like her own private paradise. But now it was June. Doros had arrived, and his mother was ready to get out of there.

I need to walk in the sun. Breathe fresh air. Look at the sky. And no matter what Alexander says, I will find a way to ride a horse again some day.

***

Morning light filtered through the four windows, striking the faces of Alexander, Niko, and Lycos as they pulled stools close together and waited awkwardly for Theodosia, sitting up in her bed, to initiate the conversation that she had been dreading.

As a young man just turned sixteen, Niko seemed especially uneasy. It was only Theodosia's second encounter with him, because her confinement had begun immediately after she arrived at the farm. Since then, her only visitor had been her husband… when he wasn't off in Athens laying the foundation for his new shipping business.

Alexander finally got things started. He reached over, brushed a loose strand of hair from Theodosia's brow, lifted Doros from her lap, and showed him to Niko and Lycos as the baby set up an energetic bawl.

"Say hello to your little brother," he said.

Lycos's face brightened with an eleven-year-old's curiosity. Light-brown curls still flopped over his forehead, just as Theodosia recalled from their first meeting at her villa, four years earlier.

"He's all wrinkly and red," the boy said. "Will he always look like that?"

"No," Alexander said, "he'll soon be a normal babe, and not long after that he'll be chasing you all over the house."

Lycos grinned up at Alexander. "Will he chase Ni-ko-laos, too?"

"Not likely. Niko's a bit old for chasing."

"Look," Lycos exclaimed, "his fists are purple and clenched."

"They'll loosen up by tomorrow."

As Alexander and Lycos kept talking over the baby's loud cries, Theodosia observed her husband's stubbornly silent first-born son.

Niko's nearly black eyes, set deeply into his skull like Alexander's, struck her as cold and emotionless. His knife-straight black hair and olive-toned skin did nothing to soften his overall image.

He must take after his mother, because—except for those eyes—it's hard to see much of Alexander in him.

Alexander held the baby out to Niko. "Would you like to hold your new brother?"

"No."

"That's understandable for now, since he's so small and fragile, but you'll want to get to know him soon, I'm sure." Alexander's smile didn't waver. "You looked a lot like that on your first day of life."

Niko jumped up from his stool, walked to the closest window, and gazed at the chestnut tree. "My mother certainly looked better than *her*."

"Your mother was tired, too, right after you were born." Alexander returned Doros to Theodosia's arms. "But very happy that you were there."

"She wasn't happy when she died."

Alexander's face darkened. "This isn't the time to talk about that."

"When then? You never want to talk about her." Niko pivoted and pointed at Doros. "Guess you'd rather hear that wretched creature screech."

His voice—in its tone and inflection—is just like Alexander's. Its rhythm, too, but that's where the resemblance ends.

"Some things," Alexander said, "are best left in the past."

"Like you left Mother and me in the past?"

Doros screamed louder, and Theodosia could have done the same. Instead, she soothed him, and herself, with a cuddle.

"Enough, Niko." Alexander's face clouded. "We'll have no more talk of that today."

Niko stalked to the door and yanked the curtain aside. His sandals clomped more loudly than necessary as he went down the stairs.

***

Ignoring the slaves at work in the orchard, Nikolaos dropped onto the dirt patch where he had taught Lycos and Myrine to speak Aramaic a year ago. He wrapped his arms around his knees and buried his face in them.

Mother was much more beautiful. How could Father forget her so fast?

"We need to talk." It was his father's voice, a few steps away.

Nikolaos did not raise his head.

How can he stand to touch that woman? He can't possibly love her.

"I hate her," he muttered into his knees. "Hate every Roman alive."

"And you hate Syrians, too, as you've told me many times."

"Not the way I hate Romans."

"Sounds like you hate everybody who's not Greek."

"I like Jews, but they don't live around here."

It was a few moments before Alexander replied. "You mustn't be rude to Theodosia, Niko. She doesn't deserve that."

"Does she deserve to live, when Mother died giving birth?"

"I believe she does. Please don't tell me you were hoping Theodosia would die giving me another son."

"Why do you need another son?"

"A man can never have too many sons." Alexander crouched, put his arm around Nikolaos, and pulled him close. "I loved your mother, Niko. I held her in my heart through a lonely decade of slavery, with no idea where she was and no way to search for her. I took no other woman during that time."

Nikolaos made no reply.

"You told me once—" Alexander retracted his arm. "You said you understood what the word 'celibate' means. Now I wonder if you really do."

Nikolaos kept quiet as his father went on.

"I cherish the memory of Antibe and our brief time together, both before and after you were born. My love for her will last until the day I die. But Theodosia is my wife now and the mother of my second son. I won't ask you to love her as I do, but I must insist that you respect her. It's not her fault that your mother died."

Nikolaos propped his elbows on his knees and laced his fingers.

"Theodosia's life hasn't been easy either," Alexander continued in his infuriatingly calm voice.

"Lycos said she had a grand villa by the sea."

"She did."

"And a huge strongbox loaded with coins and gold bars and boxes filled with jewels."

"That, too."

"She owned lots of slaves, didn't she?"

"Thousands."

"Well, to me that sounds like a pretty easy life. Owning Lycos. Owning Stefanos. Owning *you*." Nikolaos lifted his head and jutted his jaw. "How can you forget that, Father?"

"I haven't forgotten it, but I have forgiven her. You can do the same."

"No, I can't."

"Or you don't want to."

Nikolaos glared at him. "Mother never believed you were dead. She told me that every time I asked about you. She always said you'd come to Syria and rescue us."

"And I did. I went to Syria just as soon as I could. Unfortunately, your mother died before I got there. And remember… if it hadn't been for Theodosia's efforts, I wouldn't even have known where to look for you. Certainly wouldn't have had the rubies that purchased your freedom."

Got to learn more about those rubies.

"You're saying I'm in her debt."

That makes it even worse.

Alexander's voice grew harsher. "Theodosia wouldn't say that, and neither will I. But she'd appreciate some sign that you've forgiven her, just as I have."

"I won't ever forgive her, and yes, I do wish they'd died yesterday. Both of them. The fewer Romans in the world, the better."

Alexander's eyes burned holes in him. "Doros isn't a Roman. He's my Greek son, just as you are. He was born in Greece. He'll bear a Greek name. Grow up speaking Greek. Be raised as a Greek. Theodosia agrees with me on that."

Nikolaos snickered. "Whatever you may think, Father, your baby will grow up to be a Roman. Your Roman wife will make sure of it."

"So, I guess it's a good thing that you'll be around while Doros is growing up, to make sure he's raised correctly."

Again, Nikolaos did not reply. Just let his father's sarcasm hang in the air.

"Your attitude disappoints me, Niko," Alexander went on. "I realize you've had a rough life. Known too much sorrow. Had too little time to be a child, but—"

"I wouldn't wish my childhood on any boy."

"Nor would I, but it's time to get over it. Little boys sulk and hold grudges and hope for bad things to happen to people they don't like. Responsible, grown-up men don't do any of those things."

"How would I know what responsible, grown-up men do? The only ones I've had any experience with were my two masters and their male slaves, but those were not normal relationships." Nikolaos paused for several moments before launching the verbal arrow that he had been holding back for months. "I certainly haven't had much experience with *you*."

Alexander's brow furrowed. "We traveled together from Daphne to here. That was a good experience, wasn't it?"

"Then you left me with strangers for a year."

"I've been back four months."

"You're still away for long periods of time, and when you return, you're always up there with *her*."

Alexander exhaled loudly. "'Up there' is the only place on this farm where my wife and I can spend time together. Do you understand that, Niko?"

"Stop calling me Niko!"

A wave of something resembling shock crossed Alexander's face. "Your mother and I called you Niko from the day you were born. That's the only thing I've ever called you."

"I'm a man now. You can call me Nikolaos."

"Very well. I'll do my best to call you Nikolaos, but don't get angry if I slip on occasion. A man's father does deserve some special consideration, after all."

＊＊＊

They sat side by side on the ground for a long time without speaking or looking at one another. Finally, Alexander turned his eyes back to his son.

"There's something you must understand, Nikolaos. I don't have to defend my actions over these past months or years. Not to you or to anybody else. I intend to give my family a prosperous life. That means Doros, Lycos, Theodosia, *and you*. My only regret is that I wasn't able to build a business when I was younger, because it's definitely harder to do as a man gets older."

"How old are you?"

"Thirty-three. Sounds ancient to you, doesn't it?"

"Twice my age."

"I spent my best decade as a slave, so now I have to start from scratch. If I'm lucky, I may have another ten years left. Have to make the most of them."

What a boring conversation.

It was all Nikolaos could do to pretend to listen.

"You see," his father droned on, "providing for one's family is what responsible, grown-up men do."

"Unless they're *slaves*." Nikolaos managed to spit out the word with the most derogatory and demeaning tone he could manage.

As Alexander stared up at the sky, as if seeking some sort of divine guidance in the clouds, Nikolaos braced for what surely was heading his way.

Here comes the lecture.

"There are some things" Alexander began, "that all responsible, grown-up men do, whether they're free or enslaved. They accept other people as they are and try to get along with them. They deal with life as they find it and do their best to succeed. They take the hits the world throws at them and move on."

"Isn't a man supposed to fight back when he's hit?"

"It's fine to fight back if you can, but you have to be smart about it."

Nikolaos eyed him sideways. "How?"

"Well, suppose you're in a position where it's foolhardy to resist."

"Meaning… you're a *slave*."

"Correct. A slave is ruled by a master backed by an emperor in command of thousands of soldiers who are constantly on the alert for the slightest sign of rebellion from the masses below. In the face of so much might and ruthlessness, a slave has to take responsibility for himself. It's no use pouting and whining and crying. If he's hit, it's his job to figure out how not to be hit again. He owes it to himself to survive and live as decently as he can."

"Doesn't a slave owe it to himself—to his family—to find a way to escape?"

Is Father smart enough to get that jab?

"Perhaps. But whatever a man's condition is in life, whether he's a slave who doesn't even own himself or a wealthy slave owner, a responsible man doesn't sit around sulking, making himself and everyone else miserable."

This lecture is getting tedious.

But his father wasn't finished yet. "You're sixteen now, Nikolaos. Time to act like a man, and I don't mean in a swaggering, sexual way, either."

I've heard enough.

Nikolaos rose and began to walk away.

"Don't go." Alexander remained maddeningly calm despite his son's deliberate affront. "I've waited till the baby was born to tell you something. Although now, given what I've seen of you today, I'm not sure if what I planned will work or not."

Nikolaos returned, sat, and leaned back with his eyes averted.

"Can we talk as two responsible, grown-up men?" Alexander asked. "Or do I have to keep treating you like a child?"

"I'm listening, Father."

But this better not take too long.

"As you noted," Alexander went on, "I've been away a lot lately, laying the foundation for a shipping business like the one my father owned in Corinth. He was prosperous. Successful. Able to give his wife and children everything we wanted or needed."

Like a professional pedagogue.

"I joined his business when I was your age, less than a year before you were born, so I had four years of experience before the Romans destroyed our family. That experience served me well during my decade of slavery."

Alexander paused and glanced at his son as if trying to decide whether it was worth his effort to continue. Nikolaos nodded, so he did.

"Bryaxis tells me his biggest problem isn't growing grain. The land's fertile and gets plenty of rain. Most years, his farm and others on this half of the island produce far more than the local populace consumes. The farmers could export the surplus if they had a dependable commercial system, but nobody knows which ships will sail into the port at Eretria, or when they'll show up, or what cargo capacity they'll have, or where they'll go when they leave here. Grain piles up on the docks and rots, so the island stays poor."

Finally... something interesting.

"And that," Alexander said, "is where my new business comes in. Bryaxis offers financing, as a shareholder, which means he'll own part of—"

"I learned in Daphne about shareholding and other business concepts."

Alexander smiled for the first time since this conversation started.

"See? That's exactly what I'm talking about. You found yourself in a bad situation, but you were smart enough to make the best of it. You learned something then, and that knowledge will benefit you now."

Nice when he appreciates me.

"So, here's the deal." Alexander's smile widened. "Bryaxis won't work directly with me. He'll stay here and run his farm, but he's agreed to put up half the money to get us going."

"Who'll put up the other half?"

"I will."

Father has enough money to match Bryaxis's half?

"Since we got here in February," Alexander said, "I've traveled twice to Athens. Found a ship captain willing to take a chance with me. Just rented a small office space near the docks in Eretria. It's a good start, but I can't do all the work by myself. I need a hands-on partner. A smart, talented, reliable, responsible, grown-up man ready to learn the shipping trade. Someone I can trust to manage the office while I go abroad in search of more captains."

Nikolaos digested his words in silence.

"So, I'm wondering." Alexander paused. "Are you ready to be my partner and help build our family business?"

Nikolaos's mood had brightened as his father spoke, but still he remained quiet, thinking it over.

Alexander seemed to interpret his lack of response as a lack of maturity. "Are you man enough to travel to Eretria and live there and work with me to make this new family business a success? Will you do your part? Or are you going to continue acting like a sulky boy who must be left behind with my other children?"

Nikolaos laughed. "I'm ready to be a man, Father, and your partner."

"Sounds like we have a deal." Alexander extended his hand.

But Nikolaos was reluctant to take it. "Just one question. Will *she* be in Eretria, too?"

"She?"

"*Her.* The Roman woman."

Alexander pulled his hand back. "Who?"

"Your new wife."

"Can't you say her name?"

"No."

"Say her name, Nikolaos, or I withdraw my offer."

What's the use of being a free, grown-up man if someone still can force me to do things I don't want to do?

Alexander gave him a hard, flat stare.

"If you wish to journey with me to Eretria and become my partner, you must say my wife's name. If not, you'll stay here on the farm, and I'll find someone else to work with me."

Nikolaos drew a deep breath and slowly exhaled it. "Very well." A long pause. "Theodosia."

"That's better, but let's be clear about one thing. As my partner, you must give my wife the respect she deserves. I won't ask you to call her 'Mother,' but you must use her name. Not *she*. Not *her*. *Theodosia*. Will you agree to that as a pre-condition for forming our new partnership?"

If I must.

"I suppose so," he said, "and in return will you promise to call me *Nikolaos* from now on?"

"Yes, I'll do that. I promise. So, any more questions for me?"

"Will Lycos, Doros, and… *Theodosia* be going to Eretria, too?"

"Not at first. I asked Bryaxis—and he agreed—to let them stay here a couple more years. They'll be safe and comfortable in the country while you and I grow our business in town."

Perfect!

"Well, then— Yes, Father, I happily accept your offer."

***

Alexander and Theodosia lay in each other's arms, savoring the afternoon's peace and quiet as Doros napped in his blue cradle by the bed. After a while, Alexander kissed the top of her head. "I had a good talk with Niko this morning. A talk with *Nikolaos*. He's excited about our new partnership."

"But not about your new wife and son."

"He'll get over that."

"Get over hating us?"

"Don't jump to conclusions."

"I'm not. I've known for months how Niko feels about me, and now it's easy to see he feels the same way about Doros."

"You've known?" Alexander rose on one elbow. "How?"

"Lycos and Myrine spent lots of time with him this past year. Recently, they concluded that I needed to hear what he's been saying about me. Since Lycos doesn't come upstairs and Myrine does, they agreed she should tell me."

"Tell you… what?" Alexander's face changed.

"How Niko decided, a long time before I got here, that I must be an awful person. A Roman witch who cast a spell over you so you'd forget his mother. A cruel, vindictive monster who kept you chained up in her villa so you couldn't escape and come to rescue them. And other speculations of that sort. No matter what Lycos said to persuade him otherwise—and Myrine says Lycos did try—Niko apparently believes all that and more."

"How dare that girl upset you." Alexander sat up, pulled on his sandals, and gave signs that he was headed for the door.

In his cradle, Doros awoke and began exercising his lungs. Ignoring the various aches that lingered in her body, Theodosia eased her legs over the edge of the bed and lifted him to her breast.

"Myrine didn't tell me that to upset me," she said to Alexander's back. "She and Lycos just wanted to make sure I was prepared for what they felt sure was coming."

"I'll talk with Bryaxis. His slave had no right to meddle in our affairs."

"Leave Bryaxis out of it, please." She propped against a pillow and patted the mattress. "Please come back and sit with Doros and me."

Alexander paused with his fingers wrapped around the curtain and looked back at her. Despite his annoyed expression, he did not walk out.

Theodosia adjusted the baby in her arms. "Ever since Bryaxis assigned Myrine to look after me, she's been my only companion, and despite her lack of training, she's a good servant. Don't get her in trouble with her master. A more productive thing would be to explain what I've done to make your son dislike me so much, and what I can do now to make it right."

"It's nothing you've done, my love, it's who you are."

"A Roman."

"That's a good place to start."

"A Varro."

"That, too, but it's also much simpler." He released the curtain and came back to the foot of her bed. "No, I'm wrong. It's not simple at all."

"I didn't think so." She offered Doros her breast. "Tell me what *it* is."

"I'll tell you what I believe after all my talks with Nikolaos, not just today's. He blames your family for breaking up his family."

"*His* family? Meaning *your* family in Corinth?"

"*My* family, yes. *Our* family in Corinth."

"You're saying… Niko blames *my* family in Rome for breaking up *your* family in Corinth?"

"That's it."

"But not a single member of my family was anywhere near Corinth when that happened."

"I know that, and so does he. Intellectually, Nikolaos understands your family had nothing to do with the disaster that befell our family."

"So, why blame us? Especially me, since I was just a child at that time?"

"Hatred isn't always rational. It's just there. In my son's mind, *you are a symbol of Rome.* You and your family *are* the Roman empire. You *are* the brutes who enslaved us. You *are* the ones who sold him and his mother to the Syrian master who beat her and raped her when Nikolaos was just a little boy. And so, to him you *are* responsible for her death in childbirth."

"Makes no sense whatsoever."

I think Alexander's wrong.

"Not to you," he said, "not even to me, really. But to Nikolaos it makes perfect sense."

Theodosia studied her nursing baby's face and said nothing.

There's something more going on—something worse than just a general hatred of Romans—in Niko's head and heart.

After a while, she raised her eyes. "I suspect there's a lot more to *it* than that. I think Niko holds a very deep and personal grudge against me."

"Well, for sure he resents you and your brother for keeping me at your villa for so long that I couldn't get to Daphne in time to rescue Antibe while she was alive."

"That's what Myrine said."

"Well then, yes, she did get that part right."

"But neither Gaius nor I ever thought or said, 'Let's keep Alexander a chained-up prisoner at our villa so he can't go rescue his family.' Nobody's mind operates that way, not even the most brutish Roman's."

"No, my love, neither you nor your brother ever said or thought that, but the resentment is planted deep in my son's soul. And the truth is—whether the chains that held me on your property were literal or figurative, whether you and your brother meant to hold me there or not—that is exactly what each of you did."

This is becoming painful.

Theodosia eased her legs over the edge of the bed and settled Doros into his cradle again.

"Why didn't you warn me?" she asked at last. "All those times I talked about making a happy home for you, Niko, Lycos, and the children we would have together. You knew this day was coming. You could've prepared me for it while we were in Sicily."

A shadow crossed Alexander's face. "I owe you an honest answer, but—" He closed his eyes. "Not sure I can find the words."

"Don't bother. I've already figured out the answer. You were afraid I wouldn't leave Siracusa."

It was a while before he looked at her. "Would you have come with me if you'd known the whole situation with Niko and," he gestured around the room, "the living conditions that were waiting for you here?"

Theodosia blinked back tears. "I love you, Alexander. I would've followed you without a second thought into the fires of Hades."

Wordlessly, he knelt before her and began massaging her bare feet. She welcomed his touch but needed to clear the air of one more thing.

"I'm still determined to make a happy home for you and our children. And don't worry, I'll do my best to get along with Niko. But please, please, please… promise me you'll keep him away from Doros."

CHAPTER 7

The Roman woman's constantly crying baby was ten days old, which occasioned a twilight naming ceremony beside a bonfire on the west side of the farmhouse.

Nikolaos gritted his teeth as the flames crackled.

Just what we needed, a second annoying brat in the family.

He jutted his jaw as he watched his father take the screaming infant from his wife's arms. And trot him around the circle of family members and slaves. And heap praise on the gods for the boy's birth. And pile on thanks for his survival through the treacherous first few days of life. And gush over him as a much-loved second son. And swear in the name of Apollo—*Why Apollo?*—to raise him in the proud traditions of his Greek ancestors. And then, at the end, officially announce that his name was Doros.

Doros. What a joke. Not much of a gift to anybody.

Once this traditional Hellenic ritual was finished, the Roman woman lifted an unusual, twisted silver amulet—a snake with a gaudy little ruby in its mouth, no less—from the front of her stola and kissed it before transferring its delicate chain from her own neck to her baby's.

From his days in service to the Roman family in Daphne, Nikolaos knew the amulet was called a *bulla*. Doros would wear it for good luck during his childhood and remove it at the next big ceremony of his life, the one that celebrated his arrival to manhood. This was a Roman tradition, not a Greek one, but the Roman woman had insisted on it and, of course, Alexander had agreed.

He'll do anything to make that damn woman happy.

***

After the naming ceremony, Doros's family joined Leios Bryaxis in the kitchen for supper with Stefan and Iocaste, who had come for the celebration and were staying overnight. Not only was this Theodosia's first chance to see them together, as a married couple, but also her first visit to the kitchen.

It's nice in here. I should insist on eating downstairs more often.

Bryaxis occupied a stool at the head of the table. Alexander and Stefan took the positions of honor next to him on each of the two benches. At Alexander's side, Theodosia held Doros on her lap, while the massively pregnant Iocaste filled the opposite space beside her husband.

At the end of that bench, Niko showed more interest in tormenting Myrine when she passed by than in conversing with the adults at the table.

On Theodosia's right, Lycos was his usual cheerful self as he toyed with the silver snake on Doros's chest and shook his long curls in the baby's face to make him laugh.

Hebe the cook, who had served as Theodosia's midwife, labored now by the hearth as Myrine poured wine. The only illumination came from the fire and a few oil lamps affixed to the walls. Warm light glanced off the faces around the table as they talked and ate and interacted with one another.

Iocaste was a month away from her own birthing day. She grunted a few times and grabbed Stefan's hand for support as she struggled to find a comfortable position on the hard bench.

"Was it bad?" she asked Theodosia at one point.

"Yes, but the pain fades and then there's a beautiful baby to keep you busy."

"I'm larger than you," Iocaste said, "so maybe it'll go easier for me."

"Don't be too sure." Stefan rubbed her enormous belly. "My son's gonna be a whole lot bigger and a whole lot meaner than Alexander's."

Leios Bryaxis clapped a gnarled hand on his shoulder. "Stefanos, you'll need at least three or four strong boys to keep things under control on that property you just bought. Daughters are fine if you got 'em—and believe me, I know 'bout daughters—but only sons will help you prosper."

Stefan kissed Iocaste's hand. "Three or four strong sons, coming right up."

Theodosia lifted the chain over Doros's head and slid his bulla across the table to Iocaste. "Do you know what this is?"

Iocaste picked it up. "A viper to keep him safe."

She's Greek. She would know that.

"That viper," Theodosia said, "not only protected Alexander and me on our journey, but it also helped us have our baby."

"It's pretty." Iocaste inspected the amulet. "Real unusual design."

Meanwhile, Stefan leaned across the table and studied Doros's face. "He looks like a Varro."

"No, he doesn't," Theodosia said.

"You bet he does. Never seen no nose like that on a Greek baby."

"By all the gods, don't say things like that in front of Alexander."

Why would Stefan—of all people—stir up the pot that way?

Stefan shook his head. "Ain't no mistaking that Roman nose."

Alexander stared down at his baby's face. "I see no evidence of a Roman nose. Just a cute little knob of flesh."

"For now." Stefan grinned. "He's got your Varro eyes, too, Theodosia."

"Fine if he has my eyes, but Alexander won't be pleased if his son winds up looking like my brother."

"It's our secret then." Stefan's grin grew. "He'll find out soon enough."

Dearest Juno, I hope not.

Iocaste steered the conversation to a subject that she probably hoped would be less awkward. "We've got our own secret, Theodosia. Stefanos didn't want to tell you before your baby came, but that's all past now, and since Father already spilled the beans—" She interrupted herself and glanced at her husband.

"A new property?" Theodosia gladly seized on the new topic.

"Several months back," Iocaste said, "Stefanos and I bought a couple hundred hectares of land butting up to Father's property. Got it from our neighbor. We knew his children, so the deal was easy. The old man left for his son's house in Athens a few months ago, and we moved in soon after."

Stefan drummed his fingers on the table, as if nervous.

Not something I've ever seen him do.

"The land came with a huge house," Iocaste added, "a bunch of barns, hundreds of goats and sheep, and three times as many slaves as Father owns. When we first saw it, the hills were covered with autumn crocuses. This spring, cyclamens bloomed and thrushes nested in the eaves. We love the place."

As she talked, Stefan continued to fidget.

Something's troubling him.

"Congratulations on being a landholder," she said to her former slave. "Slave owner, too. Congratulations for everything, and I do mean that."

"I traded four of your rubies," Stefan blurted.

"My rubies?"

I'd almost forgotten about them.

Niko's head jerked, which also caught Theodosia's attention.

"Stefanos and I divided them when we first got here," Alexander said. "I took four with me when I left to find Nikolaos, and Stefanos buried the rest."

"I dug up my four when I got back last September." Stefan nodded in Bryaxis's direction. "Needed to show this fellow I wasn't a worthless louse just hanging around to get my hands on his daughter and her dowry."

The old farmer's leathery face crinkled, but he said nothing.

"Father already knew you weren't a worthless louse." Iocaste rested her head on Stefan's shoulder. "He saw how hard you worked here before."

"Still," Bryaxis said, "it helped that Stefanos had his own resources."

Niko switched his eyes to Iocaste and spoke for the first time this evening. "Was that the secret you wouldn't tell me last summer?"

"What do you think?" Iocaste said.

"I think it was."

"And I think you're right."

Stefan chuckled at their banter. "The old neighbor told me his son and daughter-in-law in Athens would be thrilled to own four huge rubies."

Niko's eyes widened and, for the first time ever, focused on Theodosia.

Usually, he acts like I'm too ugly to look at. Why's he staring at me now?

Iocaste passed the viper amulet back and touched Theodosia's hand. "You did *give* those rubies to Stefanos, didn't you?"

"Of course." Theodosia replaced the amulet on Doros's chest.

Well, I didn't exactly intend them as a personal gift so he could buy an enormous farm, but—

Iocaste persisted. "You weren't expecting him to return them, were you?"

"No."

That much is true. Never thought I'd ever see them again, much less get them back.

"Has that been worrying you?" Theodosia asked Stefan.

"A bit." His face revealed a rare tinge of chagrin. "Wasn't sure how you'd feel about it."

"Well, I'm glad you put them to better use than they had before."

Even though you two are off to a great start in life, while Alexander and I have almost nothing to build our future on.

"That's good, see, because I— Because we both hoped—" Stefan muddled on. "I worried that— Maybe you didn't mean to give them to me and— Maybe you was gonna want them back once you got here."

But since you don't have them any more, you can't give them back. So I might as well put your minds at ease.

"I'm glad you're happy with the farm. Sounds like a good investment."

"Trading all four of your rubies for that property," Stefan said, "let us save every bit of Iocaste's dowry—including a big, fat bag of coins—for something else in the future. And her father *was* relieved he wasn't giving his daughter to a worthless louse."

"Pa likes the idea," Iocaste said, "of combining our two farms and maybe even buying others some day. Between us, we and Pa already own the largest chunk of land and more slaves than anyone else on Euboea. No telling how much of both we'll have in a few years."

***

The next morning, after Stefanos and Iocaste departed in their donkey cart, Alexander and Nikolaos set off on an hours-long trek on foot across the broad Lelantine Plain, which sprawled between the island's central ridge of mountains and its namesake Euboean Sea.

At one point, Alexander halted and gestured with both hands toward the famously fertile fields around them. "Seven hundred years ago, the towns of Chalcis and Eretria fought over this ground. It was the only war ever conducted on Greek soil in the thousand years between the Trojan War and the Persian invasion of Greece."

"What's Eretria like?"

"Used to be a cultural center. Acropolis. Theater. Temples. Mentioned in *The Iliad*. Not much left now of all that glory."

"Might be fun," Nikolaos said, "living in a place connected to the Trojan War."

Alexander smiled at him as they moved on down the road. "We never know where life will take us, do we, Son? Eretria has had its ups and downs, just like you and I have."

He's lots nicer when he's away from her.

"Five hundred years ago," Alexander went on, "King Darius of Persia ordered a siege of Eretria that lasted six days."

"Can you imagine what it's like to live through a six-day siege?"

Alexander shook his head. "After it ended, Darius burned the town to the ground and enslaved most of the townspeople who survived. Plato actually wrote a poem called 'On the dead of Eretria'."

"I'd like to read that."

"So would I. We'll find a scroll and read it together."

This must be how Father taught Lycos.

"So, what happened after that?"

"Eventually, a few surviving Euboeans rebuilt their town, but the Roman army sacked it again a century ago."

"Any Romans still there?"

"Just a small garrison that maintains peace on the island and guards the harbor. Shouldn't cause us any trouble."

***

Nikolaos and his father spent a couple of hours prowling Eretria's tangled streets, exploring the tumbled-down theater and other weedy piles of ancient rock, and bemoaning the pitiful state of their heritage. Some new structures, built with carved stones pilfered from the ruins, revealed a desire for progress, but most residents seemed content with the bedraggled remains.

As usual for a Greek town, not a single free woman or girl put in an appearance, but males of all ages were everywhere. The younger ones ran about nearly naked… yelling, throwing rocks, and dodging donkey carts. The older ones, including some about Nikolaos's age, were better dressed and behaved but also seemed to have nothing particularly useful to do.

Guess there's not much work to be found in Eretria.

Male and female slaves dressed in short, coarse wool chitons hustled from the market to their masters' homes, toting amphorae of oil and wine or baskets of fish, fruit, and bread, taking pains not to bump into men like Alexander and Nikolaos, who wore the longer, linen chitons of free men.

They had left the Bryaxis farm with rolls, cheese, figs, and boiled goose eggs, all of which they ate on the road. But as the afternoon waned and cooking smells wafted out from walled courtyards, they made their way to the place where Alexander had stayed during his earlier visits.

Eretria was too small to offer inns or street-side food shops, so visitors were forced to find lodging and take their meals in one of the private houses or businesses clustered near the water. Alexander paid twenty drachmas to an elderly shoemaker for a month's room and board in one of the rooms above his shop.

The shoemaker's daughter, Cilla, was about thirty and married, with two daughters. She greeted Alexander warmly and seemed to take a genuine interest in his son.

"Nice to have a young man around," Cilla said. "All our other guests are old fishermen like my husband. They eat early and go straight to bed so they can be up and out by dawn."

She set a salad, fresh-caught squid, and homemade bread on the table in her flowery, lamplit terrace as Nikolaos and his father eyed the dishes hungrily.

"I forget where you're from," she said as they dug their fingers into the squid.

"Corinth." Per a previous discussion with Alexander, Nikolaos didn't mention how long it had been since they actually lived there.

After dinner, Cilla led them upstairs. The third-floor room under the eaves that Alexander had previously occupied faced away from the water, but it did offer the rare luxury of two separate beds, two chests, and a round table with three stools.

Alexander removed his dusty sandals, stretched out on one of the beds, and exhaled a sigh of exhaustion. "A good place to be."

"Better than the farm," Nikolaos agreed.

"But not better than having our whole family together."

Nikolaos ignored that, took off his own sandals, and pretended to sleep.

***

After breakfast on Cilla's patio, Nikolaos and Alexander headed for the cobblestones that edged the shoreline, led to the docks, and gave access to a few ramshackle warehouses. Clouds and birds cruised the sky.

They strolled to the far end of the pier as an army of fishing boats marched their red-green-yellow-blue reflections across the harbor and a seagull screamed like a general in battle.

Why are gulls always so angry, so ready for war, when they spend their lives in total freedom?

The fishy breeze evoked that island-hopping journey from Syria to Euboea with his father. And even further back... a few clear memories from his early childhood.

Alexander must have read his mind. "Your mother loved the sea, remember?"

Nikolaos bobbed his head.

"I wasn't sure you would," Alexander said. "You were only four."

Only four.

The breezes were the same. The same azure sky. The same colors of the boats and cries of the gulls. Niko clutched the hem of Mother's flowing white peplos. Stood as tall as he could but barely reached her waist. Pointed to a pelican at the end of a pier. Held her hand as they moved toward it. Watched her face as she turned in Father's direction.

"I'm glad," she said, "we three could come out together this morning."

"Remember this moment, Niko." Father's voice choked as he lifted him in his arms. "Remember it for all the rest of your life."

"Yes, Father, I'll remember."

And then, still holding Niko, Father bent down and gave Mother a kiss. "Actually," he said, "we'll all remember it for the rest of our lives."

"When will they come?" Mother's voice was tense.

"Soon." Father's answer was short and even tenser.

"Any chance they might just let it go?"

"No."

Niko sensed that something was wrong. Didn't understand what. Didn't try to understand. Only knew that Father and Mother were sharing some special information that wasn't meant for him.

"What will happen—" Mother's head wobbled. "To us?"

Father buried his nose in her flying hair. Said something into her ear.

Niko never knew what it was that Father had told Mother that morning, but he did realize one thing, even then. When Father said "soon," he meant "very soon," because the Romans arrived while the family was still at the far end of the pier. A dozen legionaries in crimson-and-brass uniforms stomped out, trapping them between the wood, the wind, and the water.

Father handed Niko to Mother moments before a mountain of a soldier slapped shackles on his wrists, locked them with a rusty key, and trotted him away at the end of a short chain.

That was the last time Father and Mother saw each other.

Nikolaos looked around for his father, who had moved away.

The last day any of us saw Corinth.

Alexander was already at the mouth of the pier, heading for a trio of weathered fishermen repairing nets by the water.

Or experienced anything like the freedom of a seagull.

***

"Nice cool morning," Alexander said by way of greeting.

The fishermen squinted at him.

"Good catch yesterday?" he asked.

Nods all around.

"Maybe you can give us some information."

Alexander squatted beside them as Nikolaos drew near.

"My son and I are in town to learn about exporting from Eretria. Can you tell us if any grain goes out of here by ship?"

"No grain," said a bald man who looked like the father of the others.

"Just fish," said a younger man who was missing two fingers on his left hand. "We take most of our catches to Piraeus."

"You're talking about fishing boats." Alexander waved one hand toward the water. "Do real merchant ships ever dock in the harbor?"

All three shook their heads.

Fishermen aren't much for conversation.

"If a Euboean farmer wanted to export large quantities of grain," Alexander asked, "how would he go about it?"

"He wouldn't," said the third man, who bore a large red scar across his nose and cheek.

"It's not possible?"

"Not without bigger ships."

Alexander scratched his chin. "When was the last time a big ship came into this harbor?"

"Twenty years ago," said the scarred man.

"Maybe thirty," said the scarred man's father.

"So," Alexander said, "cargo ships *can* sail in, they just don't bother. Is that right?"

The scarred man nodded. "Something like that."

"What's the biggest ship that's ever been seen here?"

The bald man shrugged but made no reply.

"They say a bireme came in once, long time ago." The son with only eight fingers appeared to be the most talkative of the group. "We wasn't here to see it."

"Who in town," Alexander asked him, "could tell us what kinds of ships sailed into the harbor in years past?"

"Ask at the fort." The talkative one pointed past a dilapidated row of buildings that paralleled the water. "Them Romans been monitoring this harbor a whole century. They got records of everything."

Suddenly, as if by some secret signal, all three heads bent over their nets.

In response, Alexander set off at a clip toward the main street, leaving Nikolaos to follow once more. But then, instead of continuing straight on to the garrison, he turned into the alley that led to Cilla's house.

"Father, you're going the wrong way." Nikolaos lengthened his stride and caught up with him. "We passed the fort yesterday, on the east side of town overlooking the harbor."

"We're not prepared to visit the garrison just yet."

He's scared to go there.

"I'll go and ask," Nikolaos said. "I'm not afraid."

Alexander glanced up toward the unshuttered second-story windows of the houses that lined both sides of the grimy alley.

"It's not a question of being afraid, my son, but of being smart."

"But I'm free, with a parchment scroll to prove it."

Alexander touched a finger to his lips.

Embarrassing to have a coward for a father.

"Caution is always the best approach." Alexander moved on. "We'll go after our noon meal, but first, let's talk about it and develop a plan."

A plan?

"Aren't we here to do deals and get rich?"

Alexander frowned and opened the door for his son.

Nikolaos stepped inside. "Don't see why we need a plan. Let's just go there and get started."

Alexander wrapped his arm around Nikolaos's shoulders and whispered into his ear. "No matter what communications we have with the Romans right now, we'll need their cooperation once we launch our business."

"So?"

"So, let's make sure we approach them in a way that won't raise suspicions or get on their bad side from the start."

***

The garrison at Eretria was small by imperial standards… eighty soldiers under the command of a centurion charged with maintaining the *pax romana* throughout the formerly rebellious island of Euboea.

According to Cilla, men lived there for decades at a stretch, venturing out in the daytime only to march and at night only to patronize the local taverns and brothels or visit women with whom they maintained special relationships.

"But," she assured her guests as she served their noon meal, "very few respectable people in town know or care to know any of them."

***

The century-old, high-walled fortress commanded a flat promontory with a broad view of the bay. Nobody could sail in or out, or even walk the streets, without being observed by the sentries atop its tall parapet.

Two hours after the noon meal, despite the confidence displayed to his father that morning, Nikolaos's heart floundered as he walked alone up the curved, hard-packed dirt road that led to the arched Praetorian Gate. Twice along the way he paused to blot his brow and push back his damp hair.

May it please the gods, let me stop sweating once I'm there.

Trying not to shake, Nikolaos explained his errand to the guards at the open gate. Beyond the wall, a wide, paved thoroughfare bisected the compound from north to south. To the right, a squadron of men in tight formation practiced their battle maneuvers on an unpaved field, raising clouds of brown dust with every turn.

One of the guards escorted him in the opposite direction, to the left, on a side path of flat, gray-green stones between the shady verandas of a pair of single-story structures built of the same rock. Male voices poured out from both sides. A crude joke in Latin. Too-loud laughter. A couple of bawdy songs.

Must be the barracks. Or maybe the baths. Or both.

The path ended abruptly at the far end of the two buildings, where his escort deposited him outside a lower wall of that same gray-green stone.

***

The pockmarked guard at the headquarters gate laughed at the question that Nikolaos had rehearsed in Greek, hoping to avoid raising suspicion.

"The deepest hull of a ship?" The soldier's Greek carried a strong Latin accent. "Odd thing to ask." He motioned Nikolaos into an austere courtyard.

Everything in sight—the wall, the pavement, and the square, two-story headquarters building—was made of that same gray-green stone. The only color came from bunches of red flowers that peeked through a balcony railing overhead.

"Centurion Norbanus Paulinus has been in command of this garrison longer than I've been alive." The soldier's face contorted as he struggled with his Greek. "He'll have an answer for you, if anybody will."

Following the plan that he and his father had concocted, Nikolaos made an effort to sound friendly, enthusiastic, and easygoing. "Sure do hope so."

The guard clapped his hand on Nikolaos's shoulder. "My name's Fabius, by the way. What's yours?"

"Nikolaos, sir. New in town and very excited about it."

"Stay right here. I'll see if the centurion is available." Fabius walked across the courtyard and entered the building. A short time later, he emerged with an older man dressed in a red-and-brass uniform with a fancy, plumed helmet. "Our garrison commander," Fabius said in his awkward Greek.

Nikolaos smiled broadly and extended his hand. "You, sir, are the first centurion I've ever met."

Centurion Norbanus Paulinus laughed and shook his hand. "The eternal garrison commander, it seems. Been here forever." His youthful-sounding voice belied his gray hair and scrubby eyebrows. "You're Nikolaos, I understand, and you've not been here forever."

"No, sir, just arrived yesterday with my father. Before that, we stayed with a farmer on the island. Do you know Leios Bryaxis, sir?"

Norbanus Paulinus cocked his head. "I've heard the name. Never met the man."

"Leios Bryaxis's daughter," Nikolaos said confidently, as if sharing a personal secret, "is married to my father's long-time friend, Stefanos, so we felt comfortable spending time at his place."

The plan's working.

"Well, Nikolaos, I'm pleased to meet you." The centurion spoke Greek well enough. "Fabius says you've come to inquire about ships."

"Yes, sir. I need to know how deep the hulls are—of the biggest ships, I mean—that have ever come into this harbor."

"Odd thing to ask about." The centurion eyed him more closely. "Most local urchins want nothing to do with us."

"Guess that's because I'm not a local urchin." Totally at ease now and eager to show off a bit, Nikolaos deviated from the plan by switching into Latin. "My father and I are here to start a shipping business. We've traveled a lot, and we speak and write both Latin and Greek."

"That's impressive."

"But before we can get started," Nikolaos went on, still in Latin, "we need this kind of basic information."

"Where's your father?"

"He needed to sit and rest by the pier." Nikolaos shrugged. "Getting old, you know, so I decided to come on by myself." He hesitated for a moment and again departed from the plan. "I should tell you, sir, I'm every bit as fluent in Aramaic as I am in Latin."

"Remarkable language skills." The centurion's voice was warm, and he seemed genuinely impressed. "I'm sure your new business will be a success." He patted Nikolaos on the shoulder, just as Fabius had.

These two soldiers are the nicest Romans I've ever met.

"Well, Nikolaos, like your father, I'm getting old. Could use a break about now. Let's walk down to the water, and you can introduce us."

***

Alexander rose and stood stiffly as Nikolaos and Centurion Norbanus Paulinus drew near.

"Your son tells me," the officer said after a brief exchange of cordialities in Latin, "that you're about to launch a shipping business here."

"All ready to go." Alexander's voice and face were taut. "Sir."

Wish Father would relax. He looks and sounds more like a slave in somebody's dining room than a businessman eager to discuss his new shipping business with the centurion.

"Most of the ships that come into our harbor," Norbanus Paulinus said, "are on the small side."

"So far," Alexander said, "we've only seen fishing boats."

"Yes, plenty of them here, but larger carriers—true cargo ships—do show up on rare occasions. We always have to guide them in."

"Why is that, sir?"

"Submerged rocks. Plus the harbor's rather narrow. Captains tend to avoid it for that reason."

"Do some kinds of ships sail in easily?" Nikolaos asked.

"As long as they've got a guide boat, most can make it."

"I'm sure my father's glad to hear that."

Relax, Father. Breathe!

The centurion's eyes homed in on Alexander's face.

"You both speak Latin remarkably well. That's rare around here. How did you learn it?"

"I spent a few years in Rome," Alexander said.

"Your son was with you, I assume, since he mastered our language, too."

"No, sir, he's never been to Rome."

"Then—" Centurion Paulinus made a double-handed gesture of inquiry. "How?"

Alexander produced a thin smile. "Nikolaos learned his Latin from me and by talking with our many Roman friends back home in Corinth. He's got a good ear and makes conversation easily."

Father's a skillful liar, but still… it does sound like he's proud of me.

"Indeed." The centurion returned the smile and bobbed his head. "Do you speak Aramaic, too?"

"Unfortunately, I've had no chance to learn that." Alexander seemed eager to steer the conversation back to the purpose of their visit. "We tried earlier today to get information from some fishermen, but they weren't interested in talking with us."

"Small town. Not open to strangers. For sure, they don't welcome us military types."

Alexander seemed to relax a bit at that. "The whole island looks like it could use some energy and fresh thinking. We're hoping to help with that."

"I'll gladly assist if I can. Now, please tell me your name again. I'm getting old. Already forgot it."

"Alexander."

"Well, that should be easy enough to remember." Centurion Paulinus laughed. "Such a good Greek name."

Nikolaos glanced back and forth between them and laughed, too.

Father needs to stop worrying about the Romans. They're much too stupid to ever figure out who he is.

CHAPTER 8

The fifth day of February marked a year since Theodosia first moved into Bryaxis's bleak women's quarters.

Now, as then, shutters on the four windows blocked all natural light, air, and sounds. She had nothing to read. Hardly slept. Chewed her nails to the quick. Berated herself every day for not being a better mother.

Doros had passed his eighth month, and she treasured him, but not even his presence at her breast gave her comfort. Sometimes her mood actually worsened when he was by her side... a fussy, constantly complaining reminder of the fact that Alexander wasn't.

Eight months away with only two visits and four letters written at sea. Always excited about landing in some port or other. Always cheered by captains willing to take a chance on the Eretrian harbor. Always accompanied by Nikolaos, who was learning the ropes and turning out to be a useful partner.

Clearly, Alexander's enthusiasm for his venture hadn't diminished. He wrote of his dream of becoming a respected member of the Eretrian community, boosting the island economy, providing well for his family.

"What I want most of all," he had written from Rhodes in November, before winter shut the shipping lanes and his letters ceased, "is to give you the secure and comfortable life you deserve."

One thought hung over her through the long, dreary winter.

Alexander has done—and is doing—so much for me. Why can't I cheer up and share his dreams?

Perhaps it was because they'd been so happy in the early months of their marriage, despite fears of being caught, until the Sicily-to-Euboea journey a year ago ended that sweet phase of their life together.

Or because Siracusa lingered in her heart. She missed the walks around the marshes, not to mention the bright cottage and airy pergola and graceful service that Alexander had provided for her.

Or because Greek society placed so many restrictions on her. She chafed at having to eat, sleep, bathe, weave, and raise her child in this one unappealing room.

Or because Bryaxis's red-faced, deadly dull slave girl was her only companion. Myrine was good with Doros but far more accustomed to butchering pigs than brushing a lady's hair. She taught Theodosia to weave, but beyond that they had nothing to talk about. Sturdy and strong as the Amazon queen she was named for, Myrine toted buckets of hot water up the steep stairs and carried out dirty tasks without complaint, but if she had any knowledge of or interest in the world, she kept it to herself.

**

By the first of April—when Leios Bryaxis's men finally removed the heavy shutters from her windows, letting in light, air, and birdsong once again—the only thing keeping Theodosia sane was Myrine.

That remarkable change had taken place one morning early in March, when they were working silently at their looms. Theodosia later realized that she must have sighed or done something else out of the ordinary, because, with unexpected boldness, the young slave took the initiative of asking a most unusual question.

"Lady, do you know about the Jews?"

Theodosia stopped weaving, every bit as astonished as if one of the wooden looms had decided to speak up. "That's an odd thing to ask."

"Master Nikolaos knows a lot about the Jews." Myrine zipped her shuttle back and forth. "He told me and Lycos all about 'em."

"I met a couple of Jews once. It was a Jewish craftsman in Rome who created our viper amulet."

"Master Nikolaos taught us Aramaic, too. That's the language of the Jews."

Theodosia glanced over at her. "Can you speak it?"

Myrine ventured a shy smile and nodded. "Aramaic's the only way Lycos and the young master and I talk together these days."

Odd to have an actual conversation with her after all this time. And on this topic, even odder.

"My husband once told me that Niko spoke Aramaic, but I wasn't paying much attention. Don't remember how he learned it."

"Long time ago, Master Nikolaos lived in Syria with a bunch of Jewish slaves." For the first time ever, Myrine raised her eyes to Theodosia's face. "Would you like to learn Aramaic, lady? I could teach you. Might be fun."

Anything beats weaving.

***

On the Ides of June, just past Doros's first birthday, he took his first steps.

Ten days later, he was clinging to Theodosia's fingers, cruising the sun-washed room, when Myrine rushed up the stairs.

"Master Stefanos," Myrine said in Aramaic, which was the only way she and Theodosia conversed these days, "sent a slave to tell us… Mistress Iocaste is expecting another son or two." She laughed. "And the man said his master did say another son or two!"

Stefan's very sure of his virility. No daughters for him.

Four months had passed since Stefan and Iocaste's last visit. Their twin sons, Amphion and Zethus, had been born last August, and they'd only been back to her father's farm a few times since.

"You speak of them," Theodosia said in her still-basic Aramaic, "and I think of Alexander."

"He's thinking of you, too, lady. I know it."

Wish I could know that. It's been so long since he wrote.

Theodosia guided Doros toward Myrine. "He is missing his son's first steps."

Myrine knelt and encouraged the baby with widespread arms and her usual much-too-big-way-too-silly grin. The moment Doros reached her, she lifted him up and over her head, rolled backwards, and suspended him in the air like a gleeful bird.

But the quick movement hurled Doros's leather thong over his head, opening the pouch and clattering his bulla on the floor.

Once Doros was safe and steady on his feet once more, Myrine retrieved the viper amulet.

"This is so pretty," she said to Theodosia, still in Aramaic. "Why don't you make a wish on the pretty little snake?"

Theodosia shrugged and threw up her hands in her best imitation of what Niko had told Myrine was an exact imitation of a Jewish scoffing gesture.

"That is silly," she said.

Myrine laughed but wasn't deterred. "Go ahead, lady. Rub it. Make a wish. See if it comes true."

What harm could that do?

Theodosia massaged the viper amulet between her palms and switched into Greek. "I wish with all my heart and soul that Alexander would come back to me."

***

A couple of hours later, Myrine raced up the stairs once more, scooped Doros out of his cradle, and flashed her usual silly grin at Theodosia.

"Come, lady."

What on Earth?

Theodosia set the shuttle down and was wiping her hands on her chiton when an insistent male voice rose from below.

"Theodosia!"

Leaving Doros with Myrine, she made her way as fast as her shaky legs allowed, down the stairs, and into Alexander's arms.

He said nothing. Just kissed her. Ran his hands up and down her back. Caressed her hips. Pressed her close until not even a bedbug could have crawled between them. And then, after a long, silent interval, he eased away and peered into her eyes. "My dearest love. I have missed you so."

Theodosia let her tears flow. "Such a long time without news of you. I wasn't sure you'd ever return."

"How could I not return to my beautiful wife and—" He glanced around. "Where's my son?"

"Here, sir." Myrine lifted Doros into his hands. "He's a fine little man."

Alexander held the boy as easily as if he had never been away. "I've missed you, Little Man."

"He's missed you, too, sir. He's glad you're back." Myrine's red cheeks dimpled in a rascally way that Theodosia had come to appreciate. "And he's not the only one."

Theodosia's face grew warm, as it always did when she was embarrassed, but she couldn't stop staring at Alexander. Never before had she thought him truly handsome, but right now…

He's the best-looking man in the world.

"Whatever kept you away?" she asked.

"Good things. I can hardly wait to tell you." He handed Doros back to Myrine, wrapped his arms around Theodosia again, and whispered into her ear. "Any chance I could persuade my beautiful, beloved wife to come outside for some fresh air and sunshine?"

"By Juno, yes."

***

Arm in arm, they strolled to Bryaxis's apple orchard, where an expanse of wild pink perouka wove its way around the edging rocks. Warm breezes and the sweet aromas of summer filled the air as birds flitted through the trees. A couple of slaves working nearby nodded to acknowledge their presence and moved to the opposite side, as if to allow them more privacy.

"I can't recall a happier day in my life." Theodosia took several deep, luxurious breaths as they ambled beneath the well-pruned branches. "So, tell me what you've been up to."

"Nikolaos and I went to Crete five times. Rhodes twice. Epidaurus and Samos once each." He kissed her. "We must be getting better at selling our idea, because we landed every one of our contracts during the winter in Rhodes." Another kiss. "This spring, four good-sized ships sailed into the harbor at Eretria for the first time ever. Their captains all pledged to return during the harvest season. If that goes well, they've agreed to come back in future years."

"How's Niko doing?"

"He's a natural businessman. Got a solid education in Daphne."

"He'll never admit anything good comes from contact with Romans."

"No, he won't, but still… he's befriended the commander of the garrison in Eretria, a centurion named Marcus Norbanus Paulinus. Nice, helpful man."

"Nice and helpful as long as he doesn't find out who you are."

Alexander bent to her ear. "Believe me, I never let myself forget that."

They made their way back to the edge of the orchard, where she pulled him down into the pink flowers and leaned forward, inviting another kiss.

He responded as if he couldn't get enough of her.

Theodosia looked into his eyes at close range. "This may well be the sweetest moment I've ever known in my life."

His eyes twinkled. "Bryaxis has given me permission to spend a few nights upstairs with a certain lovely young woman who lives there."

"That's allowed?"

"Assuming that lovely young woman is my wife, and also assuming that nobody else's wife or daughter is around."

"Myrine's been sleeping upstairs, but she can return to her mother's room. And they'll gladly keep Doros at night, except when he needs to nurse." Theodosia pressed her cheek to Alexander's chest. "Myrine and Hebe both love him. They'll put up with his squalling to give us some peace."

"You like having Myrine wait on you?"

"She's great with the baby, and I actually do enjoy her company. I'll miss her when time comes for me to leave." She paused and tilted her head to cast a seductive eye in his direction. "I'm all set to leave right now, in case you haven't noticed."

"Hadn't planned on that quite so soon."

"But I really could leave now." She rubbed one hand across his abdomen for a few moments, then let it wander lower.

"*Ummm.* Have to find a house first."

"Make sure it's big enough to keep Niko away from Doros."

***

One hot morning early in August, Leios Bryaxis's most-trusted driver and a yoke of snorting oxen carried Alexander, Theodosia, Doros, Lycos, and Myrine in a large, two-bench wagon across the fertile Lelantine Plain to their new home in the historic seaside town of Eretria.

Doros was growing larger, sturdier, and more active by the month. An expert at pulling things off shelves in the women's quarters, he merrily made a mess of anything that came into contact with his fingers. But never before had he left the confines of the Bryaxis house, so today—eyes wide and taking in all the new sights as they rode along—he babbled, patted his hands, and pointed in delight at everything they passed.

It took all Myrine's efforts to keep him contained and entertained for a few hours in the back of the wagon.

The girl's very presence on this trip was notable, because only the day before, to Theodosia's great surprise and delight, Alexander had purchased her from Bryaxis.

Myrine had wept as she left her mother and brothers and the only place she had ever known, but now, riding with Lycos and the baby in the cargo area on a multi-layered cushion of brown blankets amid gunnysacks stuffed with clothing, she chattered on and on about the thrill of moving to town, managing the house there, helping her mistress raise Doros, and maybe even having little ones of her own some day.

From Theodosia's spot on the second bench, directly behind Alexander and the driver, she listened to the conversation going on in the rear.

"Remember how I told you, long time ago," Myrine was telling Lycos in what sounded to Theodosia like exceptionally fluent Aramaic, "I wasn't meant to spend my whole life on a farm?"

"You said that, and Nikolaos laughed in your face."

"He won't laugh when I show up in Eretria." Myrine giggled. "I'm ready to make him miserable like he always made me miserable."

"Well," Lycos said, "I was meant to stay put in one place. Hope this is my last trip forever and ever."

Around noon, they stopped for a picnic lunch and a break from the uncomfortable, constantly jolting wagon.

As soon as Doros hit the ground, he took off... barefoot and at full speed. Myrine chased him down and toted him back, howling with merriment the entire way.

Juno and Alexander, I thank you both for Myrine.

***

Alexander joined Theodosia on the rear bench as their journey resumed.

"Don't believe I told you," he said, "but the ships that sailed into port these last months have punched new life into the local economy. Farmers across Euboea, including Stefan and Bryaxis, are seeing the benefits already."

"How do you plan to handle the increased activity?"

"Nikolaos will remain in Eretria from now on, managing the office while I'm abroad recruiting more captains."

"So, he'll be at home the whole time you're away?" She made sure her face conveyed the displeasure that she felt. "For months at a time?"

"There always must be an adult male in the house, Theodosia." Both corners of Alexander's mouth turned up in an expression that didn't quite reach the level of a smile. "Imagine the scandal if I left my wife, baby, adopted son, and slave girl to fend for themselves in a rowdy seaport town."

I'd rather be alone than with an angry stepson who hates my guts.

"Don't worry," Alexander added as if reading her mind, "Nikolaos promises to be on his best behavior."

***

Six stinky oxen stomped up to the open door of Nikolaos's office, hauling behind them a creaky, too-big wagon that completely blocked the alley.

He jutted his jaw.

If a captain or a farmer showed up right now, he couldn't get in. Might not want to either.

The driver proceeded to clutter the stone floor with half a dozen blankets, five stuffed gunnysacks, three clay amphorae, and a blue-painted cradle.

Meanwhile, a piercing screech blasted the air just outside the door, topping off the annoyance.

Alexander tipped the driver, and then, once the obstruction finally departed, the Roman woman, Lycos, Myrine, and the world's noisiest baby invaded Nikolaos's normally tranquil work space.

The office was ample in size, a short block off the main street near the wharf, and easy to find on the ground floor of the two-story stone building that Alexander had purchased to serve as both the family's residence and place of business.

Nikolaos had spent the whole day on one of the stools beside the table in the center, scratching with his reed pen and shuffling through stacks of papyrus sheets. Although he could have used a stretch, he did not stand.

Don't care what Father says. Not glad they're here. Won't pretend otherwise.

Alexander pulled his son up for an embrace.

At seventeen, Nikolaos was already much taller, huskier, and stronger than his father, and very proud of it. He said nothing as the Roman woman limped toward his table.

Alexander lifted the cradle and the blankets and nodded toward the pile of sacks. "Let's take these up," he said to Myrine, "and put things away before my wife gets there."

Myrine passed Doros to her mistress and hoisted four of the sacks as Lycos picked up the fifth. They followed Alexander to an interior door leading to the residential part of the building.

***

The Roman woman entered, took a stool near the spot where Nikolaos stood, and began bouncing her unruly urchin on her lap.

"That's my place," Nikolaos said in Latin.

The Roman woman hesitated briefly then rose and settled herself and her brat on another stool.

Nikolaos remained standing. Maintained his full height. Made sure to tower over her as much as possible.

"We're a family now, Niko," the Roman woman replied in Latin, "and I think we owe it to your father to—"

"Don't call me Niko."

"Isn't that your name?"

"My name is Nikolaos."

"I'd prefer to call you Niko. It's friendlier."

"The only person alive who has a right to call me Niko is my father, and even he does not do that anymore."

"Very well." The Roman woman's lips twitched as she bobbed her head. "I will call you Nikolaos. Do you expect your baby brother to call you that, too, when he begins to talk?"

"Yes."

"Then I will teach him to call you Nikolaos. Just don't expect him to say it correctly for a few years." The Roman woman gestured to the stool she had just vacated. "Won't you sit with us and get better acquainted? You may hold Doros, if you like."

"I want nothing to do with him." Nikolaos paused for dramatic effect. "Or with you."

The Roman woman exhaled sharply. "We're going to be sharing this house, so that will not be possible."

"It's entirely possible, because you and that—" He stopped himself from saying *brat*. "You and that baby will live upstairs. I will live downstairs. We'll never encounter each other again unless you first send Myrine to ask my permission to come down."

A shadow crossed the Roman womans face, and she seemed to struggle for a response. "Doros will outgrow the women's quarters in a few years."

"So, in a few years, we'll deal with that."

The Roman woman closed her eyes and sat motionless for some time, as if digesting the rules he had laid down for her. At last, she opened her eyes, looked up, and trained them on him.

"I do not intend to stay upstairs all the time. Nor will I be a prisoner in my own home. You and I *will* encounter one another on occasion."

"My father said you'd remain up there." Another pause. "Permanently."

"He never consulted me about that."

"You'll defy him?"

"It has nothing to do with defiance and everything to do with how I choose to live my life."

"Father promised me that, once you arrived in Eretria, you'd behave as all proper Greek women do."

"The problem with that is, I'm a Roman woman."

If she thinks she can defy Father and me because she's a Roman…

Slowly, Nikolaos circled the table.

"When my father is away, I am the adult male in charge of this office, this house, and this family. I'll have full authority to enforce the rules when he is gone." He stopped abruptly and stared down at the lame, fragile-looking person cradling her baby in front of him. "You would be wise to remember that."

CHAPTER 9

Eretria was nothing like Rome, or even Siracusa, but Theodosia was prepared for that.

What amazed her was that somehow, even in this run-down town, Alexander had managed to locate and purchase a well-maintained house with a spacious upstairs apartment for her and Doros.

He knew exactly what I wanted, and he found it.

The best feature of their new "quarters" was its splendid combination of light and air. Three windows and two balconies offered views of water to the south and mountains to the north, plus tantalizing glimpses into nearby alleyways and courtyards.

On this first morning in their new home, with sunshine pouring in through the east-facing window and open balcony door, she stretched her limbs, eased her feet to the floor, and lifted Doros from his cradle to her breast.

Her spirits rose as she crawled back into bed to nurse him. "We're going to be happy here, Little Man."

The room was square, with wooden floors and the usual collection of leather-slung beds, each with its accompanying chest, plus two round wooden tables, an assortment of stools, a pair of cushioned chairs, and Doros's blue-painted cradle. Between the stairway and the fireplace, abutting the opposite wall, stood a tin tub... convenient for Myrine to carry water up from the kitchen, heat it close by, and pour it for her mistress's bath.

There were no colorful frescoes on the walls, no carved decorations, no soft textiles on anything. The place itself wasn't lovely, but such touches could be added later.

The second-best feature of her new quarters was a brand-new cithara that Alexander had bought in town and left for her to discover.

Other than finding the old one I left behind in Nero's palace, nothing could please me more.

And the third-best feature was something that wasn't there at all.

Alexander knew better than to leave a loom or other weaving equipment in here for me.

***

The sun sailed higher the next morning as Myrine bustled about with vases of purple-flowered vines for the tables inside and out.

Theodosia stood at a balcony railing, holding Doros and pointing to everything in sight as he babbled and followed her fingers with his eyes.

On each of the balconies, empty terra-cotta pots begged for flowers while stone-topped tables awaited their meals. Red-tiled rooftops stretched out in all directions, from the coast to the foothills, where the marble columns of Eretria's oldest temple still stood proud and tall, even as its main structure crumbled into the dirt.

In the narrow passageways below, male slaves in undyed chitons hustled to and fro with tools and handcarts while similarly dressed servant girls slipped in and out of their masters' courtyards. Naked children chased one another back and forth as they rolled hoops and darted into doorways.

Well-dressed free men strode through on their way to whatever important business took them to the waterfront.

But female slaves were the only women to be seen.

***

Days passed. Theodosia enjoyed spending afternoons on the shady eastern balcony. Overhearing conversations. Getting acquainted with her new cithara. Singing to Doros in Latin and Greek. Encouraging him to point to birds in the air, people in the town, and boats in the bay.

But slowly, she became aware of a quiet grumble that skipped through her head at intervals until at last it emerged, fully formed, into her consciousness.

If Alexander can rent a horse and visit farmers throughout the island and travel to other cities in Greece and sail to foreign lands...

And if Nikolaos can live and work downstairs and enjoy meals with his father and Lycos and receive captains and farmers in his office and take walks around town whenever he pleases...

And if Stefan and Iocaste can live like kings on their vast farm with a huge house and scads of barns and cotes and sties and hundreds of animals and scores of slaves...

And if Lycos and Doros can play outdoors someday and make friends with other boys and visit their friends' homes and eat with their friends' fathers and brothers and grow up to be full participants in Eretrian life...

And if Myrine can move about in the streets and gossip with the other slaves and shop in the market and mingle with the men of our family and their guests and even take a lover someday if she chooses...

Why on Earth should I—the one who, at great personal risk to myself— literally clawed back from the emperor the rubies that made all this possible...

Why should I forever be a prisoner in my own home?

***

Alexander was dressing one morning when Theodosia conjured up the tone of authority she had last used with him half a decade earlier.

"My love, I've made a decision."

He looked over his shoulder. "What's that?"

"From now on, I intend to go downstairs whenever I please."

Alexander finished wrapping his linen chiton around his torso and pinned it at one shoulder.

"I'll stroll around town, too, in good weather." Theodosia waited for him to react, but he did not, so she went on. "In the daytime only, of course."

"I thought you and Nikolaos discussed this on the day we arrived."

"He raised the issue, not me, and I did not agree to anything."

"For the sake of our family reputation and the business—"

"I did not appreciate his attempt to tell me what to do."

Alexander matched her authoritative tone. "My elder son and I do expect you to conduct yourself appropriately."

"Being trapped inside my own house is appropriate?"

"'Being trapped' is not exactly how I'd phrase it."

"Sure seems that way to me."

"'Choosing to conduct yourself with dignity' is more accurate." He tied his leather belt around his waist and pulled the loose fabric of his chiton over its top. "Ship captains will come to the office. Farmers. Townspeople. Only the gods know who might show up here in future years."

"None of that should impact how I live my life."

"Will it look professional if a client encounters you at the door?"

"I see nothing wrong with that."

"Or spots you on the stairs?" He sat on a stool and reached for his sandals.

"As long as I'm dressed, what does it matter?" She took a few deep breaths before looking back at him. "My dearest love, this room is quite pleasant."

He didn't look up. "I did my best to find a good home for you."

"I realize that, and I'm grateful to you for bringing Doros and me here from the farm. But still— I can't spend the rest of my life stuck up here."

"Other free women in Eretria leave their homes on religious holidays and feast days. You may do that, too."

"It's not enough."

Alexander made no reply, and for a while Doros's soft cooing was the only sound in the room.

"Look," Theodosia said after a time, "I've accepted that I'll never ride a horse again. That's a sacrifice I can live with. But all the more reason for me to get out and walk for exercise and for the pleasure of shopping like I used to when I lived in Rome."

"You no longer live in Rome. Free women in this culture do not go shopping. That's what slaves are for."

"I had slaves in the past, as you'll recall, and yet I still went to market."

Alexander brow furrowed, but he made no comment.

"I didn't behave like a proper lady back then," she persisted, "and that never seemed to bother you."

"You weren't my wife back then." An edge crept into his voice. "Not the mother of my baby son. We were living in your country, in your culture, in your villa. And it wasn't my place to reprimand you." He moved closer, enveloped her in his arms, and gave her a kiss that nearly dissolved her.

She pulled away, intending to protest again, but Alexander continued before she could organize her thoughts.

"I'm not asking you to do this for Nikolaos, but for Doros and me." His tone was softer now. "Do it for our future prosperity and all our sons and daughters to come."

"What I really don't understand is—"

Doros began to fuss, so she picked him up.

"Since the Romans control Greece," she went on, "why don't—"

"The Romans have nothing to do with our lives or my business."

"But why don't Roman customs prevail here?"

"They just don't." The edge returned. "Look, if you insist on acting like you're in Rome, you'll embarrass Doros. Once he grows older and goes out, he'll see how his friends' mothers behave. He won't like it if you're different."

"But he won't be like any of the other boys in Eretria, either. I'll teach him to speak and read and write Latin. I'll tell him all about our famous family and our history and our villa and—"

"That's not the best kind of education for a Greek boy."

She let a teasing note creep into her voice. "Stefan has already observed that Doros is going to have a Roman nose. And if he's got a Roman nose and a Roman family history, shouldn't he also have a Roman education?"

"If Doros shows any pretense of being Roman, Nikolaos will knock it out of him."

She gasped at that. "Nikolaos must never touch Doros."

"Not physically, no. I would never let him do that."

"Unless you're not here to stop it."

"He will not do that." Alexander caressed the top of their baby's head. "But I *have* asked my first son to help my second son learn what he needs to know to become a successful Greek merchant."

"Even if your first son hates your second son and even if it turns out that your second son has no desire to become a Greek merchant?"

Alexander made no reply.

"Understand this," she said. "I will not be subservient to Nikolaos. I will not seek his approval to move about in my own home or go outside it. And, most of all, I will not allow him to intimidate or abuse my son."

That should settle it.

But Alexander didn't seem to consider the matter settled. He pursed his lips as if giving it great thought.

"Even in your beloved Rome," he said at last, "a married woman whose husband dies or absents himself from the family home is under the legal control of her husband's first-born son, whether that son is her own or her husband's by a previous wife. And her children are under his control, too."

He's right, of course.

She carried Doros to one of the chairs by the fireplace and sat. "So, now I get a taste of what I avoided by not marrying when I had the cream of Roman nobility begging for my hand." She gave a bitter laugh. "And here I thought I'd saved myself from that fate by marrying someone different."

"It's the fate of women everywhere, Theodosia. No culture in the world offers your sex full autonomy."

"But I *was* fully autonomous at my villa."

"That situation was an anomaly. And you know as well as I do… it wouldn't have lasted." He stepped to her side and draped an arm over her shoulders. "Sooner or later, one way or another, all those rich Romans you thought were your friends were going to take you down. Do you really think either Titus or Otho cared one whit about you or—if one of them had succeeded in marrying you—would have respected your desire for independence?"

She sat without speaking as Doros nuzzled her breast, eager to be nursed.

"My dearest love," Alexander said, "please try to get along with Nikolaos."

"Of course, I'll make an effort to get along with him, for your sake. But you must realize, there's absolutely nothing about him that I like."

"You don't have to like him, just stay out of his way."

"And obey his orders?"

Alexander kissed the top of her head. "Yes."

***

Five days later, Alexander left on his first business trip without Nikolaos. The next three months were good for sea travel, he said, so he had to go.

Theodosia had not set foot in the street since the day she arrived in Eretria. But still she knew a lot, thanks to sharp-eyed Myrine, who made a point of covering a lot of territory as part of her daily routine… and always found

out everything that was going on in the house, in the office, and in Eretria…
and never failed to tell her mistress about it all.

A few hours after Alexander's departure, Myrine bounced onto the
flower-filled balcony where Theodosia was entertaining Doros by juggling
three cloth balls, which she had learned to do from the same elderly slave
at the villa who had taught her to whistle when she was a girl.

"Mistress, you'll never guess what I just learned." A sly smile appeared on
Myrine's face. "You're not the only Roman woman in Eretria."

"Really? Who else is here?"

"The centurion's wife."

"Centurion Marcus Norbanus Paulinus has a wife?"

Myrine's smile progressed to a subtler version of her usual impish grin.
"She lives at the garrison, on the second floor of the headquarters building."

"How on Earth did you find that out?"

"One of the sentries told Master Nikolaos about her, and he told Lycos,
and Lycos told me." Myrine lifted Doros to her shoulder and bounced him.

"I wonder," Theodosia said, toying with a new idea, "if the centurion's
wife would like a visitor."

***

Two mornings after his father's departure, as Eretria stirred to life, Nikolaos
walked the docks, filling his eyes with sunshine and his lungs with sea air.

The day was just dawning, cooler and breezier than normal, but already
some boats were way out on the water while others raced with shouts and
laughter to catch up in a decades-old, good-natured local rivalry to reach
the best fishing spots in the bay. As he approached the pier, he stopped cold.

At its far end, a woman with a large bundle balanced on her left hip stood
looking out to sea. Loose ends of a distinctive yellow palla flapped around
her head and neck, as did a few escaping tendrils of gold-tinged brown hair.
Her ankle-length blue stola swirled about her legs.

Although her back was turned to him, he still knew.

It's her.

His sandals soon beat the boards. "What in the name of Zeus are you
doing here?" he demanded.

The Roman woman faced him. "Probably the same thing you are."

"You've no business being out here, especially not with my father's baby."

"Where I come from, women go outdoors whenever they like, with or without their babies."

She moved toward the shore, but he stepped up and blocked her path.

"Return to the house this instant, before anyone else sees you out here."

"How can I return if you're standing in my way?"

"So, you *are* going home?"

"No." Her eyes leveled on his. "To the garrison."

"You can't do that. Most improper."

The brat began screaming and squirming, as usual, so she shifted him to rest against her shoulder. "In Rome," she said, "it's entirely proper."

"Soldiers can be dangerous."

"These soldiers are my people. My son's people. I see no reason to fear them, and with so few Romans in town, every reason to get acquainted."

"They're not your son's people. My father plans to raise him as a Greek."

She smiled at that, but just barely. "I respect your father's wishes, but Doros comes from an old, distinguished Roman line. The Romans inside that fortress *are* his people." She tried to slip sideways around him. "The centurion's wife is expecting Doros and me to join her for breakfast."

Nikolaos was about to restrain her when heavy boots came stomping down the street behind him. He looked back. A squadron of legionaries had picked that exact moment to come marching through town.

Better not have an altercation with a Roman woman within shouting distance of the Roman army.

He stepped aside. "Your husband will learn of this when he gets home."

"I doubt he'll be surprised."

***

Theodosia made her slow way up the sloping road to the Praetorian Gate.

"I'm a Roman newly arrived in Eretria," she said in Latin to the guard on duty as Doros's tiny hand reached for the shiny metal links on the man's breastplate. "The centurion's wife has invited my son and me to join her for breakfast this morning."

The first soldier handed her off to a second, who led her past buildings that smelled of sweaty men and on to a two-story structure with its own low wall and gate, a balcony, and red flowers peeking through the railing.

A third guard left her in the courtyard—where she tried to hold on to an increasingly restless Doros—as he went for permission to bring them inside.

After a while, an officer emerged and extended his hand. "A warm Roman welcome to you, Theodosia, and to your son."

Centurion Marcus Norbanus Paulinus was about fifty. Old battle scars and knobby warts covered his face, neck, and arms, but he wore his red-and-brass uniform and plumed helmet with obvious pride.

Theodosia flashed her friendliest smile. "Doros and I are grateful for your hospitality, sir."

"Aula is most eager to receive you. I am but her humble messenger."

Not all that humble, I suspect.

After a few more pleasantries in Latin, he escorted her into his windowless office, which was illuminated by a single lamp on his desk.

As her eyes adjusted, Theodosia noticed a collection of weapons on the walls and a jumble of other military gear on a shelf near the stairway.

Doros spotted them, too, and began pointing in all directions.

Norbanus Paulinus offered her a stool. "In your note, you say you're Roman—and in fact your Latin does appear to be native—yet you and your son bear Greek names." He sat behind his desk and, with visible patience, awaited her explanation.

"My husband's Greek. Born in Corinth, actually. I've adapted, or at least I'm trying to adapt, to his culture."

With luck, that answer will do.

The centurion chuckled. "I've come to appreciate the Greek men who live on this island. But I never get to meet their women, so it's a fine day when a beautiful young lady shows up in my office to remind me how lovely Latin can sound when softly and gently and correctly spoken."

A sudden rush of blood seared Theodosia's face and neck.

Not the line of conversation I expected. Must be careful.

"I'm sorry," he went on, "but you've not yet satisfied my curiosity about your family history."

She smiled again. "My history's complicated."

Without thinking too much about it, she fell back on a just-in-case story that she and Alexander had concocted two years earlier after her encounter with the nosy slave woman at The Petulant Pelican in Messana.

"I grew up with my mother's people in the town of Lecce, in Apulia, on the Adriatic. Always loved those beaches."

Hope he doesn't ask me to describe it further.

"Originally, her family came from Rome, so from my earliest years I spent a lot of time with other relatives there, which is why I sound like a born-and-bred Roman."

Maybe that will suffice.

"Still," she added, "I do consider myself to be an Apulian, not a Roman."

It's hard to lie about such a basic fact, but—

The centurion's eyes probed hers. "Aula will be disappointed. She's been hoping you'd share her love of news and gossip from Rome."

"Oh, no worries!" Theodosia laughed, perhaps a bit too loudly. "I enjoy imperial court news and gossip as much as anyone." She shifted Doros in her arms and embellished her fake history even more. "My father was a Corinthian, which is why I have a Greek name. He died not long after my birth, which explains why my mother moved back to her home town in Apulia."

"You mentioned that your husband also hails from Corinth." Norbanus Paulinus tilted his head. "That's quite a remarkable coincidence."

"Not really, sir. Alexander and I met while I was visiting my father's family there."

He appeared to search his memory. "I believe I talked with him last year."

Hope my story comes close to matching what Alexander told him.

"Don't you have another son, Theodosia? An older one named Nikolaos?"

"Nikolaos is my husband's son by his first wife. This one, Doros, is ours."

For a while, from behind his gnarled hands and flickering lamp, the old warrior played peek-a-boo with the little boy.

Finally, Norbanus Paulinus rose.

"Aula is thrilled to have another Roman woman in town. Even an Apulian will be welcome company for her after all these years alone." He helped her up, too. "Can you manage the stairs?"

Theodosia nodded. "Slowly and carefully."

Good thing he didn't ask why I limp. My old fell-off-the-roof story won't work now that I'm officially a woman again.

Moments later, as Doros rode on her shoulder past the shelf of military gear, his hand shot out and snagged a helmet. It wobbled in his fingers until Norbanus Paulinus rescued it and popped it onto the boy's head. The helmet covered Doros's eyes, but he squealed in glee, patted it, and uttered the first word that his mother was absolutely sure she understood.

"Mine!"

***

Aula held Doros on her lap until he grew restless, then she watched calmly as he toddled around her apartment, touching everything within reach and jabbering a running commentary that meant nothing to anyone but him.

A slender maid with red hair, decades younger than her mistress, arrived with a glass pitcher of cherry juice, two silver cups, and an oval pottery plate of pastries stuffed with apples and almonds in honey.

It wasn't long before every bit of Theodosia's first-visit awkwardness vanished.

Amazing to find a friend in this forlorn place.

"Do you have children, Aula?"

"Four grown sons, plus two baby girls who didn't survive. Even with their father off at war much of the time, all my boys turned into strong, brave men."

"And grandchildren?"

Aula's elegantly coiffed gray hair rippled as she bobbed her head. "The three oldest have left the army, married, and sired seven children who would be the delight of my heart if only I lived nearby. My youngest, Sextus, is just entering officer training, so no chance of marriage for him for a few more years."

"Where do the older ones live?"

"In Rome." Aula's face turned wistful. "There's nothing I wouldn't give—and almost nothing I wouldn't do—to be there while those little ones are growing up. It's my heart's truest desire."

"Couldn't your husband get a transfer back to Rome?"

"Without the help of someone high up in government, not much chance."

"The emperor?"

"Certainly, he could arrange it." Aula chuckled. "But I doubt Nero even knows the island of Euboea exists, much less a centurion named Marcus Norbanus Paulinus."

Doros came racing across the room. Still not fully in control of his feet, he stumbled and crashed into his mother's chair. An instant before his wails began, she scooped him up and held him close until his tears subsided.

"How did you and the centurion wind up in Eretria?" she asked Aula.

"Marcus was wounded in Britain, so General Vespasian sent him home to heal. The army later rewarded him with the command here."

"He served under General Vespasian?"

Aula nodded. "Best commander in the world, if you believe my husband. Marcus swears that Vespasian will be emperor one day. When that time comes, we'll travel to Rome for his coronation and ask for a permanent transfer back."

"Were they friends?" Theodosia nibbled a pastry.

"The general knew all his centurions by name, but that's as far as it went." Aula shrugged. "And many years have passed since then."

No way can I tell her how well I know Vespasian and his children.

Theodosia pivoted to a safer topic. "What does the centurion of a remote garrison like this do on a daily basis?"

Another shrug. "Whatever needs doing." Aula motioned for her slave to pour them both more juice. "A local uprising? Marcus puts it down. A robbery? He investigates it. A murder? Same thing."

"There can't be many murders around here."

"No, not many. More commonly, a couple of islanders will dispute ownership of a cow or a piece of land, and he has to straighten that out. Sometimes, a man gets thrown in the dungeon until he cools off. But in general, Marcus is not only commander of the garrison but also the local prosecutor and judge, as well as the governor's eyes and ears on the island."

"He must know everything that happens here."

Aula nodded. "Everything."

***

Theodosia soaked in a tubful of warm water as Myrine massaged clove oil into her arms and back before employing her strigil and Doros explored their quarters for at least the fifth time that afternoon.

"Her name's Aula, and she hates it here. Twenty years stuck behind those fortress walls. I can't even imagine such a thing."

"Nobody to talk to in all that time?" Myrine clucked as she reached for a soft, freshly harvested sponge.

"Just her husband and his soldiers. She never goes into town. 'Mustn't offend the locals,' she said, but I could tell by the sarcasm in her voice, she doesn't care if they're offended or not."

Briskly, Myrine scrubbed the sponge over Theodosia's back, hips, and shoulders. "Bet she's glad you showed up."

"News from Rome is what keeps her going. Her husband shares all the official dispatches with her, so we had fun laughing at the latest gossip."

"Anything you can tell me?"

"Sure, but... where to start?"

"At the beginning."

"There is no beginning, Myrine. The scandals in Rome have been going on forever." Theodosia stopped to think. "How about this? Five years ago, when I lived just north of Rome, a very, very, very ambitious young widow named Poppaea Sabina was casting her net for a certain fish we both knew. A very, very, very big fish named Nero."

Myrine's brown eyes widened. She floated the sponge on the water and reached toward the shelf of towels. "You knew the emperor?"

"I knew an enormous mass of flab wearing too many rings and too-heavy perfume to cover up the stink of his rotting teeth."

Theodosia chuckled and went on as Myrine wrapped her wet hair in one of the towels.

"Poor Poppaea. There she was, a beautiful, delicate little thing absolutely desperate to marry that blubbery body attached to a foul-smelling mouth, but, unfortunately for her, Nero was already married!"

Theodosia clutched Myrine's hands, stood, and stepped out of the tub. Once she was dry and draped in a fresh chiton, she lowered herself into one of the cushioned chairs. Myrine knelt and rubbed more clove oil into her mistress's feet and legs, stretching and flexing them as she did every day.

"Things were looking bad for Poppaea," Theodosia continued, drawing out the details for Myrine's amusement, "because the woman Nero was married to at that time—the Empress Claudia Octavia—just happened to be the daughter of his predecessor, Emperor Claudius. And that, of course, was one of several reasons why Nero had wound up as emperor in the first place. So now, given Claudia's noble birth, Nero couldn't just dump her for a younger, sexier wife like a sack of moldy grain."

Myrine laughed loudly at that. "Zeus!" she exclaimed with her usual playful grin.

"But you know, pesky details like marriage and fidelity don't matter much at the imperial court in Rome."

"Kinda seems like they'd matter more at court than any place else."

"Logically, you would think that, but you'd be wrong. Nero had already had two very public and scandalous affairs—one with a castrated slave boy and another with a slinky freedwoman—so Poppaea saw no reason why she couldn't sleep with him, too."

"Did she?"

"Oh yes, many times. While I was in Rome, gossip raged constantly around Poppaea and Nero." Theodosia relaxed as Myrine's strong fingers worked her joints and muscles. "But since then, according to Aula, Poppaea quit throwing herself at Nero and decided to marry his best friend."

"That don't make sense."

"Actually, it does, and here's where the story gets interesting to me. Poppaea's husband was a long-ago suitor of mine, a mean and aggressive military man and senator named Marcus Salvius Otho." Theodosia lowered her voice. "I didn't tell Aula any of this, so please understand… you mustn't talk to others about it either."

Myrine's cheeks dimpled. "Don't understand it enough to talk about it."

"Neither does Aula, so she's puzzled. She can't figure out why Poppaea would want to marry Otho, because—like everyone else who follows the goings-on in Rome—Aula knows Otho's a nasty bastard."

Myrine removed the towel and combed Theodosia's hair with her fingers. "Is he really a nasty bastard?"

"Absolutely the nastiest bastard you can imagine."

They both laughed.

"So," Theodosia continued, "while Aula scratches her head over this, I bet you, Myrine, can guess the real reason why Poppaea Sabina married Otho."

"She slithered high 'nough up the greasy pole to get a chance to *marry* the emperor, not just *sleep* with 'im."

Myrine's a lot more intuitive than the average slave girl.

"Slithered is right." Theodosia laughed again. "Now, all that happened a few years back, but here's the latest news. Nero's long-standing hatred of his mother—his very own mother!—is boiling out of control, while at the same time he keeps trying to strangle his most-noble empress so he can marry Poppaea. And the very best part is… this summer, Poppaea divorced Otho and sweet-talked Nero into banishing her not-so-beloved-now former husband to Lusitania."

"Where's that?"

"On the west coast of Hispania."

"Where's *that*?"

Theodosia recalled the land-and-sea sketch that Alexander had bought in Messana. "It's a large, squarish land a long way across the sea to the west of the Italian Peninsula. And since Lusitania lies even farther away—on the far-western edge of that land—it was just about as far from Rome as Nero could find to toss Otho." Another laugh. "And since it's also a quiet, remote province where almost nothing ever happens, the assignment isn't likely to turn Otho into a military hero and thus a rival for Nero's throne."

Myrine reached for Theodosia's silver hair brush. "Nice to see you laugh. You gotta do that more, for Master Doros's sake and Master Alexander's sake, too, when he comes home."

"And for your sake, too?"

"Yes, Mistress, for my sake, too." Myrine smiled as she began brushing. "And also for your own sake."

"Well, after that bit of Poppaea-Otho-Nero gossip, Aula filled me in on other news, like the doings of another old suitor of mine, Titus Flavius Sabinus Vespasianus *the Younger*, and his better-known father, Titus Flavius Sabinus Vespasianus *the Elder*."

"Fancy names. How's one tell 'em apart?"

"The father's called Vespasian. The son's Titus."

"Father, Vespasian, son, Titus. Got it."

"Vespasian commanded the legion that conquered Britain fifteen years ago. People in Rome adore him."

"Do you know all these important folks?"

"Sure do. Years ago, both Titus and Senator Otho—that's Poppaea's recently dumped former husband—wanted to marry me, but the Fates conspired against it."

Probably shouldn't tell her that, but what's the harm?

"You and Master Alexander was friends back then, too, wasn't you?"

Friends, yes, in an odd sort of way.

Theodosia shut her eyes and said nothing as Myrine kept brushing and talking.

"I bet Master Alexander was real jealous of your other suitors."

Not something to discuss with her.

"I'd love to meet an emperor some day," Myrine went on.

"No, you wouldn't. They don't tend to be nice men." Theodosia's mind wandered. "It's not impossible that Otho could wind up as emperor," she said, mostly to herself, "or else Titus could."

"They're both that ambitious?"

"Clawing at each other's throats right now, I'm sure."

"So, what you're saying is, if you'd married one of them instead of Master Alexander, you might've been the empress sometime soon."

"It could have turned out that way."

"Are you sorry it won't happen now?"

Theodosia gave that question some thought. "Rome's a dangerous place, Myrine. I'm much better off here in Eretria with Alexander, Doros, Lycos, and you."

"But not with Master Nikolaos, I think."

She's already noticed?

CHAPTER 10

By early October, Theodosia was sick every morning and eager to let Alexander know another baby was coming, but she had no way of getting a message to him. Over Nikolaos's increasingly angry objections, she now visited Aula in the afternoons.

"I learned something interesting today," she told Myrine one evening as she prepared for bed. "According to Aula, Roman garrisons around the world are laid out in the same way. The smaller ones, like here in Eretria, are almost all alike. The larger ones are different from the smaller ones, but they're similar to one another. Headquarters in one area. Exercise fields in another. Barracks, baths, dungeon… each in its own specific location. And guess what? In safe, pacified places like this, they often cut a low door into the wall somewhere inconspicuous and plant bushes on the outside to camouflage it even more."

"Bet they bolt that door extra tight."

"They're supposed to, Aula said, but with so many trips in and out each night to the bars, the brothels, and the 'friendly ladies' of Eretria—and yes, she did actually call them that—it's usually left unlocked."

Myrine folded Theodosia's green palla and stola and laid them on a shelf. "Are you thinking, Mistress, what I'm thinking?"

"Not sure what you're thinking, but I'm thinking I could slip out through the kitchen and make my way along the back alleys to that secret door in the wall behind the bushes and visit Aula every day and leave Nikolaos completely in the dark about it."

***

A few nights later, as Theodosia relaxed in her cushioned chair, Myrine knelt to massage and flex her feet and legs. Then, with her head still down, she began to talk.

"Lycos says he's in love with me."

Smiling to herself, Theodosia recalled the shy child she had first met at her villa five years earlier.

"Even tries to kiss me," Myrine went on, "but he can't unless I lean down."

"He's only twelve. Much too young to entertain such thoughts."

"I told him that. 'Zeus,' I said, 'I'm four years older than you. A really old lady compared to you.'"

"What'd he say to that?"

Myrine grinned mischievously and delivered a perfect, high-pitched imitation of Lycos's voice. "'Yeah, I know.'"

How funny.

"He's playing games with you."

"Sure did sound serious."

"Boys always think they're in love with older women. Makes them feel all grown up. Remember what I told you about General Vespasian's son?"

"Titus?"

Theodosia nodded and laughed at the memory. "Titus was fifteen and I was nineteen—and way too old not to be married already—when he first asked me to marry him."

More details than she needs to know, but again, who cares?

"Lycos says the same thing."

"He wants to marry you?"

"Says he's ready right now. Is that a problem?"

"If he were serious, it might be, but no… since he's just joking." Theodosia laid her hand on the girl's head. "Make sure you don't do anything 'romantic' with him without your master's permission. Above all, don't tell Nikolaos about it."

Myrine kept her eyes down, but her face grew even rosier than usual. "Mistress, that's another problem."

"Another problem?"

"Master Nikolaos is worse." Her voice dropped to a whisper.

"Worse?"

"Lycos just tries to kiss me, but Master Nikolaos keeps pushing me to sleep with him, and I don't want to." Myrine raised her eyes. "I *really* don't want to."

"When did this start?"

"Soon after the master left."

"Two months ago?"

Myrine nodded. "He's all over me. Every day. Every chance he gets."

"What do you mean by 'all over you'?"

"He corners me when I'm alone. Squeezes my breasts. Gives me gross kisses. Pokes his fingers into my rear end. Says I got no right to push him away or tell you about it or do anything else to stop him." Myrine shuddered. "That butt poking started way back before you got to the farm, but the boob squeezing and icky kissing is new."

"You don't have to give in."

"But how can I hold him off?" Myrine's voice hardened. "He keeps telling me he's in charge here now."

"Legally, I'm afraid, that's true."

"He says, 'Obey me or face the consequences.'"

"What consequences?"

"Says he'll flay the skin off my back."

Theodosia exhaled noisily. "That will not happen. I'll never allow it."

"Well, I can't argue with him, and you're never there when he does any of it." Tears flowed, but Myrine made no effort to blot them off her cheeks. "Mistress, how much longer before Master Alexander comes home?"

"I expect him around the middle of November. So, about a month."

***

The rainy season arrived early, well before the end of October. Slaves and donkeys still went about their chores, but children and free men vanished from the streets. No farmers or ship captains slogged through the muck to the office. Business stopped. Nikolaos grew bored and restless.

One dark morning, an hour into what should have been a work day, he went to the kitchen, where an inviting fire crackled in the hearth. He expected to find Lycos chatting with Myrine in Aramaic, as he usually did at this hour, but for once there was no sign of the boy.

Myrine was there, however, standing with her back to the door. Chopping and cooking were regular duties for the family's only slave, so… no surprise that she was in the same place, doing the same thing that she always did at this same hour every day.

Her left hand and her cleaver rose together and, for a moment, hung in the air over the bloodstained chopping block before they fell and landed with a solid *thump*. The rising and hanging and falling and thumping repeated again and again and again, with a steady cadence, as Nikolaos watched.

Smells like mutton. Good choice for a day like this.

Myrine was no more physically attractive, two years on, than when he first laid eyes on her in the Bryaxis kitchen.

As bovine as ever. But still, there's something about her.

This morning, as rain pounded the kitchen roof and her cleaver thudded rhythmically into the block, he knew what that something was.

Myrine's earthy. Strong. Sensual. Tasty. And all alone.

Keenly aware of his increased height—because on the farm last year he and Myrine had stood eye-to-eye, and now he looked down on the top of her head—he crept up behind her.

In a flash, his left hand seized her left wrist at the highest point of its chopping arc. A quick twist sent the cleaver clattering to the stone floor.

The girl gasped as his right hand snapped across her chest, mashed her left breast against her rib cage, and kneaded it hard with his fingers.

Releasing her wrist, his left hand dropped fast and pressed hard on her belly, forcing her backside against his groin, which soon developed a new energy of its own and began thrusting itself at her.

Never did anything like this before. Feels good.

Restraining her with both his arms, he rammed her soft bottom… back and forth, back and forth, back and forth.

Then, without stopping that motion, he draped his right arm over her shoulder, lifted the front of her short slave's chiton, and dug into the warm, moist spot between her legs. It was a more aggressive version of the grope-and-poke move he had often used on her in the kitchen, laundry, barnyard, and chicken coop.

From experience, he knew that whatever action she was engaged in at that moment would instantly cease. And sure enough, Myrine froze.

She wants me to take her.

The girl gave her usual gasp-and-twitch response.

Too timid to say so, but she wants it.

Even her breathing had stopped.

Wants it now.

"Bend over the block."

First time for everything.

"Master Nikolaos, I—"

"Bend over."

She remained stubbornly upright.

"Disobedience," he growled, "is not allowed."

With his hot erection pinning her from behind, he beat her breasts with both his hands, as forcefully as he could from that awkward angle. She cried out in pain, which only enhanced his arousal.

We've both waited long enough.

In the next instant, he shoved her forward, flattening her chest and face on the bloody block as chunks of mutton joined the cleaver on the floor.

It's time.

Myrine's face angled to the left as her arms flailed on both sides. "Master Nikolaos, I gotta get the stew on the fire."

Again he smacked her, across the buttocks this time and from a much better direction, which conveniently sent the back part of her chiton flying up over her plump posterior. "Not sure how I've resisted your seductions for so long."

"My mistress will not allow this." Her voice quivered.

"Your mistress has nothing to say about it." He boosted her farther up on the big, square block.

"But my master—"

"Is not here to object."

***

It ended even more deliciously than Nikolaos had anticipated, despite Myrine's sobs and trembling, or perhaps because of them.

Who'd have guessed she was a virgin?

"Clean yourself up," he commanded, "and say nothing of this."

"Yes, Master." She did not raise her face from the block.

He hit her bare backside once more for good measure and stepped away before halting in mid-stride.

Lycos was standing in the door.

Myrine's sobs quickly evolved into wails, but Nikolaos ignored her.

Instead, he drew a deep breath and swaggered toward Lycos. "How long have you been there?"

"Long enough to know what you did." Lycos's face was as red as Myrine's. "Get out."

The boy didn't budge. "You'll answer to Alexander for this."

"He won't care. He was young once. Probably did the very same thing with the slave girls in my grandfather's house."

"We need to talk," Lycos said, even though his manner suggested that talking was the last thing on his mind.

"Not in the mood to talk."

"So, get in the mood and come with me." Lycos yanked open the kitchen door and plunged out into the torrent.

For some reason that Nikolaos didn't understand, he followed him down the sodden alley, all the way to the deserted waterfront.

***

When they reached the docks, Lycos pivoted, clenched his fists, and smashed them repeatedly, with all his little-boy strength, into Nikolaos's abdomen.

"You had no right to rape her!"

From his superior height, Nikolaos grabbed the boy's wrists and lifted them to stop the pummeling. "She's been asking for it, and she enjoyed it."

Let him chew on that.

"I love Myrine!" Lycos shouted against the wind. "I want her for my wife!"

"You can't marry her."

"I can! I will!"

"She is my slave and—"

"She is not *your* slave!"

"And I will never let you have her."

"She belongs to our father."

"*My* father, not *your* father" Cold water dripped from Nikolaos's hair into his wool chiton and coursed on down his chest and back.

Why am I standing outside in a storm, arguing with this obnoxious brat?

"I'm part of the family, too!" Lycos yelled even louder.

"Not true." Nikolaos threw his hands back at him, then he leaned down and spat into his face. "You're nothing but a pathetic little runaway slave who doesn't even know where he was born or who his real father is."

"You're not so fine yourself, Ni-ko-laos. Just another ex-slave. Your father's a runaway, too, but he's also a good man who helped me escape and told me to call him 'Father.'"

As if that settles everything.

"I'm going to buy Myrine's freedom," Lycos went on.

"That will never happen." Nikolaos straightened to his full height and flexed his growing muscles. "I guarantee it."

"Well, let me tell you one thing that definitely *will* happen if you ever rape her again." Like a wolf, Lycos bared his teeth. "I will kill you!"

Nikolaos fluttered his fingers and produced a high-pitched imitation of Myrine's voice. "Zeus, I'm scared. So very, very scared."

In the next moment, using both hands, Nikolaos shoved Lycos so hard that the boy lost his balance and fell backwards onto the wet cobblestones. Then, repeatedly, he kicked him. "I'll teach you to threaten me."

Lycos yelped at each blow and struggled to regain his footing, even as Nikolaos wielded his foot as an obstacle to make sure he stayed down.

"You like pushing me around, don't you?" Blood oozed from cuts on Lycos's chin, nose, and shins. "But I'm growing up, too. Getting taller and stronger every year, and I swear—" He paused and used his sleeve to wipe away the blood on his face.

"You swear what? A little boy with such dangerous secrets shouldn't be so quick to make threats." With that, Nikolaos relented and gave him a chance to scramble to his feet.

Lycos panted as he rose. "I swear— if you don't leave Myrine alone— one of these days— when you least expect it— I really and truly will *kill* you."

***

Another blustery storm over the Aegean Sea delayed Alexander's return home until mid-December, nearly a month later than expected.

Rain battered the closed shutters as Theodosia dozed in her chair, facing the door. She jumped when, without warning, Alexander dashed through the curtain carrying a wet, shivery puppy—white with brown spots, floppy ears, and a black nose—and set him on the floor near her chair, in front of the warm fire.

"What's that?" she asked by way of greeting.

"Peace offering." He kissed her, then he grabbed two towels off a shelf near the tub, squatted, and rubbed the sopping creature until it stopped shivering and licked his hand. "I found this little fellow begging for food on the wharf at Piraeus. Couldn't just leave him there."

Doros came over to investigate.

"It's a dog," Theodosia said. "Can you say *dog*?"

"Dog."

"What kind of dog is it?"

"Brown dog. Nice dog." Doros beamed and raised his voice. "Dry dog!"

Oh, my dearest Juno, I do so love this child.

Alexander eyed his son. "Those are some mighty fine words."

"You've missed a lot, my love. First words. First steps." Theodosia petted the puppy. "What's his name?"

"I call him Socrates."

"Is he a philosopher?"

Alexander laughed. "He's the most philosophical dog you'll ever meet."

She laughed with him. "I'm sure that's true."

So then, after a longer kiss…

And a thorough update on his trip…

And the announcement of her new pregnancy…

And a lively rough-and-tumble with Doros and Socrates…

It fell to Theodosia to break all the bad news and spoil Alexander's homecoming.

He needs to hear every bit of it, and from me.

"Doros has a nighttime cough that never quits and Myrine gives him herbs and honey but nothing works so he doesn't sleep which means I don't either so I'm wiped out in the daytime and can hardly think straight…

"And Nikolaos raped Myrine in the kitchen and Lycos caught him at it and they had a big fight and punched each other in public and soldiers in town saw Nikolaos shove Lycos and kick him while he was down and his face and legs were bloody when he got home…

"And now Myrine's pregnant and too sick in the mornings to help me at the very time I need her most.…

"And Lycos is furious about the rape and insists on buying Myrine's freedom so he can marry her someday but Nikolaos turns purple whenever the subject comes up and they threaten each other and neither one will speak to the other…

"And Myrine knows what those threats are and they must be pretty awful because she refuses to tell me and neither will Lycos although I've asked him over and over so the best I can do is guess…

"And Nikolaos rages at me for going downstairs and visiting the garrison because I've made friends with the centurion and his wife and I enjoy getting the news from Rome and they're completely harmless social calls but your son rants and raves like I've dishonored the family for generations to come…

"And now that I'm pregnant again and Nikolaos knows it, he's madder than I've ever seen him before."

She stopped for a breath and looked at Alexander.

"One thing's clear. Nikolaos doesn't want me giving you any more sons."

Alexander's eyes—as hard and black and sunken as she had ever seen them—bored into hers. His bloodless lips mashed together. His face had flushed to the color of a ripe Sicilian pomegranate.

Without a word, he rose and strode to the door.

***

Nikolaos was wiping ink off his fingers when Alexander barged into the office.

"Welcome home, Father."

Never saw his face so purple.

"Successful trip, I'm sure." Nikolaos extended a hand in greeting.

Alexander ignored it. "You've upset the whole house in my absence."

"I've upset nothing."

"That's not what my wife tells me."

Of course not.

"On the contrary, I've resolved several problems created by others."

"Not according to Theodosia."

"Surely you didn't expect a positive report from *her*?"

"You raped Myrine." The old scar on Alexander's jaw twitched as it always did when he was angry.

Might know that'd be the first thing she told him.

"Never raped anybody, least of all Myrine."

"By all the gods, Son, you better not lie to me."

Nikolaos snickered. "Won't deny I had sex with the girl, but it wasn't rape. She wanted it. She asked for it. She enjoyed it." He raised his voice in another shrill parody. "Come to me, Master Nikolaos. Kiss me, Master Nikolaos. Take me, Master Nikolaos. Right now, Master Nikolaos. Faster! Harder! Zeus! Harder-harder-harder! Thank you, thank you, Master Nikolaos!"

"That's not the way Myrine described it to her mistress."

"Of course not." Nikolaos pointed to a stool on the other side of the table. "Have a seat, Father, and tell me all about your trip."

Alexander sat but did not tell Nikolaos about the trip.

"Myrine is pregnant and sick, which means she's no use to my wife, who is also pregnant and sick and needs the full attention of her servant." His voice deepened. "That baby Myrine's carrying, is it yours?"

"Maybe. Maybe not. Who's to say with a slave whore?"

Rain hammered the roof, but otherwise the room was silent.

"Years ago," Alexander said at last, "a Syrian master raped your mother. He probably thought of her as a 'slave whore,' too. You once told me how horrible it was to watch her die trying to expel that man's spawn."

Nikolaos said nothing, so Alexander went on.

"Have you forgotten about that?"

Silently, Nikolaos inspected his fingers to see if all the ink was gone.

"Answer me, Son."

"I'll never forget it."

"I didn't think so." Alexander lowered his voice. "Now listen to me. You and I were other people's property for a decade, but at no point in all that time did either of us ever sink so low as the men we were forced to serve. And I say 'men' deliberately, because Theodosia was not in that category of owner."

Nikolaos licked two fingers and tried to expunge the last of the ink.

"So," his father went on, "as an eyewitness to how badly that man treated your mother, how could you now take advantage of your position as a master and do exactly the same thing to a slave woman under your control?"

Nikolaos raised his head. "Myrine asked for it. Mother did not."

After more silence, Alexander changed the subject. "Theodosia also said you had a violent argument with Lycos. Several soldiers reported it to her."

"He slugged me first, with both fists."

"Hard to picture a skinny twelve-year-old landing many painful punches on a hefty fellow like you."

As before, Nikolaos made no reply, so his father continued.

"The guards told Theodosia that you shoved Lycos to the ground and kicked him and forced him to stay down when he was trying to get up. That's cowardly, bullying behavior."

"I had my reasons."

"What reasons?"

"To make him stop harming our family."

Alexander flinched. "I can't imagine he's harmed our family in any way."

Nikolaos remained quiet.

"Tell me," his father demanded, "how Lycos has harmed us."

"Betrayed family secrets."

"Family secrets?"

"People can put two and two together."

"About what?"

"Her history."

"Whose history?"

Nikolaos jutted his jaw. "*Hers*… and also *yours*."

"Nobody in Eretria knows anything about either one of us."

"That's not true. Lycos knows all about you and *her*. So does Myrine."

"Sure, Lycos knows about it because he lived through it with us, but he never would betray any of our secrets." Alexander's forehead wrinkled. "Who told Myrine?"

"Lycos did and—" Nikolaos gave a half-hearted laugh. "*Her*."

"You promised you'd use my wife's name."

Nikolaos ignored that.

"Between them—all three of them—they've passed on a whole lot of personal information."

His father's eyes widened. "When did this begin?"

"Last August, the day after you left, when she started flaunting herself in the street."

"Flaunting herself?"

"Usually it's in the morning, sometimes in the afternoon, but each and every day she goes prancing off to the fort." Nikolaos made flighty waves with both hands. "How do you think she met those guards who told her about my fight with Lycos?" He paused, then went on. "She hauls your son all over town, showing off his fancy viper bulla to everyone she meets."

Alexander expression grew more anxious as Nikolaos elaborated.

"Each and every day when the weather's good, she and Doros and Lycos and Myrine go to market. And, of course, they stop to gossip with Myrine's slave friends. And chat with shopkeepers. And with fishermen. And with soldiers." Another pause. "This whole town assumes your wife is a harlot."

Alexander remained stone-faced, so Nikolaos kept at it, muddling real street reports with tidbits of actual Varro lore gleaned over the years from Lycos, plus his own fantasies of patrician life in Rome.

"She entertains them with stories about herself and her noble family and her ancient villa and her black filly named 'Lamia' and her this and her that and her whatever. Doesn't take long before those details and a whole lot more find their way back to me."

"What other details?"

Damn. Father actually believes me.

"Use your imagination, Father. It's not hard to guess."

Alexander released a loud sigh. "My imagination is tired. Worn out from travel. You'll have to tell me."

Gladly, Father.

"So, at first it was just amusing tales about Doros. Why you gave him that name. How fast he learned to walk and talk. How he grabbed a helmet off the centurion's shelf and claimed it for himself. That kind of thing. But then the stories got more personal. Facts I never would have known except all my friends kept feeding them back to me."

"What facts?"

"How her son's a lot more Roman than Greek."

Father will love that.

"And how proud she is of his cute little Roman nose. And how he'll grow up well informed on his Roman family heritage."

Alexander winced, but Nikolaos didn't stop.

"And how she used to be such a grand lady. Rich. Powerful. Coastal estate. Mansion in Rome. Land. Horses. Carriages. Scrolls. Gold. Rubies. Emeralds. Pearls. Rings. Necklaces. Earrings. Silks. Slaves. Lovers. Orgies. Sex.

"And how this noble patrician sought to marry her, and that tribune, and some other illustrious so-and-so. And how she dined with the emperor and rode in litters carried by scantily clad slaves and had hot sex with this senator and that general and with their wives and their sons and their slaves."

His father's color was completely drained, but Nikolaos kept on.

"And then, absolutely the worst thing of all… One day last month, when I went to the market to buy wool for a winter cape, the fabric merchant had a question for me." Nikolaos caught Alexander's eye to make sure he was listening. "A single specific question."

He stopped and waited.

"Tell me." Alexander's voice was barely audible.

Nikolaos taunted him with more silence.

"The merchant wanted to know—" Another pause. "Were the rumors true that you and I and Lycos are lifelong slaves and that, in fact, we three actually are, still, the personal property of your alleged 'wife'?"

Alexander reacted as if Nikolaos had struck him. "I don't believe a word you're saying."

Nikolaos slouched back on his stool. "Believe it, Father."

CHAPTER 11

After Alexander left, Theodosia stretched out on her bed and fell into a deep sleep, which she badly needed.

But then, an hour later, he came back and woke her up.

"We have to talk." His face was pale now, not purple.

Theodosia shook most of the fog from her head and tried to focus as he vented what was on his mind.

"Nikolaos tells me you've been trotting around town for months, bragging about Doros and informing everyone you meet about yourself and him and all of us."

Theodosia rubbed her bulging belly and lifted her twisted left leg. "'Trotting around' isn't the best description of how I move these days."

"It's not a joke, Theodosia."

She sat up. "I've hardly gone outside this month. In such bad weather, it's not very tempting."

"You should've heeded my advice."

Slowly, her mind and tongue reacted. "I'm neither a hen in the coop nor a sow in the sty."

"No one expects you to behave like a hen or a sow."

"And I'm not a Greek woman either, no matter how much you may wish it. I'm a Roman woman and a rather unique one at that." Fully awake now, she stretched her right hand out to him.

"I'm well aware of your uniqueness." There was no warmth in Alexander's face or voice. Even worse, he refused to take her hand.

There must be some way to make him understand.

"With my father's blessing, as you know, I ran wild and free from my earliest childhood. He educated me and taught me practical skills that other girls never learned… all the while neglecting to teach me the kind of things that they did learn. I wasn't raised to be a proper lady—either Roman or Greek—for reasons that you understand very well."

Alexander stared at her as if he didn't see how her personal story related to their current situation.

"Long before you married me," she went on in a tone that made her intent clear, "you were aware of almost everything there was to know about me."

"Yes, I was."

"So, why would you expect a girl who was raised to think for herself and do as she pleased and actually did enjoy true freedom—"

"For half a year only."

"That's not true. Granted, I was a pauper during my decade in Rome, but thanks to my brother's lack of interest in me, I was a free-and-independent pauper. Did you really expect me to ease into a culture that restricts women so much and not anticipate that I'd push back in some way or other?"

"I'm just concerned about what Nikolaos has told me… that on the very day after I left, you started running around town. Chatting with men in the street. Taking Doros to the market, the fort, the docks. Showing off his amulet. Telling the locals all kinds of private information about us."

"I make conversation, that's all."

"And what do you assume the men of Eretria conclude from their 'conversations' with you?"

"That I'm friendly and like meeting the townspeople."

"No. They conclude that you're a prostitute soliciting business."

She laughed. "That's ridiculous."

"Not in Greek culture."

"Most of the people I meet seem genuinely interested in us, so I tell them quick little stories. What's the harm in that?"

"Have you ever told anyone that Nikolaos, Lycos, and I were once slaves?"

"Of course not."

His deep-set eyes narrowed. "Or suggested that we're *still* slaves?"

Theodosia gasped and stared at him. "No."

"Or insinuated that we're actually still *your* slaves?"

"Dearest Juno!"

She propped her hands on the mattress, swung her legs out, and struggled to stand. For the first time ever, Alexander made no effort to help her.

He's really upset.

His grim face confirmed it. "Several men have approached Nikolaos with questions like that. He says there are rumors about us all over town."

"Alexander." She stood steadily at last and looked into his eyes. "Nikolaos is lying to you."

"I see no reason to believe that. Maybe you confided a few of our secrets to the centurion's wife?"

"No. Never."

"I'm not trying to blame you, just seeking the truth." He hesitated. "Lycos knows everything about us. Could he be the source of these rumors?"

"Lycos is smart, and he loves you too much to take any risks with your life and freedom, not to mention his own." She licked her lips. "And by the way, you can bet he cares a lot more about you than Nikolaos ever will."

Alexander didn't react to that. "So, if Lycos isn't the source..." A long pause. "Let's go back to what you've told the centurion's wife."

"Not a lot. Centurion Norbanus Paulinus served under General Vespasian in Britain, which, of course, means Vespasian is a mutual acquaintance."

Alexander's face clouded even more, his brow furrowed, and he responded in a voice as stormy as his expression.

"I bet you told her how many times that summer Rome's most famous and most ambitious general visited your elegant ancestral villa...

"And how the general's equally ambitious son and visibly envious daughter were your constant companions...

"And how perfectly a Greek slave named Alexander served you and them as you lounged idly about, eating and drinking and gossiping the hours away in the breezy shade of your pergola...

"And how cunningly you spent that summer and fall playing Titus and Otho off against one another, all the while enjoying your great 'romance' with a gigantic, gladiator-like slave named Stefan...

"And how, in the end, that reckless behavior destroyed your famously independent life, just as it threatens to destroy our family now..."

Theodosia jumped in before he could go on.

"No, Alexander, by all the gods, I didn't tell Aula any of that."

She collapsed onto the bed and looked up into a blazing rage that she had never seen in his eyes until now.

He's angry but there's something more. He's worried. Frightened, even.

"My love," she whispered in the gentlest tone she could muster, "Aula and her husband have been kind to me, but they're the last people on Earth I'd share any of our secrets with."

"Then how have so many facts about us spread so widely around this town? Because, according to my son—whom I do believe I can trust—the people of Eretria know far too much about us."

"I told you, Niko is lying to you."

"Why would he do that?"

"To drive a wedge between you and me." She dug her fingertips into her temples. "Actually, he's been doing that for years. It seems to be working."

"Could Myrine be the source? Maybe Lycos told her too much about us."

"I doubt it." She lifted her legs onto the bed, stretched out again, and closed her eyes.

But Alexander kept on. "What have you told Myrine about your old life?"

Keeping her eyes shut, Theodosia thought about it. "A while back, I mentioned how Titus and Otho courted me years ago."

"That's it?"

"I told her a bit about them, and about Poppaea Sabina, too. We laughed at how Poppaea slithered up to Otho to make Nero jealous and maybe get her chance to be empress. And not long ago, we talked a bit more about Titus. That's all I've told her about my old life."

Alexander dropped his head into his hands. "Any chance Stefan could be the source of the rumors?"

"He knows better than to talk about any of us."

"Unless he confided in Iocaste, who gossiped with her sisters, who told their husbands, who spread around the island a series of spicy stories that ultimately reached Eretria, where people began asking my son about them."

"If that's the way it happened, how likely is it that all that gossip preserved so many of the details that Nikolaos reported to you?"

Alexander shook his head. "Not very likely."

"Which means, Stefan isn't the source."

"Probably not."

There was a long silence.

"I just thought of something else," Theodosia sat up again and lowered her voice. "Stefan and Lycos and you… all runaways, and all linked to one another by your arrival together at the Bryaxis farm four years ago. Leios Bryaxis surely does remember that, and so will all his daughters and all his slaves, including Myrine, if they're ever questioned about it."

"You're saying, if any one of us is vulnerable, we all are vulnerable." Alexander rose and paced the room.

Theodosia stood, too, and went to him. "Let's talk with Lycos," she whispered. "He's a keen observer who never volunteers anything to anybody. Whatever he knows, we'll have to pull it out of him."

Alexander smiled for the first time since his conversation with Nikolaos, and, at last, he kissed her.

"I left Socrates in the kitchen with Myrine," he said. "Promised her I'd take him out before he made a mess in there, so I'd better go do that right now. After that, I'll ask Lycos to join us up here."

"Nikolaos will blow up if he finds out that a boy of twelve—old enough to have sex and marriage on his mind—is invited to my quarters."

"He'll blow up anyway if he finds out we've been talking confidentially with Lycos about these rumors."

Not if *he finds out. When.*

***

Yapping noises in the kitchen. In the hallway. In the alley.

Nikolaos opened the office door and watched as his father clomped by under his hooded cape, dodging the worst of the mud puddles and carrying a brown-and-white puppy in his arms.

Meanwhile, he saw Lycos approach the house from the end of the alley, as if returning from an errand. He stopped to pet the puppy and talk to Alexander, then he nodded and headed for the main door.

At the very moment when Lycos's sandals began clacking in the hallway, Alexander set the dog down at the nearest corner, where it jumped up and down in frenetic circles and splashed in the water and did its business.

Just what we need. Another smelly, squally baby in the house.

After a time, Alexander came back with the muddy little mutt, dropped it off in the tiny cubicle where the family's supplies of oil and grain were stored, and closed the door.

***

Silently, Lycos slipped into the women's quarters, peeked at Doros dozing in his cradle, and dropped to the floor beside Theodosia's russet-cushioned chair. She chuckled, amused to see him still following the habit he had acquired so many years ago during his months with her at the villa.

Alexander arrived soon after. He pulled a stool closer to the fire, tugged Lycos up to sit on it, and took the other cushioned chair.

"I've been told," he said to Lycos in a tone much softer than he had used earlier with Theodosia, "that you sometimes talk to men in town."

"Only those I know." The boy's voice conveyed a noticeable shakiness. "Lots of people ask me questions, but I never say much to strangers."

Just like when I first met him. Even after all these years, there's still a scared-and-abused little slave lurking within.

"People *are* curious about us." Theodosia glanced in Alexander's direction. "And there's nothing wrong with talking to them."

Alexander's mouth turned down, but he didn't reply to her.

"We trust you, Lycos, not to betray our secrets, but we do need to know what sort of things the men ask."

"They want to know where we come from."

"What do you tell them?"

"From Corinth, and I always drop in a few of the details you gave me, so it sounds like I really did live there."

"That's good. Anything else?"

"They ask why we picked Eretria for our new business. I just repeat what you told me to say."

Alexander nodded his approval. "Anything else?"

"Why you're gone so often and for so long." Lycos smoothed his tunic. "Where you go. Who's in charge here when you're away. Things like that."

"Nothing about our past lives?"

Lycos's green eyes widened. "No, and I wouldn't say a word about that, even if they asked."

"I didn't think so." Relief flooded Alexander's words. "But it seems someone's been spreading rumors about us."

"Any idea who that might be?" Theodosia asked Lycos.

The boy signaled *no* with both his head and his hands.

"Did anybody in town ever ask a question that made you nervous or uncomfortable?" She kept her voice low and non-accusatory.

He made the same negative gestures.

"Nothing about our lives back on the Italian Peninsula or your legal status or anything else like that?"

"No, not even a single question."

"Never?"

"Never."

Theodosia looked at Alexander and lifted her eyebrows.

Maybe now he'll realize that Nikolaos lied to him.

After an awkward interval, Alexander pressed Lycos's thin forearm. "There's something else we need to talk about, and I apologize in advance, because it's going to be hard for all of us."

Juno, give us the wisdom to handle this well.

"I have to ask you," Alexander went on, "to tell me what you saw that morning when you walked into the kitchen."

Lycos's face and neck flushed as dark as the cushions on Theodosia's chairs. "It was terrible," he whispered, "and I keep seeing it in my mind."

There's that abused slave boy again.

Theodosia reached over and put her hand on his.

Alexander also flushed. "Myrine has already told Theodosia her side of the story, so there's no need for you to be embarrassed."

Lycos dropped his eyes. "Hard for me to talk about it."

"Please try." Alexander took a deep breath and slowly released it. "When you got there, where were Nikolaos and Myrine?"

"At the chopping block."

"What were they doing?"

"He was standing. Adjusting his tunic in front."

"And Myrine?"

"She was pushed way up on the block. Face down. Legs apart. Sobbing."

"What else can you tell us?"

"Her chiton was jumbled on her back." Lycos's voice shook. "Her rear end was bare and covered with blood."

"You can stop," Theodosia said quickly, "if it hurts too much."

But Lycos did not stop. Instead, the words gushed out. "She'd been cutting meat and the cleaver was on the floor and there was blood from the block squished all over her and she was sobbing and then she saw me and shook her head and waved her hand like she wanted me to go away but I couldn't move and then Nikolaos screamed at me and—" His voice cracked.

Alexander hesitated for a few moments, giving the boy time to compose himself. "What did you think had happened?"

"I didn't have to *think* about it." Lycos raised his head and stared straight at him. "I *knew* what he had done to her."

"And what was that?"

"He had raped her."

Theodosia leaned forward. "Are you sure you understand what that word means?"

Lycos lowered his eyes once more and bobbed his head. "Very sure."

"And you're confident that's what happened?"

Another nod. "I asked Myrine about it later. She said he *had* raped her, which was exactly what it looked like when I walked in."

"Did you actually see him do it," Alexander asked.

Lycos's eyes shot up. "I'd have punched him in the nose if I had."

Silence filled the room.

"So, Lycos," Alexander went on after a while, "here's where it gets even more difficult. Nikolaos told me that Myrine asked for it. He says she's always pushing herself on him, begging him for sex, and he says she enjoyed it."

"That's not true." Lycos turned to Theodosia. "Do you believe Myrine asked for it?"

"No, I don't."

"Why not?" The tremble in his voice had disappeared. Remarkably, he sounded like a grown man in charge of an interrogation.

"Because," Theodosia said, "not long before the incident took place, Myrine told me Nikolaos was pushing her to sleep with him."

"Did she seem happy about that?" Lycos's eyes bore into hers. "Like she was asking for it?"

"Absolutely not." Theodosia raised her eyes to Alexander. "Having sex with Nikolaos was the last thing Myrine wanted, and it's also the last thing that I, as her mistress, would have allowed."

***

Crouched at the top of the stone stairway, Nikolaos only caught parts of the conversation. But even so, its topic was obvious.

Lycos accuses me of rape to turn Father against me... and because he wants Myrine for himself.

The muffled voices continued, as did the infuriating yaps and yowls from the storage cubicle below. At last, Nikolaos decided that he'd had enough. He rose, pushed the curtain aside, and walked in.

The Roman woman, who was sitting closest to the fire, facing the door, was the first to notice him. "What are you doing in my room?"

Lycos leaped to his feet and clinched his fists as if ready to defend her with his life.

Alexander stood up from the other chair and swung around. Shock registered on his face. "Get out!"

"I'm your son."

"You are not welcome here."

Nikolaos pointed to Lycos. "Got more right to be here than *he* does."

"*He* was invited up to talk with us," Alexander said. "*You* were not."

"Myrine just told me—" Nikolaos interrupted himself and advanced into the room. "Father, are you going to let Lycos marry her?"

Alexander gaped at Lycos. "You want to marry... Myrine?"

"I do," Lycos said.

Alexander glanced at the Roman woman, then back at the boy. "Well, I might give you permission some day, once you're old enough to take a wife."

"That's not acceptable!" Nikolaos shouted.

Alexander glared at him. "If I say it's acceptable, it *is* acceptable."

"Myrine's pregnant by my seed. She's mine from now on."

The Roman woman stared at him, but she directed her words to Alexander.

"He must never touch her again."

"While you're away, Father, what I choose to do with a slave girl belonging to our family is entirely up to me."

"By all the gods, no!" The Roman woman slammed her palms on the arms of her chair. "Legally, Alexander, Myrine belongs to you, but she is my maid. I depend on her, and I also value her loyalty and companionship."

Emotional female drivel.

"Property matters," Nikolaos said with intentional calmness, "are for the males in a family to discuss and decide, not the females."

But the Roman woman ignored him and continued addressing her husband. "On a personal level, I like Myrine a lot. She's a good woman and a faithful, hard-working servant. I will not let your disgusting elder son rape her over and over for the rest of her life."

"I did not rape her." Nikolaos jutted his jaw.

"Yes, you did." With great exaggeration, Lycos jutted his own jaw.

Obnoxious brat.

"We don't need a child's input into this." Very deliberately, Nikolaos jutted his jaw once more.

The Roman woman rose and confronted him. "I also say you raped her."

"Father, can't you shut your wife up?" Nikolaos no longer cared to control his temper. "Whenever something bad happens between you and me—no matter what it is—she's always right in the middle of it!"

Alexander draped an arm over Lycos's shoulders. "Go downstairs, please. Nikolaos and I have a few things to discuss by ourselves."

***

The argument woke Doros from his nap. Soon he was standing in his crib, fussing, and reaching for his mother. Theodosia lifted him to her shoulder and wrapped her fingers around the small leather pouch at his chest.

Little snake, all I want—all I've wanted since our escape—is to give Alexander lots of children and raise them all in peace.

She sat on her bed with her back to the two men at the other end of the room and, as Doros nursed, overheard a very different kind of family conversation than she could had imagined.

"I hoped you'd be more mature by now." Alexander's voice was low.

"I'm a full-grown man, Father, or haven't you noticed?"

"Not talking about physical size."

"Truth be told, I function quite well as a man."

"Raping a woman, whether slave or free, does not in any way prove your manhood."

"I didn't rape Myrine, but even if I did, it wouldn't matter."

"Yes, it would matter."

"She never objects to anything I do."

"She protested to my wife."

"She *lied* to your wife, and your wife took her side."

Theodosia heard a chair scrape against the floor.

"This conversation is over, Father. I have work to do in the office."

"Sit back down. I did not invite you to come up here, but now that you are here, you will stay until I tell you to go."

From that point on, Theodosia heard little more. Not the rain pounding the shutters. Not the puppy's howls downstairs. Not even Doros's soft sucking sounds at her breast.

The silence that filled the room—and her head—was total.

What will Alexander do if Nikolaos disobeys him?

Nothing indicated that Nikolaos had taken his seat again.

Nothing indicated that he had left.

Theodosia strained to follow what was going on behind her without betraying her obvious interest in the men's words and deeds.

After a very long time, Alexander spoke again, even more quietly. "Lycos will turn fifteen in three years. At that point, if he still wishes to take Myrine as his wife, I will allow it."

"Bad idea." Nikolaos's voice was low, too. "Can't promise I'll go along."

Which means, he intends to keep raping Myrine.

"You will not be the one making that decision."

Nikolaos shattered the stillness with a harsh laugh. "Just think, Father, by the time Lycos is fifteen, Myrine could easily have three of my babies." He laughed again, even louder. "Our family will be so much wealthier!"

Sandals stomped toward the door.

Alexander can't deal with him, so I must.

Theodosia set Doros on his feet and summoned up the voice of command that she had learned to exercise as the young, determined mistress of the Villa Varroniana.

"Nikolaos."

The stomping stopped.

She rose, adjusted her tunic to cover her breast, and faced him. "You will keep your hands off Myrine."

Nikolaos was already near the door. He did not acknowledge her as she walked up behind him.

"You are forbidden to touch her ever again."

Nikolaos said nothing. Did nothing. Gave no reaction at all.

"Whether or not you think she wants it, you will leave her alone."

He kept his back to Theodosia, not speaking, facing the curtain.

"I guarantee one thing." Theodosia circled around. Placed herself between him and the doorway. Forced him to look at her. Let her words sink in. "If at any point I learn that you've abused her again—or abused anyone else in our household—you will no longer occupy a place in this family."

***

After Nikolaos departed, Doros padded barefoot around the room as their father sat, silent and unmoving, staring straight into the fire.

Theodosia went back to sitting in the chair opposite him.

"Nikolaos," she said, "is toxic."

She waited for Alexander to reply, but he remained tight-lipped.

"He's poisoning our relationship," she added. "Can't you see that?"

Still, Alexander made no response.

Doesn't he care?

"I cannot accept," she went on, "that he's in charge when you're away."

"He *is* in charge when I'm away."

Doros wandered over to his father, who playfully wrestled with him before letting him go.

"Keep him in the business if you must," she went on, "but he cannot wield authority over Doros and me, or Myrine either."

"He's my first-born son." Alexander looked into her eyes. "My love, I'm working to build something good for you and Doros and Lycos, but I'm also building it for Nikolaos. I want you all to be well-off property owners when I'm no longer here to provide for you."

"That's fine. Leave Nikolaos whatever property you like, but—"

Seems as good a time as any to tell him.

"There's been an idea floating in my mind for some time," she said.

Alexander eyed her with obvious curiosity, and possibly a bit of suspicion, but he said nothing.

"Why don't you make Lycos your business partner? He's smart and well educated, thanks to you, and even at twelve he's a lot more stable and trustworthy than Nikolaos. Once he's older, he can be the adult male in charge of us."

Alexander kept quiet, so she pushed on. "While you're home this winter, you can teach him what he needs to know."

Still no reaction from Alexander.

"I understand it's hard to move your older son aside, but he can find some other kind of work in Eretria." Theodosia's voice rose. "Alexander, for the sake of our relationship and our family's future, do it!"

Slowly, Alexander shook his head.

"Do it for Doros!" Her tone was growing harsher than she intended but, caught up in the emotion, she couldn't help herself. "Do it for me!"

Alexander recoiled as if she had slapped him.

I shouldn't have said it like that.

Never before in the five years since Alexander ceased to be her slave had she spoken to him in any way that resembled an order.

"Oh, my love, I'm sorry." She reached out to him. "I really didn't mean it to come out that way."

Alexander accepted her hand and pressed it to his lips.

"I feel responsible for everything that's happened to him," he said after a while. "My little Niko was a sweet child with a good home and parents who loved him, and then he lost it all. I can't just toss him into the street now."

"But *you* lost it all, too. Your family. Your freedom. Your place in society. You endured as many years of slavery as he did, but you didn't come out of that experience angry and bitter. You emerged with self-respect and brand-new ambitions and—"

"A lot of that had to do with you." He leaned forward and kissed her on the lips. "Without you, I'd have been a slave forever, or at best a slave forever on the run."

"No, you would have rebuilt your life, with or without me."

"Can't say I believe that."

"Well, I do. But whatever your motivation, you *are* rebuilding your life. You're highly respected in this town and on this island, and your reputation will only grow with time. I don't see why Nikolaos can't make an effort to do the same."

Doros toddled by once more, so Alexander lifted him onto his lap.

"Just imagine," he said, "that four or five years from now—for whatever false crimes they might dream up—the Romans were to sell you and me and this little fellow into slavery. Suppose they whipped you and raped you in front of Doros, and then nine months later you died screaming in pain with him at your bedside. Would you expect him to accept all that and move blithely on through the rest of his life?"

"That's an absurd scenario."

"No, it's exactly what happened to my little Niko. Why couldn't it also happen to my little Doros?"

"What I think," she said, "is that you're so eaten up with guilt, you can't stand up to Nikolaos even as he openly defies you and bullies Lycos in the streets and rapes our slave girl under this very roof and does his best to intimidate me in every way he can think of."

A corner of Alexander's mouth curled up in that familiar wry smile.

"I'm sure he thinks it's his duty—as one of the grown-up, responsible men in this family—to keep you safe."

"Keep me safe? No, he wants to control me, and you seem perfectly willing to let him do that."

Doros slid down from his father's lap and crawled up onto his mother's. For a time, she cuddled and cooed over him.

How can I make Alexander see what I see and not take offense?

"Let me put it to you this way," she said at last. "I did not escape from Nero only to be locked up again by Nikolaos."

***

Theodosia sat alone by the fire for an hour. Played peek-a-boo with Doros. Tossed fabric toys across the room for him to find and bring to her.

"You're such an energetic little man," she said at one point, just as a foul-but-familiar odor wafted out of his diaper. "And such a stinky little man."

Where's Myrine? Haven't seen her all day. She must be very sick.

Finally, she stood. Lifted Doros to her shoulder. Straightened the viper amulet at his chest. Held his feet so he wouldn't kick the baby in her womb. Pushed open the curtain. Reached the top of the stairs. Extended her right foot. Shifted her weight forward. Noticed something on the first step down.

In a flash, its details registered.

Small.

White.

Muddy.

Brown spots.

Caked in red.

Throat slit open.

Doros squealed and squirmed in her arms.

He saw it, too.

As she struggled to hold him, her twisted left leg gave way and her body swung sharply in the opposite direction.

Memories swirled in the stairwell. A foggy dawn. A beloved filly. A steep bluff. An excruciating fall. A rocky river bed. And a baby lost before it had the chance to be born.

Spinning in midair as twenty stone steps raced toward her, Theodosia crossed her arms over the little boy at her shoulder.

And pulled him down.

And braced him against her chest.

And cupped both hands over his head.

And curled her body around his.

And made her choice.

Save Doros!

PART III

ADVERSITY SHOWS WHETHER WE HAVE FRIENDS
OR ONLY THE SHADOWS OF FRIENDS.
—PUBLIUS SYRUS, 85 BC - 43 BC

CHAPTER 12

"One, two! One, two! One, two! One, two!"

Doros marched in place at dawn, barking the cadence, lifting his knees, swinging his arms in perfect rhythm.

Wearing a close approximation of a legionary's uniform—complete with a helmet once worn in battle, the gift of a veteran who had moved in with one of the "friendly ladies" in town when his service contract ended—he looked and acted as close to the real thing as a nine-year-old boy possibly could.

Just as the sun's rays crested the horizon on this Ides of July, half the garrison's soldiers emerged, single-file, through the Praetorian Gate, double-timed down the sloping drive, and formed up along the waterfront.

Catching the morning light with every turn, as they always did, each polished segment of their breastplates, each shiny dagger, helmet, and brass-and-leather shield stabbed the eyes of the two women standing together near the docks. Theodosia and Aula winced, as they always did, and looked away.

Once the entire squadron had assembled, Doros fell in behind them, as he always did, still loudly pacing his steps and theirs. It was the same routine he and they had followed every morning at this hour, through rain and shine, summer and winter, for the last two years.

As forty grizzled, real-life warriors and one small, make-believe warrior headed west, the only Roman women living on the island of Euboea crossed the road to the shade of a purple-flowered vine billowing over a garden wall.

Despite their long, dignified stolas and the modest pallas covering their heads, male passersby muttered under their breaths, as they always did.

As usual, Theodosia and Aula ignored them.

Theodosia snapped one of the purple blossoms and took several deep breaths, savoring its aroma and color and a general sense of well-being.

Life hasn't always been this sweet.

She watched her son disappear with the professionals where the road bent to make its way out of town and across the Lelantine Plain.

"Such a fine little soldier," Aula said, as she always did, "with those big amber eyes and that perfect Roman nose."

Theodosia nodded in agreement with her friend, even though she had never pointed out Doros's nose to Aula or anybody else. But still, as always, the sight of her son happily marching off with the soldiers struck a terrible blow to her heart.

What a shame Alexander insists he become a "proper" Greek businessman. He would make such a fine Roman officer.

***

These days, Theodosia's household revolved around its children: Doros, Olinda, Kronos, and Hyperion.

She still dreamed of giving Alexander more sons, but between his long absences, the death of their unborn child on the stairs seven and a half years earlier, and the further damage done to her own body in that fall, which had resulted in other miscarriages since then, the reality was plain to all. Another successful pregnancy wasn't likely.

Obviously, the gods hadn't built her the way they built Myrine, who delivered a healthy baby each year. She was pregnant again now, and this baby—her seventh—was expected in December. Myrine's oldest child, a girl named Olinda, would turn seven in a few days. With her straight black hair, and black, deep-set eyes, and olive-colored skin, Olinda's paternity would have been clear even if she hadn't been born nine months after Nikolaos raped her mother... an unfortunate circumstance that no one in the family ever talked about. Myrine was raising Olinda as a good slave mother should: teaching her to respect and obey her masters; taking her to market to learn how to identify and purchase quality food; showing her how to clean house, prepare meals, and so on.

But from the very first day of Olinda's life, Theodosia noticed that everything about their relationship seemed perfunctory. If the mother-daughter attachment was deep, it wasn't obvious in any way.

Exactly the opposite was true with Myrine's two boys, cleverly named—like three male siblings who had not survived their infancy—for the Titans.

At five, Kronos was curious, confident, charming, and smart. "I love that boy more than anyone or anything else on Earth," his mother often confided to Theodosia, and her affection was visible.

Myrine doted on Kronos. Cuddled him at every opportunity. Took him walking on the waterfront. Taught him the ancient game of knucklebones. Regaled him with tales of growing up on the farm with her brothers. Fed him the best meat trimmings from her kitchen. Invited him to go with her and Olinda to the market. Even spoke to him in Aramaic.

"It's our secret language," she would tell him with a wink to her mistress.

At three, Hyperion was timid and showed no prospect of ever developing the brilliance or charm of his older brother.

"He'll make a strong, sturdy laborer some day," Myrine often said, somewhat defensively, to Theodosia.

"Just what one expects of a Titan," her mistress always replied with a reassuring smile.

Both Kronos and Hyperion possessed their mother's permanently ruddy cheeks… a curious combination with the green eyes and soft, curly brown hair inherited from the man who, beyond any doubt, was their father.

Lycos was twenty now and in charge of the business and the household when Alexander was away. Over the last half decade, he had become not only a loving husband to Myrine—or as much a husband as one could be to a woman who was the property of another—but also a trusted and hard-working partner to Alexander.

Legally, of course, Olinda, Kronos, and Hyperion were all Alexander's slaves, following their mother's status. But Lycos was paying a monthly sum to secure Myrine's freedom, and once she was manumitted, Alexander had promised, her children would also go free, including his own unacknowledged granddaughter, Olinda.

Three years ago, as the business outgrew its original room in the house, Lycos had rented a space a few blocks away and moved his office there.

That move had worked out well for other reasons, too.

Nowadays, Lycos, Myrine, and their three children slept in what had been the original office. And now that Doros had grown old enough to spend nights by himself in the little cubicle once used to store grain and olive oil, his mother rested better in her quieter quarters upstairs.

So as Alexander prowled the Mediterranean for months at a time, seeking more ships to export the growing Euboean grain supply, Theodosia dedicated herself to educating their son.

***

It wasn't always a given that Theodosia would become her son's full-time teacher. In fact, it almost didn't turn out that way.

One warm afternoon late in July—as she sat with Doros on their shady balcony while he scratched perfectly formed Latin sentences into a wax tablet and their white linen tunics stirred in the breeze—Alexander's voice whispered in her ear as clearly as if he were standing right there, right now, giving her the bad news for the very first time.

"Come spring, I'll take him to Athens to begin his schooling."

All the family's free and slave members had gathered near the kitchen fire on a bitterly cold December morning three-and-a-half years ago… everyone except Lycos, who had left for his office.

On the floor, Olinda fed make-believe dirt food to her cloth doll.

Kronos dozed in his blue cradle by the hearth.

Myrine—swollen with the child they would soon welcome as Hyperion—already had prepared breakfast; cleared, washed, and dried the breakfast dishes and dashed out to the market; and was now coating a fresh-caught mullet with dried herbs for their midday meal.

Alexander and Theodosia lingered at the table, watching six-year-old Doros practice his knucklebone technique on the opposite side of the room.

"Come spring," Alexander whispered to Theodosia, "I'll take him to Athens to begin his schooling. A pedagogue will make sure he becomes a superb Greek citizen and orator, well prepared to take his place in the world."

"He can become a superb Greek citizen and orator," Theodosia whispered back, "right here in Eretria."

Alexander shook his head. "It's too small and isolated."

"So, I'll take him to Athens several times a year. We'll visit the Parthenon, shop in the Agora, attend comedies and dramas at the Theater of Dionysus, discuss those works with the actors and directors, and—"

"My love, you and Doros cannot go to Athens on your own."

"Why not? It would be fun and educational for both of us. Imagine all the things Doros could learn."

"He needs to learn business skills, make good contacts—"

"Lycos can teach him about the business and introduce him to all the farmers and captains who come to the office."

"That's not good enough."

"Lycos didn't have any formal education, and he's doing well."

"Yes, he is doing well, because he was motivated from the beginning to run the office and keep the books and deal with the customers. But that's a small part of what it would take for Doros to own and manage the entire operation... even if he were motivated to do so, which he clearly is not."

Theodosia glanced across the room.

Doros was still tossing square sheep knucklebones into the air and catching them on the backs of his hands, showing no awareness of their talk. Then, all of a sudden, his head popped up.

"I want to be a Roman soldier!" His too-loud voice echoed on the stone floor and walls.

Alexander frowned. His eyes narrowed. His jaw clenched.

"The one thing you will *not* be is a soldier."

Doros jumped up and marched across the kitchen toward his parents, matching the cadence of his words to the *click-clack* of his sandals.

"I want — to be — a Roman — soldier!

"I want — to be — a Roman — soldier!

"I want — to be — a Roman — soldier!"

"Especially not a *Roman* soldier." Alexander's face was turning red.

Doros glared at his father. "What other kind of soldier is there?"

"In Greece nowadays, none." Alexander rose, too, and stalked out.

"Mother!" Tearfully, Doros hurled himself into Theodosia's arms. "Don't let Father send me away! I can become a soldier right here!"

"I'll do what I can, Little Man." She hugged him close and kissed his wet cheeks until the tears subsided.

That night, after Alexander and Theodosia made love, she raised the subject again.

"Doros is only six, you know."

"Perfect age to start studying."

"I'll need him to keep me company while you're away."

"You'll have plenty of company with Myrine and her endless stream of babies."

"That's not the same thing."

"For our son's sake, my love, you *must* accept this."

"But I *cannot* accept it. *Will not* accept it." She propped herself on one elbow and tapped his chest with her fingertips. "Understand me, please. I've no intention of sending my only child off to live with strangers."

Alexander sighed and rolled away from her, as if ready for sleep. "I'm sure every mother in the world says the exact same thing when this time comes for her first-born son."

"Every mother in the world isn't prepared to make her son literate in two languages. But I *am* prepared to teach Doros to read, write, calculate, think critically, and speak with polished rhetoric in both Greek and Latin. My father did all that for me, and I can do the same for Doros."

"You're not a pedagogue."

"I can teach him as well as anyone else."

"Athenian pedagogues use traditional, proven methods."

"They whip their students."

"Only those who fail to learn their lessons." Within moments, Alexander dozed off.

Unwilling to let the subject go, Theodosia shook him awake. "How can you, of all people, give a complete stranger the authority to beat your son?"

For all the rest of that month and all the rest of that winter, she had countered his every argument.

And he had done the same with hers.

Alexander's resolve had held out for months until—after the only actual fights they'd ever had—he finally surrendered and left on his all-important spring business trip.

So now, on their shady balcony this warm afternoon late in July—as nine-year-old Doros scratched perfectly formed Latin sentences into a wax tablet and their white linen tunics stirred in the breeze—his mother ran through her mental list of how well things were turning out.

Alexander's living the life he dreamed. Traveling the world. Building his business. Providing nicely for his family.

And Lycos is prospering, too. Proving his worth to the business. Buying freedom for his wife and children.

And Doros gets better and better at everything he studies in both Latin and Greek. Even speaks a bit of Aramaic, too, thanks to Myrine.

And Myrine has three healthy children, all safe and happy at her side, with another on the way.

And Nikolaos hasn't set foot in this house in seven and a half years.

Thank you, Juno.

***

It was late October.

Nikolaos hadn't spoken with the Roman woman in almost eight years, which was fine with him, and he'd only had occasional, strained conversations with his father, which he did regret somewhat.

Two days after Theodosia Varro and her brat tumbled down the stairs, Alexander had persuaded his rich friend Zosimos, who owned both of Eretria's meat markets and half the other shops in town, to hire Nikolaos as a clerk.

Alexander also had twisted the arm of his former innkeeper, Cilla, who clearly wasn't enthusiastic about the idea and made sure her daughters kept their distance from the new boarder, to rent a room to Nikolaos.

Even after all these years, gossip still raged around the behavior of the two Roman women, the most outrageous females in town—even more notorious than the "friendly ladies" and waterfront whores who serviced the garrison's warriors, visiting farmers, fishermen, and sea captains—who walked unescorted through the streets, lounged about where women had no business lounging about, barely covered their heads, jabbered on and on in Latin, and let their clothing flap provocatively in the wind.

Gossip still raged, too, over Alexander's family's mysterious history.

And why he had kicked his first-born son out of their house.

And how he had come to select a mere boy—not even a blood relative, if you believed the rumors—to run his business office.

And about his arguments with his wife, which were easily overheard in the alley below her balcony and always seemed to focus on his too-loud, too-militaristic, younger son.

And about his inexplicably long absences from home.

Hardly a day passed that Nikolaos didn't overhear snide comments from the slaves who frequented Zosimos's meat shop in the market that sprawled just outside the eastern wall of the garrison.

In short, while everyone appreciated the prosperity that Alexander had brought to their island, speculation about his business and family dealings offered the people of Eretria an ongoing source of amusement.

In all those seven and a half years since the puppy from Piraeus turned up dead on the stairs and the Roman woman slipped and fell and lost her unborn child, Alexander never talked with Nikolaos about it. He simply ordered him out of the house. Away from his wife and child. Forever.

From that day on, Nikolaos had held his head high, labored competently in the market, and kept his mouth shut.

But still, every other morning on his way to work, he would stop at his father's house, where he always happened to find Myrine alone in the kitchen.

And so, with Alexander traveling…

And Lycos working elsewhere…

And Doros marching with the legionaries…

And the Roman woman flaunting herself in town…

Nikolaos hardly ever missed an opportunity to visit with Myrine, which gave him a chance to stay fluent in Aramaic and relieve those deep-down urges, which was almost too easy since the slave never resisted.

Clever of me to make certain of that.

Most mornings, Nikolaos picked a back route from Cilla's house to Myrine's kitchen to Zosimos's butcher shop. Anything to avoid the brazen Roman woman, her equally shameless Roman friend, and her Roman-nosed little soldier as they disgraced themselves on the streets of Eretria.

But not this morning.

***

"So," Aula said, "how are the lessons going?"

She and Theodosia stood at water's edge as the weakening autumn sun threw its first rays across Eretria's flat rooftops. Doros marched in place while fishermen slid by in their boats, glaring their disapproval as usual.

"Well enough." Theodosia smiled at her friend. "I'm proud of my boy."

"What's he studying now?"

Theodosia ticked off the subjects on her fingers. "For mathematics, he's reading Pythagoras of Samos. For ethics, Socrates, Antisthenes, Epikouros. For logic, Plutarch and Cleanthes. For history, Thucydides and Xenophon on the Peloponnesian War."

"How do you get the scrolls?"

"Alexander buys them abroad and brings them home."

"And *you* can read them all?"

"I already did read most of them long ago. My father was a serious scholar who helped me study them and enjoyed discussing them with me."

Aula's wrinkled face contorted. "I thought you told the centurion that your father died when you were very young."

Dear gods, what story did I tell him?

"Oh, he lived long enough to teach me the essentials and leave me with a good base of knowledge to build on."

Aula chuckled in her usual way, but something about it rang false.

Not the first time she's caught me on one of my long-ago lies. Better change the subject.

"Didn't you mention some time back that your youngest son would soon be moving to Athens?"

Aula's gray head bobbed in obvious pleasure. "He arrived last month with his wife and two children. I've never met those three, so right now I can hardly wait to get there."

"How old are the little ones?"

"Two and four."

"So, you'll finally get the visits you didn't have with the older grandbabies."

"I sure do hope so." Aula turned the conversation back to Theodosia's family. "Does Lycos still enjoy running the office?"

"The job's perfect for him, and from the way Alexander treats him, you'd think Lycos was his first-born son."

"He respects him a lot more, I suspect, than his actual first-born son."

Oh, my dear friend, that's not a subject we need to get into.

Aula already knew enough about the events that had torn Theodosia and Alexander's family apart.

"Alexander respects everybody," Theodosia parried.

"And, of course, given everything he's done for the island's economy, people respect him, too." Aula adjusted her stola for a better drape over her heavy breasts. "I certainly respect your husband, Theodosia, but honestly—" She broke off for a laugh. "He's such an odd duck!"

Theodosia laughed, too. "Maybe that's part of what attracted me to him. He wasn't exactly the match my friends expected of me."

To say the least.

"What I still don't understand, even after all this time—" Aula groped for words, as she always did when the subject of Alexander came up. "How on Earth did a well-bred, well-educated Apulian lady like you…" Her voice dwindled off.

Previously, whenever Aula asked about their marriage, Theodosia had managed to steer her on to another topic. But now, given her earlier error this morning, it seemed best to address Aula's unfinished question.

"How on Earth did a well-bred, well-educated Apulian lady like me wind up married to an odd-duck Greek in a run-down port town like this?"

"It's a fair question, because in all these years we've been friends, you've never told me how you happened to meet and marry your odd-duck Greek."

"That's a lengthy story, Aula."

"And complicated?"

"Mostly just boring."

Aula looked skeptical. "Hard to imagine how such a meeting—and especially such a marriage—could be boring, unless your family in Apulia encouraged you for some particular reason."

Can't recall the tale I made up for the centurion.

"My father was a Greek, too—also a Corinthian—so, of course, he didn't object if I married another man from Corinth."

"Wait. Wasn't your father long dead at that point?"

"You're right." Theodosia's heart fluttered. "But everyone in the family said he had made his wishes for me known well before he died."

"So, you're saying—" A puzzled expression crossed Aula's face. "While you were a small child... your Corinthian father specifically told others in your family... including your mother's people in Apulia and Rome... that when you were old enough to marry... he wanted you to marry a Corinthian."

"Something like that. I was too young to know, much less comprehend, every bit of what he said about me while he was still alive."

Aula looked over her shoulder toward the Praetorian Gate, from which the soldiers would soon be emerging for their march. Theodosia stared that way, too, hoping for some distraction from Aula's interrogation, but so far no one had emerged from the fort. Meanwhile, Aula pressed on.

"Your relatives in Apulia must have given you a significant dowry, since you and Alexander brought such high-quality resources to the island."

"Well, yes, my mother's family did help us get started."

What is she talking about?

"Yesterday, in the market, my maid overheard—" Abruptly, Aula stopped. "Let me just say this. There's a rumor going around that you were quite wealthy and well-connected in Rome, but Alexander was not."

"No, he was not." Theodosia kept her tone even.

"In all these years, you never told me that."

"Never saw a need to tell you."

Theodosia shifted her eyes to Doros, who continued marching in place but no longer counted his steps as he awaited the soldiers. Most mornings, the squadron already would have formed up and been gone.

"Something's delayed them," she said, awkwardly stating the obvious.

As if she were not a bit concerned about problems at the garrison, Aula stayed with her topic. "Yesterday, my girl overheard a report that, years ago, Alexander traded something very rare and special for your house."

The skin on the back of Theodosia's neck began to crawl. Sudden sweat dampened the inner folds of her stola.

Why is this coming out now, eight years after we arrived in Eretria?

"What do you mean by 'rare and special'?" she asked as lightly as she could.

"You don't know what that object was?"

"Well, of course I do." Her throat tightened. "It's just—"

"I didn't mean to frighten you, Theodosia."

"I'm not frightened, just taken by surprise."

A massive *thud* from the fort reverberated through the town, followed by heavy footfalls and a loud cheer from Doros.

"Gate's open," Aula said, as if—after following this routine for years—Theodosia could not guess what had caused the noise. "Here they come."

Doros began shouting his usual cadence. "One, two! One, two! One, two! One, two!" Then he fell in behind the soldiers.

The moment the squadron and Doros disappeared around the bend in the road, Theodosia put her hand on Aula's arm.

I need to know what she knows.

"Tell me about that rare, special object."

Aula said nothing.

"Tell me, please."

"You really don't know?"

"I'm not sure if I do. Guess I need to hear it from you."

Aula gazed at Theodosia in silence. Then, apparently convinced that her friend didn't know, she bobbed her head. "The previous occupant of your house has been telling everybody in town that her husband traded it to your husband for a gigantic, extra-fine, blood-red ruby."

Theodosia inhaled sharply.

A gigantic, extra-fine, blood-red ruby.

Trying to formulate a response, she glanced toward the water.

And then every thought in her head vanished.

Because way out there—leaning against a post at the far end of the pier, dark and scowling—Nikolaos was staring straight at her and Aula.

She was even more startled when he began walking toward them.

***

Aula had spotted Nikolaos, too. "How old is he now?" she asked.

"About twenty-five."

"Tall, strapping fellow. Good looking, too."

"Hasn't found a wife, though."

"The centurion says most townspeople keep their distance from him."

That's the second time today she's referred to her husband as "the centurion," instead of "Marcus." Is there something to be read into that?

"Like me," Theodosia said, "they'd rather avoid a confrontation."

"Still think he was to blame?"

"Who else? If you're clever and a bully, you can get away with almost killing a woman and a baby."

Nikolaos halted a few feet away, spread his legs, and planted his fists on his hips. His arms and shoulders were much more muscular than the last time Theodosia had seen him, and he stood at least a foot taller. His straight black hair was matted. Dried blood caked his short, gray tunic.

Appropriate that he works in a butcher shop.

He jabbed an index finger at Theodosia and jutted his jaw. "You're a disgrace. The people in this town are shocked beyond words."

He waited all this time on the pier to say that to me?

"If so," she replied, "they should be brave enough to tell me themselves, not send you out to do the job for them."

"And risk the wrath of her husband's soldiers?" He nodded toward Aula. "The Eretrians aren't fools, but I'm not afraid to say what they will not."

His voice sounds like Alexander's.

Aula made no response, but Theodosia stepped forward and tilted her head back to confront him.

"Why worry about *my* behavior?" She made a broad gesture with both hands. "All those people in town whose opinion you value so much… every last one of them knows you're no longer part of our family. They know your father kicked you out. And you can bet they know the reason why."

"I am still my father's son." Nikolaos looked away, as if deep in thought. "Still care more about him than you do." Abruptly, his eyes shot to hers. "Don't want your shameful behavior—or the scandals of your past—to cause him any more harm than they already have."

"The scandals of my past?"

"Oh, Theodosia Varro." He enunciated her name with care. "Theodosia Varro, your old secrets are coming back to haunt you."

In all these years, he never once used my first name, much less my full, family name. What could have made him decide to say the whole thing twice in front of Aula?

Puzzling over that, her mind returned to Aula's probing of her family history just a short time before.

Now, thanks to him, she knows my family name. She'll recognize "Varro" as Roman, not Apulian or Corinthian.

Once she realizes I lied about that, she'll wonder what else I lied about. How long before she and "the centurion" turn up everything else there is to know about me?

And everything else there is to know about Alexander?

"I'm not sure," she said at last, "that you and I should be discussing this subject right here, right now."

"Well, since we're unlikely ever to speak again…" He shrugged.

Nikolaos would stop at nothing to hurt me, but I can't believe he deliberately would put his father at risk.

How bad can my old secrets be if he's willing to bring them up in Aula's presence?

"I'm eager to hear," she said with more confidence than she felt, "how you think my past is coming back to haunt me."

"Sure you want *her* to know?"

"Aula is my friend. I keep nothing from her."

That's not true either, but he's got me cornered. I have to play this out.

"Very well." Nikolaos's smile made her skin crawl. "Yesterday afternoon, while I was butchering a goat, a woman brought a remarkable gemstone into the shop." Another smile. "A huge, unset, blood-red ruby."

For a while, Nikolaos stared down his long Greek nose at Theodosia, as if waiting for his words to sink in and for her to react.

But she didn't.

"A huge, unset, blood-red ruby," he repeated, "like the ones that, according to Lycos, you once owned and enjoyed at your fancy villa outside Rome."

Aula's words rang in her ears.

"A gigantic, extra-fine, blood-red ruby."

Now, instead of smiling, Nikolaos raised a menacing eyebrow. "Before Zosimos got there, the woman had shown off her splendid ruby to everyone passing in the street and waiting inside the shop. Scores of people saw it, including me."

"So?"

"So the woman told half of Eretria that her family had acquired that remarkable stone from Alexander, the Corinthian merchant. 'I'm looking for a buyer,' she kept saying. She planned to offer it first to Zosimos, she said, since he's the richest man in town and she needs every drachma she can get to live on, now that her husband's dead."

I don't understand any of this.

Theodosia switched her eyes several times between Nikolaos's face and Aula's as they both stared at her.

Why didn't he inform me privately?

Why come out here way before sunrise?

Why bring it up with Aula standing beside me?

Why hold off through that long delay at the garrison?

Why wait until Doros and the soldiers were out of town?

Why loiter so long to give me a few little bits of information?

Aula's earlier statement drifted in the air..

"Alexander had traded something very rare and special for your house."

Gradually, as Theodosia thought about it, Nikolaos's actions began to make sense.

His story wasn't meant for me at all. Everything he said was targeted at Aula.

He had no idea if she had heard about the ruby. Or how the old woman in the market got it. Or that it might have something to do with me. Or if she knew my family name. Or if she could tie all the facts together by herself, without help.

He wanted to make sure she grasped their significance, but he'd never be able to meet with her at the garrison. He didn't want military personnel to see him talking with her. His only way to get to her was to catch her out here with me.

Bit by bit, everything made sense… except his motive.

Why in Zeus's name did Nikolaos want to get that information to Aula?

CHAPTER 13

Alexander arrived home in mid-December, worn out from six months of travel and ready to rest. After dinner, as he soaked in the tin tub, Theodosia regaled him with Doros's latest accomplishments.

"He reads for pleasure now. Four times through Plautus' *Miles Gloriosus* and dying to enjoy it again. And just wait till you see how he writes. His Latin grammar's flawless, even when he speaks. Perfect enunciation and diction, too, although—" She winced. "I do have to warn you, he spends part of each day at the garrison."

"So, my son loves raunchy comedies about swaggering soldiers, and he spouts barracks obscenities, jokes, and jargon with a plebeian accent." Alexander reached for the linen cloth she held and dried off as well as he could before stepping out of the tub. "Perfect preparation for a Greek merchant. So, it seems, between you and the boys at the fort, I've got a Roman-army son whether I want one or not."

"That's not fair. Doros speaks and writes Greek, too, and he knows his philosophy up and down. Ask him to explain the similarities and differences between the Stoics, the Pythagoreans, the Peripatetics, and the Platonists. He's studied Homer and Plato and—"

"Does he show as much enthusiasm for *The Iliad* as for *Miles Gloriosus*?"

"Well, Homer's definitely harder for him, but look, he's still a boy. He should be allowed to have some fun." Theodosia took a fresh towel and finished drying his back. "Lycos and Myrine have taught him Aramaic, too, which they learned a long time ago from Nikolaos. These days, Doros only talks with them in Aramaic."

"Sounds like our son's not only a budding soldier but also a budding linguist."

"Aramaic and Latin could prove useful to a Greek merchant."

"Assuming I can persuade him to become a merchant." Still naked and noticeably excited, Alexander reached for her hand. "But first, my love, there are more urgent matters to attend to."

＊＊

Theodosia lay with her right arm draped over Alexander's chest and her left pressed flat under her own torso. He had fallen asleep the moment their lovemaking ended, and she—not wanting to disturb him—held that position as one arm grew cold, the other numb and painful. When at last she absolutely had to move, he stirred, kissed her in the dark, and began to talk.

"Nice to wake up and find such a beautiful lady cuddled close to me."

"You're exhausted. Been pushing yourself too hard." She nuzzled her head against his neck for a few moments, then asked a question that had been in her mind for months. "Any chance you could stay home next year?"

He kissed her again. "I've been thinking that way, too. Got enough ships lined up now to export every excess grain of wheat the Euboean farmers produce."

Bless you, Juno!

"Your wife and son," she said, "would enjoy getting better acquainted with you."

"Sons. I have two, don't forget. And since it's not likely Doros will ever be interested in the business, maybe it's time to bring Nikolaos back in."

"And Lycos? He does consider himself your third son, and he's been working very hard for you all these years."

Quite out of context, as if his thoughts were elsewhere, Alexander changed the subject. "Guess what your old buddy, Vespasian, did a few months ago."

"I haven't talked with Aula in a while, but the last time we got together she told me that the general—"

"The *governor* now."

"She said that, at Nero's command, *Governor* Vespasian had journeyed all the way from Africa to Athens while he—Nero—was touring Greece."

"Seems like the emperor looks for ways to get away from Rome, because he's growing less popular there each year."

"Aula said Nero was performing in Athens when—right in the middle of his concert, if you can believe it—"

"The illustrious Governor Vespasian fell asleep!" Alexander laughed so hard he barely could talk. "And not only did he doze off, but—"

"Aula said Vespasian's snoring all but drowned out Nero's singing."

Vespasian is the most serious and deliberate man I've ever known. How could he make a dumb mistake like that in Nero's presence?

Abruptly, Alexander's laughter stopped. "Rumor has it, Nero was about to order Vespasian's execution for treason when someone pointed out it wouldn't be wise to do that to his most competent governor."

"Especially since that governor also happens to be the most loved and successful general alive today."

"Nero probably feared the army would move against him if he killed their favorite commander. The divine emperor does have his enemies, you know, including that other old buddy of yours, Otho."

"Well, of course. Every single day when Otho wakes up, he looks in his polished-bronze mirror and sees himself wearing imperial purple. Think he could raise his own army?"

"Maybe, but it's a bad time for any kind of military uprising, given that they're already facing the prospect of war in the east."

Theodosia propped on her left elbow and peered into the shadows of Alexander's face.

"You know," she said, "I bet Vespasian made that 'mistake' on purpose."

"Why would he do that?"

"To provoke a confrontation."

"A military coup?"

"Well, he *is* ambitious, as you and I both know, and large portions of the army would follow him."

Again, Alexander changed the subject. "I have to tell you... the whole Mediterranean is rumbling over this big rebellion in the eastern provinces."

"Sounds bad."

"It's worse than bad. Two months ago, a swarm of Judean peasants slaughtered dozens of Roman soldiers in the streets of Jerusalem."

"Aula must have gotten that news, too, but I haven't seen her in months. Have to wonder what else I've missed."

"Soon after that," Alexander went on, "another rebel group armed only with spears and slingshots set a trap and ambushed a legion that foolishly got itself strung out along a narrow canyon near Jerusalem. The Jews killed officers and men alike—all but a handful of soldiers from the legion—and made off with their sacred *aquila*."

"A long time back, Father described to me how, in our entire history, that kind of rout only had happened once. It was during Augustus's reign, when Germanic tribes set a brutal trap that destroyed three of our legions. Fifteen thousand Roman soldiers died in one day, and the tribesmen carried away *all three* of their sacred eagle standards." Theodosia shivered, both from the cold and from the recollection.

Alexander pulled the blanket over her shoulders. "So, on a smaller scale, that has happened again."

She snuggled against his warm chest, ready for sleep. "Fortunately, Jewish peasant revolts have nothing to do with us."

***

The next morning, as Nikolaos carved up a goat he had just slaughtered behind Zosimos's shop, he heard the news from two slave customers.

"Your pa got in yesterday," said a gray-haired woman waiting to buy fresh goat meat for her master's table. "Lucky he beat the baddest part of winter."

Why didn't I hear about this yesterday?

"Glad he's home," said the other, who was many years younger. "Done so much good for Euboea."

"And for hisself, too. Master says Nickolaos's pa's gonna be the richest man on the island real soon."

"Folks who seen him at the wharf said his face was drawn." The younger woman frowned. "But he sure did look to be in good spirits."

"And in a great rush to get on home." The older slave grinned as she made a suggestive gesture.

But in no great rush to see me.

***

Zosimos granted Nikolaos's request for the afternoon off, so he headed for Lycos's office on the other side of town.

He opened the door, shook out his woolen cloak, draped it over a nail protruding from the wall, and surveyed the workspace. A bright flame in the fireplace. Two long tables. Assorted stools. Shelves for scrolls and cabinets for supplies. Dozens of wax tablets propped on the walls around the perimeter of the dirt floor.

Business must be good.

Lycos was sitting at one of the tables, scratching on a papyrus sheet with a reed pen. He glanced up, very briefly, but didn't stop working or even say a word of greeting.

"Where's my father?" Nikolaos demanded.

Lycos didn't raise his eyes. "Getting reacquainted with his son."

"I am his son. He is not getting reacquainted with me."

"His other son. They'll both be here later."

Nikolaos stepped to the second table and took a stool. "I'll wait."

***

The sun and its warmth had been dropping for an hour when familiar voices sounded in the street. The door swung open, and the brat strutted in—showing off his best military-style footwork—followed by Alexander. More gray showed in their father's hair than Nikolaos remembered, and he was beginning to stoop.

Looks like the old man may have started to shrink, too.

Nikolaos rose from the stool, straightened to his full height, and waited for them to approach.

Without speaking, Alexander embraced him.

I'm at least a foot taller now than he is and lots bigger all around.

"You've been in town a whole day," Nikolaos said. It was less a statement than an accusation.

"I was tired. Needed a good long night's rest."

Needed to spend a good long night screwing her.

"Well rested now?"

Alexander's lips twitched as he caught Nikolaos's eye.

He got my point.

"Are you here," Alexander asked, "for some special purpose?"

Nikolaos jutted his jaw. "My father has been away for half a year, and I wanted to see him. Is that special enough?"

Lycos stood now, too. He was also taller than Alexander, but still much slighter than Nikolaos.

No doubt they visited last evening, at the house.

Lycos glanced at Alexander. "Want me to leave?"

Alexander shook his head, so Lycos resumed his work. Nikolaos stepped behind him and peered over his shoulder as he wrote.

The little soldier marched across the room. He saluted Nikolaos and began declaiming. "Our father had a great trip! Visited ten new seaports!"

Unbearably obnoxious, even for a nine-year-old.

"Signed up fourteen more ship captains! Ready to distribute Euboean grain throughout the Mediterranean!"

"Doros is right," Alexander said to Nikolaos, "and that's—"

"And that's remarkable!" the brat shouted.

"Starting next summer—"

"Three dozen ships will sail into Eretria!"

"Which means," Alexander went on smoothly, as if a child's constant, screeching interruptions were the norm for business conversations, "more income for island farmers."

"More jobs!"

"Their sons won't have to leave for Athens to find work."

"More money in people's hands!"

"More goods for Zosimos to sell in his shops."

"A better life for everyone!"

"Yes, everyone on the island will benefit, so—"

"So we should celebrate!" The brat hopped onto a stool beside Lycos. "Even you, Nikolaos!"

Alexander took a stool opposite Doros and Lycos. "Nikolaos, since we're talking about remarkable activities—" He gestured across the table. "You and I and everyone else on this island owe a big debt of gratitude to Lycos."

No reason for me to be grateful to Lycos.

"He's run the office for seven years," Alexander said, "and done outstanding work. I want to make sure you recognize that."

Nikolaos ignored the comment. "I'm proud you're my father. Always have been proud of you."

A slow smile crept over Alexander's face. "An hour ago, Doros and I stopped by the market. You weren't there, but Zosimos told us you're the best worker in any of his shops right now. Best worker he's had in years, actually."

Is that his way of saying he's proud of me, too?

"It's obvious you've matured a lot over the last year, so I've been thinking—" Alexander dropped his eyes and studied his hands.

Unsure where this discussion was heading, Nikolaos kept quiet. For a time, there was no sound in the room except the crackling of the fire and the soft scratching of Lycos's reed pen on the papyrus.

Alexander chuckled at last, but there was no humor in it. "I'm getting older. Just turned forty-three. Don't have the strength and stamina I once did. Starting to have back troubles, and my balance isn't what it used to be either. Not sure how long I can keep up this pace. Besides, my wife wants me home."

Nikolaos held his breath.

"And this second son of mine—" Alexander pointed in Doros's direction. "Has absolutely no interest in the business. So, Nikolaos, here's a question for you."

Lycos's hand jerked. A splotch of black ink stained the papyrus. He put down his pen but continued staring at the page as Alexander went on.

"Would you care to work with us again? Become Lycos's partner? Travel in my place?"

Lycos's head shot up. He stared at Alexander. Opened his mouth. But no words came out.

***

Myrine's birth pangs began that afternoon, but still she insisted on baking bread and preparing the family's favorite fish soup for dinner.

"I'm tough," she joked between contractions as she served her master, her mistress, her husband, and Doros. "Born for this, you know. I'll be up and about early in the morning."

"No," Theodosia said, "you must take a few days to rest."

Actually, she'll do just what she said. It's what she always does.

But as Myrine moved around the kitchen, her face grew even more florid than usual. After she spilled a couple of bowls, Theodosia rose.

"Time to go lie down." She wrapped an arm around the slave's shoulders and patted her. "Olinda and I can handle this."

"You sent for the midwife?" Alexander asked Myrine.

"Yes, Master. Olinda went an hour ago to tell her."

After she left, Theodosia finished serving the men. Olinda fetched portions of soup for her brothers, who sat at a lower table off to one side.

Lycos was silent as Alexander, Theodosia, and Doros talked through dinner. He didn't even respond to their expressions of concern for Myrine.

They've been through so many of these birthing days. Guess it must feel totally routine by now.

At the end of the meal, however, Lycos raised his head and scowled at Alexander. "You should have told me first, before Nikolaos." His voice was devoid of expression.

"Told you what?"

"That you were bringing him back into the business."

Theodosia tilted her head and eyed Alexander sideways.

He gave Lycos no warning about his new plan?

"You're right," Alexander said after a while. "I should have told you first."

"You should have *asked* me first."

Alexander sighed. "Yes, I should have *asked* you first."

"I've worked for you for seven years, almost a third of my life." Lycos looked very different from the frightened slave boy of times gone by. "Never thought you'd do something this important without consulting me."

"Yes, I—" Alexander pushed his empty bowl aside. "I should have— Of course. At the very least, I should have told you first."

The kitchen fell silent. Even the slave children, wide-eyed in their corner of the room, seemed to sense that something was wrong.

"Maybe," Alexander went on in a whisper, "I was just too eager to make the family whole again."

CHAPTER 14

When the midwife knocked, Theodosia left the kitchen and led her to the sleeping chamber that Myrine and Lycos shared with their three children. An oil lamp burned on the single chest.

The midwife set her birthing stool beside the bed where Myrine lay and touched her forehead.

"Towels are over there, in the cabinet," Myrine said.

Theodosia squeezed her hand. "I'll go heat the water."

Juno, keep her safe.

***

Theodosia returned to the kitchen in time to overhear what appeared to be the final part of an announcement by Lycos to Alexander.

"—really can't stay. Best for all if I find work elsewhere."

Alexander made no reply.

Listening, but trying not to show it, Theodosia lifted the half-full pot of soup from its spit over the fire and set it on the stone floor.

"If you'll allow me," Lycos went on, "I'd like to keep buying Myrine's freedom."

Alexander's silence stretched on and on.

He doesn't need this stress.

"Of course," he said after a long interval, his voice taut.

Theodosia placed an empty iron pot on the spit. Then, with a bucket, she awkwardly brought water from the cistern outside.

She had splashed the floor a few times before Alexander rose.

"Let me help with that," he said.

As he approached the fire, one of his sandals caught an uneven edge on the floor. He tripped, failed to catch himself, and fell face down.

Theodosia and Lycos assisted him back to the table.

"That wouldn't have happened," he said, clearly shaken, "even a year ago. Definitely showing my age."

Lycos finished filling the pot. "Once this boils, I'll take it across the hall and wait outside till the baby comes." A short time later, he used several of Myrine's homespun hot pads to carry it from the kitchen.

***

For the rest of that hour and most of a second, Theodosia and Alexander kept a silent vigil. Finally, she took his hands, which were scratched and cut from breaking his fall.

"What'll you do without him?"

"Been wondering that myself."

"Couldn't you just apologize?"

"I did while you were out."

"And?"

"His mind's made up."

"Think he'd listen to me?"

"Not likely."

"We've always had a good relationship."

"I've an even better relationship with him that goes much farther back into his childhood." Alexander stared at the fire. "If I can't persuade him—"

Neither one spoke as an eerie silence descended on the house.

Hope Myrine's all right.

"There must be someone else in Eretria," Theodosia said at one point, "who can manage the office for you."

"Haven't been able to think of anyone." He gave her a thin smile. "Guess I'll do it myself. Not too old for that yet."

***

A third hour passed with no sound from the bedroom across the hallway. No screams. No cries. Nothing to signal that a baby was being born.

And then a fourth hour.

Suddenly, the kitchen door opened and Lycos walked in. His soft, curly hair tumbled over his forehead, and for the briefest moment Theodosia saw the little boy she had first met at her villa thirteen years earlier.

"Is Myrine well?" she asked.

A sour expression crossed the young man's face.

Alexander echoed Theodosia's concern. "Please tell us she's all right."

"She's all right." Lycos's nostrils flared. "Nothing wrong with *her*."

"The baby?" Theodosia asked.

Lycos didn't look at her.

"What *is* wrong?" She caught his arm as he passed.

Lycos recoiled as if he had been seared with a torch. "Everything."

He retreated to the hearth, snatched up the iron poker, and whacked at the fire. Energetically. Viciously. Over and over and over until it was roaring.

Alexander and Theodosia eyed one another but kept quiet.

After a while, Lycos faced them. "Myrine's baby is fine."

'Myrine's baby'? Not 'our baby'?

His face was crimson from the flames, or something else. "A healthy girl."

He must've been hoping for a third son.

Theodosia clapped her hands. "Congratulations are in order!"

"Theodosia and I," Alexander said, "could not be happier."

"Well, I most certainly *could* be happier." Lycos lifted the poker over his head with both hands and smashed it against the stone hearth.

Rock fragments shot out and scattered around him.

Then came another hard crash of the poker.

And another.

And another.

And another.

After a while, abruptly, Lycos swung around in Theodosia and Alexander's direction.

"Myrine's new girl has olive skin. And straight black hair. She looks exactly like Olinda."

***

Waking in the night, Theodosia sensed that Alexander was moving around the room, dressing without a lamp, as if trying not to disturb her.

Without a moment's thought, she rolled onto her side and dropped off to sleep again.

***

She awoke to early sunlight seeping through the shutters and to the sight of Myrine lighting a fire... as she always did at this hour, so the room would be comfortable when her mistress rose and dressed.

What an amazing woman. Last night, she had her baby, but here she is, sturdy and competent, going about her regular morning duties.

As the fire crackled and spread its heat, Myrine pulled Theodosia's heaviest stola from a chest and draped it over the chair closest to the hearth, to warm up. Then she went downstairs.

She soon returned with her swaddled newborn and settled into the other cushioned chair near the fire. It was the same routine that she had followed, with Theodosia's encouragement, after each of her six previous birthing days.

The baby cooed and sought her mother's breast. In nine days, assuming she survived that long, this newest member of the family would receive a name agreed upon by her father, Lycos, and her master, Alexander.

All in all, life is good.

After a while, Theodosia noted an unusual redness around the new mother's eyes. It didn't come from the cold or from sitting too near the fireplace, and it wasn't the same old ruddy color in her cheeks.

Myrine's been crying.

***

An unusually frigid dawn was breaking as Nikolaos, ready for warmth and Cilla's fresh-cooked breakfast, slung over his shoulder the big, orange-colored leather sack that he had purchased in the market yesterday afternoon.

As he reached Cilla's front door, footsteps crunched on a frozen puddle behind him. He turned—even more cautiously than normal, given the energetic activities he had been engaged in since evening—and started.

Alexander stood across the street, wearing his hooded winter cloak but without the thick wool strips that most men laboriously bound around their feet and legs at this time of year.

Looks like he dressed in the dark without a lamp.

"Why are you out so early," Nikolaos asked, "and unwrapped like that?"

"I'd rather be anywhere else in the world than here."

"Then go home and warm up."

"Not until we talk."

"About what?"

Alexander gestured toward the house. "Upstairs. In your room."

***

Theodosia climbed out of bed. "Stay put," she told her nursing slave.

Awkwardly, because one of Myrine's usual tasks was to help her dress, she removed her sleeping tunic and draped the pre-heated stola around her body. Then she settled into the chair opposite Myrine and her baby and pulled on her warm woolen slippers. "Your girl's got a good appetite," she said.

Myrine kept her eyes down.

Definitely been crying.

"What's the matter?"

Myrine shook her head.

"You should have taken it easy this morning, like I said last night," Theodosia scolded. "Every year I tell you the same thing, and every year you ignore me. You really do need to give yourself time to recover."

Myrine nodded without looking up.

"Can I get you anything?" her mistress asked in a gentler voice.

Another shake. "Olinda cared for me through the night." Her voice quivered, despite obvious efforts to hold it steady. "She'll fetch your breakfast soon and also feed Master Doros and the little ones."

"And Lycos, too?"

Myrine's face puckered at that. "If he's there, she will." Her head drooped over the infant as sobs wracked her body. "Oh, Mistress, he stomped out last night, but before that he said— right in front of the midwife, he said— he wasn't never coming back."

More fodder for Eretria's gossips.

Theodosia shifted her weight, leaned forward, draped her fingers over Myrine's shoulders, and massaged them.

But the tears continued.

After a while, the slave raised her eyes. "Later on he— did come back." She was hiccoughing rapidly now. "We had a fight— after you and the— master went to bed— and Lycos called me a— a harlot and a slut and— a whole bunch of nasty— names I can't repeat."

Theodosia sat back in her chair. "He was furious with all of us last night, not just with you." She kept her voice as soft and calm as possible. "Most of his anger was directed at Alexander."

"Lycos accused me of— lusting for sex with— Master Nikolaos for— all these many years." Myrine shook her head again. "Like I had a choice or something."

"So, you did not—" Theodosia interrupted herself, unable to complete her question.

"Not willingly. No, Mistress. Never. The last thing I'd ever want to do is have sex with that monster."

Not willingly. The last thing she'd ever want to do.

"So… how?" Even as Theodosia asked, she knew the answer.

"Oh, Mistress, can't you guess?"

"He raped you again."

An onslaught of tears jostled the baby at Myrine's nipple.

As the tiny girl's wail filled the air, Theodosia lifted her from her mother's arms and strolled with her around the room. Rocked her. Calmed her. Eased her into the well-worn blue cradle whose previous occupants had included Doros, Olinda, Kronos, Hyperion, and Myrine's three deceased children.

Finally, the baby dozed, so Theodosia returned to her chair and waited for Myrine to regain her composure, too.

"Want to tell me more?" she asked after a time.

The slave plucked a thin cloth from her tunic, dabbed at her eyes, and blew her nose.

She'll open up when she's ready.

It took a lot of face-wiping and nervous inhaling and exhaling, but finally Myrine began to talk.

***

The rented room under the eaves was little changed from that hot June day, nine years earlier, when Alexander and Nikolaos first walked into Eretria together, weary from their long hike across the plain, and found their way here to rest.

Except that now, despite shutters across the windows, the space was barely warmer than the air outside. There was no fireplace, and little heat penetrated the floor from the room below. A thick pile of blankets was all that kept Nikolaos from freezing to death at night.

The same three stools surrounded the same round table, but the second bed had been removed. The only usable light came from a small bronze brazier that Nikolaos had lit during the night and left burning when he departed.

"Smells spicy," Alexander said as they stepped in.

"Cilla buys Egyptian oil." Throughout his seven years of sleeping alone here, this exotic fragrance was the only thing that welcomed Nikolaos when he returned each evening from his bloody work in the market.

He offered his father a stool, then he walked around the bed and—on the far side, out of sight—dropped his orange leather sack. It thudded on the floor boards, but Alexander didn't seem to notice.

"What's on your mind, Father?"

Maybe we can get this over fast.

"Myrine gave birth to a girl last night." The yellow flame cast odd shadows on Alexander's face.

Nikolaos sat opposite him and said nothing.

"Mother and daughter are well," Alexander went on. "The gods have blessed us in that way."

The gods had nothing to do with it.

Nikolaos gave a sardonic chuckle. "Father, you didn't crawl out of bed before dawn on such a bitter morning and trot half-way across town, under-dressed, to tell me there's a new slave baby in the family."

"Not just for that, no."

"Look, I'll need to leave for work soon, so—"

"Lycos isn't the baby's father."

Nikolaos laughed at the absurdity of that statement.

"Oh, that's too funny! As if someone can possibly know with certainty the paternity of any given slave child."

"She's an exact, perfect replica of Olinda."

"So?"

"Everyone knows Olinda is *your* child."

"So?"

"You had sex with Myrine after I told you to stop."

Nikolaos kept laughing. "I enjoy myself, and so does she."

"She does not enjoy it."

Nikolaos shrugged. "As we've discussed before, I'm happy to do what I can to increase the family's wealth by impregnating the family's slave."

"But... when?"

"When... what?"

This kind of conversation drives the old man crazy.

"When do you visit her?"

"Whenever it suits me."

"Mornings? Afternoons?"

"Mornings, mostly. On my way to work. After Lycos leaves for the office. While your wife is out disgracing our family in the street with her marching brat and her fat, wrinkled, gray-haired friend."

Alexander blinked. "Every morning on your way to work?"

"Not every morning."

"So... when? Several times a month? Every other day?"

"No routine. Whenever I feel like it."

"Let me see if I understand. You come to our family kitchen at random moments, but always at an hour when you know our slave is going to be alone there, and you come with the explicit purpose of forcing her to have sex with you."

"Well, we never do it right away. Always talk first. I enjoy speaking Aramaic with her, because I taught her and she's gotten very good at it."

"But then, every time you come to our kitchen—after having a little fun speaking Aramaic with Myrine—you rape her."

"I excite her and pleasure her, which isn't something that Lycos seems able to do."

Alexander jumped to his feet and knocked over the stool, which banged loudly on the floor. "Now I see what all my efforts have come to. My eldest son, whom I've worked for and deprived myself of a normal family life for and exhausted myself to build a future for— That ungrateful wretch sneaks into my house when he knows all the free people are away and forces himself on a woman who is powerless to say no to him."

Nikolaos rose and lifted the stool back onto its legs. "Father, why all this fuss over a slave?"

"Myrine has a husband."

"Not a *legal* one."

"I've allowed her to take a husband."

"That doesn't make it legal."

"It's legal if I say it's legal."

"Not until he pays you every drachma he promised for her freedom."

"As I was saying… you enter my house without my permission—"

"With or without your permission, I've every right to do anything I wish with Myrine, which means that what I do with her is not rape."

"Without my approval, it *is* rape."

"I don't give a damn whether you approve or not."

Instantly, Alexander's hand lashed out and smacked his son's cheek. It was the first time that he—as a former slave—could imagine doing such a thing.

Nikolaos recoiled from the blow and seemed to need some time to recover. Finally, his shaken eyes focused on Alexander's.

"Thank you, Father, for clarifying our relationship." He managed a smile of sorts. "I understand now that *my* family no longer exists. The last member of *my* family died in childbirth in Antioch."

"You are not the only injured party. For various reasons, Lycos is now alienated from me and also from the woman he loves. As all the world can plainly see, Myrine has two daughters who were sired by you and two sons who were sired by Lycos."

"Ask *her* how that all came about. You'll discover that such a sweetly symmetrical two-by-two arrangement came about by pure coincidence."

Alexander's forehead crinkled. "I don't understand."

"As Myrine will tell you, if you care enough to ask her… Kronos and Hyperion could just as easily have been born with my olive skin and my nearly black eyes and hair."

Alexander's eyes went blank. No level of comprehension showed in his face. Nothing but sheer befuddlement.

"You really *don't* understand, do you?" Nikolaos laughed once more. "I've been having sex with Myrine the entire time that Lycos has, and even longer, actually, because I got started on her first." He paused. "Of course, none of that matters one whit now."

The furrows on Alexander's forehead deepened. His mouth twitched convulsively, and the deep, jagged scar on his jaw seemed to darken. "Why doesn't that matter?" he asked in a voice both weary and wary.

Nikolaos paused for maximum dramatic effect. "Because Lycos is gone."

Alexander's thin hand rose to his equally scrawny throat. "What?"

He really does look old.

"You heard right, Father. Lycos left town last night. Said he wouldn't be back. Said nobody in this house would ever see him again."

"I don't understand."

"So," Nikolaos said with excruciating patience, "let's see if you can understand this. I'm leaving today, too. You and your Roman wife and your bratty little Roman soldier... none of you will ever see me again either."

He let that statement hang in the air as he stepped around the bed, slung the orange leather sack over his shoulder, and stamped his way down the stairs to Cilla's front door.

CHAPTER 15

Theodosia held her tongue as the baby slept and Myrine unburdened her heart in a rare-for-her, uncontrolled rush of words.

"Soon after you fell down the stairs and Master Alexander kicked Master Nikolaos out and you was up here in bed recovering… Master Nikolaos started showin' up in the kitchen and he never made no noise and he fixed it so I didn't make no noise either, but later on the master was travelin' and Lycos never heard nothing even though he was workin' in the next room, but the worst came after Lycos moved his office and you was always with the lady Aula and Master Doros was always marchin' with the soldiers and my babies was always sleepin' and I was always alone in the kitchen."

Why am I just hearing about this?

"That's when things got really bad 'fore Master Nikolaos used to stroll in every mornin' after you was out, always wantin' to talk in Aramaic, but then it was the same thing every mornin' and he'd make the same exact hand gesture like I was a dog that had to obey and every single mornin' if I wasn't quick enough to suit him he'd wallop my boobs or my butt or do his business with me extra rough." Myrine dried her eyes on the scrap of cloth, blew her nose, and caught her breath.

"Why didn't you ever tell me?"

The slave merely shrugged.

"Answer me, Myrine. There has to be a reason why you never told me."

Tears flowed again. "He swore he'd kill my babies if I told you 'cause nobody cared and nothing bad would happen to him 'cause they was just slaves. Said he'd slit Kronos's throat first and then Hyperion's."

Dearest Juno.

"Did he threaten to slit Olinda's throat, too?"

"No, he never threatened her."

"Because she's his?"

"Guess so." Another shrug. "He kept sayin' he's such an expert butcher. 'Real handy with a knife,' he'd say. 'Little boy's throat ain't half as thick and tough as a goat's,' he'd say." Myrine wiped her wet cheeks with the cloth. "And one time he said somethin' else, too."

Theodosia forced herself to carve every disgusting detail of this repulsive story into her memory, so she could recount all of it later to Alexander.

Myrine's hiccoughs came back. "It happened one time when I told him— when I reminded him how Lycos was— payin' Master Alexander for me so— I'd finally be a free woman and— how even my children would— go free someday too and then… Oh, Mistress, take a guess what he said."

"I'm afraid to guess."

"He vowed he'd make damn sure— that Lycos never finished payin' off— all the money he'd promised the master. He said that so mean, Mistress, and— can you figure out why?"

Once again, Theodosia declined to speculate.

"Because that way— if it ever comes a time— when Master Alexander dies or for any other reason ain't here—" Myrine slowed down and managed to control her hiccoughs. "If that happens, I'll still belong to him, meanin' Master Nikolaos, and it won't just be me that's his property by law, 'cause when Master Alexander dies all my babies will belong to him too and not only will he do whatever he wants with me but also whatever he wants with them."

Unfortunately, all of that could happen exactly as he said.

"And I got the idea," Myrine went on, "that even if Master Alexander was still alive, Master Nikolaos might kill Lycos to make sure he never pays it all off. Can you see, Mistress, why I was too scared to tell you?"

Theodosia nodded, but before she could say anything, a sharp cry rose from the foot of the stairs.

"Mother!" It was Olinda's voice. Screaming. "Come quick!"

Myrine jumped up and rushed to the door, then she swung around and headed back toward the cradle for her little one.

"Go on," Theodosia said without thinking, "I'll bring her."

Moments later, supporting the newborn with one hand, bracing the other against the wall, and watching each step, she crept down to the first floor.

Might not survive another fall with another child.

***

This time, the scream was Myrine's. "By all the gods, come back to me!"

Sounds, smells, and shivers assaulted Theodosia as she reached the hall. Olinda's screeches. Myrine's wails. The stink of vomit and feces. A crawling sensation all over her skin.

Struggling not to retch, Theodosia tucked the baby into the folds of her stola, stepped to the door of the sleeping chamber that once had been a business office, and took it all in.

Myrine was bending over at the near side of her two boys' bed. Bracing her upper body on her forearms. Sweeping the floor with her hair. Keening.

"Kroonooos!

"Krooonooos!

"Kroooonooos!"

Abruptly, the slave straightened and tugged her older son's filthy body onto her breast. Rocked him. Covered with kisses his swollen, blackened face.

"Krooooooooooonooooos!

"Krooooooooooonooooos!

"Krooooooooooonooooos!"

Theodosia shifted her eyes and focused on the second boy lying on the far side of the bed.

Olinda had thrown back the stained blanket and was desperately trying to shake Hyperion awake.

Also filthy. Also swollen. Also blackened.

And still as death, just like the puppy.

Except… there was no blood. No slit throats. No knife wounds. Only two small, lifeless bodies covered with their own vomit and excrement.

Poison?

Just then, Doros walked in. "What's going on here?"

Still holding Myrine's baby with one arm, Theodosia turned her own child around with the other and pressed his wide-eyed face into her abdomen.

A few more moments later, as if there weren't enough chaos in the house already, someone pounded hard on the front door.

Theodosia maneuvered Doros into his own sleeping chamber and closed the door behind them. "Keep this shut and don't come out till I call you."

For once in his life, Doros didn't argue.

Theodosia shifted the baby to her other arm, slipped out again to the hall, and opened the main door.

Carrying her walking stick, Aula shoved her way past Theodosia.

She's the last person I need to deal with right now.

Myrine's wails continued as the stench of death engulfed the house.

Aula's nose twitched. "Did your slave miscarry?"

"No." Theodosia held up the newborn girl. "The birth went fine, but a few hours later, both of her sons fell ill."

"Odd coincidence." Aula peered into the baby's face. "Have you noticed? She's a true miniature of Nikolaos."

And so the gossip continues.

"Let's go upstairs where it's quieter," Aula said. "There's something I have to ask you in private."

"Sorry, but… too much going on right now. Can it wait till tomorrow?"

"No."

Theodosia exhaled more loudly than she intended, but she did take Aula to her quarters, settled her into one of the chairs by the fire, and snuggled the baby into her blue cradle.

Please, Juno, let this little one sleep.

Aula plunged into her topic. "What I need you to tell me is—" Suddenly, she stopped and let her eyes wander the room, where they lingered on every object as if searching for something or other.

Theodosia's eyes followed, both curious and concerned.

She came looking for specific information?

Finally, Aula turned back to her. "What happened last night?"

"No idea what you're talking about."

"Lots of people reported it."

"Reported what?"

"What happened in the street."

Theodosia scratched her head. "In the street?"

"A big fight just a block away."

"Well, after the baby was born last night, Myrine and Lycos had an argument, but—"

"This was two men."

"I didn't hear any of that." Theodosia's skin went clammy. "Not with the shutters closed."

"Everyone else had their shutters closed, too, and they all heard it."

Everyone else in the neighborhood? In the whole town? In the fort?

"Wasn't loud enough to wake me, for sure." Theodosia caught herself digging at a rough cuticle on her left thumb. She forced herself to stop and spread her hands on her lap. "I slept soundly all night."

"What everyone heard was a long, loud, angry fight between Alexander and his son."

"Nikolaos?"

"No. It was Lycos, according to all the reports."

"All the reports?"

"Dozens of people said Lycos shouted at Alexander, and vice versa."

"Lycos and Alexander have never shouted at one another in their lives."

Until last night in the kitchen, but she doesn't need to know about that.

"Everyone said it was Alexander and Lycos." There was no hint of doubt in Aula's voice. "They all agreed it went on and on for a dreadfully long time. You must be the only one in town who *didn't* hear it."

"That's not possible. Alexander was in bed with me all night."

"But if, as you say, you slept so soundly and didn't hear a big commotion in the street, how would you know if he was in bed with you or not?"

Theodosia made an effort to laugh. "Believe me, I know when my husband's in bed with me and when he's not."

Except… he did get up and dress and leave in the dark, but I most definitely am not going to tell her that.

"Where is Alexander now?"

"I don't know. He went out a while ago."

"Will you swear he was with you the whole night?"

What else can I do?

"Of course."

***

Alexander didn't come home all day. Didn't show up for meals. Didn't send word of where he was.

And neither did Lycos.

But Theodosia had no time to worry about them.

In the morning, she, Myrine, Olinda, and Doros washed the boys' bodies and wrapped them in new linen before working side by side to clean out the messy, smelly sleeping chamber where they had died.

Through the early part of the afternoon, with the sun at its warmest and the ground its softest, they took turns digging a deep, rectangular hole not far from the kitchen door.

Later in the afternoon, they buried the little corpses head to head and covered them with loose soil.

Finally, as the sun set and Olinda sobbed and Doros stoically watched, Theodosia and Myrine stood together beside the grave with their arms wrapped around each other, propping each other up, chanting a traditional Greek mourning prayer before going in to bathe and rest and eat and grieve beside the kitchen fire.

Since Kronos and Hyperion were slaves, no report to the government officials was needed.

***

Theodosia was deep in sleep when Alexander entered the bedroom. It took a while before she roused herself enough to speak coherently.

"You spent the whole day and much of the night in Lycos's office," she said at last, "but you couldn't find time to send me a message?"

"I didn't spend the day in Lycos's office." His tone was flat. "Nor any part of the night."

Theodosia waited, but no clarification came, so she kept probing.

"Have you heard what happened here this morning?"

Alexander made no reply.

"Two terrible things took place in this house," Theodosia said.

Alexander kicked off his sandals but said nothing.

"Aren't you curious to find out what they were?"

Something else is wrong.

"Both of Myrine's sons suffered violent deaths," she said, "and Aula spent an hour interrogating me about your whereabouts last night."

More silence.

"I didn't know what to tell her," she went on, "so I lied. I covered for you." Still he held his tongue.

"But now you need to tell me where you were."

He tugged his woolen himation over his head. "Out."

"Doing what?"

"Searching."

As before, she waited for an explanation that didn't come.

Instead, in the dark, Alexander splashed his face and torso with water from the bowl on the table, toweled himself dry, donned his cotton sleep tunic, crawled into bed, and kissed her.

"I love you, Theodosia."

Without another word, he rolled away from her.

But she was wide awake now, and even more worried, and unwilling to be ignored.

"Who have you been searching for?"

"Nikolaos." He spat the name.

Nikolaos has disappeared?

"And Lycos, along with—" Alexander stopped.

Lycos is missing, too?

"Along with—" she repeated. "Who else is missing?"

"Not who. What."

Theodosia held her breath until at last he broke the news.

"Our cache of gold and silver coins. All our business profits. Our entire life savings."

She rose on one elbow. "What are you saying?"

"One or the other of them—"

Alexander rolled back toward her, found her hand, and pressed it to his lips. "And I truly have no idea which one it was—"

He shivered. "All I know is, either Nikolaos or Lycos dug up everything we had buried under the office floor and stole it all from us."

***

Voices echoed in the street.

Fists banged on the front door.

Feet smashed the wooden panels.

Hobnailed boots pounded the stairs.

And rancid oil from a dozen lamps befouled Theodosia's quarters as a swarm of burly shadows burst in, casting bizarre, flickering shapes on the walls. The presence of so many male bodies in her private space jolted her awake for the second time that night.

Alexander leaped out of bed to confront them. "How dare you?"

Theodosia sat up in time to see one of the men punch him in the back and shove him to the floor.

"Stop that!" She swung her legs over the edge of the mattress. "By whose order do you invade our home?"

A second man slammed his knee into Alexander's spine, twisted his arms behind him, and clapped irons on his wrists.

Last night's fire had gone out in the hearth. The room was icy cold.

Aware of the thinness of her sleeping tunic, Theodosia pulled a blanket off the bed, tossed it around her shoulders like a cape, and rose.

A third man yanked Alexander to his feet, grabbed the short chain attached to the manacles, and kicked him toward the door.

"I need to dress!" Alexander shouted as he resisted.

The soldier smacked his head. "Dressed well enough for where you're going."

Meanwhile, others ransacked Theodosia's belongings. Tossed her clothing off the shelves and out of the chests. Dug under the mattress that she and Alexander had been sleeping on.

What in Hades are they looking for?

As the chaotic scene played out and a few clear thoughts formed in her head, she became increasingly certain of one thing.

Somehow, Nikolaos is to blame for this.

Barefoot, she padded across the frigid floor to the well-muscled man who held Alexander's chain.

"What are you doing?"

The soldier snorted. "Obvious, isn't it? We're arresting him."

"By whose order?"

"Caesar's."

Nero ordered this?

She forced herself to stay calm. "My husband is not a young man. Getting rather old, actually."

"That's his problem." Another snort. "Not mine."

"But it's winter, and he's in his lightweight sleep tunic with nothing whatsoever on his feet."

The lamplit face under the red-and-brass helmet twisted into a smirk but didn't bother to reply.

"What's the charge?" Theodosia demanded.

"Ask him." The smirk grew more pronounced. "He knows."

"No!" Alexander yelled over his shoulder. "No idea!"

"Shut up, Greek." The smirking soldier boxed his ears, then tossed him through the door.

Theodosia watched, stunned, as the brute threw her beloved husband down the steep stairway.

By the time the entire group had stomped out through the front door into the street, she was sure of three more things.

These soldiers are not from our garrison.

Not the ones Doros has been marching with.

The soldiers we know would never do this.

CHAPTER 16

Mother!" Doros raced up the stairs in the dark. "Some shitty bastards just dragged Father into the street! In chains!"

"I know. Did you recognize any of them?"

Shivering, Theodosia felt through a pile of clothes that the soldiers had knocked off a shelf until she found her warmest woolen palla.

"No. They're not from our garrison. These assholes are new."

"Stop talking like you spent the night in the barracks."

She draped the long palla over her night tunic and pulled Doros under it, too, so they could share each other's body heat.

"The centurion will tell us why Father was arrested, don't you think?"

"I'm sure he will."

And even if he won't, Aula will.

Operating purely on instinct as she hugged Doros close to her, Theodosia felt for the leather strap around his neck.

By old habit, she squeezed the pouch to make sure the viper amulet was still there. And then...

"Doros, where's your bulla?"

He slipped out from under her stola, opened the pouch, held it upside down, and shook it. Nothing clattered on the floor.

"Mother, the damn viper's gone!"

Just like our fortune.

***

The sun was well up over the waterfront opposite the Praetorian Gate when Nikolaos joined a crowd of sullen, restive men, each one grumbling and grousing under his breath.

"What's he done to deserve that treatment?"

"Merely improved the life of everyone on this island."

"Damn Romans wouldn't care if we all fell back into poverty next month."

"We could storm the garrison to get him out."

"And wind up dead."

"Or in chains alongside him in their stinking dungeon."

Of course, nobody in the group dared to grumble and grouse too loudly or make any aggressive moves, because dozens of well-armed legionaries paced atop the fortress wall while dozens more guarded the perimeter at ground level… each and every one of whom appeared to take as his personal mission in life to stop any sign of uprising by the men beside the water.

No other Romans were visible.

Except her.

***

Twice this morning, the Roman woman had limped down the street and stumbled up the driveway to the Praetorian Gate. Both times, she carried a heavy-looking gunnysack and a folded garment made of thick, gray fabric.

That's Father's hooded woolen cloak.

Each time, after a bit of conversation at the gate, she left with nothing to show for her efforts.

An hour after her second trip, she returned once more with the sack, but now her brat accompanied her, carrying the cloak. Apparently, not even the would-be Roman soldier—who for years had marched in lockstep with the soldiers at this garrison—could convince the guards to let them in, because he and his mother departed soon after.

Nikolaos left, too, and returned well after lunch, but no one had news of his father.

Finally, late in the afternoon, the Roman woman appeared for a fourth time, alone and with nothing in her hands. And then, at last, after an extended discussion with someone on the other side of the gate, she was admitted.

***

For what seemed an hour, as both the light and the temperature dropped, Theodosia stood shivering inside the Praetorian Gate.

At last, a soldier she had never seen before emerged from the headquarters.

"You're new here," she said to him in Latin as pleasantly as she could.

"Every man new here."

No warmth resonated in his voice, and she knew, even from that short statement, that his Latin wasn't native. Besides that, his dull chain armor was only the most basic part of a regular legionary's flashy uniform.

"I wish to speak with Centurion Norbanus Paulinus."

"He order back Athens."

Really bad Latin. Must be one of the auxiliaries the army hires when there aren't enough regulars to staff every garrison in a region.

She switched into Greek. "Who has taken his place?"

The auxiliary brightened at the chance to speak his own language. "Centurion Secundius Rufinus is in command of this garrison now."

"When did this happen?"

"Yesterday afternoon. We have replaced the previous century."

Theodosia gaped at him. "You've replaced the *entire* century that was stationed here before? All eighty men?"

The auxiliary nodded. "They sailed for Piraeus last night, two hours after we arrived, on the same ship that brought us here."

"And the wife of Centurion Norbanus Paulinus?"

"She's gone."

"For a few days?"

"For good."

Without time to say farewell?

"Why?"

The man's lips twitched. "Not allowed to say."

"And my husband? The man they arrested in the night?"

"Our centurion questioned him."

"For what reason?"

Another twitch. "Not allowed to say."

"Surely he doesn't believe my husband committed a crime."

"Not allowed to say."

"But Alexander—that's his name, you know—is a very important man on this island."

"Our centurion said that."

They know who he is now, but how far back will they probe?

"I'm a Roman citizen, sir, and a citizen's spouse is always given special rights."

"Your husband has no rights."

"No rights?" Theodosia pressed a palm to her forehead and dug her fingers into her scalp, which for hours had seemed ready to split wide open.

"Our centurion said that, too."

The only reason he'd say that is if he knows Alexander's an escaped slave.

Somehow, she refocused on her mission, despite her aching head and quavering voice.

"My husband must be freezing, because they hauled him off in his sleep tunic with nothing on his feet. Surely your centurion will let me bring warmer clothing for him."

For a few moments, the auxiliary hesitated, then he bobbed his head. "Stay here. I find out."

"Please ask if I may provide hot food as well."

The auxiliary returned. "Our centurion says bring food and clothing tonight. You may return with food each day your husband is here."

Relief washed over her. "Oh, sir, thank you!"

"We inspect everything. No ropes. No knives."

She touched his arm. "How soon may I see him?"

"That will not be permitted."

He removed her hand from his arm, placed his own hand on her back, and escorted her out through the Praetorian Gate.

***

Nikolaos lingered in the crowd as the sun cast its last rays over the sea and the winter night closed in.

The Roman woman returned a fifth time, balancing a steaming bowl on the thick layers of Alexander's cloak while her brat handled the bag.

Myrine's fish stew.

By now, the men's usual angry objections to her behavior had turned to grudging appreciation.

"After all these trips, she must be exhausted."

"Can't imagine how she manages to carry so much weight."

"And without spilling hot soup all over herself."

"She *is* still shameless but admirable, too, in her way."

"Do all the women in Rome make this kind of effort for their men?"

"I'd like to think my wife would go to so much trouble for me."

The Roman woman and her brat passed the bowl, the cloak, and the sack to the guards at the Praetorian Gate. Then, without a glance at the throng of murmuring men, they headed home.

Right at that moment, a young fisherman—whose name Nikolaos didn't know but with whom he had struck a pricey deal earlier in the day—strode up to him and nodded.

Nikolaos returned the nod and slung his orange-colored leather sack over one shoulder.

Soon they were sitting in a little yellow fishing boat, paddling under cover of darkness across the icy waters of the Bay of Eretria, bound for an unpopulated stretch of coast north of Athens.

***

Five days had passed since Myrine gave birth to her newest daughter, whom—in the unexpected absence of both her husband and her master—she was calling "Anthousa."

Four days had passed since Lycos disappeared, Kronos and Hyperion died, and Alexander discovered that his fortune was gone.

Three days had passed since Doros lost his bulla and his father was arrested.

Two days had passed since Theodosia began carrying food to Alexander.

One day had passed since Olinda and Doros accompanied Myrine on her first postpartum trip to the market.

This morning, the three went back to the market, but they returned with more than the usual fish and winter grains.

***

On the second floor, beside the warm fire, as Anthousa alternately dozed and fussed in her blue cradle, Theodosia sat by herself and eyed this newest family member from the comfort of her favorite cushioned chair.

Anthousa. Flower. Ironic name. Most likely she'll grow up to be as homely as her sister.

On the ground floor, a door slammed.

And Aula's right. Anthousa does look exactly like Nikolaos.

Sandals clattered on the stairs as Doros sprinted up from below and burst in, followed closely by Olinda. Both of them dropped to the floor between the cradle, the chairs, and the fire.

"Still haven't found your bulla?" Theodosia asked her son. "It's such a bad time for that thing to go missing. Have you looked for it?"

Doros ignored her, as he often did these days. "Mother, listen." His voice was quieter now. "You'll never guess what we learned at the market."

"No?" She brushed a lock of hair from his forehead. "So, you'll have to tell me. Or… Olinda would you like to tell me?"

The girl's eyes were bloodshot. As always when Theodosia addressed her, she replied with nothing more than a motion of her head. This time, her answer was an especially jerky, negative shake.

For perhaps the first time in his life, Doros lowered his voice to a whisper. "It's bad news, Mother."

As if things could possibly get worse.

Myrine came upstairs and joined them then, and lifted Anthousa into her powerful arms. Then she settled into the chair opposite her mistress, still following the venerable custom that kicked in whenever she brought a new baby into the family. Her eyes were bloodshot, too.

Doros glanced at Myrine. "Want me to tell her?"

Myrine shook her head. "Best I do it."

Some new horror?

"Lycos is dead, Mistress." The slave had barely gotten that out when her face crumpled. Quickly, she offered Anthousa her breast, pulled a thin cloth from the belt of her chiton, and covered her eyes as the tears flowed.

Theodosia opened her mouth but found herself powerless to speak.

"Woodcutters discovered his body yesterday," Doros continued the story in the darkest tone his mother had ever heard from him.

He's beginning to see there's more to life than make-believe soldiering.

"They found him in the forest just outside town." Doros sniffed and rubbed his nose on his sleeve. "Dumped in a gully beside the main path. Not covered up with leaves or anything. Whoever killed him must have wanted him found, because the woodsmen actually stumbled over his body. They loaded it into their cart and hauled it to the garrison."

A memory stirred from thirteen years earlier.

General Vespasian and his three children, on their first visit to Theodosia, were enjoying lunch under the pergola at her villa.

And Domitian, the general's youngest, kept racing toward the cliffs overlooking the Etruscan Sea.

Until Alexander—Theodosia's newly inherited, vigorously attentive slave steward—proposed a solution that caused Rome's greatest living military hero to respond with a remarkable level of courtesy.

"If you wish, sir, I can find a playmate for him."

"Yes, please."

Which led to her very first encounter with Lycos, another newly inherited slave, a previously abused little boy.

From that point on, she had marveled as—under Alexander's gentle care and skillful tutelage—that frightened child grew into a quick-witted youth, and then into Alexander's trusted partner, and then into Myrine's loving husband, and then into the devoted father of their two boys.

Witnessing that transformation had been one of the most gratifying experiences of Theodosia's life. But now...

Lycos is dead. His sons are dead. And no telling what they're doing to Alexander in the garrison.

***

Early on the penultimate day of December, Theodosia went back to the Praetorian Gate, carrying yet another steaming bowl of stew. A strong wind had whipped up overnight, complicating the task of carrying the bowl while keeping her stola and palla modestly wrapped around her.

The crowd that had gathered by the water at the start of this ordeal no longer showed up. And so, for the last ten days, at that same hour and without witnesses, she had handed the bowl to a guard and accepted back the previous one. But this morning, there were no guards on duty.

Carefully, she set the bowl and its heat-protective cushion on the ground, readjusted her palla, and pushed on the gate. It was locked.

Three rounds of loud banging were required before a soldier she had never seen before opened the door.

"I've brought today's meal for my husband," she said.

"He's not here." This fellow wore the same chain mail and displayed the same provincial accent as the other auxiliaries, but his Latin was better. "They took him away last night."

"Took him?" Fears raced to her tongue. "Who? Where? How?"

"Our second-in-command took him to Athens. Via Piraeus, of course."

"Why?"

"To stand trial."

"But he's committed no crime!"

"That's for Governor Vibius Galarius to decide." The soldier flashed a read-something-into-this-if-you-can smile. "Isn't it?"

He began closing the door, but Theodosia grabbed its edge with both her hands and stopped the motion.

"Tell me, please." She scrutinized his face. "What's he accused of?"

The soldier dodged her eyes as, one by one, he peeled her fingers off the door. "Theft," he said under his breath, "and capital murder."

***

Theodosia returned home to find a scruffy man in hard-worn clothing—a slave, as it turned out, from Stefan and Iocaste's farm—standing beside the kitchen fire, gulping down a bowl of Myrine's fish stew.

Too upset even to sit, Theodosia unloaded on her family and also on the stranger in her kitchen the disastrous news about Alexander.

And then, as four sets of horrified eyes engaged each other around the room, Stefan's slave handed her a torn, previously used sheet of papyrus.

What now?

She struggled to read past the old, scratched-out writing to the semi-literate Greek words scrawled around the edges.

Theodosia— Big problem.
Soldiers came. Took Stefanos. To Athens. For trial. For thief.
Tell commander at fort. I pay good ransom. —Iocaste

It's clear, she hasn't heard about Alexander.

"No point asking about Stefan at the garrison," Theodosia said after she'd repeated Iocaste's message to the others. "If they're taking him to Athens, he'll be gone already on the same bireme as Alexander."

Abruptly Myrine switched the discussion into Aramaic.

"Good thing they're together on that ship. Master Stefanos is stronger and tougher and younger than Master Alexander. Maybe they can escape."

Myrine's shrewd. Doros and I understand what she said, but the farm slave doesn't, so there's no way he can report us to the garrison and bargain for his freedom as a reward.

"You are right," Theodosia replied in Aramaic. "Stefan will free Alexander, as well as himself."

"Sorry, Mother, but I don't think so." Doros spoke in Aramaic, too, and with his usual confidence about military matters. "The soldiers will keep them chained to the ship's walls in separate cells."

All Theodosia heard for several long moments was the sharply crackling fire and Myrine's softly gurgling baby.

After a time, Doros stepped forward and wrapped his arms around her.

My boy comes all the way up to my shoulders now.

"Let's go to Athens," he said, still in Aramaic and also still in the new, serious-and-assertive voice that his mother was coming to appreciate. "You and me. We'll convince the governor to free them both."

"What chance would we have, all by ourselves?"

Myrine jumped in again, still in Aramaic. "Let me go with you. I know I can't talk to the governor, but there's other ways I can help, even if it's just making sure you two dress warm and eat good."

Olinda was sitting on the floor, humming, as she rocked her baby sister.

Theodosia pointed to them and continued in Aramaic.

"We can't leave your daughters here alone, and we can't take them with us to Athens."

"Mistress Iocaste will welcome them. She'll have women nursing their own babies who can do the same for my sweet Anthousa."

Yes, as shrewd as always… and also way ahead of me.

"Getting both men home could take ten days." Theodosia mulled it over. "Maybe fifteen. Might even be a month, if things don't go well. And by Juno, I doubt we even have enough money to last a month."

As her mistress dithered, Myrine took charge.

She clapped the farm slave on his back and switched out of Aramaic to address him in Greek.

"My daughters and I will ride to the farm with you today. Tomorrow mornin', you'll bring me back here."

He frowned. "But what if my Mistress Iocaste don't—"

"I grew up with your Mistress Iocaste. She'll be happy to see us, and she'll say… leavin' my girls with her is a fine idea."

***

On the morning of the last day of December, at the exact same time that Myrine was on her way back from delivering her daughters to Iocaste, Theodosia hired the owner of a small fishing boat to convey her, Doros, and Myrine to the port at Piraeus tomorrow.

Tomorrow. That's important.

The fact that the trip would take place *tomorrow* mattered a lot, because tomorrow was the first day of the month named for Janus, the two-headed Roman spirit of doorways and archways, who famously looked both forward and backward at once and offered good omens… but only—as Theodosia recalled the story from her childhood—for new endeavors begun at the start of *his* month.

"That's especially important," she said as Myrine and Doros packed essential items into their gunnysacks, "since we no longer have our viper amulet to keep us safe and bring us luck."

CHAPTER 17

Twilight settled in early on the short first day of the year as a driver from Piraeus carried Theodosia, Myrine, Doros and their bags in his donkey cart past a Roman garrison, past weedy fields between temples and tombs, past crumbling remnants of the famous Long Walls that for centuries had protected Athens from invaders, to the center of the elegantly constructed, colorfully painted, and frenetically utilized public market and gathering spot called the Agora.

Never before had either Myrine or Doros left the island of Euboea, and even though Theodosia had traveled farther in her life than they, this was still her first time in Athens, the most culturally acclaimed city in the world.

So now, snugly bundled against the cold air, standing beside their gunnysacks, they ignored their most urgent need—finding a safe place to spend the night—and gaped in amazement at the remarkable scene that loomed above them.

Most Athenians and foreigners had disappeared into their homes and inns, but in their stead, as if rising specifically to greet the strangers, the full moon shone silver-white in the soft black sky that offered a perfect backdrop for their first glimpse of the Parthenon.

It was also a stunning introduction to the towering rock known as the Acropolis, whose precipitous bluffs supported the famous temple that all three of the newcomers had heard of their entire lives.

Seeing the Parthenon's marble columns and statues by moonlight proved especially hard for Myrine. Tears welled in her eyes, as they often did these days.

"Growin' up," she said, "I heard magical stories 'bout this place, but I didn't never think I'd travel far enough to see it. Just wish Lycos and our boys was here with us."

***

They took the last available bed in The Garden Patch, an ancient firetrap of an inn wedged between two others in a narrow alley in the heart of the Agora's teeming bazaar.

The room was located up three flights of rickety stairs. With just one flimsy mattress, no storage chests, and no fireplace, it was cramped and cold but also cheap enough with a discounted, pay-in-advance rate.

Theodosia, Doros, and Myrine agreed they could tolerate it for a few days.

As she paid the innkeeper, Theodosia silently prayed to Juno for the continued health and safety of Iocaste, who not only had taken Myrine's daughters into her home but also had sent Theodosia a fat bag of gold and silver coins. "Bring my Stefanos back to me, please," was Iocaste's verbal request, as Myrine had reported when she delivered the money to her mistress yesterday afternoon.

From the rooftop terrace—which opened off their tiny room and would have been an appealing amenity in a warmer month—the innkeeper pointed out the Theater of Dionysus, sprawling in the shadows at the very foot of the Acropolis.

"Go there at midnight," he told Doros, "sit still, be quiet, and listen. They say Sophocles always strolls by."

"The great tragedian from five hundred years ago?"

My boy does love to show off his knowledge.

Still, she smiled at him. "You've got the right Sophocles, but I'd much rather see your father stroll by."

***

Father will find out who cares the most about him.

Optimistically, for over an hour—as the strap of his heavy, orange-colored sack dug into his shoulder—Nikolaos made repeated loops past the mansions of the hilltop neighborhood that surrounded the imperial governor's high-walled palace. He recalled it well from one special day years ago when Alexander had first brought him from Eretria and introduced him to Athens.

On this second morning of the new year, a frigid fog enshrouded the coast. Within an hour it began to lift, offering tantalizing hints of the views that the city's most privileged residents enjoyed in good weather.

But slowly, noting his target's few entrances, his optimism waned. The governor's immense house was built and guarded like a fortress.

No way in.

He kicked a few rocks to the other side of the street, then tossed the sack to the ground and slouched against it to consider his options.

Household slaves know everything that goes on in their master's house. Bet that's true of household guards as well.

Four well-armed men stood at the only gate that Nikolaos had seen leading into the compound. While watchful, they kept bantering back and forth, laughing at one another's jokes.

Brothel humor, for sure. Nothing stiff and stuffy about these fellows. A few nice bribes and they'll tell me how to find Father. Maybe even take me to him.

Soon, he had his plan.

Fish market's this side of the Agora. I'll buy each one a lamprey eel.

He pulled a handful of silver drachmas out of the orange sack, slipped them into the money purse at his belt, hoisted the weighty monstrosity to his shoulder again, and headed down the steep slope toward the Agora.

No way can they afford expensive eels on their salaries.

***

A block away, Nikolaos halted so fast that he almost lost his balance.

Right in front of him, climbing the same steep hill—and on the same side of the street no less—came the Roman woman, her brat, and Myrine.

What in Hades are they doing here?

He shrugged the bulky sack off his shoulder, set it down, and waited for them to notice him.

They'll not be glad to see me either. Well, too bad, because they are going to see me.

And they did.

The women stopped abruptly and stared at him as the wind tossed their head coverings and tendrils of hair blew around their faces.

But their not-so-little-anymore, would-be soldier did not stop. With an obstinate expression on his face, Doros marched on up the hill. "Nikolaos, what are you doing here?" he demanded loudly in Aramaic.

Myrine must've taught him.

Nikolaos answered in Aramaic. "I've come to free my father."

"That's what we're here for, too."

Of course, so you and your damn mother can take credit for it.

Below them, the Roman woman gawked as if she couldn't believe what her eyes were seeing.

But Myrine bounded forward with clenched fists, ready to smash Nikolaos as she smashed cockroaches in her kitchen. "You bloody butcher!" she bellowed in Greek. "You murdered my husband!"

"Shut up, Myrine. The guards are close enough to hear you."

And while they may be Romans, they'll understand her Greek just fine.

She showed no sign of shutting up. "Poisoned my sons, too!"

Regardless of the consequences, he rammed the heels of his hands into her thick breasts. "Shut up!"

Myrine's face flamed even more than normal, if that was possible, but his double-punch strike didn't faze her. She came at him even more fiercely than before.

"And you stole my master's life savings!"

He glanced at the guards, all of whom were watching the scuffle.

"That's his money you're totin' around, ain't it?" She grabbed the neck of his orange sack with one of her enormous hands and lifted it off the ground.

Nikolaos snatched it back from her and sneered. "You can't prove that or any of your other lies."

"You stole everythin' he and Lycos worked for!" she screeched. "And then—like the slimy, rapin' coward that you are—you ran away!"

At that, his annoyance turned into a rage that matched her own. "By all the gods, I'll have you strung up naked in the Agora and whipped!"

"You will do nothing of the sort," the Roman woman said in Greek from a couple of feet away. "I'll tolerate no more abuse of her."

How did she make it up the hill so fast?

"I most certainly can and will have her punished," he said, "because in my father's absence, I'm her legal master."

Myrine's eyes all but popped out of her head as she rushed him again.

Towering over her, Nikolaos locked his fingers around her wrists, jerked her back and forth, and laughed in her face.

Damn bitch thinks she's strong, but she's no match for me. Truly powerless, both legally and physically, and she needs to know it.

Before either Nikolaos or Myrine could say or do anything more, the Roman woman raised both her hands with her fingers outstretched.

"That's enough, Myrine. Hello, Nikolaos."

About time she tried being pleasant.

And she remained remarkably pleasant.

"You and we have come to the same place at the same time, so I'm guessing we've all learned the same facts and come to the same conclusions."

He glared at her. "Conclusions?"

"I bet you have concluded, as we have, that your father is in there." She nodded toward the governor's palace. "Maybe you've even devised a plan to get him out, as we have."

"I sure have, and I'll be damned if you or your snotty brat or your nasty slave are anywhere around when Father walks free."

Her face registered no emotion.

"Your father's life is at stake, Nikolaos. Saving him is the only thing that matters to me."

"And the only thing that matters to me."

"Good." She smiled at that. "So, let's cooperate and get it done."

"When have you ever cooperated with me?"

"Look, I'm truly sorry we haven't gotten along in the past, but let's do this one thing together and then we can each go our own way."

"I've no desire to do anything with you."

If I follow her lead and we get Father out, he'll give her all the credit.

"Before you dismiss my idea," the Roman woman said, "please listen."

"Not interested."

He shouldered his sack and was about to walk when she seized his arm.

"Again, I ask you. Let's go in *together* and talk with the governor. He's the most powerful man in Greece. If you, Doros, and I—*all of us together as Alexander's family*—if we appeal directly to him, he'll listen."

He shook off her hand and headed downhill.

Time to go buy those eels.

"Nikolaos," she called from behind, "this isn't a competition."

Doros ran down the slope and leaped in front of him. "You and my mother want the same thing," he said, also in Greek. "Why are you fighting her?"

Why not fight her?

"We're more likely to get Father out," the brat went on, mixing his usual intensity with a rare quiet voice, "if we work together."

Nikolaos waved a hand at the governor's mansion. "There's no way in. I've checked. Spent several hours walking around, looking for a secret entrance. It's not possible."

The Roman woman came limping down to where they stood. "You forget that my father was once the governor of Corinth. And the daughter of a former governor of Corinth does not have to sneak into the home of the current governor of Athens."

She's desperate. Knows she won't get any credit when I save Father.

She smoothed her white silk stola and tucked the flighty tendrils under her palla. Then, without another look at Nikolaos, she crooked a finger for Myrine and Doros to follow her back up the hill.

As Nikolaos watched, they approached the only gate in the forbiddingly high wall around the governor's mansion. After a brief conversation, the guards opened the gate and let them in.

∗∗∗

Theodosia, Doros, and Myrine followed the guard along the path that led to the governor's mansion. The slave then remained with the porter at the front entrance.

The moment Theodosia stepped into the Roman atrium, she felt at home.

For this to work, I have to reveal my full, true identity to the next level of gatekeeper. And I will.

Very soon, the Roman governor of Athens strode into the atrium and embraced her.

Governor Publius Vibius Galarius radiated the refined air typical of an elderly man in his position. Every last detail of his appearance—his finely loomed toga and closely shaved chin and expertly trimmed hair and perfectly groomed nails and exquisitely crafted pin and tastefully coordinated rings and smoothly polished sandals and deftly gemmed dagger—spoke of old money taken for granted and casually spent on swarms of highly specialized slaves.

He led Theodosia and Doros to a circle of red-cushioned chairs in his study. She slipped the palla off her head, shook out the natural waves in her hair, and pointed toward a series of brilliantly colored frescoes of classic Homeric battles.

"The walls of our ancestral home are decorated with murals like these," she told Doros. "Some day, I'll take you there to see them."

Vibius Galarius gestured for a slave to pour wine, which Theodosia immediately recognized as Falernian.

"It's every bit as sweet as I remember," she said as Doros savored his first taste of the upper-class Roman's favorite beverage. "Do you like it?"

Doros nodded and emptied his cup, which the slave refilled.

The governor raised his eyebrows. "You don't drink Falernian now?"

"Too expensive, but I grew up with it, so I do know what I'm missing."

Have to make sure he understands we come from the same class.

In the end, that effort wasn't needed, for it turned out that the governor had known her father decades earlier and was happy to share amusing anecdotes of two randy young patricians enjoying the high life together in Rome.

After a tediously nostalgic hour, Theodosia steered the topic back to the reason for her visit.

But that proved worthless, too, because the emperor's hand-picked agent in this all-important Greek province professed total—and for a governor, highly remarkable—ignorance of recent events on the island of Euboea, which fell entirely under his control and wasn't so very far away.

No knowledge of the murder of a young businessman.

No knowledge of the arrest of a respected merchant.

No knowledge of a prosperous farmer accused of theft.

No knowledge of the abrupt departure of the garrison staff.

No knowledge of anything.

And even worse… not only did the governor not know about those events, but he showed no curiosity about any of them, not even when Theodosia explained in great detail what had happened on the island and how it impacted her family and friends.

No interest in anything. This isn't worth another moment of my time.

At last, she finished her wine and stood. "Governor, we mustn't interrupt your day any more."

Doros bounced out of his chair, clearly ready to leave.

The governor rose, too. "You're lodging nearby, I assume."

"A modest little spot in the Agora called The Garden Patch."

His nose wrinkled. "Why there when we have so many superb inns in our better neighborhoods?"

"Well, The Patch, as we call it, is perfectly fine. We'll only be in Athens for two or three more days anyway."

Can't have him thinking we're too poor to stay anywhere else. And for sure, we won't linger much longer if things don't go better than this.

A few moments later, as they passed through the atrium, his crab-like hand gripped her arm. His disdain turned instantly to showy grief.

"Oh, my dearest Theodosia," oozed the governor, "I just remembered. Your brother was murdered some years back, wasn't he? I was commanding my legion in the northern provinces at that time so wasn't aware of it until later, but… Gods, what a horror!"

Under the pretext of arranging her palla over her hair, Theodosia slipped out of his grasp.

"I'm much more interested," she said pointedly, "in a recent murder in Eretria than a very old one in Rome."

"Well, of course you are, but still—" He grimaced. "Patricians just don't get themselves killed on the streets of Rome. So, my dear, you *must* come back to fill me in on all the details."

As they neared the door, Myrine bowed respectfully and fell in close behind them.

"I should have asked before," Galarius went on, "if you know another old friend of mine, General Vespasian. Now, Governor Vespasian."

Theodosia recalled Alexander's long-ago warning.

"Make sure nobody ever learns how close you were to Vespasian."

Her mouth went dry. "I met him once or twice. He and his family lived in Caere, not far from our villa."

"Then you must know his son, Titus. You're about the same age."

Can't tell him how often Titus asked me to marry him.

"I saw him a few times." She scrambled for a way to end this perilous conversation. "He wouldn't remember me after all these years."

Theodosia shot a glance at Myrine. Her eyes were down and her face was blank, as a well-trained slave's should be at such times, but her mistress had no doubt she was listening.

From everything I've told her, she knows that's a lie. Fortunately, she's too smart to say anything.

"What a pity," the governor said, "because General Titus happens to be in Athens right now. I would've arranged a dinner for you two if I'd known you were in town and that you once were friends."

Titus is a general now? And in Athens?

"What's he doing here?" she asked.

"Nero ordered Vespasian to Judea late last year. Titus's visit is tied in with that."

"I heard a bit about Judea but no details. What's going on there?"

"Peasant revolt. Happens in that miserable land from time to time, but this one's the worst in a century. I worked in Jerusalem for two years as a junior officer on Governor Pontius Pilate's staff, so I've been following this latest mess with interest."

"Is it as bad as that rebellion in Britain that Vespasian squashed twenty years ago?"

"Well, this one's only been going on a few months." The governor signaled for his porter to open the door. "No telling how long it will last."

He accompanied her down the path, all the way to the gate, as Doros and Myrine trailed behind.

"Just between you and me," the governor said under his breath, "Nero wants Vespasian to wreak even more havoc on the Jews than he did on the northern barbarians. He's determined to make an example of them."

"Enslave them?"

"Enslave them, sure, but also rape them, butcher them, burn their fields, destroy their cattle, smash their towns, pillage their cities, crush their army, and so on." The governor snickered. "Wiser heads in Rome have argued against that approach."

"I would hope so."

"Problem is, the Jews are not primitive, illiterate barbarians like the tribes Vespasian put to the sword in Britain. They're well-educated, smart, and shrewd, and while they may well be the world's most aggravating people, they do—like the Greeks they despise—have a remarkable culture."

"A lot older than ours, I believe."

"And more complex, which is part of the problem. They consider themselves superior to us Romans, with our shorter history and scores of gods and spirits. They won't surrender without a bloodbath on both sides."

"Are they good warriors?"

"That's the thing. The Jews really do know how to fight."

***

Theodosia, Doros, and Myrine stepped into the street.

The fog had lifted.

The sky was blue.

And Nikolaos was nowhere to be seen.

"Guess he's off to rescue Father in his own way," said Doros.

"Good riddance," said Myrine.

Good riddance, indeed.

***

That night, as Myrine snored on her pallet on the floor, Theodosia lay awake in the bed she shared with Doros, fretting over her failed conversation with the governor.

She stared at the ceiling.

Wish I'd asked him to put me in touch with Titus.

And stretched her legs.

It would've been so easy for him to do.

And tugged on the blanket.

Although terribly risky for us.

And closed her eyes.
Titus holds the key to saving Alexander.
And tried to sleep.
I'll find another way to get to Titus.
And had an inspiration.
There's one other place he could be.
And spent several more hours fleshing out that idea.
Alexander and Stefan might be there, too.
By dawn, she had finalized a plan.

***

Early the next morning—after dismissing Doros's pleas to tag along and admonishing him and Myrine to keep their distance from Nikolaos if they saw him again in the street—Theodosia hired a driver to take her to the Roman garrison that she had seen two days before on the ride out from Piraeus.

As the man's plum-color painted cart rumbled past marble temples and mud cottages, she ran through the eight-step scheme she had devised during the dark hours.

1. *Hire a driver for the whole day.*
2. *At the garrison, ask about Titus and try to see him.*
3. *Bribe the guards if necessary.*
4. *Meet the commander or his deputy if Titus isn't there.*
5. *Persuade them to let me see Alexander and Stefan.*
6. *Make sure those two are well enough to travel.*
7. *Negotiate the ransom price and pay it.*
8. *Leave for The Patch with Alexander and Stefan, collect Doros and Myrine, return to Piraeus, find a boat, and immediately depart for Eretria.*

She had paid the driver, in advance and in full, for waiting around and being available the entire day, so the first and last steps were easy.

It's those six steps in between that'll be tricky.

***

Scores of fish wagons heading from Piraeus to the Agora added pungence to the air along the road as Theodosia and her driver neared the Roman fort on the coastal plain.

No invading force could enter the port, much less attack Athens from the sea, without being intercepted by the soldiers at this garrison. But no one challenged the plum-colored cart as it made its way up the sloping driveway to the Praetorian Gate.

Just like the sloping driveway in Eretria.

Soldiers in the same flashy, red-and-brass uniforms strutted atop identical high walls. Others stood at attention by an indistinguishable Praetorian Gate.

Everything's exactly like the fortress in Eretria.

The driver helped his passenger out of the cart and pulled to the western side of the wall to wait.

Theodosia adjusted her palla, lifted her head, and approached the two guards at the gate.

"I'm here to see General Titus. He's an old friend of mine from Rome, and he invited me to visit him here this morning."

"I doubt that," drawled one legionary whose accent identified him as a native speaker of Latin, not an auxiliary, "since he's not here."

Theodosia cocked her head. "When will he be back?"

"He's never been here, so how can he come back?"

She ignored the sarcasm. "Any idea where I might find him?"

"Not at leave to say."

The second guard, also a native-sounding speaker, turned out to be friendlier and more willing to talk.

"I didn't even know General Titus was in Athens. Just assumed he'd be in Judea by now, with his father."

"I have it on good authority," Theodosia said with a brighter cheeriness than she felt, "that if he's not lodging here, he's lodging somewhere else very near here."

"Check with Governor Vibius Galarius in Athens." The nicer guard gave her a big smile. "He'll know if General Titus is anywhere around. Probably will help you find him, too."

No way I'm going back there.

She tried not to show her disappointment.

"Well, since General Titus isn't here, I'd like to speak with your commander."

"Have an appointment?" It was the first guard again.

"Not with him, no, but since I'm a Roman woman, he'll certainly want to see me."

The first guard chuckled. "Not unless you're on a mission from Caesar and can prove it."

Theodosia chuckled, too, and leaned toward him as if sharing a vital secret. "I'm definitely not on a mission from Caesar."

As before, the second guard was more affable but no more helpful. "To tell you the truth, lady, our centurion, Fulvius Viridis, never meets with civilians."

Centurion Fulvius Viridis. Must remember that name.

"Perhaps his deputy would be willing to see me."

"Most unlikely." The first guard turned his back on her.

"Sorry." The second guard actually did sound sorry. "It's just not possible."

CHAPTER 18

The plum-colored donkey cart stood waiting for Theodosia near the southwestern corner of the fort, well away from the gate.

As she approached it, inspiration struck a second time.

Aula said the smaller garrisons are all alike.

"I'll be a while longer," she said to the driver.

Guards atop the front wall faced south, toward the sea, so she set out to walk the square perimeter along its other three sides. There were plenty of scrubby bushes, but just past the northwestern corner she found what she was seeking: a low door like the one she had used occasionally in Eretria.

She pushed the shrubbery aside and tried the door. It opened.

She ducked in. Straightened her clothing. Scrutinized the area.

Layout's the same. North-south thoroughfare. Cross roads. Parade ground. Dining hall. Barracks. Baths. Verandas. Headquarters building. Low wall.

She glanced at the parapet on the opposite wall. The guards gazed outward, away from her, their attention fixed on the port of Piraeus and beyond.

And my way is clear, straight to the headquarters building.

***

A slender officer in the usual red-and-brass uniform stood with his back to her, searching through a stack of rolled purple scrolls on a deep wall shelf.

Purple parchments. Orders from the emperor.

Theodosia stood as straight and tall as her legs allowed, breathed long and deep, and set her mind for success.

"Forgive the interruption." She kept her voice low. Concentrated on sounding confident. "The guards said you would help me."

He nodded, as if to acknowledge her presence, but made no reply.

"I'm here to meet with Centurion Fulvius Viridis."

The officer still did not face her. "He never receives callers without appointments."

"I made an appointment several days ago."

At this stage of things, one more little lie can't hurt.

"He has no appointments today." The officer pulled two purple-dyed scrolls from the shelf, deposited one on his desk, unrolled the other, and began reading it.

"But someone else in this office, perhaps his deputy, told me three days ago to come back today at this hour."

"I'm his deputy." He kept his back to her. "The only one who works here."

"Then it must have been you."

"It was not me."

She raised her voice. "The reason why I scheduled an appointment with the centurion—" Abruptly, she interrupted herself.

Telling the truth and getting straight to the point usually works best.

So she reversed course. "To be honest, I came to see my husband. Perhaps you know his name. Alexander."

For the first time, the deputy looked at her.

"Alexander," she repeated. "He's a respected merchant who brought prosperity to the island of Euboea."

"We know that."

They know it. Does that confirm his presence here?

"Prisoners in the dungeon," the deputy went on, "are not allowed to receive visitors."

He is here!

"Could I send a message to him?"

A scowl creased his smooth forehead. "That's not allowed either."

She took a few moments to consider her next move.

"Perhaps it would help if you informed the centurion that my father once served as governor of Corinth."

"Irrelevant." The deputy turned back to his purple parchment.

"Please, sir, look at me again."

With obvious reluctance, he set the scroll down and did as she asked.

She extended her hands, palms up, in the ancient, eternal gesture of supplication. "Will you at least tell me one thing?"

The deputy blinked a few times.

A break in his resistance?

She stepped closer and wrapped her fingers around one of his arms. "Are my husband, Alexander, and his friend, a farmer named Stefanos, being held here?"

The deputy yanked his arm away. "Not at leave to say!" His eyes widened.

He looks remarkably familiar.

She pursued a hunch. "Any chance you're related to Centurion Paulinus, who commanded the garrison on the island of Euboea until December?"

He blinked again. And looked around. And strode to the door. And leaned out. And checked in both directions. And shut the door. And looked at her once more.

"I'll tell you my name, lady, and you can figure out the rest. I'm Sextus Norbanus Paulinus."

Sextus. Aula's sixth and youngest child. The one who did his officer training after I met her.

Theodosia took a deep breath and studied his face.

And he knows who I am.

"I will tell you what you ask, but you must promise—" Again, he looked around.

"Promise what?"

"No one must ever know that I spoke with you, much less that I told you anything."

"Yes, I do promise that. No one will ever hear about this at all."

For sure, I will keep that promise.

The young man lowered his voice. "Your husband and his friend are here for the time being."

For the time being.

Theodosia's heart raced. "Where is the dungeon?"

"Not at leave to say."

"How long will they be here?"

More blinks. "Not much longer."

"Are you saying they'll soon be set free—"

"You must go now—"

"Or sent somewhere else?"

 "And never mention my name—"

"Please, which is it?"

"To anyone."

"Why won't you answer me?"

The metal segments of his breastplate clinked as he grabbed her shoulders, marched her to the door, opened it, and shoved her out.

Theodosia resisted long enough to leave him with one important bit of information. "Tell your mother I'm staying at The Garden Patch, in the heart of the Agora."

An instant later, he slammed the door in her face.

Theodosia stood alone in the courtyard, expecting someone to come and insist that she leave the fort, but no one seemed aware of her presence.

Ten steps down the main north-south thoroughfare, she stopped and looked around. Guards atop the southern wall kept watching the sea.

In all my visits to Aula, I never asked where the dungeon was located.

A side road took her eastward, away from the headquarters, the main gate, and the secret door.

Obviously, it's underground, but how does one get in?

She kept going until she reached the eastern wall, where she turned left onto an unpaved path that ran inside the perimeter.

Then, suddenly…

Someone high up on the rampart whistled.

Someone on the ground picked up on the alert.

Someone behind her shouted. "Intruder! East wall!"

Faster than she could have imagined, a dozen soldiers surrounded her, hustled her out through the Praetorian Gate, and unceremoniously escorted her to the plum-colored cart.

Without inquiring about his passenger's peculiar methods of entry and exit, the driver carried her back to The Patch.

***

At sunset that evening, a military courier in a hooded red cloak arrived at The Patch with a verbal message for Theodosia.

"Leave Athens now," he told her in native Latin as he stood in the doorway. "Take your little soldier son. Go home to Eretria. You accomplish nothing here. You're not helping your husband's situation."

Theodosia's first reaction, after two frustrating, dead-end days in a row, was acceptance.

Good advice.

She reached into her money pouch for a small bronze coin, tipped the courier, and dismissed him.

But then, moments later...

Who was that fellow? How did he know I have a son who wants to be a soldier? And that I came here from Eretria? And where I'm staying? And that my husband is in a "situation."

From a hook on the wall, she grabbed her cloak, then she threw it over her shoulders and pursued him through the fast-darkening shadows.

Neither of them carried a lamp, so the only light came in narrow strips from shuttered windows above and around them.

A tantalizing aroma of fried fish permeated the neighborhood.

"Stop," she called as her quarry passed a closed-up potter's shop. "Please wait for me."

To her surprise, he stopped and waited.

"You speak perfect Latin." She pulled a few more coins from her money belt. "Who are you?"

"Not at leave to say."

"Who sent me that message?"

"Not at leave to say."

"Was it the governor?"

"Not at leave to say."

She flashed a silver coin—a very generous bribe—in front of his eyes. "So, then, don't say anything. Either nod or shake your head. Was it the governor?"

The courier stared at the coin and shook his head.

"Was it a young Greek named Nikolaos?"

Another shake.

"Was it an older Greek named Alexander?"

That's not likely, but I do have to try.

The courier peered down the street in both directions. Another shake.

Not the governor. Not Nikolaos. Not Alexander. Who else?

"Was it a young soldier named Sextus Norbanus Paulinus?"

Another shake.

"Or maybe the young soldier's father, Centurion Marcus Norbanus Paulinus?" She was running out of ideas.

After a long hesitation, the courier shook his head a fifth time.

That hesitation.

"Was it the centurion's wife?"

This time, the courier did not shake his head.

"Aula?" Theodosia clarified.

Finally, he nodded.

Aula!

"Oh, sir, thank you." She pressed the silver coin into his palm as relief and gratitude spread across her face in the form of a wide smile. "You may not know it, but the lady Aula is my very best friend."

Her message was carefully worded. No doubt she's doing something for us behind the scenes.

"Tell me one more thing, please." Theodosia dug into her pouch again. "Where's she living now?"

"Not at leave to say."

She flashed two more silver coins. "You don't have *say* where she lives, just walk there. Slowly, so I can follow you."

The man eyed the coins and nodded once more.

"Stop in the street," she said, "and face her house. No one will notice. I'll pass by, hand you these coins, and we'll go our separate ways. You'll never see me again, and no one will ever learn what a great favor you've done for me tonight."

***

Around mid-morning the next day, Theodosia retraced the courier's steps to a modest, one-story house in an old neighborhood several blocks outside the Agora and knocked on its bright-yellow door.

Not sure this is wise, but…

The red-haired maid who opened the door was the same one who for years had served Theodosia in Aula's sitting room. She showed no surprise at who was calling, but neither did she offer any sign of recognition.

"My mistress is not at home." She shut the door without asking, as a well-trained servant should, if she could take a message.

Theodosia knocked a second time, then a third, but nothing happened.

Back in the bustling Agora, she ducked into the shop of Athens' most famous public scribe, easily identifiable by the outline of a reed pen and the name "Balios the Scribe" burned into a wooden plank over the door. Since arriving in Athens, she had come here alone twice a day to enjoy a break from her son and her slave and all the other guests in the overcrowded Garden Patch.

On her way to the long writing table reserved for customers, she passed stacks of fresh papyrus, bins filled with reed pens and small glass vials of black ink, and shelves of new parchment scrolls. She purchased a sheet of papyrus, a pen, and some ink and sat down to write.

Aula— I need to speak with you.
Please meet me tomorrow morning before midday
in the shop of Balios the Scribe in the Agora.
It's warm and quiet with mountain tea, mulled wine,
and delicious honey cakes. My treat. —Theodosia

She returned to Aula's house and slipped the papyrus under the door. *The promise of sweets will get her there, if anything will.*

***

From his perch on a high stool behind a wooden counter, Balios the Scribe grunted in recognition.

His assistant's green wool sleeve brushed Theodosia's elbow as he set her usual morning cup of hot, spiced wine on the table. Its enticing flavor—a mixture of cinnamon, cloves, nutmeg and other aromas that permeated the shop—was the main reason she came here.

Although a tempting array of pastries sat on a nearby counter, she wasn't about to waste coins on them.

Not till Aula shows up. Then I'll gladly pay.

"May I prepare a document for you today?" the assistant asked, as he always did, with the air of one who repeats the same formulaic question several hundred times a day.

Theodosia wrapped her fingers around the warm cup, inhaled its heady vapor, and declined his offer, as she always did.

"A letter perhaps," he persisted, "or a contract of some sort?"

"I'm expecting a friend to join me. She may have something that needs copying." She smiled, more sympathetic to his plight as a peddler of writing services than he could possibly know, but she did have a very special reason.

This is how Alexander supported me in Siracusa. Helping people with their correspondence and contracts. Serving them wine and sweets. Laboring under the eye of a stony-faced shop owner.

Four hours passed with no appearance by Aula. Theodosia pushed the cold wine cup aside, crossed her hands on the table, pressed her forehead to her knuckles, and silently prayed.

Dearest Juno, I do so love Alexander, but with almost no allies or resources, I'm going to need a lot of help from you to save him.

***

That evening, about the same time as before, the red-cloaked courier reappeared at The Patch. The innkeeper notified Theodosia of his presence.

She found him waiting just outside and followed him down the same dark street, inhaling the same odor of fried fish, until he stopped in front of the same closed-up potter's shop.

"You must not go there again," he said from deep within his hood. "You put her husband in danger."

"My husband is already in danger."

"She's at risk, too."

Theodosia pressed her fingertips into her temples. "Because of me?"

"If there's news, you'll be informed… assuming you leave them alone."

"How will I be informed? Through you?"

He shrugged. "However they choose. Good-bye."

"No!" Theodosia seized a fold of his cloak.

"Let go."

Reluctantly, she did. "I must understand— Did this second message come from Aula, her husband, her son, or someone else?"

Without a word, the courier moved on down the street.

Theodosia followed. "How do you know her? Or them?"

The courier made no response, just kept walking.

"When can I see her?" she called.

At that, he tossed his cape back and swirled around. "If you don't go home—" His face was still invisible under the hood. "If you keep probing—"

A horizontal bar of light from a nearby window fell across his index finger, which was now pointed directly at Theodosia's face.

"You will never see her or your husband or your big friend again."

***

Before dawn the next morning, dressed in her warmest woolen stola and with her head and face concealed under a thick black shawl, Theodosia positioned herself at the mouth of a wedge-shaped alley straight across the street from Aula's bright-yellow door.

Nobody coming or going from the house was likely to spot her, but she could see everything that took place there.

Following her second hunch in as many days, she had come prepared to wait, but things happened faster than she expected.

Even before the sun cleared the nearby buildings, her ears detected high-pitched voices and a crunch of footsteps that stopped before they crossed through the intersection in front of the alley.

Cautiously, she peeked around the corner.

A slender young officer—wearing a red military cape exactly like the courier's—approached Aula's door and knocked. In his arms, he carried a small, well-bundled child. An older boy walked beside him.

The door opened promptly, and all three stepped in. Moments later, the door opened again and the young officer left alone.

***

Theodosia repeated her watch the next morning and several more mornings after that. The routine never changed, and soon it all made sense.

Sextus Norbanus Paulinus works at the garrison in Piraeus, but he lives in Athens near his father and mother and brings his children to spend each day with them. The courier is probably someone they all know.

***

Nothing Nikolaos tried got him into the governor's mansion or the garrison near Piraeus, yet the Roman woman had managed to talk with top-tier officials in both places. At least, that was what her brat boastfully told him when they bumped into one another in the Agora.

But he wasn't worried, because he had his own method of investigating.

In Piraeus, he had rented a room in a building surrounded by scores of bars and brothels that lined the alleys along the waterfront. The most popular of these was a rowdy joint named Sailor's Delight.

So now he spent his evenings there.

Putting his father's savings to good use…

Carousing with off-duty soldiers and sailors…

Swapping drinks and whores for useful information…

Amazing what you can coax out of people if you have an unlimited supply of money to pay for refreshments and fleshy enticements.

That was how he learned, in mid-January, that General Titus was assembling a flotilla of biremes and triremes to haul soldiers and supplies to the rebellious province of Judea.

And that was how he learned, late in January, that a Roman woman had broken into the garrison at Piraeus to chat with a well-connected young officer named Sextus Norbanus Paulinus.

And that was how he learned, early in February, that a huge, ruby-stealing Euboean farmer only had been questioned—but not tried or convicted—before he was sold to an itinerant slave trader who promptly shipped him off to a famous gladiatorial school in a secluded valley east of Rome.

And that was how he also learned, right in the middle of February, that trial had ended for a Greek merchant from the island of Euboea.

***

With stealth and cunning, Nikolaos ratcheted up the pressure on his buddies at the amusingly decorated Sailor's Delight.

By early February, two things were well known among the bar patrons.

First, if a fellow wanted to keep enjoying free drinks and his choice of slave girls or boys, thanks to the coins in Nikolaos's orange sack, he had to provide accurate, timely reports on the merchant who had been arrested in December in the port of Eretria on the island of Euboea.

Second, if a fellow brought in a friend who could offer useful details, the unlimited-drinks-and-sex-for-a-night offer was good for them both.

But still, even while dangling such irresistible temptations, Nikolaos had to spend an awful lot on wine-buying and whore-sharing to extract even the slightest bit of genuinely useful information.

None of the regular patrons or their guests were officers, so what they brought in was limited to what they had picked up by listening on their superiors, which tended to produce little more than second- or third-hand rumors.

And the guests never were warned in advance that they had been invited to experience the finest pleasures at Sailor's Delight in exchange for the treasonous act of revealing imperial secrets.

So, no wonder that it wasn't until the night of the Ides of February—when a jolly fellow named Gripus, a member of Governor Vibius Galarius's personal security detail, came in with one of the regulars—that Nikolaos finally got the full story he had been waiting for.

"I'll expect my reward tomorrow night," whispered the sailor after introducing Gripus to Nikolaos. "Nothing but the Double Duckie Delight will do."

Nikolaos grinned. "And you'll get it, assuming Gripus actually knows and is willing to tell me what you think he knows."

"He's the governor's favorite bodyguard. Present for everything. Sees everything. Knows everything."

Probably one of those joking jerks who never would let me in.

It took three wineskins, a flickering lamp, and a matched pair of Illyrian girls in a grimy, two-bed cubicle before Gripus's tongue began to loosen.

Nikolaos was careful to drink very little while still appearing sociable.

After he and Gripus had traded the wineskins and the slaves back and forth for a couple of hours, he turned to the happy fellow on the other rumpled mattress and let loose his best impersonation of a drunkard.

"Grip-pus— wha'cha know 'bout tha' crim'nal mer-chant wha' went on trial las' month?"

"Wha' crim'nal mer-chant?"

"Ol' guy from Euboea. Name's Alex-ander."

Tired of sex for once and eager for the information he was paying for, Nikolaos shoved the second girl off his bed and sent her scrambling from the room.

"Who's he t'you? Ah!" Gripus gasped as the girl in his bed, a fifteenish waif with uncombed black hair who spoke no Latin and wouldn't be likely to engage in intellectual conversation with the customers even if she did, lowered herself onto him for the third time that night.

"Jes' an ol' man I use' t' know."

"Bad news, bu— Ow!" Gripus yelped as the girl launched one more relentless assault on his not-yet-exhausted private parts. "By all th' gods, girl, don' stop!"

As Gripus savored her unabating energy, Nikolaos lounged back and inspected the Priapus decorations—a comically drawn series of male figures, each with a massive erection detailed in red paint—that covered the brown-spattered walls of the chamber.

Once Gripus was spent for what Nikolaos hoped was the last time tonight, the girl grabbed a rag to clean herself again.

No longer bothering to feign drunkenness, Nikolaos pursued his quarry. "You said it was bad news?"

It took his companion a while to respond. "Wha'?"

"You said it was bad news about that merchant arrested on Euboea?"

"Yep." Gripus released a deep burp. "Baaaaaad."

Better get it all out fast, before he falls asleep.

"You're saying… the old man was found guilty?"

"Yep. Baaaaaad."

"What charges did they convict him of?"

"Mur…" Gripus's nearly incoherent voice was fading. "An' thef…"

"Murder and theft. Both of those?"

"Tha's th' ol' me'chant. Big farm—"

"You're saying… both of them were guilty of murder and theft?"

Can't be. Stefanos wasn't around that night, and I already heard what they did with him.

"Nah." Gripus closed his eyes. "Jus' ol' man. Big farm' thef' got sent—"

"I know who the merchant killed, but what did he and the farmer steal?"

"Rub—" A loud snore interrupted the word.

Nikolaos shook him awake. "A ruby?"

"Nah, lo's more."

"Lots more. How many?"

"Ni—." Another, deeper snore.

Once more, Nikolaos woke him. "Did you say… nine?"

"Nin' fanc' rub—" Gripus grabbed the girl's buttocks as if he still hadn't had enough. "Each one bigg'r 'n redd'r 'n this swee' li'l gal's swee' li'l puss!"

Nine big, fancy rubies.

"Should'a seen the gov'nor's eyes. Them nin' stol'n rub—" In the next instant, Gripus was out for good.

***

Shortly after dawn the next day, Nikolaos knocked on the door of The Garden Patch. His head ached, his body was weary from the previous night's activities, and to save his life he couldn't have given a rational explanation as to why he was there, instead of in his bed in Piraeus, sleeping it off.

Maybe I just want to rub it in that I'm the one who dug up all the facts.

To his surprise, the brat opened the door.

"What do you want?" he demanded.

"I've news for your mother."

"She's asleep."

"Tell her, our father's been found guilty of murder and theft."

The brat's eyes bulged, and for once he was speechless.

"Tell her," Nikolaos went on, "I'll do everything I can to save him, but you two must go home to Eretria."

CHAPTER 19

Theodosia raised her face to the warm sun and inhaled the ocean breeze as a guard ushered her and Doros across the blue-and-yellow mosaic floor of Vibius Galarius's rooftop pergola, where ten blue-cushioned marble chairs alternated with oval marble tables in a wide semicircle, turning their backs to the Acropolis, facing the Aegean Sea. Spindly vines planted in pots climbed posts and looped through open supports overhead. Soon they would leaf out and shade the roof, but on this fine mid-February afternoon, they let the balmy warmth pass through.

Under better circumstances, Theodosia would have enjoyed relaxing with her son in this gorgeous place high above the frenzy of Athens, sipping Falernian with the governor, and reminiscing some more about her father.

But she and Doros had not come for pleasure, relaxation, or nostalgia.

A slim Greek slave approached, bowed, and offered his master's guests embossed silver goblets filled with wine. Along with a glass pitcher on a silver tray, he carried a white linen cloth to wipe the rims and catch any spills that might occur.

Exactly like Alexander when we first met.

The governor arrived and sat on the other side of Doros, facing Theodosia.

She steered the conversation to the reason of her visit. "You mentioned that General Vespasian's son, General Titus, is here in Athens."

"He *was* here when you and I last spoke, but you said he wouldn't remember you, so—" The governor made a fluttery gesture with his fingers.

"Governor, this is hard to say, but I wasn't entirely truthful with you. To be honest, I was afraid to tell you the whole truth."

Vibius Galarius's face darkened. "The whole truth at that time might have helped your husband. Not so sure it matters now."

"I'm aware of that."

"So now... the *whole* truth?"

"The *whole* truth is that General Vespasian and his son, Titus, and his daughter, Flavia Domitilla, used to be my very good friends."

The governor's expression didn't change. "Actually, I've known that for quite some time."

"You just forgot to mention it?"

"I didn't forget." Oddly, he smiled and changed the subject. "Did I tell you why Titus was here?"

"Something related to his father's new assignment in Judea."

"That was the truth, but only part of it."

So, now, who has a problem telling the whole truth?

But she didn't argue. The stakes in this game were too high.

"Caesar ordered General Vespasian to smash the Jewish revolt. And to do that, Vespasian needed a larger supply fleet. And to do that, he needed more rowers." The governor arched one eyebrow. "Titus came to Greece to collect rowers."

Theodosia struggled to grasp his meaning. "Collect rowers?"

"He visited many ports on his way to Judea. This was one of his last stops. He came looking for convicts, and he found them."

Slowly, Vibius Galarius leaned forward. Propped his elbows on his knees. Pressed his fingertips together. Tapped them on his lips. Peered over them. Gazed hard at her.

In an effort to keep calm, Theodosia lifted her cup and sipped.

"Thieves," the governor went on. "Murderers. Escaped slaves. General Titus scooped up every able-bodied convict he could locate."

A violent spasm sloshed the red Falernian over the edge of Theodosia's goblet. Like blood, it stained the front of her white silk stola and dripped onto the blue-and-yellow tiles.

The waiter lifted the cup from her shaking hand and offered his dry cloth.

She took it, blotted her stola, and tried to speak. "My husband—"

The governor's mouth moved, but all Theodosia caught were phrases.

"Properly tried and convicted."

That's not possible.

"Somewhere out there now." Vibius Galarius waved toward the sea.

He's done nothing wrong.

"Rowing to Judea."

He's forty-three.

"Rowing General Titus's trireme to Judea, to be precise."

Doros reached across the table and took his mother's hand, which jolted her thoughts into speech.

"He's not a young man," she said.

No response from Vibius Galarius.

"Not a strong man."

No response.

"Not used to forced labor."

No response.

"Won't survive a year."

No response.

"Or even six months." Her panic grew with each moment of the governor's silence. "He's well educated. A successful businessman. Couldn't you have penalized him in some way that wasn't a death sentence?"

Juno, make him say something. Anything.

Ultimately, it was Doros who spoke up. He released Theodosia's hand and turned to Vibius Galarius.

"My father is not a murderer, sir. Not a thief. It was his other son, my half-brother, Nikolaos, who killed our friend Lycos and stole all our money."

The governor seemed to consider his statement.

"That's a serious accusation, boy. Can you prove it?"

"Lycos and Nikolaos had a huge fight, and I can tell you why."

Let's see if the governor's interested now in knowing why. He certainly wasn't interested the first time we met.

"Quite a few free men in Eretria," Vibius Galarius said, "voluntarily testified that the fight was between Lycos and Alexander."

"They lied," Doros said.

"Why would they do that?"

"I don't know, sir, but I do know there was an old hatred between Lycos and my brother, and never any bad blood between Lycos and my father."

Doros rose then and faced the governor. "Nikolaos was the one who killed Lycos that night."

His training in rhetoric—all those hours we practiced debating and public speaking—really shows.

"It's natural that you defend your father," the governor said, "but—"

"Sir, if you'd just investigate—"

"We finished our investigation."

Visibly upset, Doros sat again.

So his mother took up the defense.

"Why wasn't I informed while your investigation was going on? I could have hired a lawyer for my husband."

"Slaves don't have lawyers."

Theodosia recoiled at this new horror.

They know Alexander's a runaway.

The governor motioned for the waiter to refill all their cups.

"Your *husband*," he emphasized, "was questioned, tried, convicted, and sentenced by Roman law."

Questioning slaves always involves torture. Always.

"So—" She forced herself to press on. "You're saying he was tortured?"

"'Appropriately interrogated' is how I would put it."

"Tortured."

"The procedures were properly handled."

"What procedures?"

Vibius Galarius took a sip. "I was there to make sure."

Alexander's haunting question came back from years ago.

"Have you ever loved someone you were powerless to protect?"

"Governor, did all this happen before or after my last visit?"

"After." There was no emotion in his voice.

She gasped. "But you knew I was in Athens and where I was lodging and—"

"You said you'd only be in town a few more days."

He's right.

How stupid I was.

"My dear," the governor said, "there were good reasons—apart from the murder of that young fellow in Eretria—why the emperor ordered your husband and his farmer friend arrested."

Theodosia's heart thumped. "Nero *personally* ordered them arrested?"

"Yes, our divine, dearly beloved emperor *personally* ordered them arrested, questioned, and tried." There was no detectable irony in the governor's voice.

"How did he know where they were?"

"Spies. Informers. People eager to win the favor of the master of the world."

"Even in tiny Eretria?"

"Especially in tiny Eretria."

As Alexander's parents told him so long ago, there's no place you can go to escape the power of Rome.

"Did Nero *personally* order you to convict them?"

Vibius Galarius bobbed his head. "Before you ever showed up in Athens. So you see, my dear, there was nothing I could do about it."

Theodosia exploded. "You could have told me! I am a free woman. A Roman citizen. The sole heir of a patrician family has property rights!"

"The two escaped slaves who were arrested in December had been the emperor's property for the last decade. You had no claim then—and you have no claim now—to either of them."

"By all the gods, I'm married to one of them."

From some shadowy spot behind a post came the *slip-slip-slip* of soft sandals.

"Not legally," said a woman's voice.

Aula. How long has she been listening? Did the governor know she was there? What's she doing here in the first place?

"There are things you never told me." Aula's stola rustled as she crept along behind the chairs. "Fortunately, my old friend Vibius Galarius kept me well informed."

Her old friend?

"All those times I shared with you the news from Rome..."

Did she know all along who I was?

"And all those famous people we gossiped about..." Aula's tone was blacker than Theodosia had ever heard it.

Or did she just find out?

"You made me think you'd never met them."

Did Nero know from the start where we were?

"You kept all sorts of secrets from me."

Or did someone recently betray us?

Aula completed her walk around the chairs and stopped in front of Theodosia. "I don't appreciate being deceived."

Was it Aula and her husband? Or Nikolaos? Or someone else?

Aula crossed her arms. "I especially don't like being deceived by someone who pretends to be my friend."

Theodosia's voice, when she finally got it to work, was stronger than she expected. "What makes you think I deceived you?"

"Because everything about your life in Eretria was a lie."

"My life in Eretria was exactly as I represented it."

"You said you came from Apulia."

"Only because I was afraid to tell you the truth."

"You said you were married to Alexander."

"We *were* married in the eyes of the gods of Greece and Rome."

"But not in the eyes of the law. And you lived on assets you had no right to possess."

"We lived on money that Alexander earned from the business he had established in Eretria, which brought prosperity to the entire island of Euboea."

"But he did not *own* the rubies that he sold to start that business and buy your house."

Theodosia gave a little moan, shook her head, and took a few moments to think. "Even if *he* didn't legally own those rubies, Aula, *I* did. They were mine by birthright until Nero stole them from me."

"Be careful," the governor cut in, "how you accuse the emperor."

"I might end up rowing a galley to Judea alongside my husband?"

"Stranger things have been known to happen," the governor said with a perfectly straight face.

"My husband and I," Aula went on, "and the governor, too… we learned everything there was to know about those rubies from Nero's couriers."

So was the centurion—or maybe the governor—sending information to Nero? Or was Nero sending information to them? Or was the information-sharing going both ways? And if so, for how long?

Theodosia struggled for a way to defend herself.

"Well, the rubies definitely were mine, and whatever I did with them—or whatever Alexander did—it was nothing compared to what Nero does every day of his life."

Aula scoffed. "How do you know what Nero does every day of his life?"

"Because I know Nero."

And maybe she doesn't know as much about me as she thinks.

"I've spent time at his court, Aula. Slept under the roof of his palace. Attended his dinners. Been best friends with some of his best friends."

None of that happened the way she'll assume, but every word of it is true.

"I'm well acquainted with Nero's tastes and habits," Theodosia went on. "The nasty things he does for fun. The way he and his buddies—"

"The couriers had nasty tales to tell about you, too."

Theodosia studied Aula's face then shifted her eyes to Doros and on to the governor. Both were closely following this conversation.

Moments later, she rose and confronted her former friend. "What 'nasty tales' did you hear about me?"

"You come from a Roman family, but you're not a real Roman, just a mongrel who couldn't have married a patrician even if one fell for you."

A mongrel, but not a—

Theodosia chuckled.

She thinks she's so well informed. Pretends she's got all the dirt on me.

Aula gave no sign of reciprocal amusement. "But still, even though everyone in Rome knew who and what you were, all the young noblemen ignored the conventions and flocked out to the country to court you, because you were so rich. And then, like a magician with some trick gone bad, you lost everything and spent years in prison."

True, and if it weren't for Alexander's quick thinking years ago, Aula would have had something even more scandalous than that to gloat about now.

"And then, as if all that wasn't bad enough—" Aula interrupted herself for a quick chortle. "You took your slave as your husband."

No reason to pretend otherwise.

Theodosia lifted her head. "Yes, I did."

Aula's face could not have contorted in greater disgust if Theodosia had confessed to marrying a house fly.

Theodosia glanced at the man and the boy, who were still sitting in their chairs. Governor Vibius Galarius squinted a bit as he stared out to sea, but Doros was watching her with widened eyes.

First time he's heard any of this. What must he think of his father and me?

Turning her back on her erstwhile friend, Theodosia took the chair next to Vibius Galarius, on the other side from Doros... a position that allowed her to watch her son's face while establishing a more personal connection to the man who held such immense power over their future.

She gave the governor her warmest smile. "As a very special favor to the daughter of a friend of your youth—"

She rested one of her hands on one of his and spoke in as relaxed a manner as she could muster.

"Please help Doros and me understand what led our family to the mess we're in. How did it all happen so fast, and why?"

The governor did not reject her hand. "May I be blunt, my dear?"

She smiled again and answered lightly. "Of course."

"It happened to *you* because you cohabited with a runaway slave."

Not the answer I expected.

"You mean, Alexander and I broke the rules, so we had to be punished."

"No, actually, that's not what I mean."

He placed his other hand over hers and looked into her eyes. Theodosia held them steady and braced herself as the governor went on.

"I'm telling you why *you*—a unique and lovely woman named Theodosia Varro—are involved in this. Under normal circumstances, you wouldn't have been impacted by it at all. Probably wouldn't even have known anything about it." His easy-going tone matched hers.

Now that Aula has withdrawn from the conversation, it's going better.

"The point I'm trying to make," Vibius Galarius said, "is this. Everything that recently happened to the man you call your 'husband' and his big farmer friend would have happened to them anyway."

"Really? Why?"

"Because not only did those two steal themselves and a slave child from Nero, but they made off with a pile of priceless rubies that also belonged to the emperor. Sooner or later, without question, those two were going to be caught, tried, and convicted."

Despite Theodosia's desire to keep the tension down, it crept into her voice. "I'm sorry, governor, but you have the details all wrong. As I tried to explain to Aula… at the time Alexander, Stefanos, and the child, Lycos, supposedly ran away, they were *my* slaves, not Nero's. They were living on *my* estate, not Nero's. And as *my* slaves, they had *my* permission to leave *my* villa with *my* rubies, which I had freely given them."

The tension, she noted, had also crept into Doros's face. His bright amber eyes blinked several times in quick succession.

He doesn't know what to make of all this new information.

Without removing her hand from the governor's, she addressed her son.

"Doros, just as you understand the reasons why Nikolaos and Lycos fought in the street that night, you must also understand and remember what I just told the governor. It's important for your future."

Silently, the boy nodded.

"Under questioning," Vibius Galarius said, "both men confessed to stealing themselves and other property, animate and inanimate, from the emperor. Even more damning, they both admitted to killing a young man named Lycos, who turned out to be that same piece of animate property that they had stolen from the emperor a decade earlier."

Too anxious to sit any longer, Theodosia withdrew her hand and stood. "This tells me more about how they were questioned than anything else."

Doros rose, too, and wrapped his arm around her waist to steady her.

"For years," she said, "Alexander protected Lycos at great cost to himself. He nurtured Lycos. Taught Lycos. Trusted Lycos to run his business. And as for Stefanos… he wasn't anywhere near Eretria when Lycos died."

"Still, they both confessed to it all."

"Under torture, anyone would confess to anything."

"Well, it doesn't really matter in the end, because either crime—murder or theft—was enough to condemn your husband and his big friend."

"With no more proof than forced confessions?"

Vibius Galarius laughed. "The evidence of theft was clear and convincing."

"You're going to have to explain that, because I don't see it."

Another laugh. "A decade ago, your gigantic slave—or your gigantic former slave, or Nero's gigantic runaway slave, or whatever he was at the time— That man traded four gigantic rubies for a gigantic farm on the island of Euboea.

In time, the old farmer who had sold that gigantic farm to your gigantic slave… well, that poor old fellow had the bad luck to die."

Theodosia found the governor's jocular attitude unnerving, but she held her tongue and listened.

"And when he died," Vibius Galarius went on, "he left those four gigantic rubies to his son in Athens. More time passed, and the son's family grew nervous. They couldn't wear the gigantic gems, or even sell them, without raising questions. And more than that, they recalled seeing painted signs all over Athens offering a gigantic reward to anyone who found and turned over to the authorities a set of gigantic, stolen rubies."

Nero posted a reward for my rubies? I thought he did that just for Stefan and me.

"So, last December," the governor continued in the same vein, "the old man's son brought those four gigantic gems to me. He explained how he came by them and ratted out the gigantic farmer—who was easy enough to catch since he was still living on that same gigantic farm—in exchange for the gigantic reward Nero had promised."

At a moment when Vibius Galarius stopped to sip and savor his wine, Theodosia leaned toward him.

"But nothing in that series of events implicates Alexander."

The governor paused long enough in his enjoyment of the wine to waggle a finger in her face. "Patience, Theodosia, there's lots more to say about it. Just days earlier, an investigation by the commander of the garrison on Euboea had turned up—"

"The commander of the garrison on Euboea is Aula's husband and—given their clear bias against us—I challenge the validity of his investigation."

The governor ignored her. "The garrison commander discovered that, a decade earlier, your 'husband' had used one gigantic ruby to start his business and another to buy a house. Many years on, that second gigantic ruby showed up in the market, with indisputable provenance."

Last November, after Nikolaos spent all that timing waiting for Aula and me by the pier, he made a great show of telling us about that woman who had brought her ruby to the market.

"None of that incriminates either Alexander or Stefanos." Theodosia's mind dug deeper into her memories of that day.

Had Aula asked Nikolaos for information the governor wanted so she and the centurion could pass it on, thereby ingratiating themselves with him and Nero?

Vibius Galarius frowned. "I haven't finished yet."

Or had Nikolaos already decided on his own to give her that information, deliberately trying to cause trouble for his father?

"Turns out," the governor went on, still frowning, "about a dozen years ago, in Syria, a man who closely resembled your 'husband' used a pair of gigantic rubies to purchase a slave from a Roman magistrate."

"That proves nothing."

"Unless you also know—" The governor interrupted himself. "I suppose it was the timing of all these revelations that made them especially notable."

"The timing?" Despite Theodosia's best efforts, her voice quaked.

"Indeed, that was the amazing part. You see, all this information came together early in December, right after General Titus arrived in Athens. And as it turned out, he was most curious to learn more."

Theodosia gripped her son's shoulders and forced her eyes to stay focused on the governor's face.

Wearing a self-satisfied smile, Governor Vibius Galarius stared out to sea. "Last December, as I mentioned, word went out from Athens to all the islands, coastal towns, and provinces that General Titus was paying a bounty for able-bodied, convicted criminals."

I was living in a coastal town, and I heard nothing about that.

"Until then," the governor said, "the dead farmer's son had been afraid to tell anybody about the four gigantic rubies in his possession. But now, that clever fellow saw a clever way to dispose of them while cleverly reaping a gigantic financial windfall."

Does he have to turn our family tragedy into a comic tale?

Doros tipped his head back and mouthed the word "asshole."

Theodosia shook her head to keep him quiet.

"So," the governor went on, "the clever son cleverly turned in not only his own four gigantic rubies but also a gigantic Euboean farmer, who was remarkably easy to locate and convict of theft and who—because of his gigantic size and strength—would make an excellent rower."

Theodosia had to restrain Doros from leaping over and attacking him.

"Ultimately, you see," Vibius Galarius continued in the same vein, "the clever son scored a triple bounty. He immediately earned one reward from Nero for returning his gigantic rubies, plus a second reward for ratting out the gigantic runaway slave, and later a third reward from General Titus for producing a gigantic convict to row one of his galleys." The governor cleared his throat, as if he were preparing for an important announcement.

Doros's shoulders tensed under his mother's fingers, but she gripped him tightly while controlling her own anger as the governor continued.

"With only a bit more persuasion," Galarius went on, "since nine gigantic rubies, not just four, had been stolen and Nero wanted all of the perpetrators in chains, the gigantic farmer pointed our interrogators to yet another escaped slave and gem thief openly living and running a business in Eretria."

They must have tortured Stefan badly. He would never have betrayed Alexander otherwise.

Vibius Galarius looked at Aula, who was lounging six chairs away, and gave her a cheery look. Then his eyes returned to Theodosia, whose heart kept thrashing about inside her chest.

"As Aula knows," he said, "we located your 'husband' in the garrison at Eretria, already professionally questioned and properly charged in the murder of a young man who had worked for him."

An old, long-forgotten memory bubbled up in Theodosia's mind.

She and Aula were relaxing in Aula's sun-washed sitting room and the maid with red hair was serving sweet-cherry juice and Doros was toddling around and the centurion's wife was confiding to Theodosia what she called her heart's truest desire.

"There's nothing I wouldn't give—and almost nothing I wouldn't do—to be back there while those little ones are growing up. It's my heart's truest desire."

And then, as on a stormy day when the black clouds part and light floods the land below, Theodosia knew exactly how and why her world had collapsed.

Trembling with a fury she could no longer control, Theodosia released Doros and stalked toward Aula.

"You set Alexander up for a murder charge, didn't you?"

Aula puffed up like an offended toad. "I would never do such a thing."

"Not only *would* you do it, you *did* do it."

"Prove that or shut up."

"You knew that Nikolaos had argued with Lycos and then murdered him, which put your husband under a lot of pressure to find the killer and settle the case. But Nikolaos quickly disappeared."

Red blotches were popping out on Aula's cheeks.

"Besides, you owed Nikolaos a favor for telling you about the ruby that had shown up in the market... and for only the gods know how many other spying assignments he may have carried out for you over the years."

Aula raised her hands to the governor, as if asking him to put an end to Theodosia's revelations, but Theodosia wasn't deterred.

"So, you came snooping around our house—on the very day Nikolaos killed Lycos's little boys, no less—looking for excuses to arrest Alexander instead of Nikolaos."

"She can't prove any of this," Aula stated in a flat tone to the governor.

"I can," Theodosia bluffed.

Actually, I can't.

Fortunately, neither one of them knows that.

"Furthermore, I know exactly what you got for lying about Alexander."

Aula's eyelashes fluttered. "What I got?"

"You got your heart's truest desire."

No way is she going to admit it, but she knows I've caught her.

"It wasn't any kind of coincidence," Theodosia said loudly enough that the governor had no choice but to hear her, "that Centurion Marcus Norbanus Paulinus was transferred from Eretria to Athens mere days after Alexander was arrested for murder."

"Pure coincidence," Aula said.

"Simply put... you and your husband betrayed me and my husband."

"Why would we do that?"

"To get out of Eretria and move to Athens. To live near your youngest son and enjoy your grandchildren while they're growing up. In other words, to attain your heart's truest desire."

Aula began cackling so robustly that Doros did the same.

"Mother, has she gone mad?"

"No, she's not mad. Just putting up the only manner of defense she can think of."

"I'm definitely not mad." Aula kept on cackling. "Just sure that nobody's going to believe lies like that, least of all Governor Vibius Galarius."

Theodosia glanced at the governor, who still gazed out over the Aegean with that same self-satisfied smile.

And then a second swift wave of realization washed over her.

Aula's right. They're old friends. He doesn't give a damn about Alexander or Stefan or me. He won't lift a finger to help us.

Her eyes dropped to Doros, who raised his hands, both of them tightly fisted as if ready for combat.

He's right, too. I have to fight this battle in a different way.

"Aula." She switched to the softest, most intimate voice she could muster. "You're one of the few people I've ever truly trusted in my life. So now I'm asking, for the sake of all the years we've been friends, please tell the governor the truth."

But Aula was silent. Wearing the same smug, indifferent expression as Vibius Galarius, she also stared out to sea.

"Aren't we friends?" For all Theodosia's efforts to control her emotions, her eyes grew wet. "Haven't we been friends for a long time?"

Aula swiveled and, with her own blistering eyes, absolutely withered Theodosia. "I am a proud, *honorable* Roman woman. And we proud, *honorable* Roman women do not befriend trash. Certainly not the kind of mongrel trash who marry their slaves."

Shaking again, and again changing course, Theodosia made a move that on any previous day of her life would have been unimaginable. She limped over to Governor Vibius Galarius's chair, positioned herself in front of him, and dropped to her knees. Sharp edges of the blue-and-yellow floor tiles gouged her bones as she stretched her arms up to him. Pain and humiliation coursed through her body. It was almost more than she could bear, and yet...

So little compared to the pain and humiliation that Alexander has endured and will continue to endure.

Maybe for the rest of his life.

"Governor, I can't live without my husband. Can't stand to know he's suffering. So I beg you, very humbly, to use your influence, please. Intercede with General Titus or General Vespasian on Alexander's behalf."

"This is disgusting." Aula's tone was sour enough to curdle goat's milk.

But the governor remained mute.

Theodosia crawled closer, lifted the hem of his robe, and kissed it.

His silence says everything. He has no intention of helping us.

Completely desperate now, she sat back on her heels, right at his feet, and stabbed her fingernails into the wine-stained, white-linen breast of her stola. With a single swift, slashing movement, she tore it open.

She tilted her head back, baring her neck and chest in the old, pleading gesture of captive to captor.

"If you won't use your influence—if you don't care to help us—please use your dagger to kill me now."

Behind her, Doros cried out and Aula clucked her ongoing disgust.

Several yards away, a shocked glass pitcher sailed off the waiter's tray, hurled itself furiously across the floor, and shattered into smithereens on the mosaic tiles.

But Vibius Galarius merely rolled his eyes.

"I will not kill you, Theodosia."

For several moments—each of which seemed to Theodosia to last a lifetime—he regarded her without a trace of sympathy.

"However," he said at long last, "I can tell you this. Your 'husband' *will* die at his oar, and your gigantic former slave *is* already dead. He succumbed two months ago under interrogation."

Tears scalded Theodosia's cheeks as a deep ache pulsed through her body. Still on her hands and knees, she retreated backwards from the man who could do everything and would do nothing.

Dearest Juno, I've disgraced myself.

She bent low, pressed her forehead to the hard tile floor, and covered her head with her hands.

Vibius Galarius rose. His robe swooshed past her.

I've disgraced Doros, too.

Aula's clothing rustled across the pergola.

I've disgraced my father and every one of our ancestors.

Out of nowhere, a metallic object clanked on the tile floor.

And I've accomplished nothing.

As Aula's soft sandals *slip-slip-slipped* toward the stairway leading down to the governor's private residence, her final words drifted back.

"The woodsmen found that thing on the dead man's body."

Doros pounced on the metallic object. "Mother, look."

Theodosia raised her head and tried to see through her clumped-together eyelashes. "What is it?"

"My bulla, except some damn bastard cut the ruby out of its mouth." He held it out to her.

Theodosia took her beloved little snake and pressed it between her palms.

"Careful," Doros said, "those mouth edges are sharp now."

"They're not hurting me."

Gradually, the calm and clarity that had been missing in recent months resettled over her heart and mind. Her eyes and cheeks slowly dried, and for the first time since Alexander's arrest, she was at peace.

She returned the viper amulet to her son. "Do you know what this means?"

"Without the ruby, it means nothing."

"No, my darling, its power never was in the ruby, but in the snake itself, which is ours once again."

Doros helped her up from the floor. "So, then, you tell me. What *does* it mean?"

Theodosia wrapped an arm around his shoulders and kissed the top of his head. "Having our little viper back means… it's time for a journey to Judea."

CHAPTER 20

The decrepit cargo ship *Minoan Spirits* pitched and rolled and creaked and cracked through the last of winter's storms, carrying Theodosia, Doros, Myrine, and—to their mutual dismay—Nikolaos. After several futile attempts to book separate passages, they had ended up together on the only civilian vessel in Piraeus with a captain willing to brave not only the late-winter weather but also a nasty war at the Judean end of the trip.

Theodosia and Nikolaos had experienced sea voyages before, but neither Doros nor Myrine had ever sailed at all until they left Eretria.

And so—while spending the last few days of February and all of March on the stormy eastern Mediterranean was nobody's idea of a pleasant journey—Myrine stayed busy and happily distracted by teaching Theodosia and Doros to speak basic Aramaic. Since both of them were motivated to learn it and needed something interesting to do to pass the time, they soon managed to communicate among themselves in that challenging new tongue.

Captain Hatzidakis, the *Minoan Spirits*' venerable Cretan owner, had been sailing his whole life. And while his ship wasn't much to look at, every other captain that Theodosia talked with in Piraeus had vouched for his ability to convey her and her family safely to the far southeastern corner of the great sea.

At each island where they stopped, he restocked their food and water, but comfort, sanitation, and privacy on board were nonexistent.

Every night, tucked into a sliver of space between piled-up sacks of merchandise in the middle deck, Theodosia, Doros, and Myrine shared a blanket and a thin sleeping pallet. Somewhere down below, in the lower cargo area where the crew slept, Nikolaos had found a spot for himself.

Whenever weather permitted, all four spent their days on the top deck, where the women kept their distance from Nikolaos, despite Theodosia's intense longing to peek inside the orange leather bag that he kept constantly at his side. But Doros did talk with his half-brother, turning up useful bits of information that he reported back to his mother.

"Nikolaos insists," he said one night as he snuggled in between her and Myrine, "that Stefanos didn't die in Vibius Galarius's dungeon. He thinks the governor sold him to a gladiatorial school on the Italian Peninsula."

"Wouldn't surprise me." As always, the boat's rhythmic rocking had Theodosia on the edge of sleep. "Several people in Rome tried to buy him from me for that very purpose."

"Did Master Nikolaos say where he learned that?" Myrine sounded wide awake.

"He laughed when I asked. Said I was too young to know more."

"Mistress, I don't see why the governor would lie to you 'bout that."

Theodosia rolled to one side and propped her head on her folded arm. "Because he lied to me about everything."

Doros yawned. "What'll you tell Iocaste after we get back to Greece with Father?"

"Good question. No good answer." Theodosia was ready for sleep. "Probably just that she—and we—may never know for sure what happened to her beloved Stefanos."

***

Nikolaos was convinced the rickety old ship would never stop rocking. Never stop leaking. And never, ever reach land.

Almost a month in this wretched tub. Must be a better way to get to Judea.

However, if there actually was a better way to get to Judea in weather like this, nobody seemed to know about it.

Finally, after a lot of complaining to Captain Hatzidakis, Nikolaos accepted his fate. He spent his days squatting at the rail. Clinging to his orange leather bag. Constantly drenched in rain and sea spray, throwing up the remains of his miserable meals.

Still, he's taking me where I want to go. Can't be much longer now.

Shortly before they left Piraeus, the Roman woman had urged him to go home. "Keep the business going. Give your father something meaningful to return to." Nikolaos had made a rude reply that ended the conversation.

But one good thing did come from that exchange. Through a smart series of dumb-sounding questions, Nikolaos wormed it out of her that she, Doros, and Myrine were headed to Caesarea Maritima, the seaside city built a century earlier by King Herod the Great, which was now a major harbor and the official seat of imperial government in Judea.

She'll appeal to the Romans again. Throw herself at their feet again. Beg and plead with them again.

But, as he knew from Grifus and his other drinking-and-whoring pals at Sailor's Delight, that approach hadn't worked for her with the Roman governor in Athens, before whom she had only embarrassed herself.

Why expect better results from the Roman governor in Caesarea?

Meanwhile, Nikolaos—with his excellent proficiency in Aramaic and his superior knowledge of Hebrew culture—would burrow deep into the Jewish community in Jerusalem.

As he had with the soldiers and sailors in Piraeus, he'd make friends who could tell him which ship his father was on. He'd learn the ship's schedule, the name of its captain, and when it would next be in port, perhaps even the exact bench where each galley slave was chained.

He dreamed of slipping onto a bireme, hacking off Alexander's chains, and hustling him back to the island of Euboea before any of the Romans in their fancy palaces in Caesarea realized that a rower was missing.

Father will soon know who cares the most about him.

***

The ancient, tiny Judean port of Yavne—which was Yamnia to the Greeks and Iamnia to the Romans—would not have been Theodosia's preferred destination. Not when Caesarea Maritima, just up the coast, offered the largest and most modern harbor between Seleucia Pieria in Syria and Alexandria in Egypt.

And that, of course, was why General Vespasian had chosen Caesarea Maritima for his base of naval operations in Judea.

And that, of course, was also why Theodosia was eager to go straight there and why, perversely, her desire was destined to be thwarted.

"Can't just sail like a whale into Herod's pretty little Caesarea," Captain Hatzidakis said in his folksy, oddly accented, unlettered Greek as they departed Itanos, the easternmost port on the island of Crete and their last stop before hitting open water. "Not with all them Judeans in open revolt against Rome."

"What in Hades does their shitty revolt have to do with us?" asked Doros, who treated Hatzidakis as the grandfather he had never known.

"Well see, youngster, it all started with them Judeans going dagger-to-dagger against their own top dogs that rule the temple."

The old seaman laid his wrinkled, sun-splotched hand on the boy's arm while at the same time winking at Theodosia.

"Them top dogs in Jerusalem is way too friendly to Rome for the rest of them Judeans to stomach. And them Judeans knows—'cause they've seen 'em in action all their lives—that them Romans lording it over 'em from their highfalutin palace in Caesarea is all a pile of crooks. So last year, see, when a whole lotta Greeks like me and you—what them Judeans look down their noses at and call 'pagans' or 'gentiles'—so them Greeks took to peddling pigeons for sacrifice right on the front doorstep of them Judeans' most sacred spot in Caesarea, which meant that them—"

"Why can't we sail straight into Caesarea?" Doros demanded.

Hatzidakis released a throaty laugh. "Right now, see, the harbor's packed with Nero's big ships, so unless your ma's willing to pay some kind of colossal fee for special access or unless she's wanting to risk being swamped by them monster triremes, it's best to go somewheres else. Easy enough to travel by land from Yamnia to Caesarea."

"Mother," Doros wailed, "tell him we have to land in Caesarea."

Hatzidakis's wind-burned eyes crinkled at the corners. "Well, see, we could head for the port at Joppa. It's heaps bigger than Yamnia and loads closer to Caesarea."

"So, let's do it."

"Fine, youngster, 'cept they got hundreds of them rebel pirates infesting the waters off Joppa, and so unless we—"

"Mother!"

Myrine sneaked up behind Doros, draped her chin over his shoulder, and enveloped him in her sturdy arms. "It's just not a good idea, Little Man. Your ma hired Captain Hatzidakis to get us there safely. Can we all agree to be wise and take his advice?" Doros leaned back against her breast and nodded, as he usually did when she asked him for something.

As always, Juno, thank you for Myrine.

***

Theodosia's eyes never left the orange leather sack as Nikolaos slung it to his shoulder, leaped over the rail of the *Minoan Spirits* into shallow water, and vanished into the multi-hued commotion of porters on shore, each one screaming and elbowing others aside in his zeal to carry Captain Hatzidakis's cargo and his four passengers' belongings up the muddy path into town.

Doros followed his brother over the railing, to his mother's dismay, then he scrambled across the dunes and crawled up the cliffs where, for a considerable length of time, he bounced around on the headland above the sea that finally had delivered him to Judea on this first day of April.

Poor boy nearly went stir-crazy on board that ship for so long.

Despite the cutting wind and the ceaseless drizzle, Theodosia remained on the top deck. Kept an eye on her son. Inspected the town's square, squat buildings. Restrained with one hand her wildly flapping palla and stola as her other hand secured the pouch containing their viper amulet, which she had sworn to keep at her bosom until Alexander was in her arms once more.

Can't risk having Doros lose it again.

She relished the crisp smell of this new land, a welcome change from the unwashed crew and the rancid air of their sleeping space.

The scenery was intriguing, too. Captain Hatzidakis had told her to look along the coast for white shells that had washed up over centuries, forming piles taller than a man's head. Weathered boulders and wind-bent grasses crowned the bluffs. As on the Italian Peninsula, Sicily, and Greece, the gods of wind and water had teamed up over centuries to flog and shape this coastline.

To save money when they first arrived, Myrine had announced her plan to haul all the family's gear into the town of Yamnia by herself.

"You know I'm strong enough," she said when Theodosia objected.

But as soon as the gangplank hit the muddy shore, two brawny porters emerged from the crowd, raced to where Myrine stood guarding their bags, and grabbed them out from under her.

Theodosia and Myrine followed the men to a nondescript square where several dozen scruffy donkeys waited, each one hitched to a uniquely painted cart as his human master chatted with the other drivers.

Theodosia listened to the jabbering cacophony around her.

And here I thought I was ready to handle Aramaic.

After a rough start, Myrine settled up with the porters and arranged for a ride to Caesarea in the most eye-catching donkey cart imaginable, an extra-bright one covered with fancifully painted red, orange, and yellow flowers.

As the driver loaded their gear, Theodosia took a closer look at the buildings that surrounded Yamnia's treeless dirt square.

Off to one side stood a small Greek sailors' temple, a remnant of their era of unchallenged dominion over the sea.

Graphic signs dangling over doorways testified to the presence of the typical waterfront businesses: an inn, a bath house, two bars, and a brothel.

A flock of mud-caked sheep ambled through the filthy streets, bleating as if abandoned, while dung-fouled dogs scrapped and snarled in their fierce competition to sniff the new arrivals and urinate on their bags.

No children were visible and—except Theodosia and Myrine—no women.

Any others around are probably confined to the brothel.

Yamnia gave every indication of being a good place to get out of fast, despite its two thousand years of continual use by Phoenicians, Greeks, Egyptians, and Jews.

Doros ran down the hill and into town at the exact moment when Nikolaos and his orange sack reached the assembly of donkeys and drivers.

Might as well make one last attempt at familial solidarity.

"We're headed for Caesarea in this lovely thing," Theodosia called cheerily in Greek from the bench of their distinctive cart. "Come with us, Nikolaos, and let's all rescue your father together."

Nikolaos jutted his jaw, tossed his sack onto the bench of the cart closest to him, and climbed up beside the driver.

"To Jerusalem," he said in Aramaic.

PART IV

No one knows what he can do until he tries.
—*Publius Syrus, 85 BC - 43 BC*

CHAPTER 21

Rain dripped from Adin's hair, nose, and blue-dyed robe. "Nobody in Caesarea has rooms to spare," he said in Aramaic, "but there's plenty in Jerusalem."

There were no rooms in Messana either, but Alexander and I managed to find one.

From the cargo area behind the bench where Theodosia, Doros, and Adin, their young, square-faced donkey driver, were sitting, Myrine continued questioning him. "You're sure about no rooms in Caesarea?"

"Positive," Adin said.

All four of them bounced as the cart hit a deep rut, splashing mud into the air on both sides.

Soon after they left Yamnia—or Yavne, as Adin called it—the drizzle had turned into a cold downpour. According to Captain Hatzidakis, wet springs were typical in Judea. The rain would likely continue throughout April.

"How much farther," Myrine asked, "before we gotta decide?" With her longer experience speaking Aramaic, she conversed quite well with Adin.

Thank the gods she's here to handle things.

Theodosia caught much of what they said but lacked the confidence to respond. Doros seemed content to let their slave negotiate with the stranger.

"Another couple of hours," Adin said. "This path takes us to the main north-south highway. You'll need to make your decision by then."

North to Caesarea Maritima—where Vespasian, Titus, and Alexander are—which has no rooms. Or south to Jerusalem—which offers us no benefit—but has plenty of rooms. Why is there never a good choice?

"Jerusalem's closer. Safer, too, for now." Adin's voice was grim. "The Romans in Caesarea got the crazy-fire in their eyes. Crucifying our men. Raping our women. Selling them and their little ones into slavery."

Not smart of him to talk politics with strangers, even if he does take us for clueless Greeks who just happened to sail into a war zone.

Adin pulled off the path to let an oncoming cart pass. "Three days ago," he said as they waited, "a bunch of us drivers carried a dozen Persian merchants from Yavne to Caesarea. Took hours to find them all rooms, scattered among nine inns. Not likely anybody has space now, unless you're willing to share a cave with some of our local bandits."

Doros tested his Aramaic for the first time. "Bandits?"

"Crawling all over these hills." Adin pointed to the rolling, treeless terrain. "By night, they rob and kill travelers. By day, they sleep in caves. We've always had road robbers, although Herod the Great clamped down on them, but over the last year they've grown bolder and more vicious. It's our own fault, really."

Now Doros attempted more than simple mimicry. "Why is that?"

"Because we chased the Romans out of Jerusalem."

"Was that a good thing?" Doros asked.

"Sure, except for the fact that they kept the bandits in check." Adin jumped from the cart and tugged his donkey back to the path. "These days, nobody protects travelers on the roads."

Theodosia turned to Myrine and spoke in Greek. "Ask if he knows of a family in Caesarea that might be willing to take us in for a few days."

Myrine translated.

Theodosia watched Adin's lips as he rambled through a few options.

"My sister and her husband are expecting their first baby any day. Otherwise, they probably would put you up. There's an old lady who opens her house to travelers, but it's full now. Or, if you don't mind paying for a longer ride, a farmer with a big place on the far-north side of town rents rooms." Adin stopped and shook his head. "Well no, that's a bad idea."

Doros followed up, still in Aramaic. "Why is that a bad idea?"

"Like most people around here, the farmer hates both Romans and Greeks."

Doros slumped on the bench. "Looks like we are out of luck."

Theodosia ventured her first words in the new language in a real-life setting. "We must not give up," she told her son in Aramaic.

Adin looked at her. "You speak Aramaic, too?"

She nodded. "I need practice."

"You'll get plenty of that around here. So, how did you Greeks come to speak the language of the common people of Judea?"

"Long time ago, a man taught—" Theodosia pointed backwards. "Myrine."

The only good thing Nikolaos ever did as part of our family.

"And Myrine taught—" More hand gestures. "Doros and me."

***

Gradually, the rain tapered off. The sun emerged. And still, Adin's donkey trudged on, up and down through the muddy gullies and thinly vegetated hills of this coastal-desert landscape.

At last, they spotted a line of horse-drawn wagons, pedestrians, mounted riders, and donkey carts moving both ways on the busy road from Caesarea to Jerusalem.

Which city to pick?

As they neared the junction, Adin touched Theodosia's arm. "Here's another idea. Now that my sister is married and living with her husband, my parents might put you up. Passover just ended, so your presence won't complicate things for us."

"What is Passover?"

He ignored her question. "There's no extra sleeping space in the house, but the roof is better anyway."

Doros wrinkled his nose. "You sleep on your roof?"

"This time of year, we sure do. Rain comes in the daytime, but the nights are clear and comfortable. We'll be sleeping up there all summer."

"Where is your house?" Theodosia asked.

"On the corner where this road meets the road to Caesarea. We'll be there by evening."

"How far from town?"

"An hour if we walk. Much quicker in the cart."

"I worry," Theodosia continued, "maybe your parents will say no?"

Adin laughed. "Not if you folks hate the Romans as much as we do."

***

On the northwest corner of the Caesarea junction, Adin jumped from his cart, opened a wide gate in a stone wall, and led the donkey into a large courtyard where geese honked at one another and pecked for grain between the paving stones.

Theodosia, Doros, and Myrine left their bags in the cart and followed Adin into the house. As he introduced his parents, Oren and Judith, Theodosia's eyes scanned the main living space.

Rough-hewn beams dictated the width and rectangular shape of the room. Iron bars over small windows offered security but little light or protection from the elements. The mortared brown stone foundation matched a floor of the same color and construction. Everything was dark, and even in the late afternoon, oil lamps hanging in the center of each plastered wall barely lit the space.

The family had no wooden furniture, not even a stool. On the floor to Theodosia's left, a set of padded rectangular mats made of dried reeds surrounded a larger, flatter, round one. To her right at the other end of the rectangle, three long sleeping mats of the same material lay side by side.

They eat and sleep on the floor, all together in the same room. Or, in good weather, on the roof. And now, if we're lucky, we'll get to do the same.

Oren and Judith listened while Adin explained the travelers' predicament. "They hate the Romans, too," he said, as if that justified taking them in.

Actually, we never told him that.

But Adin knew his parents well. Oren's loose black-and-white garment rustled as he extended both his hands. "You are welcome in our home."

Judith wore a green headscarf over a simple brown dress that was tied with a rope at the waist. Like her husband, she was barefoot.

Her forehead furrowed as she exchanged glances with Oren, but in the end she shrugged and pointed to the dining mats. "Make yourselves comfortable. After our prayers, we will join you for a modest supper."

Happy to have understood most of what they said but reluctant to speak Aramaic with them just yet, Theodosia turned to Myrine.

"Tell them we are grateful," she said in Greek, "and most fortunate to find such a good place to stay and such fine people to stay with."

***

Myrine toted their bags from the cart to the roof as Judith, Oren, Adin, and Esther, the family's elderly slave, left for a private prayer room in the back.

Doros helped Theodosia lower herself onto one of the padded dining mats, then he stepped over her inflexible left leg and sat beside her.

In the center of the round serving mat stood an oddly shaped ceramic pitcher and a few small, chipped pottery cups.

Doros inspected the wide funnel and strainer built into one side of the pitcher. "Never saw anything made like this," he said in Greek, then he poured wine from the spout on top into two of the cups.

Theodosia took her first tentative sip of Judean wine. "It's definitely not Falernian," she whispered to her son in Greek.

The family reappeared and dropped onto their mats.

Myrine came down from the roof. At Esther's nod, she followed her to the courtyard. Soon, she returned with a large bowl of soup, which she set on the serving mat. Esther entered with a basket of bread and a bowl of grains that, as Judith explained, had been cooked with goat's milk and fresh figs.

Oren prayed over the food in a language that Theodosia didn't recognize as Aramaic, then he dipped a chunk of bread into the common soup bowl and popped it into his mouth.

Judith and Adin did the same.

Moments later, Theodosia and Doros followed their lead.

No plates. No individual bowls. No spoons.

Between bites, Oren turned to them. "What brought you across the sea to this unfortunate place at this unfortunate time?"

Juno, help me hold my own—linguistically, socially, and politically—with our Judean hosts.

"To rescue my husband from the damn Romans."

With Doros and Myrine's help, she had memorized that sentence while their hosts were off praying. *Damn* was the strongest word any of them knew in Aramaic.

"You are Greeks," Judith said with a slight smile, "but still you hate the Romans. Truly, you are welcome in our home."

Thank you, Juno.

∗∗∗

While Esther and Myrine collected the leftovers, Theodosia and Doros followed Judith for a tour of the courtyard.

Downspouts on every side conveyed rainwater to several cisterns and to a tall fig tree growing just beyond the gate, near the road.

On the southern wall, a two-story stable sheltered the family's assortment of goats and geese, plus their only donkey, from rain and sun.

"Why do you have a two-story stable?" Doros asked Judith.

"You'll see," she answered.

The northern wall supported a half-covered, half-open kitchen with in-ground storage for amphorae filled with olive oil, shelves bulging with pottery jars of various sizes, and several fire pits. Two of them had built-in iron griddles, while others featured hooks for hanging pots.

An outside stream fed a trench that carried water through the wall to irrigate a vegetable garden inside the courtyard.

Doros hopped around the cultivated beds, gushing in Greek about the unusual plants as his mother and Judith inspected the kitchen.

Meanwhile, Esther and Myrine entered and washed the dirty food bowls in a tin tub that they filled with water from the kitchen cistern.

"Esther sleeps over there." Judith pointed to a mat under a covered section in a back corner. "Your girl can fetch a mat for herself."

"Myrine must stay up on the roof with me. I need her help at night."

"In this land, slaves do not sleep in the same area as family members." Without giving her guest a chance to object, Judith set off for the western edge of the courtyard. "We are fortunate to have our own *mikveh,* fed with living water from the stream."

Anticipating her direction, Doros dashed ahead.

"Look, Mother," he shouted in Aramaic, "an outdoor bathtub!" He pointed to a set of rocky stairs that led down to a deep pool lined with much-smoother stones and filled with water.

Judith reacted sharply. "Our *mikveh* is not for your use. It is only for our ritual cleansing. Gentiles must not defile it. Esther will get you a basin."

"I promise," Theodosia said in Aramaic, "we will not touch it."

"But we haven't bathed since Athens," Doros grumbled in Greek.

Theodosia wrapped her arms around him, even as she nodded at Judith and gave her a reassuring smile.

"We are guests in her home," she whispered in Greek. "Very lucky to have found this place, so we don't want to lose it. And remember, we're doing this for your father."

***

Following Esther, Doros helped Theodosia up the external stone stairway to the roof, where they found an uneven wooden floor extending over the house and stables, all of it surrounded by a waist-high parapet.

It's the Judean-peasant version of a pergola, with livestock odors instead of sea breezes, but at least we won't roll over the edge in our sleep.

Oren and Adin were already stretched out, several yards apart, on long straw mats like those in the house below them, face up to the clear night sky.

Doros darted into that unusual second-story shed over the stable. "Now I see what this is," he said in Aramaic.

When observed from the roof, the covered area's purpose was clear: daytime shade for the humans on hot summer days and storage for their sleeping mats and other goods in the rainy season. Myrine had even stashed her family's gunnysacks there.

Doros brought two mats out of the shed, tossed them to the floor between Oren and Adin, helped his mother settle onto one, and made himself comfortable on the other.

Theodosia lay back, draped her shawl over her torso, cradled her head in her hands, and stared in awe at the horizon-to-horizon bowl of stars.

Never saw anything like this before. Not from the cove at my villa. Not in the mountains of southern Sicily. Not even on the Etruscan Sea. It has to be the most magical night sky ever.

"Is it true," Doros asked after a while, "that all the Jews hate all the Romans?"

"Most do," Oren said, "but nobody hates them as much as the Zealots do."

"The Zealots?"

"They're the most anti-Roman of all our sects," Oren said.

"Basically, they're assassins," Adin said. "Even the Roman soldiers try to stay out of their way."

"You're not Zealots," Doros asked with a laugh, "are you?"

Oren also laughed at that.

"No," he said, "we're simple Jews who pray and purify ourselves and honor the Sabbath and try to live worthy lives."

They wouldn't tell us if they were Zealots.

But Doros persisted. "Don't some Jews get along with the Romans?"

"Some do." Adin lurched upright, as if the subject were painful to him. "Take the greedy Sadducees. Despite their old money and rich landholdings and political power, they use their coziness with the Romans to make themselves even richer and more powerful."

Judith dropped her mat beside Theodosia's. "The rest of us spend our lives just getting by so we can pay the Sadducee tax collector."

"But you have a nice house," Doros said, "with a garden and animals and a servant."

"It's been a rainy year," Judith said. "Things are good right now. But when the rains don't come and the stream dries up and the garden withers, we can't pay our taxes and also feed ourselves, much less Esther and our animals. Then the tax collector threatens to confiscate our land and lock us away until we pay."

"And, of course," Oren said, "the money he takes from us never does any good for the common people of Judea. The Sadducee takes his cut, gives some to the Temple to keep the priests happy, and sends the rest to Rome."

"Why send money to Rome?" Doros asked.

"Poor Nero needs more money." Judith's voice dripped sarcasm. "Jews who have been to Rome say he has to build himself a few more palaces and send a few more armies out to crush a few more ancient civilizations."

There's a lot of truth in that.

"I don't understand," Doros said, "how the Sadducees can force you to pay tribute to Nero."

Judith snickered. "When their best friends and allies are men like Pontius Pilate and Gessius Florus, it's easy."

"Who are Pontius Pilate and Gessius Florus?"

"Two of the worst procurators Rome ever inflicted on us," Oren said. "Thirty or forty years ago, when Pilate was in charge in Jerusalem, we called him Pontius the Lightweight. He meant well, I guess, but he mismanaged everything he touched."

Adin interrupted his father. "Tell them about the carpenter."

"I will. Pontius the Lightweight was cozy as bedbugs with the Sanhedrin."

"What's the Sanhedrin?" asked Doros.

"Our supreme religious body." Oren released a soft sigh. "In their dubious wisdom, they hauled a popular reformer from Galilee before Pontius the Lightweight, insisting that he be tried and executed."

"People who were there reported that Pilate didn't want to do it," Judith added, "but in the end he crucified the man and created a martyr."

"These days," Oren added, "the reformer is long gone, but cult groups of his followers keep popping up around Judea and Galilee."

"Our family is not part of it," Judith said, "but we know some who are."

"His cult has reached Greece, too." Theodosia spoke slowly, trying to get the words right. "And also Rome, from what I hear."

Adin looked at her. "The Nazarene has followers in Rome?"

"Poor people and slaves." Theodosia tried to recall what Aula had told her. "Nero blamed them for a bad fire three years ago, so there may not be as many now as before."

Better not show too much knowledge of the situation in Rome.

"You spoke of another—" She forgot the word she wanted in Aramaic. "What is the title of that man Florus?"

"Procurator," Oren said in Aramaic.

Theodosia nodded. "Please tell us about Procurator Florus."

Oren sighed again, louder than before. "Florus was actually worse than Pontius the Lightweight. He was a cruel, corrupt man who got the appointment because his wife was close to Nero's wife or mistress or whatever she was."

He's talking about Poppaea Sabina.

"That was also three years ago," Adin said. "Not long after he got here, Florus ordered his soldiers to raid our Holy Temple so he could send even more of our gold to the emperor."

"We thought Florus was awful," Oren said, "even before his men massacred tens of thousands of Jews last year."

"Is he still the procurator?" Doros asked.

"No," Oren said. "Nero yanked him back to Rome a few months ago, for stirring up so much hatred here."

"Good riddance!" Doros shouted, as if there were nobody on the face of the Earth he could possibly hate more than a Roman procurator.

My smart boy.

But Theodosia's mind was running fast in another direction.

A new procurator might be persuaded to help me find Alexander.

"Who is the procurator now?" she asked.

"Marcus Antonius Julianus." Adin spit out all three names.

Marcus Antonius Julianus. Must remember that name.

"Is he any better?" she asked.

Adin laughed. "He has only been on the job fifteen days and already we loathe him."

No doubt the new procurator is very busy right now, but I'll find a way to meet with him in the next few days.

As Theodosia relaxed and turned her eyes back to the heavens, a shooting star burned its bright arc across the sky.

Instinctively, she reached under the shawl and wrapped her fingers around the pouch that held the viper amulet. With or without its ruby, her little snake always offered comfort and hope.

Either Vespasian, Titus, or Procurator Marcus Antonius Julianus will help me get Alexander off that ship.

CHAPTER 22

Jerusalem!

The thousand-year-old City of David crouched atop its flat-rock fortress like a hunchbacked survivor of too many battles, showing little evidence of energy or spirit.

And yet, according to Captain Hatzidakis, throughout this old, hardscrabble land, a brand-new generation of fearless Hebrew warriors kept themselves busy slinging rocks and hurling spears at their detested rulers from across the sea. And in truth, even on this wet April day, it did seem that every adult male in Judea was on the north-south highway, moving from one village, one town, or one province to another.

It had taken Nikolaos two decades to get here, and as he and his sullen driver approached the high walls from the north, he couldn't help thinking of his Jewish friends in Daphne, who had talked endlessly of Jerusalem and would have traded all the rest of their enslaved lives to share this road with him and the other travelers.

***

The sun was out by the time the driver pulled under a tall stone gate in Jerusalem's third set of massive walls and stopped at the intersection of two muddy lanes. "This is Small Market Street in the Lower City." Those were the first words he had uttered since Nikolaos stepped into his cart in Yamnia, hours earlier. "Best place to find food and a room."

Silently, he accepted the coins Nikolaos handed him and drove off.

Nikolaos stood amid a jumble of buildings, clutched his orange leather bag, and surveyed his surroundings. Aromas of baking bread and cooking meat filled the air as weavers, potters, fabric dyers, basket makers, and other craftsmen labored in shops on all corners of the crossroads. No trees or open space softened this section of Jerusalem. Every one of the square, squat structures rubbed elbows with its neighbors in a solid brown mass of stone.

He spotted a sign above a door a block away. Soon, his Aramaic and a few coins secured a room and breakfast at a run-down inn named Divine Glory.

Father would appreciate the irony.

***

As a proud Greek, Nikolaos wasn't impressed by the Jews' revered Second Temple. Sure, it was big. Even when seen from outside the walls, its high, white-marble, gold-crowned sanctuary dominated the city and surrounding hills and valleys. But he had seen many temples, from the Parthenon in Athens to the shrine of Apollo near his master's home in Daphne.

Greek temples are always more elegant and better sited.

As a gentile or "pagan"—a word he especially detested because it belittled his faith in the many gods of Greece—he wasn't allowed to enter the Temple, but quick peeks through the arched doors revealed a bustle of market stalls, money changers, and other commercial activities surrounded by long, columned walkways and vast expanses of colorful pavement.

Not a bit better than the Agora in Athens.

Another landmark that his Jewish friends had talked about was the Antonia Fortress, which King Herod "the Great"—and they always laughed when they called him that—had foisted on them and named, in his ingratiating way, for Roman General Marc Antony.

Even more than the Temple, Nikolaos wanted to visit the Antonia, as it was called, and the grand palace that Herod had built for his own use whenever state matters forced him to leave his preferred homes in Caesarea and Masada.

He found the Antonia connected to the Temple by another wide swath of pavement. He walked its perimeter. Gazed up at the four rectangular towers at its corners. Admired its intricate stonework.

But after a time, he began to sense that something was wrong.

A fortress should teem with soldiers, as a market teems with shoppers.

He made another loop around the structure. Looked closely. Pushed and pulled the locked-tight wooden doors. There was no movement. No sign of human presence. Fire scorches on the walls. Stones torn off. Only mangy dogs in the street outside.

Just as the Antonia was easy to spot, Herod's palace also should have been quickly located on its rocky platform above the western wall. But Nikolaos had to prowl the area before finally identifying the remains of three towers surrounded by an immense pile of rubble. Tumbled-down marble blocks. Fallen columns. Blackened beams. Hacked-up floor boards. He lowered himself onto a cracked pillar lying perpendicular to the street and stared at the devastation.

How in Hades did this happen?

***

In the time that Nikolaos sat there, scores of men in long robes with knotted belts and a variety of head coverings walked the same broad boulevard that Herod and his royal entourage had traveled a century earlier to reach the grand palace whose ashes now blew in the wind.

Nobody else stopped to look at the ruins. Not a single person even made eye contact with him.

After a while, he rose and approached a man passing by with two boys who appeared to be his sons. "Whatever happened to the palace?" he asked, deliberately polite and in his best Aramaic.

"It burned," said the man.

"I see that, but— Why?"

"Because we set fire to it."

Did I understand that correctly?

"You set fire to your own palace?"

"Never was ours, Greek."

Even here, they can tell I'm a Greek?

"Wasn't it built by your people?"

"Herod the Tyrant inflicted that monstrosity on us. Impoverished us to build it. And then, after he died, the Romans took it for themselves."

Nikolaos pointed to the wreckage. "You say *you* did this?"

The man nodded.

"You, *personally*?"

"Yes," the man said, "I *personally* burned down Herod's palace."

"I also *personally* burned it down," said his older son.

"So did I," said his younger son.

The man clapped his hands on each of his boys' shoulders. "Every Jewish male in Jerusalem *personally* burned it down. The Romans can't blame any one of us, because we all did it."

So they'll slaughter or enslave all of you, instead of a few.

"When was this?" Nikolaos asked.

"Last summer," the older boy said. "We killed a lot of Roman soldiers, too."

"But the gentiles in Caesarea started it!" shrieked the younger boy.

His father nodded again. "Greek swine insisted on sacrificing birds to their false gods, smack in front of our synagogue."

The Jews hate the Greeks, too? Not just the Romans?

"Next thing," the man went on, "they built a shop beside the synagogue and deliberately blocked the street so our people couldn't get to worship. We objected, of course, but the Romans always favor the Greeks over the Jews, so the bastards just stood back and smirked and watched as those filthy pagans butchered every Jew in Caesarea."

There's one reason why they hate us.

"That's not all," the man added. "For two years, that damn Procurator Florus bled our people dry. Didn't care if we starved. Last year, we finally had it with the taxes, the corruption, the desecration." His voice rose. "We protested loudly and aggressively for a long time."

"How did the Romans react to that?"

"Said they'd teach us a lesson."

"And...?"

"They plundered our temple." The man's body shook with fury.

"Defiled our temple," his older son said.

A couple of other passersby stopped to listen.

"What did you do after that?" Nikolaos asked. "Protest some more?"

"We sure did." The younger child bounced up and down. "And guess what that damn Florus did then."

"No idea."

"He ordered his men to slaughter our people!" The boy hoisted an imaginary sword from an imaginary scabbard, enthusiastically swirled it around his head, and with an ear-splitting cry rammed it into Nikolaos's gut.

"The soldiers," said the boys' father, "chased down every man, woman, and child in the marketplace and chopped them to pieces."

"A few got away," the older son said, "but the Romans followed them into their homes and killed them along with their families and servants."

His father's voice was taut. "Four thousand Jews died right here in the Upper City."

Nikolaos whistled. "All around the same time?"

Three more men paused in the street.

"All on the same *day*," the older boy emphasized, "and then that damn Florus had other men arrested, including some that hadn't even been in the market, hadn't even protested—" His face contorted as if he couldn't bring himself to tell the rest of the story.

So his father finished it for him. "That damn Florus ordered his soldiers to flog and crucify those peaceful Jews right out here in the streets."

Five more men joined the crowd.

The younger boy seemed eager to compete with his brother in who could tell the most gruesome story. "There was another slaughter in Egypt, an even worse one, if you can believe it! Our people were fighting the Greeks in Alexandria and—"

"That was the gentiles' fault, too," called one of the newcomers.

"Quite right." Someone else picked up the story. "The Romans themselves murdered every last Jew in Alexandria. Male or female. Old or young. Guilty or innocent. Free or slave. It didn't matter to them."

"Then last autumn," the older boy said, "in our great scholarly city of Lod, some shithead Roman general flogged and crucified dozens of old men who hadn't even raised a hand in protest."

"He razed Lod, too," his father said. "Don't forget that."

"And then Damascus." It was the younger boy again. "The Romans killed thousands more Jews there, too."

At least two dozen other men had gathered now, all of them nodding and muttering as they clustered at the edge of the ruined palace.

"Our fighters occupy Masada now," shouted one of them, "and the fucking Romans will never get it back!"

"Last November, at Beth-Horon—" The older son stopped and pumped his fist in the air. "Our forces destroyed the entire Twelfth Legion."

"Using only rocks and spears!" The younger boy also pumped his fist.

Grown men in the crowd began pumping their fists now, too.

A defiant grin spread across the father's face. "Six thousand professional Roman soldiers turned tail and ran at Beth-Horon."

"But not us!" yelled yet another newcomer. "We chased 'em down and killed every last one! Captured their eagle, too, and we still have it!"

"Forgive our joy," the boys' father said with no trace of apology in his voice, "but on that day our heroic Jewish fighters delivered the Roman army its worst defeat in a century."

"Worst defeat ever!" yowled a voice in the growing throng.

No wonder Nero wants this insurrection squashed.

Nikolaos recalled what Captain Hatzidakis had told him. "I understand that, two months ago, the Romans killed thousands of Jews outside another port."

"That was Ascalon!" cried a young man. "My uncle was among those killed there."

"And they're still at it," said the older son, "all over our undefended villages in the north."

"I'm proof!" yelled a fellow who was missing an arm. "I'm a survivor of Roman carnage in Galilee!"

What a bloody mess.

"But we're fighting back." The father's tone was chilling. "We overran their garrison here and—"

"Killed every Roman we could get our hands on!" a new arrival hollered. "Inside and out!"

Explains what happened at the Antonia and why there are no legionaries in Jerusalem.

"We grabbed all the weapons they left behind!" screamed another.

"Now the Romans are holed up in Caesarea," the older boy said, "plotting their revenge."

"For a while," his father said, "we controlled Caesarea."

"They'll try to snatch Jerusalem back, too," another man said.

"But we'll stop 'em!" shouted an especially angry voice in the distance.

"Our *Siqari'im*," the father said, "broke into Herod's fortress at Masada. Killed scores of soldiers and brought masses of armor and spears back here."

Siqari'im was a new word to Nikolaos, but he guessed its meaning from the Latin equivalent.

Sicarii. Dagger men.

"They're our bravest fighters!" exulted the younger boy.

Soon, every man in the street was howling in chorus.

"Romans, die!"

"They will fail!"

"Kill the Greeks!"

"Death to pagans!"

"Liberty for Judea!"

"Take back our land!"

Someone behind Nikolaos started a chant that he didn't understand. Others took it up as even more passersby joined in.

Soon, the entire Upper City pulsed to a single angry rhythm.

Nikolaos turned his eyes back to the ruins in the ancient city that his Jewish friends in Daphne would have died to see one more time. And then, without another word for the bitter father and his two warmongering sons, he slipped away from the bawling crowd.

Have to find Father and get away before this place explodes.

***

As Nikolaos fled down the steep steps toward the Lower City, his nose once again picked up the aroma of roasting meat. He followed it to an open-air cookshop near the Divine Glory, where he ordered two sausages with bread and a cup of Egyptian beer and decided to engage in conversation with the middle-aged man turning a spit over the fire.

"You are Jewish?" he asked in Aramaic.

The cook gawked as if a three-headed sea monster had walked up to his counter and begun to speak. "You are not."

"No, I am not."

"I knew that."

"How did you know it?"

"You don't look Jewish, and you don't speak Aramaic very well."

"I learned it as a child in Syria."

"And you haven't spoken it since."

"Only with friends."

"Your friends are not Jewish."

"No."

"That explains it."

Nikolaos paid him and took a stool at a small street-side table. Soon the sausages arrived, hot and fragrant, with a crisp-crusted round of bread that tasted so good he immediately ordered another.

First decent food I've had since Athens.

He was polishing off the second sausage when the cook came around the corner of his stall with a bowl of olives.

"I was rude. It's a common failing of my tribe." The cook set the olives on the table and took the other stool. "My name is Shimon."

"I'm Nikolaos. Just arrived from Athens."

"You're not a Greek from Galilee? Didn't grow up in Tiberias?"

"Don't even know where that is."

"Glad to hear it." Shimon helped himself to an olive.

Nikolaos studied his face.

There's something different about this fellow. He's not sweet-natured like the Jews I knew in Daphne, but also not rabid like those at Herod's palace.

Shimon chewed the olive for a few moments, then spit its pit onto the ground. "Just off the boat from Greece and you head to Jerusalem?"

"Got here this morning."

"Not a very smart move."

"Why? I found a place to stay, a place to eat, and—"

Shimon cut him off with an impatient hand motion. "We Jews *hate* you Greeks, and that, my gentile friend, is an understatement."

Best ignore comments like that.

"I'm looking for a man," Nikolaos said. "Once I find him, we'll both leave."

"In Jerusalem there are many men, although—sad to say—not nearly so many as a year ago."

"The Romans are holding this man captive in Caesarea."

"There are no Romans left in Jerusalem and no Greeks other than you. So, of all places, why did you come here?"

"Assumed I'd be safe while I—"

"There are no safe places left in Jerusalem—"

"I understand that now, but—"

"Or anywhere else in this land."

"I *thought* I'd be safe here while I searched for him."

"What's so special about this man that you sailed the great sea in March—and into a war zone, no less—to find him?"

Nikolaos glanced around. Except for a trio of bored-looking donkeys tied to a post, the alley was deserted. And aside from the burned palace and fortress and the angry crowd still chanting in the Upper City, Jerusalem didn't seem like a war zone.

Can I trust this fellow?

He inspected Shimon's face.

I've got to find someone here to trust.

"The man I'm searching for is my father. He's a prisoner on an imperial ship."

"In other words, a galley slave."

Nikolaos nodded. "On one of General Vespasian's warships."

"So, then, go to Caesarea. That's where the Romans and their ships are."

And also the Roman woman and her brat and her atrocious slave.

"Too many Romans there, and not one of them will help me."

"You're expecting the Jews of Jerusalem to help you?"

"I hope they will."

Shimon snorted. "Why?"

Because the Jewish slaves in Daphne were the only people who ever showed any kindness to a motherless Greek slave boy.

But he didn't say that.

"Because the Jews hate the Romans as much as I do. Especially now that the Romans are preparing to crush you."

Shimon made a few loud clucking sounds. "The emperor thinks he's dumped his Jewish problem onto Vespasian, but there are many other factors he doesn't know about. It's a very dangerous political situation."

"Involving the Jews?"

"A very dangerous political situation *completely* involving the Jews."

Something I need to understand if I'm to survive here and succeed.

"Can you explain it to me?"

Shimon raised his eyebrows. "How much time do you have?"

***

Darkness was falling on the Lower City.

For five hours, taking breaks only to serve other customers, Shimon had poured into Nikolaos's head more details than he could possibly remember.

Names of kings and priests and procurators.

Centuries-old feuds, rivalries, and conspiracy theories.

Friction between the provinces of Judea, Samaria, and Galilee.

Wars, murders, mass killings, famines, destroyed temples, and rebuilt temples.

Proven and unproven charges of corruption and high crimes by Roman and Jewish officials.

Traditional religious sects and newer splinter groups—the Essenes, Edomites, Pharisees, Sadducees, Zealots, *Siqari'im*, and followers of something called the Fourth Philosophy—some of them murderous and all with competing beliefs and political ambitions.

So much worse than I expected.

Stunned, Nikolaos sat without speaking as Shimon's too-long, too-grim lesson in Jewish history and culture ground to a close.

"These factions," Shimon concluded, "with their endless infighting, can't agree on even the most basic defensive strategy against the Romans. They've divided our people and aggravated our relationship with Rome while hampering our ability to fight off Vespasian's legions and the modern war machine he's assembling."

I was foolish to come without understanding at least a bit of this, but I'm here now, with a job to do.

"Isn't there someone you know—or know of—here in Jerusalem or elsewhere, who has a good relationship with the Romans?"

Shimon dug his fingers into his hair and massaged his scalp, as if that would help him remember. "One man comes to mind," he said. "Happens to be a Pharisee, and a remarkably rich one at that."

"The sect you said enforces strict adherence to Jewish laws and identity?"

"Exactly. Sanctimonious, self-righteous purists who hold themselves up as a counter to the growing gentile influence on our land." Shimon snorted again. "The Pharisees are bitter enemies of the Sadducees. That's *my* tribe."

"Tell me about this Pharisee who gets along so well with the Romans."

"He's not much older than you are. Better educated than most of them. He spent a year in Rome, so he understands the Romans and seems to get along with them."

"Think he'd be willing to talk to me?"

"Maybe." Shimon shrugged. "For sure, he knows what it's like to ask for help."

"What do you mean?"

"I mean… this young Jew somehow managed to appear *in person* before the emperor in Rome to enter a formal plea on behalf of our people. And he accomplished that feat by enlisting the support of Nero's wife, no less."

"Amazing." Nikolaos stared into Shimon's face. "Do you know him?"

"My kind and his don't mix, remember?" A sour laugh. "He came back from Rome two years ago and is rising fast these days in political circles."

"Does he live in Jerusalem?"

"His family's here. I can't say if he's in the city or not. Might be in Caesarea. His father, Matityahu, can tell you how to find him. Assuming he wants to."

"Does this Mat-at-ya— Does he live near here?"

Shimon pointed to the top of the rocky cliff that separated the Lower City from the Upper City. "Head back that way tomorrow morning. Anyone up there can point you to the house of Matityahu, but I doubt you'll have any trouble spotting it."

"Can I trust this Matta-ya-yu? Can I trust his son?"

"You trusted me." Shimon smiled for the first time that afternoon. "And I'm just a simple Sadducee with a cookshop. So, do you want the name of this well-connected young Pharisee or not?"

With nothing to write on, Nikolaos memorized the name as Shimon pronounced it.

Yosef ben Matityahu.

CHAPTER 23

On the eastern side of Caesarea, surrounded by crowds too dense for Adin's cart to penetrate, Theodosia tapped his shoulder. "You can let us off here. We'll walk on in."

She draped her white silk palla over her head, dropped its long ends down her back, and turned to Doros. "People say King Herod's 'new town' is a small-scale imitation of Rome and Athens."

"But it's even more important, Mother, since General Vespasian is here."

Meanwhile, Myrine knotted the ends of her undyed cotton headscarf under her chin. "We sure do hope so, Little Man."

Thus protected from the wind and disapproving eyes, the women followed the boy through masses of people and animals that threatened to overwhelm Herod's proudest achievement.

Along the walkways, clusters of toga-clad Roman citizens and tunic-clad functionaries bent their heads together, as if sharing imperial secrets.

In the alleys, laborers and merchants in flowing red, blue, and green robes—Jews, Greeks, and Arabs—tugged on balky camels, strings of over-burdened donkeys, and coffles of newly enslaved Jews from rural Galilee.

On the streets, Roman officers on horseback galloped through, singly and in pairs, forcing pedestrians to jump aside to avoid being trampled.

And everywhere they looked, every man who had the power to do so was elbowing everyone else out of his way.

As in Yamnia, there were no other women and children. No hint of softness. No humor. Caesarea and its Roman rulers were busy ramping up for war.

***

The house of Matityahu stood so tall and so proud in the morning sun that Nikolaos had no need to inquire about its location. As Shimon had predicted, nobody could miss the majestic three-story structure in its fine Upper City neighborhood.

A thin, wrinkled, long-bearded, and gentle-eyed man wearing the off-white, belted, knee-length tunic of a slave responded to his knock.

"Is this the home of Matityahu?" Nikolaos asked in his best Aramaic.

The slave bowed.

"My name is Nikolaos. I am a Greek from Athens."

Might as well make that clear right up front.

"Is your master in?"

Wordlessly, the slave ushered Nikolaos into a hall whose stone floor was punctuated by tilted squares of light from windows high above. He offered him a seat on a marble bench and disappeared.

Moments later, in walked another thin, wrinkled, long-bearded, and gentle-eyed man.

But for the clothing, I'd take them for brothers.

Over a plain linen undergarment, a sleeveless, deep-brown woolen mantle flowed unbelted from this man's narrow shoulders to his slippers. A long, brown-and-white scarf with white fringe fell from a squarish head piece.

The newcomer extended a hand with gnarled, swollen joints. "I am Matityahu. Welcome to my home."

This is the warmth I expected to find among the Jews of Jerusalem.

"My name is Nikolaos." He rose and took the proffered hand. "I am a stranger in your city."

"Strangers who are peaceful and well meaning are always welcome in the City of David."

***

Theodosia's family trio finally drew near the water's edge of King Herod's masterpiece "new city." Admiring each wonder they passed, they strolled his double-colonnaded promenade; exclaimed at his expansive, human-built harbor; gaped across the water at his marvelous "floating" palace; climbed the steps of his high-arched, multi-columned Temple of Roma and Augustus;

and peered out through its perfectly positioned windows toward the naval biremes and triremes rocking peacefully on the blue water.

"Your pa's on one of those ships," Myrine said to Doros. "I hate being so close without seeing him."

Doros's eyes swept the harbor. "Me, too."

Before they reached the palace that served as Vespasian's headquarters, Doros dashed off toward a group of soldiers marching down Caesarea's main street. Theodosia and Myrine pursued him into the polyglot chaos, where once again they struggled to avoid the sweaty humans, the puddled mud, and the horse, camel, and donkey droppings. Finally, they spotted him many yards away, strutting his steps behind the legionaries.

He will find a way to be a soldier.

"Keep an eye him," Theodosia yelled. "I'm going on to the palace."

"If we get separated," Myrine yelled back, "Doros and I will meet you at Adin's house."

***

Matityahu led Nikolaos to the most luxurious room he had seen since leaving his master's mansion in Daphne where, as a slave, he was never allowed to sit.

Tasteful tapestries graced its walls. Elegant rugs embellished the highly polished, intricately laid wooden floor, which in itself was finer than any surface Nikolaos had ever walked across. A thick cushion in a rich shade of green enveloped his hips as he lowered himself onto one of the marble chairs.

Meanwhile, Matityahu inspected him with the calmest eyes that Nikolaos had encountered in a long time.

Have to make sure he sees this stranger as peaceful and well meaning. And polite. And humble. And trustworthy.

A second slave handed Nikolaos a goblet. He had no idea what kind of wine it was, only that it was sweet and slid smoothly down his throat.

Matityahu gestured for Nikolaos to speak first, and he complied.

"I arrived in Jerusalem yesterday, sir. My Aramaic is poor. Please be patient as I try to explain why I am here."

Matityahu nodded but remained quiet.

"I traveled all the way from Athens to find a man who I believe is your son."
He'll never know that's not the truth.

"I have two sons," Matityahu said. "Which one are you seeking?"

"The one who spent time in Rome. His name is—and please forgive me if I do not say this right—Yosef ben Matityahu."

His host raised his eyebrows. "Is Yosef so well known abroad?"

"My Jewish friends in Athens, the ones who taught me to speak Aramaic—"
Close enough to the truth.

"They told me of a well-born young man from Jerusalem who, as they recalled it, was on especially good terms with the Romans in Judea."
A bigger stretch.

"Yosef is the one you seek." The old man's already-wrinkled brow wrinkled a bit more, and for a moment Nikolaos thought he might laugh. "My other son," he went on without laughing, "is much more sensible."

"I'm sorry, sir, but I know nothing of him."

"Of course not. It is unlikely that anyone would journey from a foreign land to speak with my other son."

"Because he is so sensible?"

Matityahu's knobby fingers combed his beard. "More than any other Jewish sect, we Pharisees hold ourselves apart from the pagans who have invaded our land in recent centuries. My son Yosef does not care much about that, but his brother is more scrupulous."

"What you're saying is… Yosef will not mind talking with me."

"He will not mind." A thin smile. "But there's more I would tell you. The most important thing for a Pharisee is knowing and abiding by the Torah."
Just as Shimon said.

"And since a Pharisee father's most important job," Matityahu continued, "is to ensure that his sons can read and interpret the Torah, I personally instructed both of mine."

"Your sons are fortunate."
More fortunate than I was.

"I only tell you this, young man, because it means I am qualified to attest that both of my sons are intelligent. Both are quick and clever. Both are fluent in Hebrew, the official language of our Temple and Sanhedrin, and also in Aramaic, our popular regional language. Both are proficient in Greek, which our Roman masters employ in their attempt to govern what they call their eastern provinces." Matityahu paused, sighed, and shook his head. "Unfortunately, common sense is not a shared family trait."

A subtle way of advising me that Yosef is foolish?

"From what I hear," Nikolaos said, "Yosef is a highly regarded diplomat."

"True, and also—while only thirty—our top military general." The old man's voice rippled with something that sounded like pride.

But, as Nikolaos knew from his own experience, it was very likely something else.

Irony. Does Matityahu really think and talk so much like my own father?

***

Theodosia's white silk stola, which she had bought in Athens for her first visit to Governor Vibius Galarius, had been torn and stained with wine even before the voyage to Judea. And its condition didn't improve in the gunnysack.

She had reversed it when dressing this morning, so the red blotch and ripped fabric weren't so prominent, but now, after two hours in Caesarea's crowds and heat and stink, it was also a sweaty, twisted mess. Without a complete re-dressing, straightening it was impossible.

Making things worse, after the brisk walk across town and the long stroll around the harbor and the hurried chase after Doros, her legs hurt.

But still, she raised her chin and stepped up to Herod's door with one hand over the viper amulet that hung under her clothes, between her breasts.

Give me strength, little snake, and please, dearest Juno, let them recognize me as a Roman woman.

"I am Theodosia Varro," she announced in her finest patrician Latin to the guard at the door, "here to visit Procurator Marcus Antonius Julianus."

The guard's mouth curled up, but he said nothing.

"I am quite sure," she added, "that he will want to receive me."

"The procurator is not available today." His tone was respectful.

"Then I will speak with his deputy."

"His deputy is also not available today."

Theodosia blinked a couple of times. "Any chance the procurator or his deputy will be available tomorrow?"

"Most unlikely."

He sounds like a native Roman.

"Please, sir, it's urgent that I meet with one of them today or tomorrow. You see, this is an emergency, because—"

"There's a lot going on here, lady, as you can—"

"I've traveled a very long way to get here, and— I really must ask— Must insist—" She floundered to a stop and took a deep breath.

"Civilian business," the guard said with the patience of one who answers the same question on a daily, or perhaps hourly, basis, "is on hold for the duration of the war."

"On hold for—" She gasped. "No! I'm a Roman citizen, and my husband—"

"No one will see you today." He motioned her away from the door so two men could pass through. "No one will see you tomorrow."

"Isn't there a spot where I can sit and wait, just in case?"

"The reception hall is already overcrowded."

Like everything else in Caesarea.

"Please, sir, let me in. I'll find a place to wait. I promise to sit quietly. Won't disturb anybody."

"It's not possible."

"But it's important."

"We're preparing for war, lady." His eyes bore into hers. "Don't you understand? General Vespasian's three legions are about to launch a full-scale invasion of Galilee, and that's all that matters."

"Is the general currently in Caesarea?"

"Not at leave to say."

***

"Last winter," Matityahu continued, "Yosef was appointed general of the Jewish army in Galilee, or governor-general, to be precise."

"That's a great responsibility."

If he's commanding the Jewish army, maybe he's not so close to the Romans.

Matityahu chuckled in a way that resembled real mirth. "It certainly is a most unusual job, since there is no Jewish army in Galilee or anywhere else."

"How can someone be a general in an army that doesn't exist?"

Matityahu chuckled again, with considerably less humor. "The friend who told me of Yosef's new command also mentioned a Zealot plot to kill him."

"Why?"

"He's Jewish, so the Romans don't trust him. And since he's thought to be closer than any other Jew to the Romans, the Zealots hate him."

"And maybe other Jews don't trust him either."

"You're a shrewd young man, with your whole life ahead of you. I, on the other hand, have little time left." Matityahu gave another chuckle, a very sour one this time." I have written to Yosef that my dearest wish is to lay eyes on him once more before I die. I don't know if he received that letter. If you do manage to speak with him, will you give him that message?"

No better way to make this old fellow trust me.

"Of course. And, sir—" Nikolaos stopped, as if considering whether or not to confide his own secret. "May I also share a personal matter with you?"

"I would be honored."

"My own father's life is at stake, sir. He's a captive of the Romans in Caesarea."

Matityahu was silent for a few moments. "I am sorry to hear that."

"Actually, that's why I came to Judea. To find him and set him free and take him home."

There was a longer silence, followed by a rustle of fabric and slippers as Matityahu rose from his chair. "I'm not sure how you expect me to help you."

"I believe your son can help me." Nikolaos stood, too, and looked into the old man's eyes. "Please tell me how to find Yosef ben Matityahu."

"My son's location is a secret for the duration of the war."

"You can trust me, sir."

"We have many spies in this land."

"I am not a spy, sir."

"Too many assassins."

Must break down his defenses.

"Surely, sir, you don't think I'm an assassin."

"In these modern times, it's hard to know whom to trust."

"Please trust me, sir. I'm not an assassin. Not a spy. I just want to find my own father and get us both out of this land before it blows itself apart."

And that, for sure, is the honest truth.

Nikolaos made his voice as soft as possible. "My only interest in your son is that I believe he can help me find my father."

Matityahu hesitated a bit more. Fiddled with his fingers. Combed his beard again. And then he nodded. "Go to Galilee, Nikolaos. Go to the town of Tiberias. My son moves in and out of there. It's the best place to catch him."

Tiberias.

"And get there soon," Matityahu went on, "because, if the Romans don't kill Yosef first, the Zealots surely will."

***

At last, the guard at the main entrance to Herod's palace gave in and handed Theodosia off to another soldier, who led her down a long, black corridor to the tightly packed, vaulted-ceilinged, scarlet-frescoed reception hall.

She provided her name to the soldier in charge and squeezed into the only available seat, a narrow space on a hard bench between two green-robed Arabs who eyed her with disgust from both right and left, then quickly stood and together retreated to the opposite end of the room.

As far as they can get from me.

Afraid of missing her call, she stayed put for the rest of the morning and the entire afternoon. Skipped her midday meal. Didn't even take a break to find a public toilet.

Every now and then, the officer in charge summoned a petitioner. Perhaps a dozen in total all day. As the sun was falling, aching from hunger and thirst, Theodosia left the palace with all the others who had not been called.

And in the growing darkness of Caesarea's empty streets, with no sign of Myrine or Doros waiting for her, she paid an unknown donkey driver to carry her to Oren and Judith's home.

***

It took Nikolaos three days to find and make a deal with the only donkey driver in Jerusalem who was willing—for five times his usual fee, paid in full in advance, with no guarantee of safe delivery—to take a passenger into war-ravaged Galilee.

Uri's extra-large wagon was a bonus, even though two donkeys were required to pull it. Wider and longer than a normal cart, its cargo area had enough space so both men could sleep there during their time on the road.

Not having to pay for inns will offset his absurd charge.

***

Over the next three days, the same scenario played out in the reception hall. Not one of the other petitioners—all men, of course—was willing to share a bench with Theodosia. And not once did the officer in charge call her name.

Still, there were two big improvements.

Doros stayed "at home" under the watchful eyes of Judith and Esther.

And Myrine accompanied Theodosia… to bring her food from a nearby cookshop, to keep men from snatching her bench when she needed a break, and to ensure her safe return each evening.

Right in the middle of the third afternoon, Theodosia turned to her slave, who had been standing behind her for hours. "You're so patient, Myrine. Most women would be jumping out of their skins by now."

Myrine's eyes filled with tears. "You and Master Alexander gave me the best things ever in my life, Lycos and our boys." She glanced around the room and bent low, close to Theodosia's ear. "There ain't nothing I wouldn't do for you, Mistress," she whispered. "I'd kill for you, if need be."

***

At sunrise on the rainy fourth morning, Nikolaos and his driver rolled through Jerusalem's outermost walls onto the same north-south highway that had brought Nikolaos from the Yamnia junction.

"Even in good times," Uri said, "only a Greek would go to Tiberias."

"I've heard it's a great resort area."

"Used to be, but once you luxury-loving pagans took it over—"

"You luxury-hating monotheists can't stand to be there."

"Got that right. We remember the Sea of Tiberias as it was decades ago, when it was a nice, clean, Greek-free place."

Have to ignore his insults.

"I thought it was called the Sea of Galilee." Nikolaos wedged his orange leather sack between his feet and the solid back-support wall of the bench.

Don't want that thing bouncing out on the road.

"Depends on who you talk to."

"As with everything else in this country."

Uri laughed. "Got that right."

Around mid-morning, they passed the turn-off to Yamnia and continued north toward the Caesarea intersection.

"Lots of inns in Caesarea," Uri said, "but they've been crammed full of shit-faced Romans for months."

"So, let's push on as planned and pull over somewhere for the night."

"Notice the stash of knives down there." The driver pointed to the same secure area under the deep bench. "We'll need 'em to fight off the bandits."

***

On the rainy fourth morning, during Theodosia and Myrine's daily trek from the edge of Caesarea into town, something happened.

At first, it seemed so ordinary that it barely caught Theodosia's attention.

They were struggling amid the usual crowds in the blocks near the palace when a pair of uniformed officers on horseback splashed through, scattering pedestrians in their wake. Theodosia, with her bad legs, barely managed to scramble out of the way. Furious, she glanced up and recognized, under one of the red-and-brass helmets, a face she had not seen in eleven years.

Titus!

He was older and heavier, and his features revealed a focus and fury never present in the young man who had courted her. But, for sure, it was him.

By the time her mind registered Titus's identity, he and his companion had pounded on into the next block. Theodosia could not possibly catch them, but the sighting confirmed one thing.

Titus and Vespasian are here.

She looked at Myrine. "You'll never guess who that closest rider was."

"Who?"

"General Titus. He's in Caesarea."

Myrine stared intently down the road at the fast-moving but flashily helmeted horsemen. "If General Titus is here, don't that mean General Vespasian is here, too?"

"Probably."

Myrine wrapped her fingers around Theodosia's arm and gave it a gentle shake. "So, Mistress, stop worrying about the procurator. Aim for the generals."

***

In the middle of the afternoon, as Uri's donkeys plodded north through a downpour, Nikolaos noticed a bright, florally painted cart pulling off just past the Caesarea turnoff, at its northwest corner.

I've seen that one before.

Its driver jumped down, opened a wide gate in a stone wall, and tugged his donkey under a huge fig tree into the courtyard.

Hard to forget those flowers.

Then he remembered.

That's the one she hired in Yamnia.

Just beyond the intersection, they passed a boy resolutely marching—and dripping—on the right side of the road. Nikolaos turned to get a better look.

Father's little soldier.

Quickly, he glanced back at the house. It took a few moments before all the details registered—the cart, the gate, the house, the tree, the boy—but once they did, they burned themselves into his memory.

Now I know where they're staying. Northwest of the Caesarea turnoff. A one-story stone house. With a covered area on the roof. And an unusually wide gate. And a tall fig tree outside the walls.

***

Much later on that still-rainy afternoon, as yet another donkey driver carried Theodosia and Myrine east out of Caesarea, they spotted Doros. Swinging his arms. Lifting his legs. Shouting his paces. Marching west toward Herod's city.

Theodosia told the driver to stop.

"What on Earth are you doing?" she called to her sopping-wet son.

"Keeping in practice. Staying tough."

"Did Judith let you out? Or Esther?"

"I let myself out."

"You can't march all alone in the road like this. It's not safe."

"I'm not alone. There's people out here. Loads of soldiers."

"You know what I mean."

He pouted. "So, where am I supposed to practice?"

"Listen to your ma, Little Man." Myrine hopped off and prodded him into the cart. "Remember what Adin said about bandits? This just ain't a real smart thing for you to do."

***

The next day, after Nikolaos and Uri spent a soggy night in the wagon well north of the Caesarea turnoff, their trip slowed considerably.

Without warning, thousands of Jerusalem-bound Jewish refugees— women, children, and old men journeying south on foot or donkey from the harassed villages of northern Galilee—came face to face on the narrow, rocky, muddy road with thousands of Galilee-bound Roman troops.

"King Herod sure didn't plan ahead," Nikolaos said, "when he built this miserable excuse for a highway."

"King Herod never planned ahead for anything," Uri said, "except his own comfort and pleasure, which is why many Jews believe he actually was a Greek."

As always, Nikolaos ignored the insult. "Isn't there a better route?"

"If there were, we and everyone else would have been on it long ago."

I'm starting to understand why he charged me so much for this trip.

Every mile was filled with Romans raucously berating the Jews, insisting that they get off the road, move over, leave.

As if they have somewhere else to go.

The Jews shouted back, of course, as did the occasional Arab or Greek caught in the middle. For hours and miles and days on end, Aramaic dueled with Latin, Arabic, and Greek in a frenzied, brain-frying cacophony.

The already-too-hot April air reeked of unwashed bodies, plus all the urine and excrement those people and animals dumped along the roadway. Flies and dung beetles were everywhere. At the head of each caravan, mounted officers led hundreds of archers, lancers, cooks, servants, and donkey carts heaped high with everyday supplies. Behind them, miles-long caravans of the biggest wagons and horses that Nikolaos had ever seen hauled an ominous array of the world's oldest and most modern weapons of war through Samaria's lush farm lands and Galilee's soft green hills.

Once or twice each day, Uri had to pull off and wait hours for the Roman war machine to pass. He and Nikolaos used the time to hunt lizards and hares, which they roasted in the rain over sputtering campfires. When the normal traffic flowed, they moved with it. When it stopped, even for short periods, they crawled under the wagon for naps. After dark, they fitfully slept with knives in their hands.

And through it all—every day and every night, waking or dreaming—the same series of thoughts ricocheted wildly inside Nikolaos's head.

Between the sea voyage in March and the land journey in April, these have been the most miserable months of my life.

Never again will I put myself through something like this.

Not in any place. Not at any time. Not with any person. Not for any purpose.

***

By the time the rains began to subside, Theodosia had tried every approach she could think of, without success. If Vespasian and Titus actually were in Caesarea, as she was starting to doubt, they must have put themselves off limits to non-military visitors.

Unfortunately, the palace guards she spoke with never seemed to feel at leave to tell her anything. Legionaries at the gate of the growing tent city inside the Hippodrome refused to discuss the generals' whereabouts and eventually ordered Theodosia and Myrine out of their sight.

So they had taken to standing back from the main street, watching as uniformed officers galloped through the crowd. No further sign of Titus.

But still, there was something new in the air. Over the last few nights, the *Siqari'im*—whom Oren described to her as "professional assassins armed with curved daggers, radical ideas, and old grudges"—had begun sneaking into town, slitting throats, disemboweling men, and vanishing into the darkness.

At least a dozen armed legionaries turned up dead every morning, but nobody ever saw the killers, who came out of nowhere and struck everywhere.

Survivors of attacks who made it back to the tent city warned their buddies and reported the attacks to their commanders, who issued orders to stay inside after sundown. To no avail, of course. The temptations of the city's bars and brothels were just too great.

Desperate to make some kind of progress, Theodosia decided on a different, much-riskier tactic. From this point on, whenever an officer—who might be Titus, or might know Titus, or might be able to get to Titus—came galloping through the crowd, she would no longer stay out of his way.

Dressed as a Roman matron, hard to ignore in her red-stained white stola and palla, she would stand resolutely in his path and dare him to run over her.

Force him to slow down.

Force him to stop.

And *see* her. And *look* at her. And *converse* with her.

Myrine tried to talk her out of it. "You've been broke up enough times in your life. Two bad falls already. Why take more chances now?"

"I'll be fine."

"Not if somebody's big horse kicks you."

"That's most unlikely."

"So, what happens to Master Doros if you die out here in the street? Or to Master Alexander?" For the first time ever, Myrine raised her voice to her mistress. "Neither one of 'em's ever gonna forgive me if I let you get yourself killed."

***

More than any other person Nikolaos had met in Judea, Uri enjoyed expounding his war theories.

"It's clear what's going on," he said one hot—and finally dry—afternoon as he tied his donkeys to a scrubby tree by the side of the road on the southern border of Galilee.

He joined Nikolaos in the shade under the wagon, where they spent a couple of hours flicking away the usual creepy-crawlies while waiting for the latest north-bound military caravan to pass and fuming at the streams of pedestrians and donkeys that raised clouds of dust while trudging in the opposite direction through the rough vegetation.

"Glad it's clear to you," Nikolaos said.

"Very clear." Uri grinned. "Ever since General Vespasian moved into Ptolemais from Syria, he's given his soldiers free rein to torment the villages of northern Galilee."

"Why them?"

"They're the closest to his camp. And isolated. And vulnerable."

"But what's the point? Why do it?"

"The wily old man is playing strategic games. By slaughtering so many Galileans and enslaving so many others and chasing all the rest south to Jerusalem, he deepens the fear of Rome in every Jewish heart."

"How does that benefit him?"

"Nikolaos, you really are a typical Greek, aren't you? Been so long since the Romans conquered your little city-states and in the interval you got so fat and lazy that now you can't even strategize the tiniest bit about war."

"Which means, obviously, that I have to defer to your superior wisdom and experience. So I repeat: How does that benefit Vespasian?"

Uri expelled a loud breath, as if some dagger-wielding Zealot were forcing him to share his most brilliant insights with a moron.

"When people get scared," he declared with as much patience as he seemed capable of, "they don't think straight. And when they don't think straight, they don't fight well. And when they don't fight well, they surrender too quickly. And when they surrender too quickly, Vespasian and his pompous-ass son and all the other bloody bastards that they brought along with 'em can ship hundreds of thousands of Jews off into slavery and get themselves out of this worthless, snake-and-scorpion-infested land a whole lot faster."

Grudgingly, Nikolaos nodded. "Makes sense."

"And also," Uri went on, "if the City of David crowds up with old men and useless females and children from the north, that means they've got a whole new problem on their hands. How to feed 'em all and house 'em all and keep 'em all safe if—or, much more likely, when—the Romans decide to turn their attention to Jerusalem."

"So, if all these people heading south are survivors, who's left in the north to fight the Romans?"

"There's bound to be plenty of strong young men there still, and you can bet that Vespasian—that sneaky ol' Roman fox—is planning his big take-no-prisoners assault on at least one of the region's fortresses."

"Galilee has fortresses?"

"Sure. Lots of 'em. Centuries ago, our ancestors surrounded their main towns with tall, sturdy walls to protect 'em from marauders. Most are still standing, either in whole or in part."

"Can Vespasian capture them all?"

Uri shrugged. "Look at the forces he's mobilized on this side of Galilee. Then imagine what we can't see coming down from Syria in the north."

***

On the next-to-last morning in April, a blast of military horns drew even more people than usual into the streets of Caesarea, where civilians jostled with the regular array of merchants, free laborers, slaves, and pack animals.

And, of course, Theodosia and Myrine—still hoping for another glimpse of either Titus or Vespasian—were in the thick of it.

Scores of mounted couriers emerged in a thunderous rush from the Hippodrome, the sports venue that was now filled with army tents, to the great dismay of racing enthusiasts like Adin.

"We're fanning out all over Judea," the nearest courier announced in Latin, "to spread the word that our beloved and divine emperor has ordered General Vespasian to crush all resistance."

He repeated his announcement in Aramaic, which Theodosia found mildly amusing.

I bet these monotheistic Jews just love hearing how the "divine" Nero has mandated their destruction.

Myrine leaned to Theodosia's ear. "I know you told me Vespasian is Rome's best general, but didn't you also say he slept through the emperor's concert in Athens?"

"Snoring loudly the whole time." Theodosia grinned at her. "But Nero needs a win right now. He'll forgive anyone who can beat the Jews."

"Over the winter and early spring," the courier continued in his most stentorian tones, "General Vespasian traveled the land route from Greece.

He crossed the Hellespont, took command of the glorious Fifth and Tenth Legions, and marched them both to Antioch."

"Why Antioch?" Myrine asked.

"It's a major city directly on his route here."

The courier's voice swelled even more over the heads of the crowd. "Soon after, the fabled Fifteenth Legion—proudly under the command of General Titus—joined his father's legions in Ptolemais, a mere two-day ride north of here. All the soldiers and supplies that arrived by ship in Caesarea are now in Galilee."

"Now we know why," Theodosia said to Myrine, "after all this time, we haven't been able to locate Titus and Vespasian. They never were here."

"But you saw General Titus that day."

"I *thought* I saw him. Maybe I just *wanted* to see him."

"And here's the best news yet!" The courier shouted even more vociferously. "Agrippa the Second has added two thousand Jewish soldiers from his own palace guard!"

Myrine looked puzzled. "Agrippa the Second?"

"Oren mentioned him to me. He's their local king. Called a client-king, because he's under Nero's thumb and has no real power of his own."

"Why would he support the Romans against the Jews?"

"Guess he wants to end up on the winning side."

Myrine frowned. "But if he and two thousand Jewish soldiers supported their own people, wouldn't they have a better chance of beating the Romans?"

"They might. Agrippa, however, would have an even better chance of traveling to Rome as the primary trophy to be marched in chains through the streets and then ritually strangled to death at the end of Vespasian's triumphal procession."

"The Romans do that?"

"They do that."

The courier's big black horse began to sidestep, as if eager to move along. His rider, however, had one more message for the people thronging the streets of Caesarea.

"Jewish rebels and all who consort with them—" He thrust his spear toward the sky as the horse lunged forward. "Prepare to die!"

CHAPTER 24

Nikolaos's horrible journey finally bore fruit on the afternoon of the tenth day of May in a nondescript two-room building situated atop a low hill in the Galilean resort town of Tiberias.

From Uri's insults, he had learned that this western shore of the Sea of Galilee was famous for its white beaches and hot mineral springs. Over the last fifty years, these natural features had drawn spa-loving Greeks from Alexandria and Antioch, first as visitors, then as permanent residents whose walled settlement further enhanced its appeal to sybarites from around the Mediterranean, thus attracting even more of them.

Uri considered the place unclean, due to its abundance of gentiles, and also because it had been built over an old Jewish cemetery.

As a cultural anomaly, Tiberias was loyal to Rome—and thus relatively safe from Vespasian's calculated harassments—which was, Nikolaos assumed, why the governor-general had chosen it for his temporary headquarters.

In the antechamber, two aides confiscated the knife that Uri had given him but agreed to set his orange-colored sack against a wall in the main room.

Governor-General Yosef ben Matityahu rose from a sun-washed desk and extended his hand.

His thin face and hawk-like nose clearly came from his father, but they were paired with shorter hair, a beard still dark, a brow still smooth, and much-less-gentle gray eyes. His plain brown mantle echoed the unpainted wood in the room, and the only evidence of his military rank was a sword in a scabbard hanging from his belt.

Matching windows on the east and west walls provided air and light to the central part of the room, where two wooden stools faced each other across the desk. Everything else lay in deep darkness.

Even before Nikolaos's eyes adjusted to the contrasty light, he sensed the presence of more guards. Ultimately, he counted six standing in the shadows—one behind the desk, one beside the door, and two flanking each window—all well armed and watching his every movement.

Not exactly a relaxing atmosphere for a get-acquainted conversation.

"I would never have expected," Yosef ben Matityahu said in heavily accented Greek as he offered his guest a seat, "to find a Greek left in Tiberias with hairy enough balls to walk in here like you just did."

How in Hades did a Judean Pharisee learn to talk like a Greek sailor?

Nikolaos decided not to match his colorful language. "The donkey driver who brought me here from Jerusalem mentioned that Tiberias has a large Greek population."

"Tiberias *had* a large Greek population," ben Matityahu said, "until some local shits decided to take care of the problem."

"I don't understand."

"Last year, before I got here, a group of Zealots crept into town and massacred scores of Greeks they considered Roman sympathizers. Those who survived either fled or are keeping their heads well down."

Wonder why Uri, with all his chatter, never told me about that.

Yosef ben Matityahu stared out the window toward the inland sea. "There were times when peace between our two peoples might have been possible."

"It's not possible now?"

"Is peace ever possible among rats who delight in biting each other's heads off?"

Time to change the subject.

To mark that switch, Nikolaos began speaking in Aramaic. "I visited your father in Jerusalem."

Yosef ben Matityahu's head jerked. His body stiffened. "Why?"

"Searching for you, I found him."

"What did he tell you?"

"That I'd find you in Tiberias."

"Which was supposed to be a secret."

Nikolaos ignored that. "He doesn't look well."

"Worries too much about me."

"He asked if I'd give you a message."

"What message?"

"He hopes to see you again before he dies."

Ben Matityahu shrugged. "He wrote me that months ago."

"He said you hadn't replied."

"Who has time to reply?" The governor-general leaned forward and inspected Nikolaos. "Why were you searching for me?"

"I learned in Jerusalem that you have a good relationship with the Romans."

"That depends. With the Romans in Rome? Yes. With the Romans in Judea? No."

Nikolaos took a few moments to absorb that information. "In particular, I was hoping you had a good relationship with General Vespasian."

Unexpectedly, the governor-general guffawed. "Haven't met the man yet, but I do expect to meet him soon."

"So," Nikolaos went on after a startled pause, "you actually *do* have plans for a meeting with General Vespasian?"

"That's not what I said."

"Guess I missed your meaning."

The governor-general's amusement vanished. "Oh, my young friend."

There's only four years between us.

"My young friend," he repeated. "Our ragtag Galilean fighters are taking on Rome's Fifth Imperial Legion, Rome's Tenth Imperial Legion, and Rome's Fifteenth Imperial Legion—in combination with the large and excellent Syrian army and the lesser might of our puppet-king, Agrippa the Second— all under the command of the much-feared General Vespasian and his blood-thirsty son, General Titus. There could be as many as sixty thousand warriors assembled outside Ptolemais, just a day's march from here."

"I knew that."

Some of it.

"*Sixty thousand*," ben Matityahu emphasized, "infantry and cavalry and archers and lancers, along with unknown numbers of slave laborers and engineers with the skills and equipment to level forests and mountains, build roads, set up camps, and deliver every weapon known to modern man. Ballistas. Scorpions. Catapults. Siege towers. You name it. They've got it."

"Traveling up from Jerusalem," Nikolaos said, just to say something, "I saw thousands of Roman soldiers, plus Vespasian's war machine."

The governor-general propped his elbows on his desk and tapped his chin with his fingers. "Traveling up from Jerusalem, did you also see thousands of Jewish infantry, cavalry, archers, lancers, laborers, and engineers?"

Nikolaos shook his head.

"Did you see *my* war machine?"

Another negative shake.

"And that's just half of our predicament," said ben Matityahu.

"What's the other half?"

"Jewish soldiers are very brave." Ben Matityahu nodded as if confirming something he assumed Nikolaos already knew. "Very. They're brave, fearless, passionate, reckless, and disorganized... novices."

"But they have—"

"The Romans are also brave and fearless, but they're not novices. Not passionate. Not reckless. Not disorganized. Every Roman soldier is a cool-headed, highly disciplined, well-trained, and professional... killer."

"Isn't that what you're training your men to be?"

"I cannot train my men to be something they don't want to be."

"But—" Nikolaos hit the top of the desk. "Damn it, man, your fighters destroyed an entire Roman legion a few months ago."

"Oh, yes, we're ferocious fighters when some dumb-ass general spreads his legion out in a long, narrow valley, handing us hundreds of opportunities to slaughter his men from above and literally inviting us to cut off his rear flank, which we did. And even in less-favorable conditions, we're ruthless with our slings, rocks, and spears."

Slings, rocks, and spears?

Again, Nikolaos said nothing, so ben Matityahu went on.

"We're also ferocious fighters among ourselves. Over generations, we've mastered all the tricks of stabbing each other in the back, leveling each other's villages, and burning each other's crops and orchards."

What Shimon was talking about.

"Not to mention our knack for slaughtering luxury-loving Greeks in spa towns."

Is that irony inherited from his father, too?

The governor-general rose, stepped to the eastern window, and gestured for Nikolaos to join him.

The sun currently dropping in the west cast vivid shades of rose and purple across a single enormous cloud that lay reflected on the smooth, deep-blue surface of the Sea of Galilee.

Looks so peaceful. Who would ever guess?

Cooler air blew through the room as the day waned.

Ben Matityahu took a deep breath of it, then he clapped a hand on Nikolaos's back and, with the other, gestured toward the tile roofs of Tiberias.

"Galilee has over two hundred towns and villages more or less like this. In the last six months, from those towns and villages, I've assembled ten thousand fighters. Recruited every able-bodied male above the age of twelve, including some foolish volunteers as old and frail as my father."

Are the Jews that desperate?

Ben Matityahu draped his hands over his head. Frustration dripped from his voice as he went on. "I've done everything in my power to get my men ready for the onslaught that's coming. Fortified every village. Rebuilt walls around the major towns. Stocked them with weapons, food, and water. But I know one thing. As soon as they come up against Rome's superior numbers, training, discipline, equipment, supplies, and commanders—" His voice broke.

Nikolaos craned his neck out the window for a wider view of the town, intentionally giving ben Matityahu time to compose himself.

"Tell me," Nikolaos said after a while, "why you expect to meet General Vespasian, even without plans to do so."

Ben Matityahu hesitated, as if considering how to answer. Then, with an index finger, he drew a straight line across the dusty window ledge.

"This war will not end in a draw. Either my army will defeat Vespasian's—" His finger thumped above the line. "Or Vespasian's army will defeat mine." His finger thumped below the line. "Either Vespasian will surrender to me—" Another thump above the line.

"Or you will surrender to Vespasian." Nikolaos thumped below the line.

Ben Matityahu had recovered enough to give him a lopsided grin. "Are you a gambling man? Some oddsmakers would say that's a smart bet."

"I'm not a gambling man. Merely stated the other half of your equation."

Once it was dark, Yosef ben Matityahu dismissed his guards.

Odd time to do that if he fears an assassin.

A lamp sat on a shelf, but the governor-general made no effort to use it. The only light in the room came from stars over the Sea of Galilee.

Another hour passed. Then two. Nikolaos was now calling him "Yosef."

Why would a general preparing for war spend so much time with someone not involved in that war?

But Yosef seemed genuinely interested in his guest's history, and Nikolaos held back only the most unsavory details.

"That's quite a tale," Yosef said when the long, complex story was finished. "So the Romans destroyed your father's life twice."

Nikolaos shrugged. "I may bear a bit of the blame, too."

"None of us is entirely guilt free." The starlight caught Yosef's smile.

Is this how friends confide in one another?

As the hour grew late, Yosef waxed philosophical.

"You and I grew up in very different worlds, Nikolaos. I've no personal experience with either slavery or poverty."

"Be grateful."

"I am. My place in society was secure the day I was born. I've accepted the Pharisaic doctrine, as my father wanted, even though I think much of it is crap. He and I never built a good relationship."

"Just like Father and me."

"At least you two can start over after you free him. Unfortunately, my rigid father has no use for 'adaptable' men such as me. His other son's a purist, and thus his favorite. My dear brother could out-Pharisee every other Pharisee in Jerusalem, including our father."

"We never had such lofty, principled disputes in our family. Our arguments always felt very territorial."

"But you're Alexander's first-born son. Didn't that give you special status?"

"It should have, but then *this* happened." Nikolaos waved one hand in the air. "And then *that* happened." He waved the other. "And then something *else* happened."

"Doesn't sound to me like you're to blame. Your father went to great effort to bring an outsider—a *Roman* woman, of all people—into his family."

"And then she gave him his favorite son."

"And after that, you had no chance."

"No chance." A decade of anger rushed back. "The Roman woman and her loud, obnoxious offspring absolutely conspired to shut me out."

Yosef ben Matityahu clasped his hands behind his head. "What do you hope to achieve by securing your father's release?"

"Prove I'm the one who cares the most about him. The one most worthy of his love. The one most entitled to inherit—"

"Freeing him should do the trick."

"Damn right it should." Nikolaos drummed his fingers on the desk. "Now you understand why I *must* meet General Vespasian. Why I *must* be the one to save my father. Why I *must not* allow her and her brat to free him."

"Well, as the son of an old man who deserves more attention from me than he is currently receiving… I do understand."

Nice to have a friend to confide in, at last.

The last trace of tension vanished. "So, Yosef, would you consider allowing me to go to war with you? To be there when you finally do meet Vespasian?"

"Food, water, and security are scarce and costly in Galilee."

"I can pay my way."

Thank the gods there's plenty of Father's money left.

"Will you also fight with us?"

Nikolaos thought about it. "I've never been a warrior, but I am a skillful butcher and—given my history and how much I despise the Romans—I'm sure I could chop one of them up as easily as a spring lamb."

Suddenly, the night air reverberated with deep voices.

Zealot assassins? Siqari'im?

Without a sound, Yosef rose, pulled his sword from its scabbard, and retreated to the blackness of the corner behind him.

Now I see why he won't use a lamp at night. Nobody can tell he's in here.

Crickets sang in the bushes outside. Bullfrogs croaked in a nearby marsh. Roosting birds fluttered under the eaves. And the voices slowly faded away.

Nikolaos sat still until it was clear they were gone.

Yosef returned to his stool. "Before you get too excited about butchering Romans, tell me how you assess the threat to my people."

"Almost certain disaster."

"Do you fully understand how my people feel about your people?"

"Ten days on the road with a gentile-hating donkey driver gave me plenty of evidence of that."

"How do you expect my Jewish fighters to react when a Greek unexpectedly pops up in the middle of our revolt against the Romans?"

"I'm accustomed to being suspected of something or other."

"Prepared to watch your back?" Yosef's eyes glimmered.

"Quite used to watching my back."

"Give me your word that you'll never betray us."

"I give you my word. I'll never betray you. You can trust me."

***

Spring rains were over. Temperatures rising fast. Sand blowing everywhere.

Adin reported normal activity on the road to Caesarea. A lot of regular comings and goings but no new deployment of military forces.

On the tenth day of May, with no reason to go into town, Theodosia and Doros decided to take a late-afternoon walk along the western side of the north-south highway. Her legs needed exercise to keep from stiffening up, and he needed to burn off energy.

Donkeys and pedestrians jammed the road heading south, but Theodosia moved carefully at her own pace along its scrubby, rock-strewn edge.

After following her for a while in the same direction, which ultimately would, if they kept at it long enough, take them to Jerusalem, Doros came up beside her. "I'm going to march," he said.

"Fine, but don't get too far ahead of me."

Some distance on, Doros raced back toward her, pointing to a clump of stunted trees off the road to the right.

"Mother," he said in Greek, "there's two strange fellows over there."

Theodosia's eyes followed his finger.

In the shadows under the trees crouched a pair of hairy men in plain gray robes, so still as to be almost invisible amid the rocks and shadows.

"Jewish fighters, I bet," she said. "Watching to make sure Roman agents don't slip into their holy city with the refugees."

A dusty gust swirled up and over the road from the very spot where the men squatted in the dirt.

Theodosia lifted her light-blue palla to keep the worst of the grit out of her mouth and nose. Then she took her son's hand and, without speaking, led him into the pack of humanity hurrying to reach Jerusalem before dark.

Safety in numbers.

Half a mile farther on, she detected motion under a different cluster of trees to the right. Bushes rustled. Sandals with wooden soles clicked on the paving stones. Men's voices—no more than two or three—began softly chanting words that meant nothing to her.

Operating on instinct, she bent over Doros. "Run back to the house."

For once, he didn't argue. Without hesitation, he pivoted and took off on the same rough ground, running against the flow of humans and beasts.

More clicks came up behind her.

Distracted, she stumbled and knocked off one of her own softer, leather-soled sandals… the kind that didn't click on the rocks.

She bent to pick it up, stepped off the roadway to pull it on again, and tried to reverse course by threading her way across the lane to the less-crowded other side, where she could turn back toward her only refuge in this land.

Two scholarly looking Jewish men wearing quality robes, neat beards, and round, high-sided caps were also heading north on foot. As she pushed her way through the crowd toward them, they slowed their steps and eyed her with obvious curiosity.

I may be the only gentile woman they've ever seen.

Intrigued by this chance encounter with Jews who were neither peasant farmers nor Galilean refugees nor donkey drivers, she briefly made eye contact and smiled at them.

Both men halted, returned her smile, and gestured for her to walk in front of them.

The hairy lurkers were gone from the spot where Doros first had noticed them. So, both tired and relieved, Theodosia slowed her pace again.

The two men who had allowed her to cut into their lane stepped around her, as if needing to reach their destination as fast as possible.

Instantly, the clicks and chants returned, more numerous than before. Close. Loud. Ominous.

Dust clogged Theodosia's lungs. Her heart pounded. At no time in the last eleven years—not since her nighttime escape from Nero's palace in Rome, from his warship at sea the next day, or from his soldiers in Palica a week later—had she felt more at risk.

A swarm of smelly, hairy, gray-clad men engulfed her, surging in from both lanes, each one with a long, glinty object protruding from the folds of his robe.

These are no ordinary freedom fighters.

Theodosia recoiled from the death she knew was coming.

A couple of paces away, the *Siqari'im* lunged forward, plunging and twisting their long, curved, gleaming blades deep into the spines of the two men who had paused so courteously to allow a gentile woman to step into their line of traffic.

Did my action slow them down? Make it easier for the killers?

The victims fell into the dirt. Spewing blood. Screaming in pain.

Or give them some kind of cultural excuse for murder?

Without hesitation, the *Siqari'im* yanked their daggers out of the bodies and thrust them in again, over and over with increasing force and fury, tearing apart the heads and shoulders and necks and torsos of their fellow Jews.

Blood washed over the smooth paving stones.

And over Theodosia's feet.

Two round caps sailed away to safety in the roadside weeds.

As if seeking their own refuge from the horror, bright chunks of crimson flesh flew up and clung to Theodosia's face and arms and to the light-blue palla over her head.

***

The next morning, after a private, pre-breakfast conference with her hosts, Theodosia asked Myrine to call Doros down from the roof.

"Neither one of us," she said in Aramaic when he joined her on the floor, "will set foot on the road again until the war is over."

Dismay flooded her son's face. "I can't stay inside forever."

"If I can, you can." Her lips twitched. "And it won't be forever, just until this miserable situation ends."

"And when will that be?"

Theodosia had no idea, so she guessed. "Fifteen days or so."

"I can't stop marching for fifteen whole days."

"It's too dangerous," Oren said, "for any of us to be out there right now."

"Except for me." Adin exuded a young man's confidence. "I'll keep driving the cart. Earn money. Keep up to date with what's going on in the north."

"Then I'll go with you," Doros said, "and learn how to handle a donkey."

"You most definitely will *not*," Theodosia said. "We owe it to your father to stay safe so we can rescue him when the time comes."

"But we'll all starve!" Doros wailed.

"No, we won't starve." Judith dropped onto her dining mat. "We've got our goats. Our geese. Our garden. Our dates. Our figs. Our stream. Our irrigation system. We have plenty of grains and nuts and oil on hand. Even some wine. No reason to go to market for anything until this is over."

As Myrine and Esther served breakfast, Theodosia smiled to herself.

Alexander would appreciate the irony that a Jewish home offers two Romans our best chance of surviving this Roman-Jewish War.

"We'll make good use of the time," she promised Doros. "It's been months since your last lesson, and—"

"I'm done with lessons."

"None of us are ever done with lessons. There's always more to learn."

"But we have no scrolls or wax tablets."

"You already know how to read and write. No need for scrolls and tablets."

"Then… how?"

"We'll educate one another." With one hand, Theodosia gestured to herself, Doros, and Myrine. "Remember how Myrine taught you and me to speak Aramaic?" With both hands, she expanded the loop to include Oren, Judith, and Adin… all of whom were already in on the plan. "Well, each of us here is a smart, interesting person who knows a lot about—"

"How will I practice marching?"

"You won't for a while."

"Mother!"

"Oren and Judith have agreed to teach us about the Jewish religion and culture."

"And you'll teach us whatever we don't yet know about the Greeks." Judith's tone insinuated that she might already know far more than she cared to about the Greeks.

But, of course, we'll not say a word about the Romans.

"Best part is," Theodosia said, "we'll do all this learning and teaching in Aramaic. Imagine how fluent you and I will be when this war is over."

A mischievous gleam entered her son's eyes. "So, from that point on, people will take us for Jews?"

Adin mimicked that gleam as he helped himself to a chunk of Esther's fresh bread. "Oh, you probably won't be *that* lucky."

"Best of all," Theodosia went on, "you can practice your rhetoric in both Greek and Aramaic. Become an even more persuasive speaker in two languages."

Actually, he can practice in three languages, but our hosts won't know when he's declaiming in Latin, as opposed to Greek.

"Time passes fast when you're busy." Despite Oren's somber face, he still managed to wink at Doros. "You'll see."

"We'll all learn from one another." Theodosia was ready to end the discussion. "Make good use of the days ahead."

"Until Father is free?"

Myrine set a bowl of nuts and goat cheese in front of Doros.

"Yes, Little Man, until that fine day when your pa walks through the door and lifts you into his arms."

CHAPTER 25

Doros squirmed on his sleeping mat. "I can't stand this much longer." It was yet another bright, starry, boring night late in May and—as they had done every seven days since arriving two months ago—he, Theodosia, and Myrine were in voluntary isolation on the roof, consuming only fruit, cheese, nuts, and bread from sundown to sundown so their hosts could cook, eat, and conduct their Sabbath rituals without interference from the gentiles in their midst.

At the top of the tall fig tree, a large owl hooted, as it always did around this hour. On occasion, the bird swooped out in silent-but-lethal pursuit of some small rodent going peaceably about its business in the dark.

A perfect metaphor for this nasty war.

"I'm tired of it, too," Theodosia replied to her son, "if that makes you feel better, and I bet Myrine is, too."

"Not tired, Mistress, but I sure do miss my kitchen. Esther has such a strange way of fixing food."

Doros sat up. "Hardly any traffic on the road these days."

On her adjacent mat, Theodosia rolled toward him. "Everybody with common sense is inside, keeping their heads down."

"So, if everybody's in and nobody's out, why can't I march?"

His mother lay still. Stared at the heavens. Begged Juno for a good excuse to keep saying no, but not even the goddess came up with one.

He does need to exercise. Burn off some energy.

"Not tomorrow," she said. "We mustn't offend our hosts on their Sabbath."

His voice brightened. "Day after tomorrow?"

His mother hesitated a few moments more. "Yes, but for one hour only, early in the morning while it's cool. And before you set foot outside these walls, you must tell Myrine or me, so we can keep an eye on you."

***

"Siege is inevitable," Yosef said.

He and Nikolaos were riding side by side through the barren Galilean desert on a fifteen-mile-long path beaten into the ground over centuries by untold thousands of donkey hooves. Behind them, also on donkeys, Yosef's six guards and two aides followed them to Jotapata, the strongest of all the region's ancient fortresses.

Jotapata. Memorable name.

"There are only two unknowns," Yosef continued. "How long this damn war will last and how many Jews will die before it's done."

"Plenty of Romans will die, too, which is fine with me."

By first light on this next-to-last day of May, the heat was already horrid, and the nights offered little relief either. Yosef's guards never left his side, even to sleep, so for the last fourteen nights, all seven of them had squeezed into one large chamber in an inn, leaving Nikolaos to share with the aides a hot, windowless storage cell. The worst had come last night, when—after enduring one more Jewish Sabbath and finally learning the name of the primitive fortress where the governor-general would make his stand against the Romans—Nikolaos's mind bounced from one nightmarish scenario to another, leaving him wide awake for hours as the aides snored on their mats.

Yosef leaned toward him now with an odd smile. "Can you keep a secret? If so, I'll share one bit of information that my spies reported this morning."

"You hid our destination from me all this time, which was fine under the circumstances, but who exactly do you think I would squeal your latest secret to, way out here in this vast, empty desert?"

"Good point." Yosef laughed. "So, here's the news. Vespasian and Titus are said to have a special blood-lust in their eyes these days."

"Because your *Siqari'im* have killed so many of their fighters?"

"I doubt it. Mostly, I suspect, it's because they're shitty losers and gluttons for glory."

"And because they're looking to make an example of you."

Another laugh. "They'll do the same with you, my young Greek friend."

"*Pffffh*. Those two wouldn't know me if I sneaked into their tent and spit in their faces."

"They'll know you by the time the siege is over."

That's my plan.

"Jotapata," Yosef said, "is my best chance to turn the war in our direction."

"Why Jotapata?"

"It's a natural fortress. Deep, steep canyons on two sides and long views across the hills to the sea. In Galilee's entire history, no attacker has ever crept up on Jotapata and caught its residents by surprise."

"Were the old fortifications good enough?"

"No," Yosef said. "Not even close, so one thing that's been happening there over these last fourteen days was that my men significantly raised and strengthened the wall."

"Does Vespasian know that's where your army is gathering?"

"Not yet, by all reports. He'll figure it out soon enough."

"Can he overrun Jotapata?"

"He'd prefer to starve us out. To prevent that, we stockpiled enough animals, grain, and water to last the town's normal population, plus our fighters, for a year. We did that in other places, too, but we stashed a whole lot more in Jotapata than anywhere else. Plus plenty of lumber and nails."

"Sounds like you've thought of everything."

"Problem is, Vespasian has had his men chasing the Galileans every which way for months. Thousands made it to Jerusalem, but thousands more—those who didn't leave in time—arrive in Jotapata every day."

"To consume all the food and water you had stocked for a normal-size population."

"Exactly. And once the siege begins, nothing more will come in."

Big risk I'm taking.

"Many lives, including yours," Yosef said, as if reading his mind, "will depend on the courage and toughness of my fighters."

Nikolaos waggled his head. "Ironic, isn't it, that a Greek from Greece should journey all this way to cast his fate with the Jews of Jotapata."

"Just don't ever give my men a reason to distrust you."

***

On the first day of June, Nikolaos stood atop the parapet of Jotapata's newly heightened and refortified wall, studying the terrain in every direction and assessing its natural and human-built defenses.

Straight ahead, a rocky trail pitched sideways, dangerously downward, as it curved around a high, broad knoll before straightening into a thin strip of land that offered the only possible access to Jotapata.

Behind and below the parapet, the old town sprawled across a flat, triangular-shaped rock surrounded by deep canyons and sheer cliffs.

The Jews who, long ago, had picked this spot for their northernmost citadel not only had built a strong rampart across its sole vulnerable side but also lower stone walls along the back edges of the triangle, apparently to keep buildings and people from sliding into the chasms.

Until now, no one had ever thought Jotapata needed better defenses.

Because no one ever anticipated Vespasian.

He turned his eyes again to the tilted trail and the narrow land bridge that their party of ten had crossed the day before yesterday. Since then, several thousand more Jewish peasants had made the same risky trek.

Yosef had assigned Nikolaos the task of finding each newcomer a place to sleep in the town's already crowded, single-story buildings. He was doing the job as well as possible without attempting to make friends. And—not a surprise either, based on Yosef's warning—the refugees showed no wish to be his friends. Still, he felt little need to watch his back, because the Jews of Jotapata seemed much more anxious to survive this war than to kill him.

***

Shortly after dawn on the third day of June, everything changed.

As before, Nikolaos stood on the parapet atop the rampart looking forward, but this time his heart insisted on thrashing about inside his chest.

Because dozens of soldiers on horseback had just crested the knoll from the west—each one wearing red-and-brass armor so highly polished that it caught the rising sun and threw back a blinding glare—and advanced until they formed a double line that completely blocked the land bridge.

Vespasian hadn't arrived yet, but his message was clear. From now on, no one would enter or leave Jotapata without his permission.

I made a big mistake in coming here.

Other soldiers came along the tilted path with whips raised over strings of naked, chained-up slaves, who immediately began removing the largest rocks.

Jewish slaves, no doubt, carted in by their Roman masters to build a level road around the knoll, so even more Jews can become slaves.

Turning around, Nikolaos scanned the steep canyon walls behind the town. The very same landscape that for centuries had protected Jotapata from intruders now turned the place into a death trap.

Too late for me now. There's no way out.

***

Centurion Doros marched each morning on the north-south highway.

In a gray tunic with red embroidery, he led the soldiers of his imaginary century. Back and forth he strutted and shouted, head held high under a clay-pot helmet. As his left hand defended his torso with a leafy shield cut from lower branches of the fig tree, his right hand hoisted a stick sword, ready to slay any foe who opposed him.

Theodosia and Myrine took turns under the shady section of the roof, alert for Zealots who might think of ending his dream of a military career.

***

In the coolest, earliest daylight hour of what would surely become a very hot day, Doros enticed Myrine to descend from the roof and enlist in his make-believe army.

"Come on down!" he hollered from the road. "Give it a try!"

With a bit more encouragement, Myrine complied.

At first, Doros giggled at her fumbling attempts to march, then he began teaching her professional moves.

Theodosia watched from the roof until her turn came.

"Mother, you can do this, too!"

"No, my legs are too stiff."

"They'll get better with exercise."

"My bones are thirty-three years old. Not sure they can take it."

"But it's such great fun!"

"Myrine," Theodosia called, "is it really fun?"

Myrine leaned backwards and looked up, her face flushed with exertion and merriment. "Yes, Mistress, it's real fun!"

A rare thing for any of us these days.

So down Theodosia went.

Doros cut her no slack, either, but barked orders to the fullest capacity of his lungs. "One, two! One, two! Backs straight! Strong steps! One, two! One, two! Heads up! Strong steps!"

For the first couple of days, she felt silly, but Doros clearly loved having actual people, instead of phantoms, at his command. And as her muscles grew accustomed to the activity, Theodosia found herself looking forward to it.

Every morning from that point on, Myrine and her mistress were out in the road, following Centurion Doros's orders, marching, laughing, and taking pleasure in the physical exertion. Whenever a pedestrian or donkey cart approached, they stopped, modestly pulled their shawls over their heads, and caught their breath.

***

A day after Vespasian's initial show of force, heavy footfalls pounded the ground with all the energy that well-fed, well-muscled men could produce. They shook the land bridge. Shook the rampart. Shook the buildings. Shook the very cliffs on which Jotapata stood.

Yosef said they always do that before they attack, to intimidate their targets. It works.

During the next hour, three large polished-gold eagles soared over the knoll, each on a tall standard held aloft by its legion's standard bearer.

Waves of foot soldiers swarmed over the knoll, too, each one armed with his *gladius* and *pilum* and stomping as hard as he could.

In the town behind the wall, people of all ages poured out of nearby buildings into the central market place.

Others surged through the streets from the back part of town.

Voices rose on every corner, screaming for their governor-general to say or do something.

But Yosef ben Matityahu wasn't available. He and his aides spent the day in their headquarters, leaving only the guards at the gate to calm the crowd.

By sunset, at the crest of the knoll, multicolored flags fluttered atop a big black tent, while rows of smaller beige tents blanketed the landscape all the way to the farthest visible hills.

***

For three days, every woman, child, and old man in Jotapata huddled in their assigned shelters as Vespasian's three legions and their allied forces, all sixty thousand stomping men, pounded the ground with that now-familiar, but no less nerve-wracking cadence.

Before dawn on each of those days, scores of Jewish fighters, each with his homemade helmet and sling, climbed the stairs to the parapet where, during the night, other men had piled hundreds of sling-sized stones, larger rocks, and spears.

Up on the wall again, Nikolaos stood apart from the Jewish defenders, as was his habit, watching a stream of catapults, ballistas, onagers, and scorpions lumber around the knoll on that newly widened, perfectly level road. Behind them came two wagons so loaded with boulders and other projectiles that four stout horses were required to pull each one.

At last, after hours of intensive preparation—unloading everything off the wagons and arranging the machinery, boulders, and other projectiles in some pre-determined order, all of which was carried out, of course, by the same chained-up, naked slaves—other things began to happen.

Six ballistas rolled forward and stopped short of the land bridge.

Six teams of soldiers lifted immense, bolt-like metal projectiles from one wagon into the torsion-powered machines.

Six operators cranked the winches and then, in perfect unison, let fly their ferocious missiles.

Six deafening crashes hit the wall below the parapet.

Six thousand screams erupted inside Jotapata.

Nikolaos had known the hits were coming, so he did not scream. Instead, with both hands, he gripped the edge of the parapet and awaited the inevitable crack and crumble beneath him.

But nothing cracked. Nothing crumbled.

His eyes swept the multitude of Romans on the ground before him. Not a man moved. The ballista operators stood still. No more rocks flew.

Confusion must have registered on his face, because the Jewish governor-general walked over to his side.

"That round was just a test," he said. "Vespasian's checking out our wall."

"I bet he's impressed."

"I bet so, too, and with good reason." Yosef's voice pulsed with blatant satisfaction. "It's the best defense against his war machine that anyone could have built."

***

Once it was clear that the first barrage was over, thousands of women raced from nearby buildings into the town square. Shouting. Crying. Tearing their hair. Carrying or clutching their children as if a mother's arms had the power to protect them from Roman devils.

Clamoring men packed the rooftops. Stretched their necks to see around others. Climbed the only tree in town to get a better view.

Wailing babies added to the uproar as everyone awaited words of comfort from their reclusive governor-general.

Nikolaos descended the stairs but stopped halfway down to watch.

As he surveyed the crowd from that elevated position, he recognized a sister and brother who had arrived a few days earlier, orphans whose parents had been killed, two of a handful of survivors from their ravaged village.

He had helped them find a sleeping spot but hadn't seen them since.

Despite the frenzy of that day, he and the girl had talked a bit, and even that brief conversation showed she had a quick wit and a bright mind.

He recalled her unusually bright eyes and clear skin, plus the wavy hair that billowed around her face. There was a delicacy to her features and frame that he hadn't seen in any of the other females in Jotapata.

She stood silently now, holding her little brother's hand.

For a long time, Nikolaos stared at her, hoping she would look up.

What was her name? Atarah? Anat? Asenat?

Finally, it came to him. *Arona.*

Yosef passed Nikolaos on the stairs, stopped on the third step up from the ground, raised his arms, and called for silence. Almost instantly, the Galilean peasants hushed before the aristocratic young Pharisee from Jerusalem, on whose narrow shoulders lay their hope of survival and freedom.

Yosef took his time. Waited until all were quiet. Built a level of tension and suspense that commanded the attention of everyone in the square. And once he began speaking, he enunciated his words with care, projecting them well into the crowd.

"This, my friends, is how the enemy announces his intention to kill us. But our faith is deep. Our defenses are strong."

How eloquently he speaks when the moment demands it. Easy to see why he was chosen for this assignment.

"We are clever and well prepared. We will defend ourselves with courage and intelligence. We will remain brave, resolute, and calm."

From what I've seen, all that is true.

"And remember, the enemy has his problems, too."

Sixty thousand warriors, plus their animals and slaves, need lots of food and water. Supplying won't be easy in the middle of nowhere. Not even Vespasian can conjure up water in the desert.

"So today I make this promise to you. The Romans will not conquer us quickly or easily. In truth, they may never conquer us at all."

Wildly, the crowd began to cheer. "Yosef! Yosef!"

"Because we have a greater force on our side."

"Yosef! Yosef! Yosef! Yosef! Yosef!"

"The One who created the world—"

"Yosef! Yosef! Yosef! Yosef! Yosef!"

"And gave his laws to Moses on the Mount—"

"Yosef! Yosef! Yosef! Yosef! Yosef!"

"And guided our people from slavery to freedom—"

"Yosef! Yosef! Yosef! Yosef! Yosef!"

"He will make Vespasian rue the day he marched his army to Jotapata!"

***

When the attack finally began at dawn, under a cloudless, pink-tinged Galilean sky, not a soul in Jotapata was surprised.

Nikolaos returned to the parapet and, along with Yosef's sling- and spear-armed fighters, watched as Vespasian launched his first real assault on Jotapata.

At one blast of a horn, hundreds of crimson-clad foot soldiers stomped forward.

The wall trembled.

At two blasts of the horn, the soldiers sidestepped into tight, precise formations.

Refugees scurried to their shelters.

At three blasts of the horn, still in formation, the soldiers marched onto the land bridge.

Doves flew off the parapet.

At four blasts of the horn, an elegantly uniformed officer rode into view, accompanied by a mounted standard bearer who carried, high above them, a shiny gold eagle.

A long, lusty cheer rose from the troops surrounding the officer.

From his position on the far end of the wall, Governor-General Yosef ben Matityahu looked down into the market square behind the gate, where masses of Jewish fighters listened to the Roman roar and awaited his order.

"It's the Fifteenth Legion!" Yosef shouted to those below. "Led by the old general's vicious spawn."

Titus.

Facing in the opposite direction, Nikolaos propped his forearms on the parapet and leaned out as far as he dared, eager for a glimpse of this Roman who was not much older than he.

I have the strongest feeling… he's the one who'll help me save Father.

The towering black plumes of Titus's helmet swayed as his high-spirited black horse pranced beneath him.

With a joyously menacing flourish, the young general swept his polished sword out of its scabbard, brandished it over his head, and sliced it down through the air.

As if waiting for that highly visible, physical signal, the fighting men of Rome's Fifteenth Legion screamed their distinctive war cry.

***

At what felt to Nikolaos like the perfect moment, Yosef's fist rose in the air, swirled a couple of times, and sharply fell.

A perfect parallel to Titus's actions, minus the helmet, horse, and sword.

Down below, as Nikolaos watched, teams of strong men slid the equally strong wooden bars and shoved the gate open.

Meanwhile, fighters at the top of the wall aimed their slings and spears outward, toward the Romans.

The first wave of Jewish warriors swarmed through the gate and spread out, holding their spears in offensive position.

The second wave followed, carrying only knives, slings, and rock-filled pouches on their belts.

At that point, Yosef joined Nikolaos at the parapet. "We're about to see the Romans' famous 'tortoise' in action. Watch how fast they disappear into it."

On the land bridge, a centurion barked an order that snapped his legionaries into defensive positions.

Each soldier on the inside of a squadron raised his shield over his head.

Each soldier on the outside of a squadron set up a barrier with his shield and positioned his sword so that any fool who ran into it would be skewered.

"I'd heard of the *testudo*." Nikolaos preferred to use the Latin word, even if Yosef didn't know it. "Never expected to see it an action. How on Earth do they do that so fast?"

"Years of practice."

***

"Now that we don't go into Caesarea," Theodosia said as she made her slow way up the stairs, "we never hear any news." After an hour marching behind Doros on the road, she needed a drink and some rest.

Myrine followed with a pitcher of goat milk. "Adin said there's a siege just gettin' started at some old fortress in the north."

"What I still don't understand," Doros said once they reached the roof, "is how spending all this time here helps us rescue Father."

Theodosia collapsed onto a mat in the shady area over the stable and released a deep, relieved sigh. "We're staying safe, which is what he would want. Once the war's over, we'll go get him off that ship."

"And while we wait, Little Man, we exercise." Myrine handed them each a cup of milk. "It don't do nobody no good—not your pa and certainly not us—to let ourselves get fat and lazy."

***

"Be brave, my love," Theodosia whispered to the stars that night. "I'm coming for you."

Juno, please keep him strong.

Little snake, keep him healthy, too.

But slowly, as the days passed, even though Theodosia never admitted it to anyone but herself, she was losing hope.

Nothing that Adin reported gave any indication that the siege of the old fortress town in Galilee was nearing its conclusion.

And she knew that only when that siege was over—when Vespasian and Titus returned victorious to Caesarea—would she finally get a chance to talk them into releasing Alexander.

Meanwhile, throughout the routine of eating on the floor, sleeping on the roof, not going downstairs on the Jewish Sabbath, and marching in the road each non-Sabbath morning, she dedicated herself to ensuring Doros's safety and sanity through a series of increasingly challenging intellectual exercises.

CHAPTER 26

The siege of Jotapata dragged on for fifteen days. Then it was twenty. Then thirty.

By day, the Romans hurled boulders up at the wall, while the Jews slung stones and threw spears down from the wall.

By night, the Jews rolled those boulders into the canyons and repaired the damage to their wall.

By day, the Romans clear-cut the surrounding forests and constructed a ramp to widen the land bridge.

By night, the Jews set fire to the wooden foundations of that ramp.

By day, the Romans built a battering ram and maneuvered it into position.

By night, the Jews reinforced the outside of their gate by piling up sacks filled with chaff to blunt the impact of the ram.

By day, the Romans pulled the sacks aside with long, hooked poles and rammed the gate.

By night, the Jews washed their clothing and, at dawn, threw it over the wall to drip, taunting the Romans with how much water they possessed.

By day, the Romans approached in their *testudo* formation, searching for soft spots in the wall.

By night, the Jews toted oil to the top of the wall and, at dawn, heated it over open fires.

By day, the Jews poured boiling oil onto each attacking *testudo*, scalding the Romans through their segmented metal armor.

By night, the Jews slaughtered oxen for food and hides.

By day, the Romans constructed a normal-height assault tower.

By night, the Jews set fire to the siege tower and built wooden frames over their wall and covered them with still-wet oxen hides.

By day, the Jews sheltered behind those tough hides—so wonderfully resistant to the Romans' javelins and flaming arrows—as they further increased the height of their wall, raising it to the greatest extent possible.

And so it went for a month. Neither side gained much of an advantage.

But then, at some point early in July, the Romans began work on a new assault tower, one clearly designed to reach the top of Yosef's final wall.

***

Nikolaos ducked under a low lintel inside the building that served as the resistance headquarters.

Thirty-seven days into the siege, this was his first visit to Yosef's private chamber. A desk, a sleeping mat, and three stools were the only furnishings that fit into this space, and the front room he had just passed through was not much larger.

He stepped around the mat and approached the desk where the governor-general sat scratching with a reed pen on a sheet of papyrus. Another sheet, already rolled and sealed with reddish-brown wax, lay on the dirt floor.

He's writing letters? To whom?

"Our water supplies," he announced in Greek, "are almost gone."

Yosef didn't look up. Didn't stop writing. Didn't reply.

Nikolaos dropped onto a stool. "Who else knows?"

"Every Galilean knows summer's not the rainy season."

"That's not an answer."

Again, Yosef ignored him.

"Are your aides aware?"

"A few." Yosef lowered his pen and raised his eyes. "How did you find out?"

"Got curious this morning and inspected the cisterns. Nobody was around to stop me."

"I've reassigned the guards."

"Not enough water left to guard?"

"The men were needed elsewhere." Yosef rolled his second letter, dripped wax over its edge, and stamped it with his signet ring. "What's it to you?"

"Like everyone else here, I'm hoping to survive."

And right now, up on this hot ledge, thirst is a bigger threat than Vespasian.

"When will you tell your people?" Nikolaos asked.

"Not until I have to."

Nikolaos nudged the scroll on the floor with his foot and pointed to the one still lying on the desk. "Looks like two lucky individuals are about to get letters from Jotapata."

Abruptly, Yosef rose and closed the door, even though they were the only ones in town who spoke Greek.

Have I stumbled onto a secret even greater than the lack of water?

"Every so often, a courier from Jerusalem slips in and out." Yosef matched Nikolaos's level gaze. "The Sanhedrin needs my report."

That accounts for one scroll, but not two.

"A gambling man," Nikolaos drawled, "would wager that your brave courier comes and goes through the east canyon."

Yosef's only response was an enigmatic smile.

***

Around midnight—eight days later and a full forty-five days into the siege—with only a quarter moon to light his way, Nikolaos crept through the deserted streets of Jotapata.

With no oil left for lamps, the mud-brick houses lay dark around him.

The town reeked of human bodies and excrement, replacing similar smells that had disappeared when the last bone-thin ox and donkey were slaughtered, as much for their hides as for their stringy meat.

The stink of human death was in the air as well, even though people who died from wounds or natural causes were promptly buried in shallow holes in the ground near the back walls.

Nikolaos stopped at Yosef's headquarters and opened the door.

Good thing none of these old buildings have locks.

His eyes adjusted. Nobody was present in the room where Yosef regularly met with his aides to plan their next day's tactics.

Good thing the aides sleep elsewhere.

He felt his way past a table toward the governor-general's private chamber.

The door was ajar, so he angled his ear and listened. The only sound emerging from the room was a deep, steady snore.

Good thing he's exhausted.

Nikolaos removed his sandals. Pushed the door. Tiptoed past the mat and its slumbering occupant. Reached the desk. Raised and lowered his hand several times until at last it landed on something round and hard.

A scroll ring.

His fingers confirmed the sharp edge, distinctive shape, and crinkly texture of a rolled-up sheet of papyrus.

On the mat, Yosef snorted and turned over.

Nikolaos froze with his hand on the scroll.

Yosef shifted whatever was serving as his pillow and, within moments, resumed his rhythmic snoring.

Silently, Nikolaos lifted the scroll and eased his way out of the room, leaving the door ajar, as he had found it.

No one must ever know—or suspect, or guess—that I was here.

He tied the scroll to the strapped-on money bag inside the breast of his tunic, replaced his sandals, and headed for the low wall that kept Jotapata from sliding into its eastern canyon.

***

Straddling the wall, Nikolaos gazed past the dark town to the widened land bridge and the taller, nearly complete siege tower and the alert torch-carrying sentries who finally had put an end to the Jews' nightly sabotage and on to Vespasian's tent city where sixty thousand slumbering soldiers no doubt dreamed of slaughtering the stubbornly resistant occupants of Jotapata so they could bid farewell at last to Galilee's scorpion-infested desert.

Also asleep, most likely, in the big, black tent at the top of the knoll, were the father-and-son generals whom the Fates had destined, even if they didn't know it yet, to help Nikolaos rescue his own father.

Time to go and get it done.

He swung both legs to the outside of the wall and was about to lower himself into the chasm when he heard a scraping noise in the grain-storage building behind him. He glanced over his shoulder.

A female figure emerged and approached as if she knew he was there.

Arona.

Silver light glanced off her face, her bare feet, and the ripples of her hair as she boldly walked over to him.

"You're the Greek," she whispered, "who has been helping Yosef ben Matityahu. Thank you for your kindness to my brother and me."

More than a girl, she looks like a ghost, which she may soon be.

Nikolaos swung his legs again, back from the abyss, and landed silently on the ground beside her. "My name is Nikolaos."

"I'm Arona." She was smaller than he remembered. Barely reached the middle of his chest. "What are you doing here?"

"Couldn't sleep," he lied. "Needed fresh air."

"Me, too." Her eyes and teeth glinted as she smiled. "You did the best you could for us, but it's impossible to rest in that room."

"The grain dust bothers you?"

"Not so much as the vermin."

He smiled back. "Jotapata could use a few cats."

"But they've all been eaten." A shiny tear tracked down one of her sunken cheeks. "We need more water, too."

Not something a child should have to worry about.

"Better yet," he joked to distract her, "more wine."

"Do you believe," she asked, obviously not distracted, "we've got enough water to hold out?"

He turned his eyes in the direction of the sleeping Roman army. "What I believe is that Vespasian will soon tire of this game and turn his legions loose on an easier target."

"No." She shook her head. "You don't believe that."

Smart girl.

"Admit it, Nikolaos, you don't. Not really."

"What makes you think I don't believe what I just said?"

"Because you avoided my eyes when you said it."

Maybe too smart for her own good.

He forced himself to look at her again. "Well, no matter where my eyes happen to wander, I do believe what I said. Why would Vespasian keep us penned up here much longer?"

Actually, he has plenty of reasons, but why frighten her further?

"Because he knows we're almost out of food and water."

"Vespasian would have no way of knowing that, even if it were true. Yosef has tricked them into believing we have plenty of both."

Arona lowered her head. "The Romans destroyed my village. I've seen what they do." Her voice trembled. "First, they kill all the men, then they take the women and children as their sex slaves."

A girl of thirteen knows about sex slaves?

Unwelcome memories of his mother's Syrian rapist inserted themselves, unbidden, into his mind.

After a while, Arona lifted her eyes to the crescent moon, whose soft light picked out even more tears there and on her sunken cheeks.

I could stay here and protect her.

She tilted her head to look at him.

Save her from Mother's fate.

Parted her lips a bit.

But if I do that, I'll have no chance to rescue Father.

Licked her cracked, shriveled lips.

Of course, it's possible the Roman woman can save him by herself.

Shook out her stringy, unwashed hair.

No, I must be the one who does that.

He made no response to Arona's transparent attempts at seduction.

She's offering herself to me if I'll stay to defend her.

Soon, without another word, she retreated to the door she had come from and disappeared from view.

Had she stayed, I might have, too.

But she vanished into the night, and so did he.

***

Nikolaos spent several anxious hours in the dark, not sleeping, clinging to a narrow, rocky shelf just a few yards down from Jotapata's back wall, hundreds of feet above the floor of its eastern canyon.

As the earliest glow struck the precipice beneath him, he plucked sweet-tart berries from one of the sturdy bushes that the Sanhedrin's intrepid courier must have used in his comings and goings and cast his eyes around, looking for a way to get to the land bridge.

Before long, he spotted a rocky outcrop barely wide enough for one foot. Then another just beyond. Then a third. The fragile path went up in spots, down in others, and up and down again until the whole way was obvious.

Rock by rock, holding tight to the bushes, he could make his way out of the canyon.

He wiped the berry juice off his fingers onto his already-filthy cotton tunic and checked to make sure that both his money bag and Yosef's scroll were still secured to his torso.

Father, here I come.

***

"Halt!" A guard on the expanded land bridge flourished his sword and thrust it at the man climbing out of the eastern canyon.

"I'm unarmed," Nikolaos said in Latin as the blade homed in on his throat. "Carrying a message from Governor-General Yosef ben Matityahu."

"What message?"

"A letter."

Two more soldiers ran up. One of them tackled Nikolaos and threw him face-down at the edge of the abyss. He tried to rise, but a heavy knee smashed him flat, pinning him to the ground.

"It's a Jewish trick," the first guard muttered.

"It's not a trick," Nikolaos huffed into the dirt, "and I'm not Jewish. I'm a Greek from the Greek island of Euboea."

"What's a Latin-speaking Greek from Greece doing here in Galilee?" demanded the man who was holding him down.

Nikolaos managed to turn his head to the right, facing the vast empty space he had just crawled out of.

They could toss me right over and no one would ever know.

"It's a long, complicated story." He made sure his Latin sounded as clear and idiomatic as possible. "And for sure I'll tell you absolutely everything you want and need to know, but first you've got to get your fucking knee out of my backbone."

The third soldier laughed at that. "He does look more Greek than Jewish, and he speaks Latin better than any Jew I've ever met."

Footsteps sounded on Nikolaos's left, where he couldn't see.

"Sir," the first guard said, "this canyon rat claims he's brought us a letter from ben Matityahu."

"Is that true?" asked a raspy voice.

"Yes, sir," Nikolaos said. "Governor-General Yosef ben Matityahu's very own, personal letter is squashed down here under me—with its big scroll ring cutting into my ribs and thus keeping me from breathing—and as I told this moron whose knee is about to slice me in half, I've a useful and interesting story to tell if he'll just let me up."

"Let him up," commanded the raspy voice.

The knee lifted from Nikolaos's back. Carefully using his hands and knees, he managed to stand without toppling into the canyon.

He first noticed the semicircular red crest on the older soldier's helmet, then the deep scars on his face and neck, which marked him as a battle-tested veteran.

This is the man who will take me to Vespasian. Or Titus. Or both.

"Give me the letter," said the centurion with the raspy voice.

"My orders are to deliver it into General Vespasian's hand."

"Strangers aren't allowed in the big tent."

"The letter will make no sense unless I'm there to explain it."

"Hand it over."

"Without me present to explain it, the general will not understand its significance." Reluctantly, Nikolaos pulled out the scroll.

The centurion seized it. "That's for him to decide."

***

Nikolaos soon found himself transferred to a fourth soldier, who hustled him past double lines of fierce-faced figures standing stiffly at attention outside the black tent with multicolored flags, and on past rows of smaller beige tents to an isolated green one in a distant area of the encampment. Wooden poles on each end supported its sides, which were secured by ropes to stakes in the ground. Its loose canvas rustled in the wind.

The soldier stopped and motioned for Nikolaos to go inside.

He ducked under the flap and looked around. Filling the large space were coils of rope, clay amphorae of various shapes and sizes, and piles of overstuffed gunnysacks spilling grain from their splitting seams.

Unseen, rambunctious creatures scurried among the sacks.

Hope they're just field mice, not full-size rats.

"Make yourself comfortable." The soldier stood at ease just inside the flap.

It was hotter than Hades. Little air or room to stretch out. But Nikolaos dropped to the ground, leaned against a coiled rope, and promptly dozed off.

*　*　*

Hooves outside the tent. Clanking swords. Sandals in the scrub. Shadows on the canvas. The sounds and shapes jolted Nikolaos awake.

A moment later, the centurion with the raspy voice lifted the flap and held it high so another man could precede him.

A younger officer entered and stood with his legs apart, left hand propped on his hip, right hand dangling a helmet resplendently adorned with the thick tail of a black horse. Every detail of the newcomer's red-and-brass uniform, his confident chin, his proud bearing, and his impeccable grooming announced: I am a very important person.

The guard inside the tent snapped to attention and saluted crisply as Nikolaos scrambled to his feet.

General Titus.

"Where did you get that letter?" the young general asked in Latin.

"From the desk of Governor-General Yosef ben Matityahu, sir. Within the walls of Jotapata."

We're exactly the same height.

"How did you get in there?"

Not much difference in age either.

"I entered with Yosef ben Matityahu before the siege began."

"How did you get out?"

Nikolaos told him.

"Does he know you left?"

"By now, probably so."

"You say you're not Jewish."

"That's correct, sir. I'm Greek."

General Titus looked skeptical. "Tell me in your very best Greek how you traveled from Piraeus to Judea."

Nikolaos described the dreadful *Minoan Spirits* voyage in such detail that no one could possibly doubt he was a native speaker of Greek.

"I also speak Aramaic, sir," he said as he concluded his tale, "which is how I've conversed with the Jews of Jotapata."

General Titus raised his black eyebrows. "Impressive language skills. Have you read the letter that you carried out?"

Nikolaos shook his head. "I can't *read* Aramaic, sir."

"Actually, it's written in Hebrew."

"Can't read that either. Besides, the letter was sealed when I received it and also when I turned it over to the centurion."

"And that's how he delivered it to me." Titus nodded to the centurion. "Good man." He turned back to Nikolaos. "You're to come with me, *um—* What's your name?"

"Nikolaos, sir."

"Do you know what information the letter contains?"

"No idea, sir."

***

Squinting in the sunshine, Nikolaos strode alongside General Titus, whose flashy red cape and horsetail crown blew wildly about in the desert wind, and studied him out of the corner of his eye.

High, smooth forehead.

Full head of black, wavy hair.

Dark-gray eyes.

Sharply arched nose.

Typical Roman coloring and features.

"We have a Jewish prisoner," Titus said, again in Latin. "An old, scholarly Pharisee, if you know what that is."

"I do."

"He's stupendously annoying. Goes out of his way to tell us how vastly superior his one Jewish god is to Jupiter and all our other gods combined. Constantly berates us for invading his land. Claims he can't work—can't even travel!—on the day he calls his Sabbath. Refuses to eat certain foods that we can't live without." Titus chuckled. "He's lost some weight since we captured him last fall."

Happy to share a joke with a general, Nikolaos laughed outright.

"I've lost a good bit of weight myself these past forty-six days. This tunic didn't always hang on me like a dirty sack." Then, suddenly aware that General Titus wasn't laughing along with him, he sobered. "Does your Pharisee speak Latin?"

"No, but like my father and me, he's proficient in Greek, so that's how we have our entertaining conversations with him."

Why's he telling me this?

"The only thing keeping the old fellow alive," Titus continued, "is that he's highly literate in both Hebrew and Aramaic, as well as Greek. Whenever we capture a courier or intercept messages, he earns his keep."

"He cooperates with you?"

Titus shrugged as if the Jew's willingness to cooperate were a matter of little concern. "He's aware that one incorrect detail—any small missed or misinterpreted nuance that could change the course of this war—will inevitably result in his most painful death."

No doubt that same thing could be said of me, too, right now.

"Let me guess," Nikolaos ventured. "He has translated for you the letter that I carried out of Jotapata."

"Correct. He gave it to us in Greek, both verbally and in writing, which is why my father wants to speak with you."

***

Observed up close and in a more leisurely fashion, the imposing black tent from which General Vespasian was directing his siege bore no resemblance to any structure that Nikolaos had ever seen before.

Its heavy fabric had been stretched so high into the sky and staked so solidly into the ground that, unlike his green supply tent, it barely rippled in the wind despite much greater exposure.

Only the multicolored flags at its peak and the red tassels dangling at its corners and canopy were allowed to exercise freedom of movement.

Nikolaos followed Titus through the same double row of fierce-faced guards into a shady vestibule, then farther on to darkness.

His first two flittering impressions of the interior were basic.

Circles of light. Odor of oil.

But gradually, more details came clear.

Desks. Tables. Stools. Chairs. Partitions. Rugs on the desert floor. Slaves with palm fans. Red-and-brass uniforms. Red cape on a chair. Horsetail helmet on a stool. Older man at the largest desk. Immense lamp beside him. Face visible in the widest circle of yellow light. General Vespasian.

The younger general saluted his father and introduced the man at his side. "Nikolaos is a native speaker of Greek, sir," Titus said, "but he's also proficient in Latin and Aramaic."

Nikolaos's heart nearly burst from his chest.

All my efforts have paid off. This was worth every bit of the risk. Father will soon go free, and there'll be no denying who made that miracle happen.

Rome's greatest living military hero seemed equally euphoric. "Rome is grateful to you, young Nikolaos!" he boomed.

How ironic. It wasn't Rome I was trying to help.

But Vespasian went on. "The information you brought to us from Jotapata will save the lives of many of our soldiers."

Nikolaos looked at him and spoke boldly. "Will it also save the lives of the people of Jotapata?"

"No." Vespasian steadied himself on his palms as he rose.

"I hoped," Nikolaos lied, "that my actions might win mercy for them."

Not true, but it sounds good.

Vespasian actually growled. "There can be no mercy for the leader of the Jewish resistance and all others who oppose Rome."

Silence fell in the tent as Nikolaos studied the rug under his feet.

Maybe he'll choose to show his gratitude in a more personal way.

After a while, Vespasian cleared his throat. "I summoned you here to tell us the exact current situation inside the walls of Jotapata."

"From the letter," Titus added, "we have a good sense of how things are, but we need to hear it from you."

Nikolaos looked up again and nodded.

"Our guest has been through a lot and is tired," Titus said to his father. "What say we all sit and take refreshment while we talk?"

Vespasian pointed to a table surrounded by wooden chairs and gestured for a slave to bring wine. After Titus and Nikolaos were seated, with full goblets in hand, the elder general joined them.

First time I ever got to sit and "take refreshment" with important Romans.

"Here's the kind of information we need," Vespasian said. "How much food and water does ben Matityahu have left? How many of his fighters remain alive? What is their condition? Are there any known weaknesses in his wall or other defenses?"

And then came the question that Nikolaos was waiting for.

"How in Hades did you get out?"

Nikolaos lifted his cup and took a sip. It was good wine.

This might actually be enjoyable if I'd had a bath in recent months.

"I told you," Titus said, "about the elderly Pharisee who had translated the letter for us. Through him, we have ben Matityahu's personal report of conditions inside those walls. It's a credible account, written not for us but for his superiors in Jerusalem."

Vespasian downed the entire contents of his cup in one gulp and then burped, quite extravagantly. "Your own account, must concur with his. If it does not, we will have to reconsider what to do with you."

"However," Titus said in a much lighter tone, "if your report *does* confirm what he wrote, your immediate reward will be a hot bath, a good meal, and a Jewish wench to keep you happy while we smash what remains of Jotapata."

CHAPTER 27

Shortly before sunset, Adin jumped from his cart in the courtyard. "Jotapata has fallen!" he shouted. "It happened early this morning! Couriers just reached Caesarea!"

Up on the roof, Judith gasped, while Oren choked on his goat's milk.

Theodosia covered her face with her hands and tried not to show her joy. *So now, Vespasian and Titus can return to Caesarea.*

Her son stood at the edge of the roof, watching a flock of vultures soar against the orange sky before settling into a nearby tree. Their caws were the only sound as the sky darkened.

Does Doros realize what this means? We'll soon take his father home.

Some time later, Adin climbed the stairway and tossed a mat onto the floor beside his mother, who was steadily weeping. "They held Vespasian off for forty-seven days." He shook his head. "Forty-seven long, miserable days."

Everyone else had eaten already, but Myrine set lentils, figs, bread, and a cup of milk before him.

Adin gulped the milk. "Before dawn, a group of Roman soldiers somehow found a back route into the old fortress. They slipped through town in the dark, slit the guards' throats, and opened the main gate. That bastard Titus personally led the soldiers who crushed the defenders in less than an hour."

"Any survivors?" Judith asked.

"Only women and children," Adin said, "and you can bet that each and every one of them has been raped today."

"How do you know that?" Doros walked across the roof and looked down at Adin. "That can't be possible."

"It's more than possible." Adin's voice shook. "It's certain."

"It's what Roman soldiers always do," Oren said.

***

Two mornings after the fall of Jotapata, General Titus swaggered into the green supply tent like a lion that had just finished devouring his prey… quite the opposite in demeanor from the scrawny Jewish girl who had spent an entire day and night cowering in a corner among the coils of rope, naked but for a thin shawl her captors had allowed her to keep, crying for hours and screaming every time Nikolaos touched her. The general ignored her noise.

Probably had so many captive women these last two days, he doesn't even hear them any more. Wonder if Arona was one of them.

Titus clapped Nikolaos on the back. "Everything you told us about Jotapata was true, down to the smallest detail. You've earned our trust, our gratitude, and a hot, soaking bath."

A military orderly entered with a flock of male slaves toting a deep tin tub, buckets of steaming water, towels, a fresh tunic, and a new pair of sandals.

In her corner, the naked girl cringed even more.

***

The orderly who had supervised Nikolaos's bath now led him to the headquarters tent. Relieved to be clean and better dressed, he stood at the entryway until the younger general noticed him and beckoned him forward.

"Sir," Titus said in Latin to his father as he drew Nikolaos into a circle of uniformed officers, "you'll remember this brave Greek who smuggled that letter out of Jotapata."

Vespasian was standing in front of his desk.

On the ground before him, trapped inside that red-and-brass circle with his hands tied behind his back, a disheveled man knelt in a wash of yellow light.

Yosef survived.

The instant Nikolaos entered that circle, the man he had considered his friend raised his head. No visible emotion crossed Yosef's face, but his eyes were blazing torches.

And now he's my enemy for life.

Vespasian extended a hand. "On behalf of Rome, young man, General Titus and I thank you. We will find an appropriate way to reward you."

You can reward me by releasing my father.

But he didn't say that, because Vespasian hadn't stopped talking.

"However, before we discuss your reward..." The general's voice was warm and encouraging. "I do have a request."

For Father's freedom, anything.

"Are you willing, my young Greek friend, to perform one more invaluable service to Rome?"

I never intended to perform any service to Rome.

But he didn't say that either. Instead, he nodded.

"Excellent!" Titus clapped him once more on the back.

With the tip of one sandal, Vespasian prodded the man on the ground in the yellow light at the center of the circle.

"Just today," he said, "we found this wretch and another equally grubby one hiding in a cistern, surrounded by the dead bodies of more than three dozen of their fellow Jews, all either murdered or suicided. We're counting on you to identify him for us."

Yosef stared at Nikolaos. General Vespasian stared at Nikolaos. General Titus stared at Nikolaos. All the other officers in that red-and-brass circle stared at Nikolaos.

Nikolaos found himself trembling like a little boy in his mother's arms at the end of a long a pier in Corinth at the moment when big men in red-and-brass uniforms stomped toward them and slapped shackles on his father and locked them tight and dragged him away.

Vespasian's voice shook him out of it. "Do you know that man?"

Somehow, Nikolaos managed to blot out the brutal memory and refocus his mind on the equally brutal present. Again, he nodded.

"Very good!" boomed the top commander of the entire Roman army in Galilee, Samaria, Judea, Syria, Egypt, and the rest of northern Africa. "Now, use your lips and your tongue to answer me. Where did you first meet him?"

A victorious general makes a better ally than a defeated general.

"In Tiberias, sir."

"Under what circumstances?"

Do I dare confess to Vespasian that I cozied up to Yosef because I hoped he would lead me to... Vespasian?

"I had personal matters to discuss with him."

"When was this?"

"Two months ago."

"Since then, where have you seen him?"

Nikolaos gazed into the eyes flaring up below him.

Yosef may not speak or understand Latin, but he knows what's going on here.

Once again, his lips and tongue ceased to work.

"Where else have you seen him?" Vespasian's tone was a knife edge.

Father's fate.

"Inside the walls of Jotapata."

"What was he doing there?"

And my own.

"Commanding the resistance, sir."

"What were *you* doing there?"

Nikolaos scrambled for an excuse. "I was sweet on a Galilean girl." He swallowed. "Her name's Arona. She took refuge in Jotapata with her little brother, and I— I was— I hoped— to ensure their survival."

"Fine." Apparently satisfied, Vespasian prodded the captive again with his foot. "So, now you will tell me this man's name."

"He's the governor-general of the Jews."

Vespasian grunted. "I asked you for his name."

What will he do to Yosef if I confirm his identity?

Vespasian's lips twitched. Eyes narrowed. Mouth turned down.

What will he do to me if I don't?

The silence grew ominous.

No other way to save Father... and myself.

General Vespasian cleared his throat. "We're waiting, Greek."

I've betrayed Arona twice now, in very different ways.

He took a deep breath.

One more betrayal hardly matters.

"Yosef ben Matityahu."

***

Outside the tent, Titus slapped Nikolaos's back a third time.

"My father and I will grant any request you make." He released a loud, merry laugh. "Within reason, of course."

"Well, there is one thing—"

"Excellent!" Titus's boom sounded exactly like Vespasian's. "But right now, neither one of us has time to deal with it."

"But—"

"You understand that, I'm sure."

"But—"

"Here's what we're going to do." Titus reached inside his breastplate and pulled up a leather thong sewed to a small leather pouch.

Exactly like the brat's amulet pouch.

Titus extracted a silver rectangle and handed it to Nikolaos, who squinted to make out the embossed design.

A man's face.

"My parents gave me my bulla," Titus said, "when I was nine days old. That's my father's portrait. There's no other bulla like it in the world."

This is my reward?

"The day after tomorrow," Titus went on, "Father and I will arrive in Caesarea for two days of celebration with our officers." He grinned. "Two days of bedbug-free beds, Judea's finest food and wine, and the most voluptuous whores in town." The grin widened. "No more scrawny, screaming captive bitches for us."

Nikolaos eyed the amulet. "You're *giving* this to me?"

"Oh, no, you'll return it to me." Another jubilant laugh. "Now listen to me as closely as if your life depended on it. You will show up at Herod's palace in Caesarea during that short, two-day window. You will present my bulla to the guards, and just as soon as you do, they'll admit you into my presence."

"And then we'll discuss my reward?"

"Correct, but remember—" The laughter subsided. "This offer is good for *two days only*, starting the day after tomorrow. Show up three days after tomorrow and your only reward will be a Roman general's bulla."

***

Early the next day—three mornings after the fall of Jotapata—Nikolaos approached the only donkey cart available for hire in the military camp. The driver was repulsive—with a mangled foot, a badly inflamed eye, and skin covered with purple pustules—but there was no other choice.

"I need to get to Caesarea by sundown," Nikolaos told him.

Sit as far away from him as the bench allows.

"Nope." The man clawed at his crotch. "Two-day trip."

"I'll double your fee if you can make it by tonight."

"Paid in advance?"

"Of course."

The man scratched his neck, crawled onto the bench, and motioned for Nikolaos to do the same. Money changed hands, and off they went.

Now, there's only one thing left to do.

As the donkey struggled to satisfy his master's demand for speed, Nikolaos tilted his head and eyed the itchy driver.

Bet he could come up with somebody.

"Any chance you know a competent man willing to do dirty work for pay?"

The driver spit over the side of the wagon. "It's wartime. Lots of fellows looking for odd jobs." He gave Nikolaos a meaningful look. "Any kind of odd job, including murder."

"Someone good at following orders and keeping his mouth shut?"

"There's plenty like that roaming the countryside. Sleeping in caves. Robbing refugees. Killing Romans in Caesarea."

"How would I find one?"

"Double my fee again, pay in advance again, and you'll have your pick."

"Deal."

***

Three mornings after the fall of Jotapata, for the first time in two months, Theodosia donned her now-grimy white silk stola and palla and rode into Caesarea with Adin. Doros remained behind in Myrine's care. As Adin waited nearby in his brightly painted cart, Theodosia took a few deep breaths of sea air and walked up to the gilded door of Herod's palace. The pre-siege crowds were gone. Nobody was there except the legionary on duty.

"Have General Vespasian and General Titus arrived yet?" she asked in a voice full of hope.

Heavy-lidded eyes inspected her around the nose guard of a red-and-brass helmet. "If they had, this town would be full of petitioners."

Probably assumes I'm a camp follower.

She smiled. Didn't care. "But they will be here soon, won't they?"

"We expect them tomorrow, or possibly the day after tomorrow."

***

Night was falling on the outskirts of Caesarea when the itchy driver halted his exhausted donkey in front of a rock wall. "Who wants to earn some money?" he shouted into the air.

He did not, Nikolaos noted with relief, climb down from the bench.

He wants to make sure he can get away fast, if need be, and so do I.

Immediately, as if drawn by some ancient battle cry, several dozen reed-thin men in tattered tunics emerged out of nowhere.

Dirt-caked bodies crowded around the cart. Elbowed each other aside. Clamored for Nikolaos's attention. Devoured him with their hungry eyes. Engulfed him in their collective stench.

Filthy fingers with long, blackened nails plucked at the clean tunic that the Romans had given him yesterday after his bath.

How to choose from this lousy lot?

As Nikolaos puzzled over his dilemma, another man came forward from behind a bush and stepped to one side, well apart from the others.

The newcomer was sinewy and scruffy, too, with matted hair and a badly torn tunic, but he conveyed a sense of strength and confidence that none of the others could match.

In his left hand, a scimitar blade caught the last lingering ray of sunlight.

None of the others have shown such a weapon. He's making sure I see it.

"Looking for work?" Nikolaos asked in Aramaic as he pointed to him.

The man nodded but said nothing.

"You'll follow my orders and hold your tongue about it?"

Another silent nod.

"I won't tell you my name," Nikolaos said, "and I won't ask yours."

Another silent nod.

"Aren't you even curious about the job?"

By way of answer, the man raised his blade and crossed it over his chest.

***

Four mornings after the fall of Jotapata, Theodosia returned to the palace, leaving Doros in Myrine's care once more.

She approached the same guard at the gilded door. "Can you provide an update on the travel schedule of General Vespasian and General Titus?"

"You'll be happy. They're due to arrive later today."

He remembers me from yesterday.

"That's wonderful."

"I'm sure they'll want to see you tomorrow." Amusement brightened the man's face. "The couriers report they're in exceptionally good spirits."

Still thinks I'm either a camp follower or a street walker.

His reward for that information was a sincere, sunny smile that bubbled straight up from Theodosia's heart. "Thank you, sir. I'll be back tomorrow."

Oh, my dearest Alexander, we are so close to going home.

***

The morning after Nikolaos's nocturnal arrival in Caesarea—four mornings after the fall of Jotapata—a barber cut his ragged hair. A fabric merchant sold him a blue silk tunic. Other shopkeepers provided sandals, an expensive silver bracelet, an unusually sharp dagger, and a leather belt with a clever slit that concealed the blade under the blousing and folds of his new tunic. He took his purchases to the city's opulent Roman-style baths, where he indulged in hot-and-cold plunges, professional nail grooming, and massages by a pair of slinky slaves who eased his weariness before helping him dress.

After forty-seven days under siege, I've earned this.

He enjoyed a meal of fresh-caught squid in an outdoor cafe with a fine harbor view, then a first-time-ever saunter along Caesarea's breezy promenade, followed by a stop at the classic Temple of Roma and Augustus and a leisurely stroll on to the famous "floating" palace of Herod the Great.

Another structure I've always wanted to see.

A guard at the gilded front door eyed him with suspicion until he pulled the rectangular bulla out of its pouch and handed it over.

"That's General Vespasian's face, see? It belongs to his son, General Titus."

The guard inspected the amulet. "How did you get it?"

Perfectly reasonable question.

"General Titus gave it to me two days ago in their camp outside Jotapata, as a token of gratitude for my help in ending the siege. He said, if I showed it to you, you would take me right in to see him."

The guard returned the bulla to Nikolaos. "I'm sure he'll be glad to see you tomorrow."

"Not today?"

"Unfortunately, the generals have not arrived yet, and by the time they do—assuming they get in tonight at all—it will be too late for anything but a bath, a dinner, a speedy screw, and a good night's sleep."

***

Five mornings after the fall of Jotapata, as was now her regular practice, Theodosia left Doros in Myrine's care. Adin carried her to the edge of shimmering-hot Caesarea, but the crowds in the streets were now so thick that he couldn't drive in close or stick around to take her home.

As always, Theodosia did her best to avoid the foul humans and slimy droppings as she made her way across town to Herod's palace.

This time, the guard seemed surprisingly eager to answer her question. "They arrived last night," he offered before she even asked it.

Perfect.

She adjusted her bedraggled clothing and lifted her head with all the pride she could muster. "Please inform General Vespasian and General Titus that their old friend Theodosia Varro has journeyed across the sea to—"

"Sorry, they're busy today."

"But yesterday you said—"

"The generals gave orders. They're not to be disturbed today."

"With so many people in town hoping to see them?"

"A couple of things came up." The guard winked. "Big, heavy, sensitive things that needed to be attended to without delay." His language grew even more casual, as if he were bantering with a prostitute with whom he was well acquainted. "Real urgent, ya' know, just wouldn't wait."

Theodosia gazed at the mass of bodies she had just pushed through.

"Look, *lady*." The guard leered as he emphasized the honorific. "Ya' gotta show up real, real early tomorrow, long 'fore the crowd gathers, 'cause tomorrow's the generals' last day in Caesarea."

"They're only here for two days?"

"After tomorrow, they're splitting up." The guard bobbed his helmeted head. "Going in opposite directions."

"What?" Blood rushed to her face, as it always did when she was flustered or frustrated. "Why?"

"Really think I'm gonna tell ya' military secrets?"

"No, but—" She looked soulfully into his eyes. "Surely you can say where they're going from here."

The guard bent to her ear. "General Titus," he whispered, "south to Alexandria. General Vespasian, north again, back to Ptolemais, then on to Syria for a strategy session with the governor there."

"Thank you," she whispered back.

Tomorrow's my only chance. Hope nothing goes wrong.

***

Donkey carts were impossible to find in the jam-packed streets, much less to hire, and there were none on the outskirts of the city either. So Theodosia walked all the way back to the house, where she found Myrine and Judith standing together at the junction, awaiting her return. Theodosia was still far down the road when Myrine began running forward.

"Master…!" she screamed in Greek.

I can't understand her.

"Master Doros…!"

Still can't.

"Master Doros is…!"

Something about Doros?

"Master Doros is missing!"

The instant Theodosia caught the final word, her mind went numb.

Missing?

"Master Doros is missing!!" Myrine's cries reverberated in the stifling air as she raced toward her mistress. "Master Doros is missing!!!"

Doros is missing?

"Master Doros is missing!!!!"

Theodosia's eyes lost their focus.

In the road ahead, Myrine's red face and brown tunic dissolved into a two-toned blur that slowed and slowed and slowed some more the closer she came. With every few steps, her wails grew longer.

"Maaster Doroos is missing! Maaaster Doorooos—!"

That's not possible.

Theodosia's mouth opened.

"Maaaaster Dooroooos!"

He's out marching.

Her lips moved.

"Maaaaaaster Doooroooooos!"

Or hiding somewhere.

Her words evaporated.

"Maaaaaaaster Dooooorooooooos!"

Or playing a game.

Her muscles locked up.

"Maaaaaaaster Doooooorooooooooos!"

Teasing me.

At last, fully depleted by the stress and exertions of recent days, Theodosia collapsed into the road, crashing hard onto knees whose old injuries raised their voices and screamed along with Myrine. Within moments, the slave was at her side, bending over her, keening as loudly as she had on that dreadful day when she found her own beloved boys dead in their bed.

"Maaaaaaaaaaaaaaster Doooooooorooooooooos!"

Little by little, Myrine's tear-stained face came into focus.

"He was here when I left," Theodosia said. "How can he now be gone?"

The slave's howls melded with her answer.

"Oooooo nooooo, I dooooon't knooooow!"

"Have you looked?"

"Mistress Judith and I—" Myrine panted. "We checked everywhere—"
More panting. "But noooooooo sign of him! Nooooooooo footprints!"

How can this be?

Myrine switched into Aramaic. "The gaaaaate was ooooopen!"

Theodosia responded in Aramaic. "The gate was *not* open when I left. I
remember closing it."

Judith reached them now. "The gate *was* closed when I left for market."

Theodosia turned her head and stared down the road.

I'd give my life to see him marching toward me right now.

"Oren and I went out to look in all directions," Judith said, "and he'll go
searching again as soon as Adin gets home with the cart."

"Soooo-ooooooh, Mistress, it's aaaaaaaalll my faaaaaaaulllt!"

Theodosia's eyes shifted to her slave. "Why is it your fault?"

"It's my jooooob to waaaaatch him, but it was sooooo waaaaarm and I—"
Myrine dropped to her knees, too, and swayed back and forth. "I doooozed
in the shaaaade on the roooof." Wailing even louder, she bent to the ground.
"Mistress, you've sooooo maaaaany reeeeeasons to whip meeeeeeee."

Theodosia rejected that idea with a wave of her hands. "We've both told
him how dangerous it is out here. He never listens, not to me or to you."

"That boy's a handful, for sure," Judith said, as if to affirm that Myrine
wasn't to blame.

***

Adin and Oren returned after dark, following a futile, three-hour search in
the cart along all stretches of road.

At that point, too worn out even to change out of her stola and palla,
Theodosia climbed the stairs to the roof, dropped onto her sleeping mat, and
pulled the viper amulet from its pouch at her breast. Carefully, she pressed
her thumb against the knife-sharp edges of the gaping hole that the ruby
had occupied before someone dug it out of its setting.

Why was I wearing this today and Doros wasn't?

CHAPTER 28

Loud pounding. A strong male voice speaking Aramaic. "Open up!"

Theodosia awoke, remembered, and rejoiced.

Someone found my boy. Thank you, Juno!

The heavily clouded sky offered no light as she pulled on her sandals and palla and groped her way down the stairs to the courtyard.

Oren followed with a lamp and opened the gate.

Meanwhile, Myrine came from the kitchen to stand with her mistress in the shadows beside the stable wall.

Impressions of the man outside filtered through the yellow lamplight.

Lean. Tough. Matted hair. Torn tunic. Scimitar blade in his hand.

Oren must have seen the blade, too, because he immediately tried to shut the gate.

But the stranger lunged through. "I came for the Roman woman."

"We are a Hebrew family." Oren's voice was calm.

"The Roman woman whose brat thinks he's a soldier."

"We're ordinary Jews. We do not shelter Romans in our home."

"You damn well do."

"He is right, Oren." Theodosia stepped into the light. "I am here."

Oren and Judith will kick us out at daylight, but that's the least of my worries right now.

"Roman bitch." The intruder brandished his blade.

"How did you know I was here?"

"Your brat told me that and a whole lot more shit." He grabbed her upper arm. "You are coming with me."

Oren bumped his hand away. "Why would she do that?"

"Because she wants to see her brat again."

The intruder thrust Oren aside and knocked the lamp from his hand. Myrine leaped out of the shadows and retrieved it before the flame died.

"Her brat's full of crap, by the way," the man went on. "Heir to a rich, noble family, he says. General Vespasian's his mother's friend, he says. The general's gonna hunt me down and kill me, he says." The intruder laughed. "Oh, right, I'm sure he will do that."

Through the fabric of her dirty and now slept-in white stola, Theodosia squeezed the pouch holding the viper amulet.

Doros is alive. Bless you, little snake.

"When did you find him?" she asked.

"Yesterday morning."

"That *is* when he disappeared. Where was he?"

"Mile or so out yonder. Marching to Caesarea, he said, to sign up with Vespasian's army." The stranger cackled. "For such a proud, mighty soldier, he sure made it easy for me and my boys to grab him."

"Tell me what he's wearing."

"Gray tunic. Red embroidery."

They do have him.

"Is he safe?"

"Come and see for yourself."

"No, Theodosia." Oren's words were barely audible, as if he hoped the other man wouldn't hear. "You must not go with him."

"Oh, yes," said the intruder, "this Roman bitch—and her money bag—*must* go with me."

Theodosia recoiled. "All by myself? In the middle of the night? Carrying money?"

Now the man chortled. "I'll take care of the money."

Her mind searched for options and found none. "How much do you want for my son?"

"Everything you got."

"But we cannot survive in this land without money, much less rescue my husband and take him home, which is what we came here to do."

Do I have to choose between saving Doros or saving Alexander?

"You want your brat to live, don't you?"

I will not make that choice. I'll take them both home with me.

Myrine returned the lamp to Oren, then she slipped an arm around Theodosia's waist. "Master Oren is right," she said in Greek. "Don't go."

"Fetch my money bag."

"No, Mistress, it's too dangerous."

"That's my decision to make. Obey me."

Myrine's bare feet padded up the stairs, headed for a gunnysack that they had tucked away, months ago, at the bottom of the stack of mats in the covered storage space over the stables.

Meanwhile, the intruder's smelly, hairy body loomed over Theodosia.

"You're a Zealot!" she exclaimed in Aramaic.

"Nah, nothing so useful to society." Another cackle. "Now, stop the guessing games, bitch, 'cause if me and you don't haul in by sunrise, my boys will slit your brat's throat."

***

"If me and you don't haul in by sunrise, my boys will slit your brat's throat."

The man's threat hung in the cool predawn air. He hadn't said another word since they left the house. A hint of light outlined the eastern hills as he hustled Theodosia off the north-south road then shoved her west onto an uneven path. After a short distance, her left leg gave out and she collapsed onto the dry, flinty ground.

Still not speaking, he scooped her up and bounced her around clumps of pines and scrubby bushes and toted her over piles of rock and on and on in what seemed like circles until they reached a huge boulder at the bottom of a hill, where he dashed with her into a well-concealed cave.

Nobody else would ever find this place, even if they suspected it was here.

He carried her a long way back in total darkness.

I can't see a thing. How can he?

Finally, he dumped her on a flat rock and yanked the palla off her shoulders. It *whooshed* softly as he held its ends and spun its length in the air. Having thus created a rope, he used it to tie her wrists tightly behind her back.

"That hurts," she said as the strong silk fibers dug into her skin.

"Shut up."

She watched in silence while he built a fire halfway between her and the entrance. When that was done, he crouched near the flame, dumped the contents of her money bag onto the floor, and stacked the coins for counting.

"I'm hungry," she said after a time.

The man sprang to his feet, strode across the space between them, and slapped her face. In the next moment, he untied a strap that was wrapped several times around his left wrist.

"I wasn't gonna do this," he said, "but—"

He jammed the strap into her mouth, secured it behind her head, and—with a gratuitous punch to her chest—flattened her against the rock.

Stunned, choking, and retching at the raw-leather bitterness in her mouth, Theodosia said nothing more and made no further move.

Eventually, however, clear thoughts began to emerge.

He only tucked the strap under itself in back. Wasn't long enough to tie properly. I should be able to knock it loose.

Unseen creatures rustled in the darkness even farther back.

Bats? Rats? Wolves?

A loud drip-drip-drip drummed the floor.

It's as dark and dank as a crypt in here. A perfect place to die.

Turning only her eyes, she studied what she could see of the cave. Its walls were smooth, its uneven roof barely high enough for a man to stand upright.

Stefan would crack his head for sure. Alexander, too, most likely.

Tears welled.

Oh, my love—

But she shook them off.

Stay focused.

Nevertheless, Alexander lingered in her mind.

Today's my last chance to rescue him and I'm tied up in a cave and a brute's got all my money and I don't have the remotest idea where Doros is.

As her abductor counted the coins, she came to realize other things.

He's alone.

Courage returned.

No other "boys" here to slit anyone's throat.

Awareness surged.

He never calls Doros "your son" or "your boy." Only "your brat" or "the brat."
Even while speaking Aramaic, he's using the Greek word "brat."
Only one other person in the world has ever called Doros a "brat."

After a while, Theodosia's captor scooped all the coins into her money bag and tied it to his belt. Ominously, silhouetted against the fire, he lumbered over to where she still lay flat on her back and kicked her in the ribs.

"If you move from this spot, Roman bitch, I'll kill you when I return."

Then he stalked out of the cave.

***

The sun was rising when Nikolaos arrived at the gilded door. Once again, he presented General Titus's bulla to the guard and requested an audience with either or both of the conquerors of Jotapata.

Preferably both.

"They're not receiving visitors at this hour," the guard said.

"I'll wait."

A waterfront bench offered a fine view of biremes and triremes sailing in and out of the harbor in the early-morning light.

Chance to relax and enjoy some of the day.

Several hours later, after a series of unproductive follow-up requests and with no good reason provided for the delay, he left to find something to eat.

***

An hour passed. Maybe two. The fire flickered and died as the amount of natural light behind the boulder at the mouth of the cave increased tenfold.

Sun's high in the sky, and he's not back yet.

Theodosia sat up on her rock, shifted her bound wrists to a slightly more comfortable angle behind her, and looked around.

The visible front part of the cavern was empty but the darkest part in the rear was not. She willed herself to see farther than she had before.

Back there, where all those unseen-but-energetic creatures still scurried about, way back beyond a line of curiously long, dripping rocks, an odd object—an inert, rectangular shape—caught her eye.

Almost without thinking, she began rubbing her right shoulder against the leather strap at the point where it crossed her cheek and ear.

Over and over, back and forth, up and down, she worked it until, after a final violent shake of her head, the gag loosened and fell out.

"Doros!" Her call ricocheted between the walls and the floor.

No telling what dangerous or disgusting creatures that will stir up.

But she called again and, as if in response, the bundle wriggled.

She shouted louder. The bundle wriggled again.

Another shout, another wriggle, again and again and again.

By all the gods, he's alive!

In the next instant, Theodosia wrenched her elbows outward. Once, twice, three times, four, and still the twisted-silk rope held fast.

Dearest Juno, please help me do this.

Using only her shoulders, neck, and feet for support, she arched her back, lowered her tied-up hands to the rock beneath her, and sawed the knot against its jagged edge. With each pass, the stone sliced her arms, which grew so wet and sore that she soon realized they were the only things being cut.

Eventually, she concluded that no divine help was coming.

Juno can't hear me so deep in this Judean cave.

She stopped sawing, sat up, and stared at the seeping walls. The skin on her back and shoulders was seeping, too, obviously with blood.

It must be midday by now. Maybe even afternoon. Titus and Vespasian's last day in Caesarea and my last chance to rescue Alexander.

Behind her in the darkness, Doros kept thrashing about.

"I'll get you out soon," she called to him, "I promise."

But he made no verbal reply.

He's gagged, too. If only some little guardian snake would slither by to help.

And with that, inspiration struck.

Her chin snapped down against her chest.

Her lips plucked at the neckline of her stola.

And her own words to Alexander returned from a decade ago.

"You don't really believe in guardian snakes."

Her neck stretched forward to its limit.

Her tongue slid under the thin leather cord.

And Alexander's eyes twinkled in her memory.

Her teeth closed on the cord.

Her jaws tightened and pulled.

And nothing happened.

Several times, she jerked her head until, at last, the little pouch flew out from between her breasts.

It soared high over her right shoulder.

A metallic object hit the stone floor behind her.

And Alexander's voice rang in her ears.

"Oh yes, Mistress, I do. And I boldly predict that by the end of this trip, you'll believe in them, too."

She lowered herself onto her left side.

Mustn't knock it out of reach.

Carefully, she slid backwards across the rock, tearing and bloodying her stola even more until, at last, the fingers of her right hand grazed the viper amulet, wrapped themselves around it, and touched the ragged lip that once had held a tiny ruby.

Doros warned me the edge was sharp and—bless the gods!—he was right.

By pressing her elbows together as far as they would go, she managed to hook the viper's mouth onto the stretched-tight strip of silk that constrained her hands and began popping each individual thread of the rope.

A dozen small, precise cuts. Two dozen. Three dozen. Slowly, the rope began to weaken. A couple dozen more cuts reduced it to a single slender filament, and then, finally, with a quick yank of both wrists, her left arm burst free. She pulled both hands forward and flexed her numb fingers.

Now, at least, I can work in front of my body, not behind.

Despite that advantage, it was hard to carry out the same task with her left hand. And although the edges of the viper's mouth were worn down, no longer as sharp as before, the silken knot lay close to the inside of her right wrist, perilously near the veins.

Risking disaster with each cut, she kept going until the rope finally fell away from her right hand.

Bless you, little snake.

***

The rectangular shape wriggled as Theodosia approached.

"Stay still," she said. "That awful man might yet come back to kill us."

Operating blindly in the darkness, her fingers felt all over Doros's body, searching for the outermost end of the winding cloth that enveloped him or, failing that, for some other place to start unwinding.

"It's not a terribly tight weave," she said in an effort to assure him that he would soon be free. "A mix of wool and linen, it seems." Her first big discovery was a hemmed edge at his ankles. "Here's an end that's not tied in with the rest."

She untwined that piece as far as she could until it disappeared under another strip of fabric just above his knees, at which point she had to begin anew to hunt for a different hemmed end. It turned out that every strip was braided, and thus buried under another, so no true loose end ever turned up.

Is this some traditional Judean shrouding technique, or just a deliberate attempt to guarantee that Doros never could work himself free?

"Looks like I'll have to have to roll you," she said after a while. "Make some kind of noise right now, to let me know you can breathe."

A snort of sorts emerged from deep within.

"What a beautiful noise!" She patted him through his shroud. "Now, my darling, please don't do that again except to tell me that you can't breathe. I'm going to roll you over and over across the floor, all the way to the front entrance if I have to, unraveling every loose piece I come to, but if you make that noise, I'll take it as a signal to stop."

The bundle wriggled again.

Theodosia kissed his muffled head. "And I'll take *that* as a signal to go."

***

Early in the afternoon, after a satisfying meal of fried flounder and a sweet local wine, Nikolaos showed up again at the gilded door.

"The generals," said the guard, "are on their midday break."

"I don't understand." Nikolaos tried to keep his anger in check. "General Titus specifically told me that presenting his bulla would get me right in."

"Too many people trying to see them today."

"Did everyone come with a general's bulla as a guarantee of access?"

The guard produced a forced-looking smile. "Imperial business will always take precedence over personal business, as I'm sure you understand."

Not really.

"Do they even know I'm here?"

Annoyance replaced the false smile. "I personally delivered the bulla to General Titus this morning. He said he'd see you as soon as possible."

"'As soon as possible' must mean something different in Rome."

"No, it doesn't, but it doesn't mean 'immediately' either."

Nikolaos pointed to the harbor-facing bench where he had spent the morning. "I'll be over there, and if you promise to whistle at me when the time comes, I'll stop pestering you."

***

Burial shrouds piled up near the dead fire.

Theodosia kept rolling Doros across the floor, over and over and over toward the mouth of the cave, working each length loose, finding new ends beneath, slowly making her way through the long cloths that constrained his arms and legs, until she had it down to a single piece around his head.

And then, at last, even that was gone.

Doros spit out the wad of cotton that had been wedged into his mouth and yelped with joy. "Thought I would never, ever get that damn thing out."

Exhausted, Theodosia bent over, hardly able to consider her next move.

But Doros leaped to his feet. "Let's go rescue Father!"

***

Mounds of rocks. Patches of trees. The glaring-hot afternoon sun.

Much closer now to dusk than to midday.

"It was dark when he carried me here," Theodosia said. "I've no idea how to get back to the road."

They shaded their eyes and began searching in circles around the cave.

Another precious hour passed before they found their way to the road and set off toward the north, headed for Caesarea against a crush of Jerusalem-bound pedestrians, donkeys, and carts.

All trying to get to there before the bandits come out of their caves.

"Let's stop at Adin's house," Doros said as they approached it. "You're all bloody, and I'm famished."

"No time for that. The generals probably won't receive visitors after sunset."

"Why don't I run on ahead to tell them you're coming?"

"No, let's stay together. I can't risk losing you again."

Sweat soaked her clothing. Pain rampaged through her legs and up her back. Heat stifled her lungs. She had to stop repeatedly to catch her breath as strangers gaped.

Juno, if you can hear me now, we really could use some help out here.

Soon, a cart rumbled up behind them.

"Doros!" Adin shouted.

"Mistress!" Myrine cried. "We've been riding back and forth since dawn. Thought we'd never see either one of you again."

Thank you, Juno.

***

The sun hovered slightly above the sea as a sharp, two-fingered whistle rousted Nikolaos off his bench.

By all the gods, it took the idiot long enough.

The guard escorted him between a pair of gray-smoking torches. Down a long, windowless corridor. Past a series of unlit cubicles. Through a scarlet-frescoed reception room filled with blazing bronze lamp trees, storage chests, and scores of benches and stools. Out onto a tessellated tile terrace overlooking the harbor, where Generals Titus and Vespasian, elegantly attired in their red-and-brass regalia, sat in huge marble chairs on an elevated platform of the same stone beneath a dark-green awning.

There was no seating or shelter for petitioners, but several military aides stood at ease behind their superiors. Titus rose, stepped off the platform, and offered his hand. "You look rested, Nikolaos."

Nikolaos bowed, came forward, and accepted the handshake. "So do you, sir. Thank you for seeing me."

"At this hour, we're only doing it because we promised to." Titus returned to the chair beside his father.

Does he think I just got here?

"It's late," Vespasian said without a trace of warmth in his voice, "and we've been at this all day, so tell us quickly what reward you want for helping end the siege."

Nikolaos had rehearsed this moment, but his imagined scenario always assumed a relaxed-and-grateful pair of generals eager to compensate the man who had made their victory possible with almost no loss of Roman lives... not a tired-and-grouchy pair of generals bored after too many hours of listening to an endless series of petitions.

From the start, his presentation veered badly off course.

"My request has to do with my father, sir," he said to Vespasian. "He built a successful shipping business on the island of Euboea and—"

"Where's that?" Titus asked.

"North of Athens, sir, and over the last decade, he became a celebrated, prosperous member of the community. But then, quite abruptly, without provocation or cause—"

Vespasian frowned. "We've no time to hear your father's entire life story."

"No interest in it either." The younger general's gaze drifted toward the huge orange ball sinking fast into the blue water.

"My apologies," Nikolaos said, "but I'm afraid you really can't—"

"So, get on with it." Vespasian slapped his hands on his knees.

"Sir, my father is a rower on one of your ships." Nikolaos gestured toward the harbor. "Somewhere out there, most likely—"

"A galley slave?"

Titus switched his eyes back to Nikolaos's face. "A common criminal?"

"No, sir, he's not a criminal. He was arrested and convicted by mistake, so I'm asking that you—"

"Roman justice doesn't make mistakes," said Vespasian.

"Roman courts get it right every time," said Titus.

Nikolaos fell silent.

Hard to argue with a pair of generals.

After a while, Vespasian cleared his throat. "Where was he convicted?"

"In Athens, sir."

"My old friend Vibius Galarius—*Governor* Vibius Galarius—must have handled the interrogation and trial."

"I'm not sure, sir, but if you'll give me a chance to—"

"What was he accused of?"

No point in lying. They'll find out soon enough if they pursue this.

"Theft and murder, sir, but he didn't do either of those things."

"How do *you* know he didn't?"

Nikolaos shrugged. "Because I know my father, sir."

Titus leaned toward his own father. "Must be one of the convicts I picked up on my way here. There's at least two dozen ships out there he might be on."

Vespasian looked at Nikolaos. "Vibius Galarius is a good man. Knows what he's doing."

"I'm sure that's true." Nikolaos licked his lips. "But, sir, if you'd only take a few moments to meet my father and speak with him—"

Titus interrupted with a boisterous laugh. "We barely have time to speak with you! We're doing this as a favor, because we said we would."

Nikolaos blinked.

They should be doing it willingly, not grudgingly.

"At Jotapata," he said, his voice rising in frustration, "you *promised* I could have any reward I wanted, within reason. Well, generals, I'm asking for my father's freedom. Under the circumstances, that is entirely reasonable."

Vespasian glowered at him. "*We* are the ones who will determine what is reasonable and what is not."

"Besides," Titus said, "imperial captains have better things to do than go crawling around their stinking oar decks trying to locate a single, specific, filthy rower so we can invite him into the palace for a chat."

CHAPTER 29

The sun had set. The crowds were gone. Gray smoke from a pair of flaming torches drifted into the night sky. Guards flanked the open door. And for the first time ever, Adin was able to pull his cart up to the entrance of Herod's palace and tie his donkey to a post near the door.

Myrine eased Theodosia down from the bench, clucking over the cuts on her arms, her blood-soaked stola, and her overall state of exhaustion.

"I borrowed two of Esther's kitchen knives." She pointed under the seat. "Want to take one in with you?"

"I could have used it in the cave." Theodosia adjusted what remained of her stola. "Shouldn't need it now."

"I'm gonna nap while you're in there. Been an awful long day." Myrine turned to Adin. "Mind if I stretch out in the back of the cart?"

Adin shook his head. "Go ahead. I'll find a spot in the grass and do the same. Won't be far away, so call if you need me."

Meanwhile, Doros marched up to the guards, clenched his fist, and smacked it across his chest in a crisp military salute.

"General Vespasian and General Titus are expecting a visit from my mother, Theodosia Varro. She hails from a very important Roman family, which means you must admit her right away."

He took several steps back and performed a series of intricate maneuvers as the soldiers chuckled.

"I'm going to be a general, too, so you better follow my instructions."

"With those moves, boy," said one guard, "I have no doubt."

Theodosia joined her son. "Are the generals available to see us?"

"No," said the other guard. "They're currently with a Greek petitioner who waited all day."

"We can wait, too."

"Afraid not. The generals gave orders to admit no one else. Just as soon as the young Greek leaves, they're going upstairs for dinner."

Doros shot his mother a knowing look, then he dashed through the open door and disappeared.

***

Nikolaos took a chance and raised his voice even more. "I'm not asking you to chat with my father, sir. I'm asking you to give him justice."

Vespasian's face darkened even more. "You dare question Roman justice and the judgment of Vibius Galarius, the man whom the Emperor of Rome personally chose to serve as the Governor of Athens?" He turned to his son. "I've heard enough."

"Me, too. Time for dinner." Titus yawned and glanced up at the black sky. Then he reached for a leather pouch that one of his aides was holding and held it out to Nikolaos. "Our standard payment to spies and traitors."

"But, sir, that's not—"

"Thirty silver talents."

"That's not why I did what I did."

"Take it or leave it."

As Nikolaos pondered his options, sandals smacked loudly on the interior side of the terrace door. Two guards lunged into an energetic scuffle with a small figure, who then slipped through their hands and raced outside.

Moments later, and just as abruptly, the brat stopped in his tracks.

How in Hades did he get loose? Damn incompetent bandit.

The brat marched up to the generals' platform, snapped to attention, executed some professional-grade movements with both of his hands and both of his feet, clenched his right fist, and with it smartly struck his chest.

He's got his military crap down pat.

"Centurion Doros reporting for duty, sirs!"

"Centurion Doros?" Vespasian's scowl vanished. He rose, stepped down, and actually laughed.

"Sir!" Doros struck his chest again. "I have journeyed a great distance—all the way from the grand port of Piraeus across the frozen sea to this war-torn land—in the company of my exceptional mother, who, by a remarkable blessing of the Fates, is also a special friend of yours."

And excellent rhetorical skills.

Vespasian's face evolved from amusement to astonishment. "A special friend of mine?"

"Sir!" Doros struck his chest again. "And a special friend of your esteemed son as well."

A ripple of mirth slid over Titus's lips. "Tell us more, Centurion Doros."

"Sir!" Doros struck his chest again. "My mother and many generations of her noble family—which, of course, also happens to be my own noble family—lived in a fine coastal villa north of Rome. She has often told me of her cherished friendship with your beloved daughter—a lovely young woman named Flavia Domitilla, if I remember correctly—and how deep their friendship grew during that extraordinary year when your two equally illustrious families came to know one another."

And nearly perfect Latin.

Titus and his father exchanged quizzical looks.

"What's your mother's name?" the younger general asked.

"Sir!" Doros struck his chest again. "Her name is Theodosia Varro, and she is the great-granddaughter of the most brilliant, most erudite, and most famous scholar in the entire history of the world."

And a gift for hyperbole.

"Theodosia's here?" Titus's mouth fell open. "In Judea?"

"Sir!" Doros struck his chest again then gestured with that same hand toward the corridor. "I left her right out there, at the very door of your palace."

Vespasian turned to one of the guards. "Find Centurion Doros's mother and bring her here."

Shit.

***

Moving even slower than normal, Theodosia followed a guard along the same hallway she had walked so many times in April, and through the same scarlet-frescoed reception hall where she had spent so many frustrating hours and days, and to a door she had never seen open before, and out onto an unlit terrace where vague shapes moved about in the dark.

A thin shaft of light from inside soon picked out more details.

Half a dozen uniformed men. Nikolaos. Doros. The two generals.

"Your son is quite the talker," Vespasian said by way of greeting as he extended both his hands and wrapped her in his arms.

Theodosia's eyes filled with tears.

Are all those things I did in the past now forgiven?

Vespasian's left hand, as he pulled it away, grazed her blood-caked back. His right hand brushed one of her scraped-up forearms.

"What have you got all over you?" he asked.

She angled toward the light and lifted both arms so he could see the cuts and dried blood. "My apologies for showing up like this, but it's been a difficult day, and I've had no time to bathe and change."

"What happened?"

She was about to tell him when Titus came forward and, as if he hadn't noted her condition, kissed her cheek.

"Looks like your boy's dead set on being a soldier," he said.

"He is, but—" She stopped and blotted her eyes. "His father won't hear of it."

"His father?" Vespasian asked.

"Doros's father," Nikolaos interjected without looking at Theodosia, "is also my father."

He doesn't have the guts to face me.

"Your father," Titus said, "the galley slave?"

Nikolaos nodded. "My half-brother and his mother—this woman—came here for the same reason I did."

Vespasian switched his eyes to Theodosia. "Your husband is a convicted thief and murderer?"

"Convicted, yes, but entirely innocent. He didn't commit either one of those crimes."

Nikolaos still didn't look at her. "I told them that."

Titus glared at him and exhaled noisily. "And I asked how you knew it."

"And I gave you my very best answer."

"And your very best answer was not good enough."

Theodosia pointed toward the reception hall. "If you'll find me a place to sit in there, I'll give you an answer that *will* be good enough."

The guards arranged five stools in a circle between two light trees. Doros helped his mother settle onto one of them, then he sat next to her. Nikolaos faced them, leaving an empty stool on each side of him. None of them spoke.

Meanwhile, Vespasian and Titus remained outside, conversing with their aides. After a time, they all came in. The generals took the two remaining stools, giving Theodosia her first good look at her old friends in eleven years, as well as a perfect position to watch their faces.

They've changed a lot since the night of Nero's big competition, and so have I.

"The first thing," Vespasian said, "that General Titus and I need to know is the name of this mysterious man we're talking about. The father of both Centurion Doros and—" He waved a hand at Nikolaos. "Your name, again?"

"Nikolaos, sir."

"Ah yes, Nikolaos. So, Nikolaos, tell us your father's name."

Doros jumped up and saluted again. "Sir, our father's name is Alexander!"

Nikolaos's eyes shot daggers at him. "He didn't ask you."

"Alexander," Vespasian said. "I seem to recall a man of that name."

"It's the same man," Theodosia said. "I married him in Sicily."

Vespasian waved a hand to dismiss his aides, who promptly left the room, leaving only a few guards much farther away, at the opposite end.

Glad he didn't force me to have this discussion in front of strangers.

"I should be shocked," the general said, "but I'm not. Nor am I surprised."

"Nor should you be." Despite the hunger that had given her a headache, Theodosia smiled. "Not if you recall him from *those* days."

Vespasian rested his elbows on his knees and leaned toward her. "I do recall him from *those* days."

"Then I'm sure you agree that he could not possibly have committed either one of the crimes he was accused of. He's neither a murderer nor a thief."

"Under the right circumstances, Theodosia, anyone can do anything."

"That's true, but—" She concentrated on making her case. "As you'll also recall, I owned a set of gold-and-silver goblets with matching serving pieces."

"A viper design," Titus said, "with very large, fine rubies." A wistful look crossed his face. "My recently deceased sister once coveted them."

"She did indeed." Theodosia smiled at him. "Those were the same rubies that Nero later accused Alexander of stealing from him. But at the time Alexander left my villa, those rubies were my property, just as he was. And I had freely given them to him, just as I had freely given him permission to leave my villa. So, he didn't steal my rubies, and he didn't steal himself."

"Did you tell all this to Governor Vibius Galarius?"

"I made an effort to, but by the time I got that chance the trial was over and Alexander was convicted and sentenced. I never could explain anything when it might have mattered, because the very first action the commander in Eretria took after he arrested Alexander—"

Her voice broke, and it wasn't an artificial effort to move them. She needed a few moments to compose herself, but even then she couldn't look up.

"The very first thing the centurion did was torture him."

"By law, that's how we question slaves," Titus said. "And since, legally, Alexander was still a slave, the centurion followed proper procedures."

Wish we had time to debate the rightness or wrongness of that.

"So there Doros and I were," she said instead, "struggling in the bitter January weather to bring Alexander warm clothing and hot food from home, when in fact—as I found out much later—they already had him stretched naked on a rack in their freezing dungeon."

Neither of the generals said anything, so Theodosia kept talking.

"After his first confession—when they tortured him into admitting to the murder of a young man whom he actually had been protecting, sometimes at personal risk to himself, for over a decade—they shipped him off to Athens so Governor Vibius Galarius could torture him again and force his second confession to a theft that never happened."

The men remained silent, so she went on.

"By the time I learned all this, Alexander was already rowing a ship—rowing *you*, Titus, as I understand it—across the sea to Judea."

She stopped and raised her eyes to the generals, who exchanged looks.

"I'm going to be blunt," Titus said after a time. "Even if I believed your story, and I'm not sure yet that I do, there's no way I can spare a single rower from the fleet."

"He's right," Vespasian said. "Every slave must be well conditioned and prepared for any sailing condition. A ship can't leave port without the exact number of rowers needed for its oars, plus a few extras as backup."

"But now that your siege has ended—"

"Jotapata was our first major battleground, not our last," Titus said. "This war will go on for years, and I can't be out hunting more convicts. We have to make do with the rowers we have."

Not what I needed to hear.

"And anyway," Vespasian said, "a murder charge is more serious than a charge of theft. Can you address that problem, Theodosia?"

Through her stola, she wrapped her fingers around the viper amulet, which rested once more in its pouch between her breasts.

Little snake, give me the strength and wisdom to get this right.

"With a bit of assistance from Nikolaos," she said, "I can."

***

Nikolaos frowned.

So now, after telling her sad, sorry tale to the same generals whose trust I risked my life to earn, here comes her predictable attack on me.

"Nikolaos." The Roman woman's eyes bored into his. "Are you planning to tell them, or shall I?"

"Tell them what?"

"The whole story of how you murdered Lycos."

"I did not murder Lycos."

"How you launched your plot by picking a fight with him."

"I did not pick a fight with him."

"On a street corner in the middle of Eretria, not far from our house, where you knew half the people in town could hear you two shouting."

"Stop making things up."

"In the darkest hour of night, when noises carry a long way."

"Total nonsense."

"Because you knew your voice sounded exactly like your father's."

"Nobody ever told me that."

Can't stand the way she twists the facts.

"And everyone would assume it was Alexander arguing with Lycos."

"Why would I want people to assume such a thing?"

"Because you knew that, if you planted the idea that they had argued in the night, Alexander would be blamed when Lycos turned up dead the next day."

"You really think I would set my father up to be accused of murder?" Nikolaos jutted his jaw. "Really?"

"I don't *think* it. I *know* it."

"How would I gain by doing that?"

"You imagined yourself jumping in, whether he was merely accused or actually convicted. You would show up as the great hero come to save him."

Nikolaos looked from Titus to Vespasian. "Generals, this is absurd."

"No doubt," the Roman woman went on, ignoring him, "it seemed a fine plan until things got out of hand. Charges you never anticipated. Torture. Forced confessions. And before you knew it, your father was convicted and sent to his likely death."

Nikolaos kept talking to the generals. "Everything she says is a lie."

But the generals paid him no attention.

So the Roman woman persisted. "How did you kill Lycos, anyway?"

"I didn't kill him, and you're just talking in circles."

"Did you stab him through the heart? Bash his head in with a rock? Strangle him with your belt? Poison him like you poisoned Myrine's sons?"

Nikolaos leaped to his feet. "General Vespasian, this woman is hysterical."

The Roman woman instantly produced one of her I-know-everything-and-you-know-nothing laughs. "I bet you strangled him. You were always so much bigger than Lycos. So much stronger. So much meaner."

"Lycos was a grown man when he died." Nikolaos looked at Titus. "Man enough to defend himself. And my father's wife has always been fucking nuts."

Titus raised his eyebrows. "Go on, Theodosia."

"Grown men *can* be strangled." She pointed at Nikolaos. "You used your belt, didn't you? Readily available. Thick and strong. Neater than a knife. Very little blood to clean up."

"Generals, don't listen to this stinking pile of donkey shit!"

Again, the Roman woman laughed. "Speaking of donkeys—"

Nikolaos addressed Vespasian directly once more. "This madwoman thinks it's funny. Do you see anything funny in it, sir?"

Vespasian made no response. Totally ignored him.

This isn't going well. I may have to get out of here soon.

"After work," she droned on, "you took your employer's cart and donkey from the market. Later, after the street fight, you loaded Lycos's body into it."

"I did not."

"You hauled his body out of town and dumped it where the woodsmen were sure to find it. And to top that off, you planted fake evidence."

"There was no fake ev—" Abruptly, Nikolaos stopped.

Must be more careful. That answer could suggest I actually was there.

"You left Doros's bulla, which you had stolen from him some time before, on top of Lycos's body, so no one could possibly miss it."

General Vespasian interrupted her to ask a question. "Who was this Lycos fellow that was murdered?"

The Roman woman's face puckered. "You'll remember him, too, from *those* days. A small, curly-haired slave boy at my villa." Her voice cracked.

Sure, get emotional. Make 'em feel sorry for Lycos.

"Alexander used to bring him to play with Domitian under the pergola."

"Yes, I do remember him." Vespasian nodded. "Sweet child."

"Lycos escaped with Alexander and from that point on was a much better son to him than this miserable—"

"Lycos was an interloper in our family," Nikolaos said. "He had no right to be there."

Once more, she ignored him and addressed the generals. "Lycos grew into a hard-working partner to Alexander and a fine husband to—"

"But *he* attacked *me* that night in the street. *I* did not attack *him*."

"That may well be true," she admitted, "and with good reason, since he had just found out you'd been raping his wife for years."

"She was *our* slave, not *his* wife."

"Oh, Nikolaos, do you really want the generals to hear those sordid details? I'll happily tell them all that, too, if you won't."

***

Theodosia plunged in now without waiting for a response from Nikolaos or either of the generals. "The day before Lycos was murdered, Nikolaos stole all our money. Everything we had saved over ten years. He dug it all up out of the floor. I had to borrow from a friend to travel to Athens and on to Judea."

Nikolaos began pacing between the lamp trees.

He's acting like a skittish, cornered rabbit.

"General Vespasian," Nikolaos said. "General Titus. How many lies are you going to let her tell?"

"So far," Titus said, "I've seen no evidence that she's lying."

"You've heard no proof of her claims either."

"Proof may yet come," Titus said. "Please go on, Theodosia."

"Once we learned of Alexander's fate," she said, "all of us, including Nikolaos, decided to make this journey to rescue him."

"That was risky," Vespasian said, "but admirable."

"It would have been even more admirable if we could have worked together. I tried to get Nikolaos to cooperate with me, but he always refused."

Titus looked at Nikolaos. "Why?"

"I couldn't see how she and her brat— How she and her son could help." Nikolaos set off on another lap between the lamps. "A war zone is no place for women and children."

"Stop pacing," Vespasian said. "You make me nervous."

As Nikolaos returned to his stool, Doros spoke up for the first time.

"That's not why he refused."

"No?" Vespasian's mouth turned up. "What insights do you have for us, Centurion Doros?"

"He's much too young," Nikolaos said, "to understand any of this."

"My insights, sir?" Doros rose. "General Vespasian." He saluted again. "General Titus." Another salute. "Would you like to hear the truth about our family?"

He paused and waited until both generals nodded.

"Thank you, sirs. Well, the truth about our family is this. Nikolaos hated Lycos. He hates my mother. He hates me. He hates everybody our father loves. He's jealous of anyone who means anything to our father. He wants *my* father to love *him* and no one else, including *me*."

Theodosia smiled to herself.

All that rhetorical practice up on the roof.

"My father and mother," Doros continued, "tried to give us a normal family life, but Nikolaos wanted none of it. May I tell you, sirs, some of the things he did?"

Vespasian and Titus exchanged glances before nodding again.

Doros lifted the index finger of his right hand.

"Nikolaos killed our puppy."

He paused, then lifted a second finger.

"Nikolaos killed Lycos."

Another pause, then he lifted a third finger.

"Nikolaos killed Lycos's little boys."

Another pause, then he lifted a fourth finger.

"Nikolaos tried to kill my mother and me when I was just a baby."

So glad we worked on gestures and repetitions and pauses.

Doros left all four fingers in the air and waved them. "And, sirs, that's not all." He lifted his left index finger.

"Nikolaos raped our slave for many years."

Another pause. Another finger lifted.

"Nikolaos stole all our money."

Another pause. Another finger lifted.

"Nikolaos stole my bulla—which he knew half the people in Eretria would recognize—and planted it on Lycos's body to make our father look guilty of murder."

Another pause. Another finger lifted.

"And, as my mother has told you, Nikolaos's only motivation for trying to save our father from the galley is that he wants credit for doing it."

Doros paused again and waved all eight fingers in the air. "Generals, I know you're both asking... *why?* Why would any man do such terrible things to his own family?"

My marvelous little orator.

The hour was late.

Theodosia's stomach growled.

Nikolaos's face had flushed purple.

The generals shifted on their stools, but neither one interrupted Doros.

"Well, sirs, I'll tell you why." Doros lowered his hands and paused even more dramatically. "It's because he wants Father to love him and nobody else. He wants to turn Father against Mother and me. He wants Father to hate us as much as he hates us. To sum it up in a single word, generals, Nikolaos is *poison.*"

With a final flourish, the boy smacked his fist to his chest once more and returned to sit beside his mother.

Vespasian stared at Theodosia. "Is all that true?"

"It is an accurate description of our lives these last ten years."

Titus scratched his neck. "Sounds like one of the old Greek tragedies."

"Yes," Theodosia said, "and there are two more series of events that even Doros isn't fully aware of."

"Tell us," Vespasian said. "We'll make time."

Theodosia smiled her gratitude. "So, here's the first. Over a decade, with superb help from Lycos, Alexander built a successful shipping business. Together, those two brought prosperity to the entire island of Euboea. Alexander became the most respected citizen in Eretria, and no one, not even the Romans at the garrison, suspected he had been a slave. Along the way, he invested the last two of those big rubies—which, as you'll remember, I had freely given him—to grow his business and buy a comfortable house for our family."

"That's an impressive story," Vespasian said.

"I think so, too, but as Doros told you, Nikolaos couldn't stand to see Alexander value Lycos so much. It drove him mad that Alexander loved Doros and me. And for some reason, he blamed *us* when Alexander reacted to his violent behavior by banishing him from our home."

Theodosia glanced over to see how Nikolaos was reacting. Except for its purple color, his face was expressionless.

Never saw him so unresponsive. Something's going on in his head.

"At some point," she continued, "Nikolaos took it upon himself to become the town gossip. He made it his business to share our secrets with anyone who would listen, things that nobody outside our family should have known."

She took a moment to catch her breath and think.

"Don't forget all those nasty rumors," Doros said.

Theodosia nodded. "Yes, Nikolaos made up a lot of sordid stories about the time when Alexander and I lived under the same roof at my villa, even though we had nothing even close to a sexual relationship back then."

"And the ruby in the market," Doros prompted again.

"Nikolaos went out of his way to let the wife of the garrison commander know when one of the big rubies—the very same stone that Alexander had used to purchase our house—showed up in the market. He spread the lie that Alexander had stolen that ruby and others."

"And," Doros kept prompting, "how it wasn't just ordinary people in town who believed his lies."

"Right. The Romans at the garrison believed them, too, even though they had been our friends for years. And then Nikolaos had the gall to tell Alexander that *I* was the source of all the gossip and rumors."

Vespasian turned to Nikolaos. "What have you to say for yourself?"

"Why bother saying anything? It's clear you're not going to believe me."

"Come on, young man, if you're as innocent as you say you are, tell us your side of things."

After a time, as Nikolaos remained silent, Vespasian addressed Theodosia again. "You said there was a second series of events."

Theodosia reached for Doros's hand. "Will you fill in any gaps in this story that I have no way of knowing?"

Gravely, her son nodded.

He looks as grown-up as I've ever seen him.

"Since March," she began, still holding his hand, "Doros and I and our maid have been lodging with a generous Jewish family that lives beside the main junction outside Caesarea. We've shared their meals. Slept on their roof. Learned their language and history and culture."

"They've taken really good care of us," Doros said.

"Thanks to that wonderful family," his mother went on, "even as the war raged and they grieved at the fall of Jotapata—and even though they told us that they didn't like Romans and Greeks—we felt safe in their home."

"They sound like nice people," Vespasian said. "Perhaps we can reward them for their kindness to you."

Theodosia gave him another grateful smile. "But yesterday morning, while I was right here, hoping to see you, Doros vanished from our Jewish friends' house. Our servant looked for him. Our hosts looked for him. I looked for him." She squeezed her boy's hand. "But he was gone."

Titus's lips twitched. "It appears you found him."

"Yes, I did, but not easily." Theodosia raised her arms so they could see her cuts and dried blood once more. "Very early this morning, not long after midnight, a bandit barged into the family's home. He knew my name and said he was looking for me. He took all the money we had left and forced me to go with him on foot."

"You went out in the night," Vespasian boomed, "all alone with a Judean bandit?"

"He said his gang would kill Doros if I didn't go with him."

Doros jumped in. "Except there never was a gang, just that one man."

"He hauled me to a cave," Theodosia continued, "somewhere off the road to Jerusalem, tied me up, and left. I didn't know until hours later that Doros was there, too. Gagged. Enshrouded. Abandoned. Left to die."

"For a whole day," Doros said, "I could hardly move or breathe."

Theodosia looked back and forth between Vespasian and Titus, neither of whom seemed inclined to rush her story.

"Doesn't it seem strange to you," she asked at last, "that a Judean bandit would break into a Judean home for the specific purpose of kidnapping a gentile boy? And doesn't it seem even stranger that he would go back for that boy's mother—whose name and background he knew before he got there—and demand all her money as ransom for her son?" Slowly, she trained her eyes on Nikolaos. "How likely was that to happen unless someone had told the bandit where we were so he could go and get us."

"You're insinuating I did that." Nikolaos stood so fast that he knocked his stool to the floor. "Generals, this is absurd. As with all this woman's other accusations, she has no proof." He bent over to pick the stool up.

"You're right about that, Nikolaos," Theodosia said. "I have no proof at all. Just one tiny, telling clue."

CHAPTER 30

Nikolaos focused his eyes on the Roman woman and laughed.

She's crazy. They're not going to believe that.

But apparently, Vespasian did. "What clue?"

"One little word." She returned Nikolaos's stare.

"What word?" Vespasian asked.

"Brat."

"Brat?" Titus laughed now, too. "What kind of clue is that?"

"An excellent one. You see, ever since Doros was born, Nikolaos has called him a brat. No matter what language he's speaking—Latin, Greek, or Aramaic—he never calls him 'Doros.' It's always 'the brat' or 'your brat.'"

The brat bobbed his head. "Nikolaos used to call Lycos a brat, too. Lycos told me that once, to make me feel better."

"Until today," the Roman woman said, "no one else—other than Nikolaos—has ever called Doros a brat. But during the night, first at our Jewish friends' house and later on the road, the bandit kept threatening my son. Doros would die, he said, if I didn't hustle along. The bandit's gang would slit Doros's throat, he said, if we weren't there by sunrise."

Nikolaos took his seat again. "As she admitted, that proves nothing."

"Let her finish," Vespasian said.

"Except," she went on, "instead of using Doros's name, the bandit called him 'the brat' every time. Using the Greek word, no less. 'They'll slit the brat's throat.' 'Your brat will be dead by sunrise.'"

"The bandit called me a brat to my face, too," said the brat, "just like Nikolaos does."

"So, here's the question," the Roman woman continued. "Why would a Judean bandit pick such an uncommon word to describe a child he barely knew, unless he'd heard someone else call him that first?"

"By all the gods, what a stupid question." Nikolaos jabbed a finger in her direction. "This woman despises me, and her brat despises me, and yes, I do call him that—in both Aramaic and Greek—because the word fits. He's an obnoxious, loud-mouth brat. Those two and their slave girl have schemed against me for years, trying to make my father hate me as much as they do."

"That's a lie," said the Roman woman.

Nikolaos turned to the stone-faced generals. "Just because I refer to my half-brother as a brat, that doesn't mean I hired a bandit to kidnap him and his mother and tie them up in a cave and leave them to rot. She can't prove a single thing she claims."

There followed a long silence that the Roman woman finally broke.

"Again, you're right," she said at last. "I can't prove any of this."

Nikolaos threw his hands into the air. "So, why are we even discussing it?"

But, of course, she never lets logic deter her.

"You're clever, Nikolaos," she said, "and you don't leave many tracks, but that doesn't mean my suspicions aren't well founded."

"Nothing you've said tonight is true."

"Actually, it's all true. I know that, and—even more important—you know it, too."

Under the folds of Nikolaos's tunic, the dagger nudged his thigh.

I'd kill her this instant if there weren't so many armed men in the room.

"So," the Roman woman went on in the tone she always used when she was about to stab Nikolaos in the back, "rather than ask the generals to rule against you—and in time of war the empire does give them great legal powers—I'm going to appeal to your better nature, your sense of honor."

"Because you can't prove anything."

"You're Alexander's first-born son, and—" With obvious fakery, she made her voice break. "Your father is the best, most honorable man I've ever known, which makes me believe there must be goodness and honor in you, too."

She's trying to set me up for something.

"So, here's our situation," she said. "On the one hand… General Titus can't spare a man from the oars. On the other hand… your father is getting old."

Nikolaos scoffed. "He's only in his forties. Not old at all."

"Forty-three is too old to row a warship. He wasn't well before and now, after months of hard, physical labor—" She let another false quiver enter her voice. "We don't even know if he is still alive, but if he is—and if the generals are willing and able to locate him—"

Here it comes.

"*You* can be the one who saves him." Her eyes glistened. "*You.* Because I don't seem to be able to."

If Arona's tears didn't move me, this woman's surely won't.

"Actually," she continued in her put-on weepy way, "you're the *only* one who can save your father at this point, and he *will* know—because I'll make sure he knows—all the good things you've done and all the many ways you've sacrificed to save him."

Can't tell if she's trying to sound sincere or sarcastic.

"What, exactly," he demanded, "do you want me to do?"

For the briefest moment, she hesitated. "Take his place."

Nikolaos laughed again. "Row a galley for nine and a half years?"

"No one can force you to do it." She made her lips tremble. "It's *your* choice."

"Glad you see it that way, because I choose *not* to row a galley."

"Please." She stood and took a few shaky steps toward him. "You're young and strong, and when it's over you'll have plenty of time to rebuild your life. Even if your father survives the full ten years, he won't have any time left."

Nikolaos rose, too, and looked down at her. "Neither the gods on Mount Olympus nor the demons in Hades could make me do what you just suggested." He gestured toward the corridor. "You and I need to talk. Privately."

Fatigue showed on the Roman woman's face, but she nodded. "Doros, while I'm away, tell the generals how you learned so much about the military."

***

The Roman woman's stomach rumbled loudly, annoying Nikolaos as he led her toward the far end of the dark corridor, where the gilded door still stood open, the same two soldiers still guarded it, and the fiery torches still filled the night air with smoke.

But something new had shown up since he entered the palace at dusk.

A donkey now waited patiently in the street, hitched to that same bright cart that Nikolaos had seen pass through a wide gate under a tall fig tree at the northwest corner of the Caesarea junction.

How convenient.

He stopped a short distance away from the door, leaned over, and whispered into the Roman woman's ear. "I cannot and will not do what you proposed back there."

"But that's the only way to free your father."

Maybe she'll cooperate if I speak her name.

"Trust me, Theodosia, it's not." He made a huge effort. Smiled at her. Patted her shoulder. "I have a plan to rescue Father another way."

"There is no other way." Abruptly, her body lurched to one side as if she were fainting.

Can't let her do that. Need her alert and on her feet.

"Yes, there is." He seized her upper arms to keep her from falling. "I have friends in Jerusalem who know men in Caesarea who can get him out. But to get to Jerusalem in time, I'll need to take that cart."

"My driver, Adin, will carry you." She waved vaguely toward the harbor. "He's out there somewhere, sleeping in the grass."

"No time to look for him, and to make this work you must go with me."

"No." She slipped from his grasp and collapsed onto the floor. "I haven't eaten in over a day. Been awake since midnight. Walked halfway to Jerusalem and back. I can't do another thing tonight."

"You can, and you will." He pulled his dagger and tapped its blade on her arm before returning it to his belt. "Now, just keep quiet."

He repositioned his hands, lifted her to her feet, and guided her out.

"She's exhausted," he said to the guards, "so I'm taking her home. If the generals send for me, tell them I'll be right back."

***

Theodosia's body throbbed with pain as Nikolaos lifted her to the bench and jumped up beside her. He slapped the reins, and the cart jolted forward. Feeling both numb and dumb, she sat still as they rode through the empty streets of Caesarea. There was no moonlight, but as usual the stars were out.

After a time, slowly regaining her wits, she curled her left hand over the back of the bench and turned her head toward Nikolaos. He was steering the cart with both hands, holding one rein in each, allowing the donkey to track back and forth from one side to the other.

Not the way Adin does it.

Twice, Nikolaos almost drove into a ditch.

His mind's elsewhere.

He hadn't reacted to her first small movements, so she angled a bit more and let her eyes wander behind him, then down.

Myrine wanted to nap in the back.

And sure enough, there she was. Stretched out. Eyes wide open. Bracing herself with one hand as the other pointed to the open area beneath the bench.

Where she stashed Esther's kitchen knives.

With her left hand, Theodosia made a stay-still gesture.

Soon they were on the open road, rolling toward the north-south highway.

"Nobody's following us," she said to Nikolaos as they approached the junction. "If you don't need me anymore, why not let me off here?"

Instead of stopping, he began curving through the intersection, heading south toward Jerusalem. "You and I," he said, "are going to Yamnia."

"Aren't we going to Jerusalem to find friends who can free your father?"

"From Yamnia, we'll catch a boat to Greece."

Why would he want me along on a boat to Greece?

"And abandon Alexander and Doros?" Anger produced a flash of lucidity.

He won't want me along. He'll kill me before we reach Yamnia.

She barely had time to process that thought when something tapped her right hip. Without moving her head, she turned her eyes down. A shiny blade glimmered on the bench beside her. She eased her hand back and wrapped her fingers around its handle. Despite her stealth, Nikolaos reacted. His right hand, which still held one of the reins, grabbed her wrist.

"Don't even think of jumping out."

"No way I'd jump from a moving cart." With her right hand, she whipped the kitchen knife up between them. "We're going back to Caesarea."

"What shit is this?"

Nikolaos's equally encumbered left hand struck out for her weapon, but she jerked it away.

He released her wrist, switched both reins to his left hand, and with his right reached for the dagger in his belt.

"Myrine!" Theodosia yelled.

Instantly, the slave rose up and grasped Nikolaos's neck with her own large, powerful right hand. Caught off guard, he wobbled on the bench.

Taking advantage of his loss of focus and control, Theodosia snatched both reins from his left hand and pulled the donkey to a stop while they were still in the intersection.

Meanwhile, Myrine hoisted the second kitchen knife over his left shoulder and pointed it at his heart.

"Always knew that someday I'd get a chance to kill you, Master Nikolaos. Didn't think you'd make it quite so easy."

"Drop the knife, Myrine," he said, "or you're a dead woman."

Her only response to that was a laugh. Then she addressed Theodosia. "Remember, Mistress, I once told you I'd kill for you if need be."

"I do remember."

"Is this the time?"

"It might be, but wait a bit. Hold him nice and tight for now."

In the next moment, Theodosia yanked the dagger from Nikolaos's belt and hurled it far out into the desert.

This was her first time to drive a cart, but she knew the intersection was wide enough for a circular turn in front of Adin's house.

I've been watching an expert do this for months.

As Myrine's right hand immobilized Nikolaos's head and the knife in her left hand hovered above his chest, ready to kill him if need be, Theodosia aimed the cart west, toward Caesarea.

＊＊＊

"Mistress," Myrine said before they reached the outermost edge of the city, "you got any objection if I practice my carvin' techniques? I'm kinda rusty after half a year away from my kitchen."

"Can't see why not. Just don't make any sudden moves, and keep me informed at each step."

"Sure will. So now, to start, I'm gonna access the meat."

Theodosia stopped the cart and leaned forward to watch. Beads of sweat glinted on Nikolaos's forehead.

He's seen how well she handles a blade.

With all the precision of the butcher that she had been for most of her life—and with her right hand still clamped securely around Nikolaos's neck—Myrine's left hand dragged the point of her knife down the front of his tunic. Smoothly, she stuck it into the fabric above his belt and pulled the blue silk taut, away from his body. A quick snap of her wrist opened a sizable hole near his navel.

"Now I understand," she said with a dry chuckle, "why the gods gave me so much more skill with my left hand than with my right."

"You really think they planned all this?" Theodosia chuckled, too.

"They control everythin' in our lives, don't they?"

Reversing course, Myrine sliced the blade up through the stretched-out silk until she reached its finely stitched hem, right next to Nikolaos's gullet. A fast outward twist sliced clean through the folded layers, dropping each severed half of the tunic and leaving his chest exposed.

"What the fuck are you doing?" he roared into the night. "Theodosia Varro, make her stop!"

"You only call me by my name when you want something from me."

"That first cut," Myrine said, "was for all the times you groped me. Remember, Master Nikolaos?"

She leaned over his shoulder for a few moments, as if contemplating her next moves.

Meanwhile, Theodosia kept observing.

"And this one's for all the times you raped me." Myrine inserted the sharp point into the skin above his nipple, but offset to the right from it, and made a vertical slice.

The wound was superficial but still, blood oozed out.

Can't believe I'm letting her do this.

Moments later, Myrine cut a second oozing line to the left and parallel to the first. "That's for Hyperion."

Panic spread across Nikolaos's face. "Stop her!"

"Now, Mistress, don't get alarmed, but this next one's gonna do a lot more damage."

Silently, Theodosia nodded her approval.

Myrine flipped the knife to its long edge and carved a deeper horizontal slice between the two oozing vertical lines, turning them into an H directly above his heart. Blood spurted out this time.

"Know who that was for, Master Nikolaos?"

He stared straight ahead, as if seeing his own doom in the darkness, and said nothing.

But Myrine insisted. "Come on, Master Nikolaos, take a guess."

"Lycos?" he whispered.

"Oh no, Lycos comes last. That one was for Kronos. You do remember him, I'm sure."

She readjusted her grip on the knife handle and leveled its tip straight into the bleeding cross-bar she had just carved.

"Now… it's Lycos's turn."

"Hold it right there," Theodosia said. "Let's get on into town."

She drove until she spotted the palace directly ahead. Again, she halted the donkey and turned to watch Nikolaos's face.

He knows Myrine won't miss his heart.

"Do you have anything to say before I give Myrine permission to dispatch you to Hades?"

A wry smile crossed his lips.

Looks just like Alexander.

"Only that I'll wait for both of you there and rape you every single day for the rest of eternity." And then he shut his eyes.

He may be an absolute bastard, but to his credit, he hasn't flinched.

Myrine's knife held fast, poised to strike.

"Tell me when, Mistress, and I'll do it."

Nikolaos made no sound.

But Theodosia couldn't turn her eyes away from Alexander's son.

I actually do see a lot of his father in him.

"No," she said after a while. "Keep that knife in position and don't let him move. There's a more appropriate fate awaiting him at the palace."

***

"Mother!" Doros rushed into the street and helped Theodosia out of the cart. "Father's here, and he's been asking for you."

She stepped over to the guards and pointed to Nikolaos, who remained on the bench, immobilized between Myrine's tightly gripping right hand and her knife-wielding left.

"Take that man into your most secure custody," she said, "and let the generals know he has returned. They'll decide what to do with him."

***

Doros tugged his mother along the unlit corridor.

"The generals didn't want you seeing him—and smelling him—like he was, so their slaves gave him a bath and clean clothes. Then Adin, Father, and I ate supper together. We were all starved."

As am I.

Summoning what was left of her strength, Theodosia followed Doros into the too-bright reception hall, where every lamp tree blazed and red-and-brass shapes swirled with the scarlet frescoes.

She clung, squinting and dizzy, to her son until the vertigo passed and she could identify individuals in the room.

Around the perimeter... a ring of guards and aides.

By the door that led to the terrace... the two generals.

Beside a table in the center... Adin.

And there, right next to Adin and supported by him—*Truly remarkable, really, given how much the Jews hate the Greeks!*—stood a fragile figure with sallow skin, ragged hair, and a shapeless, graying beard. Open sores and fresh bruises covered every visible part of his body. Thick crusts encircled his ankles and wrists. A short, white slave's tunic hung from his spindly frame.

Bless you, Juno. He really and truly is alive!

***

Crinkles at the corners of Alexander's eyes were his only initial response as Theodosia ran her fingers through his damp hair, wrapped her arms around his bony shoulders, and tenderly kissed his cracked lips.

After a series of deep, racking coughs and a nervous glance around the room, Alexander's own fingers, arms, and lips began to respond.

Adin stepped aside so they could hold one another. The room fell silent until Theodosia found her voice.

"Oh, my dearest love. Doros and I have come to take you home."

Out of nowhere, a too-loud shout broke the magic of that moment.

"I don't want to go home!!!"

Alexander and Theodosia pulled back from one another and stared at their son. Gasps rippled across the chamber.

As if unaware of the distress he was causing, Doros marched forward, matching his words to his steps as he had done once before, years earlier.

"I want— to serve— with General— Titus.

"It is— what I— was meant— to do.

"You know— that too— Mother— Father.

"All I've— ever wanted— was to be— a soldier."

One clear thought, and only one, formed in Theodosia's head.

I have not journeyed so far and struggled so hard to rescue my husband, only to lose my son at the same place and time.

Nobody in the room moved. Everyone looked at her.

I must say something.

Experiencing an uncanny sense of detachment—as if somehow her eyes had sprouted wings and were now flying around near the vaulted ceiling— Theodosia watched herself struggle to respond.

Watched the guards watching her.

Watched Myrine slip into the room.

Watched Doros cross his arms in defiance.

Watched Adin support Alexander once again.

Watched the generals converse with a pair of aides.

And then, as the silence lengthened, the right response came to her... a single perfect question with the power to end Doros's military ambitions once and for all.

"Have you asked if General Titus actually *wants* you in his service?"

"No, Mother, I haven't, but I'll go find out right now."

Doros executed an abrupt pivot, marched toward the generals, and came smartly to attention. The sharp salute that followed resonated in the great hall.

"Centurion Doros at your command, sirs!"

Titus grinned. "So, Centurion Doros, what's this all about?"

"Seeking permission to remain with you, sir, to serve in any way you can use me—either as your Aramaic interpreter or one of your aides, or even as your servant—until such time as you judge me ready for training to become an officer in the Roman army."

Juno, please don't let him take my boy.

Unlike his son, Vespasian remained stern. "How old are you, Doros?"

He knows what it means to be the parent of a young child.

"Just turned ten, sir. Will General Titus accept me into his service?"

Vespasian hesitated. "First, you need to ask your father's permission."

Doros's face drooped. "He won't give it."

I sure do hope not.

"Unless—" Doros's eyes lit up. "Will you go with me to ask him?"

For a few long moments, Vespasian regarded him with solemn eyes. "Both General Titus and I will go with you. After all, we did come back down here tonight specifically to greet your father."

Moments later, the highest-ranking officer in Nero's imperial army extended his hand to a man who had spent the last five months chained to a bench in the bowels of a warship and who also—fourteen summers earlier, under a breezy pergola on the coast north of Rome—had served the general and his children countless cups of Falernian.

"Greetings, Alexander." Vespasian's tone was noticeably warmer now.

The great general's hand hung in the air, but Alexander seemed unable to raise his eyes, much less his own hand.

To encourage him, Theodosia placed one of her hands on his back and rested the other on a small, uninjured portion of his forearm. Meanwhile, on the other side, Adin kept him steady.

There's only one reason why Vespasian would come downstairs tonight to see Alexander, much less offer his hand.

She looked at Vespasian but spoke to Alexander. "It seems the general may be about to give you a most precious gift."

Vespasian smiled at her and nodded in a highly meaningful way.

Her heart soared. "Oh, my dearest love, he's granting you your freedom!"

At that, slowly and shakily, Alexander accepted the general's hand.

"Thank you, sir." His voice quavered, too. "I'm forever in your debt."

For a time, he clung to Vespasian's hand like a lifeline.

Which is how it must feel to him.

"You owe me nothing, Alexander. This happy result is entirely due to your wife and sons." The general's words were a bit unsteady, too.

He's a good man, also touched by the emotion of this moment.

"I say that," Vespasian continued, "because—in the most curious but ultimately the most effective way one could imagine—the three of them did work together to secure your freedom."

"My *sons*?" Alexander glanced around the room. "Is Nikolaos here?"

"Nikolaos *was* here, earlier today." Vespasian paused, as if weighing his words. "He has volunteered to serve out the rest of your sentence."

"Volunteered?" Theodosia whispered.

"My aides offered him two options, Theodosia. That is the one he chose."

Instant death, no doubt, or rowing for nine-and-a-half years. Either one's a fitting punishment for all he's done. But I'll keep my promise to him. Alexander will never learn what led Nikolaos to make this sacrifice.

Timidly, for perhaps the first time in his life, Doros looked at Alexander. "Father, I ask your permission to remain in Judea and serve General Titus as part of his legendary Fifteenth Legion."

Alexander's dark, deep-set eyes lingered on his son's face. "Have you considered how difficult it will be for your mother and me to leave you behind when we depart for Greece?"

"I only know it's the right thing for me to do."

He hasn't considered us at all.

"Were you in on this?" Alexander asked Theodosia.

"No. I'm not happy about it, but also not surprised, and neither are you."

Alexander turned to Titus. "Are you willing, sir, to accept Doros into your service?"

"As my youngest and most enthusiastic aide and interpreter, I am."

Doros abandoned his military bearing and began jumping up and down. "Father, does that mean you'll say *yes*?"

Stiffly, and with the help of both Adin and Theodosia, Alexander lowered himself onto the stool behind him and gestured for Doros to come closer.

"There's no turning back once you've made a decision like this." His frail fingers clutched Doros's arms. "I truly do wish you'd consider a more uplifting occupation, rather than give yourself over to a life of hardship, violence, and war."

"I was born for a life of hardship, violence, and war. And… glory!"

After another fit of coughing, Alexander touched Adin's arm, while still addressing his son.

"Were you born to fight and kill the Jews, some of whom have now become your friends?"

Doros tilted his head back to look up at Adin.

"No, Father, I don't want to kill Adin and Oren and Judith and Esther." His face puckered. "I don't want to kill anyone, really."

"But that's what it means to be a soldier." Alexander's eyes never left his son's face. "It's not just marching in the street and saluting your superior officers and sharing raunchy jokes in the barracks. It means killing people, including many who never harmed you in any way."

Doros dropped his eyes and said nothing.

Alexander waited a frighteningly long time before turning to Theodosia. "Forgive me for this, but who am I to tell him he can't follow his heart?"

In a louder voice, he addressed his son. "Doros, if that's what you want to do with your life—if hardship, violence, war, and maybe even occasional glory are what will make you happy, and if General Titus is willing to accept you as his aide—then *yes*, my beloved son, you *do* have my permission."

"Thank you, Father!" Doros turned and dashed across the room to Myrine. "I'm going to be a real soldier!"

"So I heard." She hugged him. "I'll miss you, Little Man."

"I'll miss you, too!" He ran back to Theodosia. "Oh, Mother, I am so happy! My life is complete!"

Famished and exhausted in every possible way, Theodosia moved a stool next to Alexander and collapsed onto it. She embraced Doros, then pulled the leather pouch up from inside her stola.

"This is yours." She draped the cord around his neck. "I pray the gods it keeps you safe and brings you back to us someday, alive and well."

Doros slipped the viper amulet from its pouch and held it aloft. "This little snake saved my life today! Mother's life and Father's life, too!"

He sped around the room, showing his bulla to all the military men. "It used to have a ruby in its mouth, but we know that didn't matter, because none of us died!"

He finished his victory lap and came back to stand by his parents.

"So, my son—" Alexander coughed again. "What's the lesson for life to be learned from this experience?"

"Always wear my good-luck viper and never, ever lose it again."

Alexander produced one of his wry smiles. "I guess that's as good a lesson as any." He lifted Theodosia's hand and kissed it.

Vespasian, in turn, patted her shoulder. "Titus and I have early departures in the morning. Can't wait around any longer."

"You're all welcome to stay in the palace tonight," Titus said, "and for as long as you need. Bathe, eat, and relax until you've recovered enough for your journey home. I'll make sure the steward takes good care of you and provides enough money to get you back to Greece. And there'll be a properly stamped manumission document waiting for Alexander in the morning."

Titus pointed at Doros.

"Tomorrow morning, if you're still determined to become a soldier, and if your parents still agree to it, meet me at dawn beside the horses in the street. You'll ride with me and a few other officers to Alexandria."

He's never even sat on a horse.

But Doros saluted. "Sir, I'll be there!"

After the generals and their aides and guards departed, Theodosia crooked her finger at her son. "Do you *really* have to do this?" she whispered close to his ear.

"Mother," he whispered back, "I *really* do."

She eyed him. "You know how I feel about it, but I won't stop you."

"I'll write you every day, I promise."

"Once or twice a month will be fine." She blinked back tears. "And there's one more lesson for life that I'd like to leave with you."

Without releasing Alexander's hand, she wrapped her other arm around Doros's shoulders. "You're happy right now, because you think you've caught your dream, and I truly hope you have. But be a realist, please. Don't succumb to the delusion that your joy will last forever. Don't get too comfortable or content or satisfied with your life, because something will always come along to shake it up."

Alexander wrapped an arm around Doros, too. "What your mother's trying to say is, life will lead you in some direction or other, but you'll never get there, because life is a process, not an end point."

Theodosia gave in and let the tears flow.

"Your father and I have learned that lesson through our own strange, complicated lives, and we know it will be the same for you. But also, we're proud of you and confident that you're smart enough and talented enough and flexible enough to adapt and thrive."

"And honorable enough," added Alexander, "to be a good man who brings credit to our family."

Theodosia closed her wet eyes, kissed her boy's forehead, and with that set him free to continue his journey through life without her.

— The End —

KEEP READING!

The Ruby Ring,
the third book of
The Ruby-Viper Trilogy
is available on Amazon.

Find links to all three books
and lots more information about the entire series at:
MARTHAMARKS.COM

HISTORICAL NOTES

In writing *The Viper Amulet*, it was fun to continue telling several interrelated stories from *Rubies of the Viper*, not just those of my fictional characters—Theodosia, Alexander, Stefan, Lycos, and Nikolaos—but also of General Vespasian and his son, Titus, two of the most important historical figures of the second half of the first century AD.

I also enjoyed introducing another historical figure who looms large in the time and place of this novel. Known to history as Josephus, he is identified here by one of two English versions of his Hebrew name, Yosef ben Matityahu. (The other is Joseph ben Mattathias.) I decided to portray him as a sardonic, acerbic, and raunchy-talking aristocrat in order to humanize a man now remembered mostly as the stuffy, traitorous, and self-serving author of *The Jewish War*, *Antiquities of the Jews*, and *The Life of Josephus*. He will reappear—and much of the rest of his story will be told—in *The Ruby Ring*.

My biggest challenge in writing *The Viper Amulet* was to get Part IV right. I aimed to capture an accurate sense of first-century Jewish life and times, but I'm not a scholar in this field, and I make no claim to professional mastery.

Besides, since this story is told through the eyes of two characters who know little of Jewish culture, their own observations and interpretations might not necessarily seem accurate to modern scholars under any circumstances. So I beg the indulgence of readers who possess more knowledge and understanding than Theodosia and Nikolaos would have had.

Still, I did work hard to get the details right, especially regarding:

• *real places*... like the ancient harbors of Messana, Siracusa, Eretria, Yamnia, and Caesarea; plus Euboea, Athens, Jerusalem, and Jotapata;

• *people's homes*... like Alexander and Theodosia's in Eretria and Oren and Judith's near Caesarea;

• *the Roman war machine*… like General Vespasian unleashed on Jotapata;

• *historical events*… like the early stages of the Roman-Jewish War—also known as The Great Revolt—of AD 66-70 (or 66-74, see below) and the siege of Jotapata, which appears to have lasted from June 3 to July 20 of AD 67.

Regarding Jotapata, we are informed solely by Josephus's *The Jewish War*, the only complete eyewitness account of the entire war, which he wrote years later in Rome. Although scholars have criticized aspects of his history, I've adhered closely to it, only departing from it in minor ways.

In my account of the early stages of The Great Revolt, for story purposes, I made up two events: Titus's trip around the Mediterranean in search of convicts to row imperial warships, and the theft of a letter from Jotapata.

I also envisioned Roman garrisons near the ports of Piraeus and Eretria, each with the standard one-gate layout used for smaller garrisons in non-hostile areas. For plot purposes, I invented a secret door in the exterior wall. Those forts and hidden doors may or may not have existed.

Likewise, I imagined distinctively painted donkey carts. Why not?

Josephus reports that an anonymous deserter betrayed the people of Jotapata, leading to its downfall. Exactly who that person was, if in fact that part of the history is true, will forever be a mystery. According to scholars, there's also reason to believe that Josephus did manage to smuggle letters out during the siege, via courier, to the Sanhedrin in Jerusalem.

The story that Vespasian fell asleep and snored at Nero's concert in Athens, which took place during his tour of Greece in AD 66-67, was reported contemporaneously and appears to be true.

Definitely true is the introduction of a primitive map of the Mediterranean by one of the first geographers, Pomponius Mela, who was born in what was then a Roman province and now is southern Spain. Reproductions of his original map can be found in the Internet.

Exact dates of events that occurred during The Great Revolt can be unclear or contradictory. I've used the best resources I could find and worked the timing details as accurately as possible into my plot line.

Historians don't agree even on the basic dates of the war. Some say The Great Revolt lasted from AD 66-70, since Jerusalem was destroyed in the year 70. Others stretch the war out to include the siege of Masada in AD 73-74, so, by that reckoning, The Great Revolt lasted from AD 66 to 74.

In the interest of keeping my novel moving along, I've suggested, summarized, and/or simplified four complex situations and events:

• *the political intrigues* that surrounded Yosef ben Matityahu during his time as governor-general of Galilee;

• *the ongoing local battles* between Greeks and Jews;

• *the internecine warfare* between various segments of Jewish society, which severely weakened their ability to resist Vespasian's war machine when it arrived; and

• *the causes and effects* of The Great Revolt.

AS REGARDS THE PASSING OF TIME...

Ancient people measured time by the sun and the seasons: dawn, morning, midmorning, midday, afternoon, midafternoon, dusk, night, midnight; hours, days, months; yesterday, today, tomorrow; winter, spring, summer, autumn; planting time, harvest time; the solstices; and so on.

They had no way to mark smaller increments than the hour, and even that was not understood or measured as we do now. At no time did they think or talk in terms of minutes or seconds, and even weeks were not noted as we do.

In writing my novels, I work around these constraints with adverbs and adverbial phrases such as *soon, immediately, for a few moments, a while later, after a time, in a few days,* or by specifying a number of days or well-understood time markers ("the Ides") within a month.

Writing about the siege of Jotapata was challenging in this regard, because we who live in the twenty-first century know that it lasted almost seven weeks, from early June to July 20. In the first century, however, Vespasian, Titus, Yosef, Nikolaos, Theodosia, and Doros would not have thought of it in those terms. Yosef famously reported that it lasted "47 days."

Likewise, ancient people had no concept of BC and AD (or, as those are also expressed, BCE "Before Common Era" and CE "Common Era"). For the benefit of readers today, I have used AD dates in my section headers, but in no way do I mean to suggest that my characters thought they were living in an "AD time period."

AS REGARDS ANCIENT PLACES AND THEIR NAMES...

In *Rubies of the Viper*, *The Viper Amulet*, and *The Ruby Ring*, I use English names for major places—Rome, Athens, Antioch, and Jerusalem; the Italian Peninsula, Greece, Judea, and Sicily—and vernacular names for small towns like Messana, Palica, Siracusa, and Yavne/Yamnia. I do use "Italia" instead of "Italy," which is the name of a modern nation, not an ancient place.

The current-day port of Messina, Sicily was known as Messana in ancient times, so that's what it's called in *The Viper Amulet*.

In the first century AD, Palica was a town in the mountains of southern Sicily, with the proud pro-freedom tradition attributed to it in this novel. Unfortunately, it did not survive the Roman era. It drops off the historical record sometime after my story ends.

The city of Syracuse, New York was named for Siracusa in Sicily. I chose to use the original vernacular name, Siracusa, so as not to set up distracting associations with the American city.

Nowadays, the island of Euboea and the fishing village of Eretria are upscale resorts popular with tourists and residents of nearby Athens. They are still known by the historical names used in my novels.

The second millennium BC (middle to late Bronze age) Judean harbor variously spelled Yavne, Yavneh, and Jabneh was Yamnia in Greek and Iamnia in Latin. In *The Viper Amulet*, the Greek-speaking characters, including Theodosia and Doros, call it Yamnia and the Jewish characters call it Yavne. Today, it's an archeological site known as Yavne-Yam ("Yavne on the Sea").

Herod's "new town" of Caesarea Maritima is now an Israeli national park.

Jotapata is a modern spelling of the old names Yodfat, Yodefat, or Iotapata. It's now an Israeli national historic site.

Thanks to an American television miniseries, many readers know Masada as an (almost) impregnable fortress where Jewish Zealots and their families took refuge after the fall of Jerusalem in AD 70. Before that, it was one of King Herod's favorite, most-luxurious palaces. Nowadays, it's a UNESCO World Heritage site.

The Mediterranean was *Mare Nostrum* ("Our Sea") in the first-century. As with the Adriatic Sea, the Aegean Sea, and the Etruscan Sea (also known as the Tyrrhenian Sea, which has the same meaning), I've used its modern English name.

AS REGARDS THE WOMEN'S QUARTERS...

In *The Viper Amulet*, I've adhered to the generally accepted view that free Greek women in ancient times lived in "oriental seclusion" similar to that of other eastern-Mediterranean societies, including some even today. This theory is based on the few writings about women's lives that have come down from that period. Some scholars argue against this theory, but I saw little reason not to reflect in my novel the commonly held belief.

AS REGARDS TRAVEL...

Nobody in the first century journeyed long distances for pleasure. Although there were roads, inns, and eateries of all sorts, getting from one place to another—even within a small area, much less across a large region—was a tough endeavor due to the presence of mountains, the threat of highway robbers, and the dangers of sailing the Mediterranean in winter.

The scenario I portrayed in Messana, where the imperial fleet had taken over every inn in town, was not uncommon. Ships didn't provide many berths, so captains accommodated their crews in port when possible.

I've done my best to capture the first-century reality of horses (ridden mostly by military officers and the wealthy) and donkeys (ridden by everyone else), donkey carts, foot travel, sailing conditions, inadequate sanitation, shared beds and rooms, and bedbugs.

AS REGARDS THE ROWERS ON GALLEY SHIPS...

One attentive reviewer of this book correctly has pointed out that the Romans did not use slaves to row their warships.

She is not wrong, but neither are the details here, which state that Titus went looking for convicts to row the extra ships he would need to transport massive quantities of men and equipment to Judea. Under the conditions described in this book, a runaway slave might also be called a "convict" or a "condemned criminal."

VALUABLE HISTORICAL RESOURCES

To anyone interested in the Roman-Jewish War and the complex time and culture in which it occurred, I recommend these books:

1. Flavius Josephus: Eyewitness to Rome's First-Century Conquest of Judea, by Mireille Hadas-Lebel, translated from French into English by Richard Miller (1993, Macmillan)

2. Apocalypse: The Great Jewish Revolt Against Rome, by Neil Faulkner (2002, Amberly Publishing)

3. The Jewish Revolt: AD 66-74, by Si Sheppard (2013, Osprey Publishing), which contains fine maps, photos, and full-color illustrations

FOR MORE INFORMATION, PLEASE CHECK OUT MY WEBSITE

— MARTHAMARKS.COM —

where you will find a wealth of additional details about
the people, places, and events portrayed in this trilogy, including:
• A map for all three novels
• A glossary of names and terms
• Suggested book club discussion topics
• My long-running blog, *The Purple Parchment*
• Personal photos from places featured in this trilogy

APPRECIATION

To JENNIFER QUINLAN of Historical Editorial, for the stunning covers she created for *Rubies of the Viper*, *The Viper Amulet*, and *The Ruby Ring*.

To BALAGE BALOGH of Archeology Illustrated, for his amazing paintings, which enhance the back covers of my paperbacks and the home-page banner on my website, MARTHAMARKS.COM. All are used with his permission.

To DONNA ROXEY, whose careful proofreading caught typos, misspellings, and flat-out dumb mistakes.

ABOUT THE AUTHOR

When I was seven, I traveled with my parents to Italy, where the ruins of the Roman Forum and the buried cities of Pompeii and Herculaneum made an indelible impression on me. As we walked the streets of Pompeii, I informed my parents that I had been there before. It was entirely familiar then, and that déjà vu feeling has been with me every time I've gone back. You'll find photos of me on that first visit to Pompeii at MARTHAMARKS.COM.

As a teenager, I devoured every novel about ancient Rome that I could get my hands on. As an adult, I've read newer fiction set in the period, returned to those same places and visited others featured in my books, and studied the history and cultures of that time. *Rubies of the Viper*, *The Viper Amulet*, and *The Ruby Ring* are the results of the fascination that began on that long-ago visit to Pompeii with my parents.

Years later, I married Bernie Marks, earned a Ph.D. at Northwestern University, and taught on the faculties of Northwestern and Kalamazoo College. After Bernie's death in 2020, I wrote and published *Betting on Bernie, A Memoir of a Marriage* (BETTINGONBERNIE.COM) and finished this trilogy.

A PERSONAL REQUEST

Reader comments and star ratings are priceless. These days, a book's success depends almost entirely on them.

A star rating takes no time at all, and an effective comment doesn't have to be long or complex. So if you wish to comment, please know that just a few sentences saying whether you enjoyed or did not enjoy a book—and why—can help both the author and the potential reader.

So I will humbly ask: once you've finished reading *The Viper Amulet*, please take a few minutes to leave an honest comment—or, if you prefer, just a star rating—to help others decide if they might want to read it, too.

At MARTHAMARKS.COM, you'll find links to Amazon and Goodreads, so you can see what people have said about *The Viper Amulet* and the other novels in this trilogy... and perhaps even add your own voice to the mix. Thank you in advance for leaving a star rating and a comment for this book!

www.ingramcontent.com/pod-product-compliance
Lightning Source LLC
Chambersburg PA
CBHW051547250626
47157CB00001B/223